RIFFING WITH THE MUSE

RIFFING WITH THE MUSE

Flynn's Crossing Romantic Suspense Series
Book 11

Yvonne Kohano

Nanokas Press

A Division of Kochanowski Enterprises LLC

Copyright © 2017

RIFFING WITH THE MUSE
FLYNN'S CROSSING ROMANTIC SUSPENSE SERIES BOOK 11

Nanokas Press/KE Press books may be ordered through booksellers or by contacting:

Kochanowski Enterprises LLC
PO Box 1274
Clackamas, OR 97015-9594
www.yvonnekohano.com
yvonne@yvonnekohano.com

Riffing with the Muse is a work of fiction. People, places, events, and situations are the product of the author's imagination. Any resemblance to actual persons, living or dead, or historical events, is purely coincidental.

Any people depicted in stock imagery provided by DepositPhotos are models, and such images are being used for illustrative purposes only.

Certain stock imagery ©DepositPhotos
Cover design: John Kochanowski

ISBN: 978-1-940738-41-3 (sc)
        978-1-940738-74-1 (e)

Nanokas Press First Edition: 07-25-2017

Also by Yvonne Kohano

FLYNN'S CROSSING ROMANTIC SUSPENSE SERIES

Pictures of Redemption, Book 1
(Serena & Dane)

Flashes of Fire, Book 2
(DK & Vince)

Naked Intolerances, Book 3
(Gabby & Rick)

Gratefully Ever Yours, A Flynn's Crossing Seasonal
Novella

Tastes and Consequences, Book 4
(Mac & Roxy)

Blooms on the Bones, Book 5
(Tess & Powers)

Wine Into Water, Book 6
(Marguerite & Deke)

Love and the Christmas Tree Nymph, A Flynn's Crossing
Seasonal Novella

Love's Touch of Justice, Book 7
(Jake & Marlee)

This Proposal Between Us, A Flynn's Crossing Seasonal
Novella

Measure Twice, Love Once, Book 8
(Geno and Agnes)

State Fair Date Dare, A Flynn's Crossing Seasonal Novella

Love's Fiery Prescription, Book 9
(Noah and Nicolle)

Love's Fiery Resolution, Book 10
(Gideon and Danielle)

Riffing with the Muse, Book 11
(Kaane and Angel)

And more to come!

Subscribe to Yvonne Kohano's enewsletter to be among the first to learn about new releases and special offers.

GET YOUR FREE NOVELLA PREQUEL at
www.YvonneKohano.com.

RIFFING WITH THE MUSE

Prologue – February

Sun sparkled off metal jewelry hanging from an intricate assembly of tree branches in the front window. It cast brilliant reflections on canvases displayed on the walls and pottery and woven items arrayed on tables. The room stood empty of people, exactly the way he wanted it.

Pulling his hat lower on his forehead and punching the glasses slipping down his nose, he glanced up and down the bustling street. At this hour on a weekday, most people had a place to be and things to do, and none seemed to note that he lingered outside the gallery. He met no one's eyes and cast his to the ground when anyone approached. He'd become a master at appearing inconsequential in public. Privacy was everything to him, and he was willing to pay the price for it.

Satisfied no one cared about his actions, he straightened and examined the interior of the shop. He didn't want an audience. Last week, someone transferred the sculpture from the window display to a pedestal deeper in the store, making it impossible to get up close and personal without going inside.

No chime sounded when he pushed open the door, a rarity on this small town's Main Street. He paused and scanned the exhibit area, expecting to see security cameras peering from corners or one-way glass framing a back office, but nothing indicated an unseen watcher. The owners obviously hoped customers would behave like civil, respectful human beings. That kind of trust was a commodity long missing in his life.

His past life. He had to get used to saying it that way. It was no longer his path. That didn't mean he still couldn't have pretty things to remind him of those times. Meaningful things, like the metal work in front of him.

A deliberate rusty patina accented exuberance in the structure. At its center stood the facsimile of an oversized guitar, upright on its end. Not just any guitar, but a Gibson Les Paul model dating back to the 1950's. He'd had one like it once upon a time, until in a fit of pique, he'd cracked it into shards over an amp in that recording studio on the Burbank strip. His action marked the beginning of the end for him, though he didn't know it at the time.

This artist captured the instrument's unique lines and markings perfectly, even in steel. Floating from the frets of the guitar, musical notes tracked the song being played. They made no sense without a score behind them, but that didn't matter. He loved the look of it, the feel of rapturous joy in what it represented. He swore he could hear its pristine electric tones.

When had he last felt that kind of sheer bliss when he struck a chord? It had been months, years even. Not that it mattered anymore. Old life.

The boys called it a dry spell, a temporary affliction he could easily overcome with dedication, or concentration, or a damn good party. From that little resort in Mexico where the tequila flowed faster than its fake waterfall and senoritas were more than happy to oblige him, to the austere snowy peaks above Aspen, he'd tried. Damn right, he'd tried. The words didn't come, the notes didn't make sense, and soon, he'd heard the whispers.

Has-been. Phoning it in. Lip-syncing because his voice was crap. No new songs in the past six years. No longer playing because he was too stoned to find the right key. Falling over a mic stand and landing on the first three rows, to the joy of surgically-enhanced women more than delighted to give him anything for the chance to say they'd had their hands all over the great Kaane Scott.

Once great. Maybe never great was more like it. Maybe he'd been fooling the world all these years. It was possible, given the star-making machine of the music industry. Plenty of dudes out there could barely sing, but they could screech and slam the strings like they knew what they were doing. Fans screamed in response and spent money on whatever crap they slung out there.

Kaane directed his feet in a path to the back counter. From his previous reconnaissance, he knew this is where the deal would be made. He'd hate to get into a long discussion about why he wanted it. But he had to have that guitar, and he didn't want anyone to take one look at him and it and make the connection.

Checking his reflection in a small mirror on the wall, he was satisfied no one would. This disguise was about as unobtrusive as he could get. Plus, he'd been out of sight and off the gossip rag circuit for long enough. He ignored the pang that idea caused. Late and never great.

His fingers hovered over the bell on the counter when voices captured his attention.

"It's the coward's way out, ya know." The gruff bass voice rang with disgust and trailed off into grumbles.

"I understand why you say that, but I have to face facts. I'm not that good." The woman's reply was no less forceful for being a breathy series of tinkling notes. She continued in a slightly higher pitch. "In fact, I'm an amateur, and if it wasn't for your friendship with my – "

"Balderdash. Ya know that any artist's work must be reviewed by a committee of the co-op before display. It wasn't my decision."

Humor lightened the woman's response. "Yes, and you execute absolutely no control over any of the others, Thomas.

Look, lots of artists have day jobs, and my only regret is if I find one, it will keep me from covering as many hours here as I have over the last few months."

The intriguing voice reminded Kaane of flowing water and wind chimes in a gentle breeze. He should make noise or call out to let them know he stood here. Instead, he leaned closer to the counter and cocked an ear toward the room out of view.

More rumbling with indistinct words followed, sounding like a question. Then, from the woman, "That man only came in a couple of times, and I don't think he was interested in my work but in me. I still shiver when I think of him, but I doubt he'll be back. Just some weird tourist."

Unintelligible snarls preceded a firmer tone. The man said, "Ya just haven't promoted your stuff properly. I mean, look at Bettie's crap. Juvenile, if you ask me. But she sells stuff, and why? She kisses up to the crowd. Your work is fine, just fine. Ya just need to work it with a little more juice, if you know what I mean."

A tsk-tsk sounded before the woman replied in full amusement. "You and Bettie have been more than generous in allowing me to hang my pieces here for as long as you have. I am sure other artists want the wall space. Everyone's been more than gracious. Just because they were all friends of my – "

"Now see here, Ms. Reed, I will not have you – "

If they were caught up in their tiff, they'd be less likely to look twice at him. He'd gladly take any advantage in the situation. Kaane's palm slapped the bell, and he jumped back when it rang out in a C-sharp, an octave higher than he anticipated.

The argument ceased mid-sentence. A rustle of bodies followed, drawing his gaze to the shadowed back area. A tall man appeared first, slightly stooped over and walking with a slow gait through an unlit passage. Kaane glanced at him, registering bristly white eyebrows in a crevasse-lined face. When his attention shifted to the woman exiting next, he forgot why he was there.

It must have been a trick of the reflected sun, but a sudden brightness framed the previously dark corner. A shimmering spotlight lit her hair in a glow of almost unnatural white-blond. Fluffy curls around her head disappeared behind her shoulders like foaming surf on the shore. She glanced in his direction and shifted away. A second later, her gaze snapped back, and a circle of surprise matched her lips to her rounded eyes. A shy smile followed before she ducked her head, but that one smile was all it took.

An angel had landed in Flynn's Crossing. A cherubic roundness to her pinkened cheeks became more pronounced as deep red lips pulled into a bow of unhappiness. A cascade of curls continued inches past her shoulders, caught at the nape of her neck by a large clip. She was short, barely coming up to the old dude's armpit, and her curves would have done Marilyn Monroe proud.

The stirrings of excitement began in his fingers, the tips itching with the urge to feel strings under them. He knew exactly which notes he'd pick to fire the first glissando up the scale from the clear bell-like sound of her voice. The notes would wander after that, as her tones did up and down with each syllable. The sparkle in the brief seconds their eyes met would fuel his creative juices. She looked away, but he still felt the jolt of those electric eyes as if they pinned him now.

Her attention focused on the old man, and Kaane wished it would shift in his direction once more. In a soft voice, she said, "I'll pick up my pieces later in the week, okay? I mean, unless you happen to sell of them before then." She gave a short bark of disbelieving laughter, but Kaane didn't think he'd ever heard a sadder sound, like the joke was on her.

The old man shook his head with fierce movements, but the young woman smiled and raised a finger over his lips as he began to speak. She reached up on tip toes and laced fingers in the white mane to pull the old guy's face down and give him a soft peck on the cheek, and damn if the dude didn't look like he was going to teeter to the floor. Then as fast as her angel wings could carry her, she was gone with a subtle creak of a distant door. Both men stared after her in the sudden emptiness.

The old man recovered first, clearing his throat and turned to the counter with spry movements that belied the earlier shuffling. "Help ya with something?" Curtness sharpened the words, as if Kaane's presence was the reason the woman sprinted away.

Hardly the kind of selling he'd preached to the girl. Kaane's gaze stayed frozen on that corridor where the angel took flight. His heart thrummed in a resounding beat, one he hoped he could replicate. Soon it fell silent, and he glanced back at the guitar, reminded of his errand.

"Ah, hi. I've been admiring this store on my previous visits and I wanted to know more about how this all works." Kaane made a circle with his fingers, indicating the shop, proud of coming up with a cover story so fast.

The old man's eyes tightened and focused on Kaane more sharply. "We're a cooperative. Artists display here, and we work here too. You an artist? We're full up."

"But, I thought I just heard – "

"Ya didn't hear nothin'. Just an artistic difference of opinion between professional colleagues. Look, ya got a portfolio or something you want to leave with me?"

Kaane took a step back. Reed. The old guy had called her Ms. Reed. It shouldn't be too hard to find her work. Why is was suddenly so important to see what she did wasn't completely clear, but then, it wasn't often that he ran into an angel. He needed a heavenly body with a desperation he didn't recognize.

"I'll, ah, look around for a while, if you don't mind. Tell me, is there information about the artists? I'm curious about the person who did that metal piece, the guitar."

The old man dropped the attitude and gave a genuine grin. "Oh yeah, DK's work. I've got a flyer here someplace. Let me look in the back. Meant to put it out there, but in all of the hullabaloo." He waved a hand in a direction Kaane took to mean the disagreement with Ms. Reed. The man's muttering continued as he disappeared.

Kaane didn't waste any time glancing at the guitar again. The urge to hold on to it like a talisman had disappeared. No, he needed something else, something to remind him of the angel. Already, the music and the words she brought him evaporated. He had to have something to hang on to, or the first hope he'd felt in forever would disappear too.

He inspected the walls for anything that said Reed. In some corners, artists had their names in large lettering or biographies in plastic frames. Others had postcards or brochures, and in his haste around the room, he knocked some to the floor. He didn't bother to pick them up. Ducking into the final alcove as he heard feet scuffing on bare concrete, he froze for the second time that morning.

'E. Reed.' The signature marked a collection of paintings in dark muted colors. Swirls, ambiguous forms, and indistinct shapes filled the frames, none with any real pattern to them. Another set of pictures crafted from a different process were stunningly realistic. Yet a third collection of smaller works looked like chalk on a sidewalk.

He glanced between the three styles, and the tingling returned, this time shaking his hands with its ferocity. The art spoke to him, but probably not the way the artist intended. He heard music, and it didn't matter if this work was any good. They were all signed by the angel, and he had to have them.

"Ah, there ya are. Found the brochure. Here it is." Paper appeared in front of Kaane's face, and he nearly batted it away as it blocked his view.

"What do you have about this artist?" He motioned to the wall in front of him, and the paper dropped abruptly.

"This artist. This one here?" The old man's voice held a tone of incredulity.

Kaane nodded, not taking his eyes off the paintings. The one with those twisting grays would make terrific cover art for an album.

The old man chuckled as if he didn't believe it. "Well, I'll be damned. Too bad we weren't a few seconds faster, young man. You just missed her. It would have made her day to know someone was interested in her stuff."

"I'll take them." Kaane shoved his hands in his pockets to keep them from caressing the nearest Reed piece. Forcing himself to turn away was nearly impossible.

The old man's eyes widened until his brushy eyebrows met his equally bushy head. "Which ones?"

"All of them."

The man's mouth fell open in surprise. Eyes narrowed and focused on Kaane as if trying to place his face. "You from around here, boy?"

Unsure which answer would garner him less attention, Kaane remembered the tourist comment. "Yes, I've been living here for a long time. I have a ranch in the south end of the county."

Sharp eyes flicked to his boots, worn and dusty enough to pass for cowboy gear, and traveled up his jeans, pausing on the holes. The jacket was similarly distressed, a cast-off found at a thrift store to aid his disguise. Resignation drew deeper lines in the old man's face when their eyes met once more.

"Let me list prices for you, son. DK's work, that's the metal stuff, don't come cheap, not since she made it big. My discovery, I'm proud to say. And the work you're staring at like you want it for your next meal, well, I am hopeful her work will be just as good – ah, I mean, important – someday."

Kaane hid his smile. He knew where the old guy was going. He didn't look like he could pay. If he slapped his plastic on the counter, the man would probably think it was counterfeit. At least the name on the credit card wouldn't draw the man's attention.

"So, what do you do, son?" Shuffling returned the old man to the counter, where he pushed through papers littering the surface. Kaane lingered behind, wondering where he'd place the chalk drawings. He hadn't done anything that could be called decorating in the house.

"Oh, you know, I take care of my ranch. Trying to dress the place up a bit, you know?" His memory lingered on the angel's perfect smile with that trace of sadness in its depths.

"Ya want the guitar too, son?"

Kaane allowed himself to smile, trusting the old man wasn't in his fan base and wouldn't recognize his trademark grin. "Yeah, throw that in too. You take plastic, don't you?"

Chapter 1

'My dearest Angel, my wish is that you use my gift to allow yourself to explore your loves, your desires, your passions. I have but one regret in life, that I did not seize opportunities and take risks when I had the chance. I see you following in my footsteps, and that troubles me.'

She wished she had the courage to crumple the pages in her hands, but this tenuous link to the past kept her from doing so. She flattened the crepe-like paper and traced the handwriting. So perfect, each letter formed as if respect for the written word drove the pen forward.

'Follow your heart. Use this time to explore, experiment, and examine life on the edge. Do things you would not normally do. Try new adventures. I hope you find a bigger world and someday, have a heart overflowing with love. Your mother would have wanted that for you beyond all else, to find a life of passion.'

Evangeline Reed sniffed, the words floating in a blur as tears filled her eyes. Passion. What did she know about passion? She thought it would find her and carry her to places she'd only read about in books. Where had this gotten her so far?

'I know how much beauty and art mean to you, my dear. Please, though, maintain balance in your life. Open your heart to love as you open your mind to opportunities and your muse to creativity.'

Her muse. She doubted she had one. Her art was proof of that. As to love, well, there was no question in her mind.

Nice men kept their distance. Weirdos, on the other hand, she seemed to attract with ease. That pervert tourist who followed her home from the gallery a few months ago, claiming to want to know everything about her work, wanted something else entirely.

'Love may not come in the form you expect. Its source may be a mystery that even disguises itself as a curse. That is the way it was for your parents, and maybe in some ways, it was true. Your father never recovered from the loss of your mother. I sometimes wonder if his accident was a welcomed end.'

Angel was even more convinced of this than her aunt had been. After her mother's death, Dad became a hollowed-out shell of himself. He threw himself into work, taking every job that came his way, not matter how dangerous the fishing or rough the seas. When he was swept overboard, others on the crew said it seemed like he didn't try to save himself.

Love. Was this what it did? Or was her family just cursed? Her mother, dead and gone too young. Her father, heartbroken and following. Aunt Jenny who, according to her own story, had bypassed her chance at love. Her regret kept her company for the remainder of her years until she also met an untimely demise.

The crack of knuckles on the wood door forced her out of her miserable thoughts. She snapped the pages along their creases and folded them with a shaking finger. She made up her mind, and she would make the best of it. She couldn't afford to give it more time.

"Hey, anyone at home?" The knocking resumed, accompanied by a cresting rise in the chattering voices outside. Angel gave the pages one last lingering look, then opened the desk drawer and slid them inside. Wiping at her eyes, she sniffed a final time and lifted her chin. Her friends would not know how much this decision cost her. She forced a smile to her face as she paced toward the door with determined steps.

Her yank on the knob revealed a raised fist. Its hand attached to a woman about Angel's height, though the resemblance ended there. Pixie features matched the elfin body, a stark contrast to the rounds and mounds Angel moaned about when she was brave enough to look in a full-length mirror. DK McGiven Cassidy looked perpetually pleased with the world, even when her husband teased her about being a little devil. The delighted gleam that came to DK's eyes when he said it took any sting out of the words.

"There you are. I was getting worried, and Roxy was about to take a cleaver to the lock to make sure you were okay. Of course, she had one in her back pocket."

DK gave Angel a hard hug and pushed past into the living room, pulling a big carton from a tote bag and spinning toward the kitchen. "Our favorite ice cream for tonight. Does that go with the menu?"

Angel chuckled, because they all knew mint chocolate chip went with any menu. She didn't get a chance to respond when she was engulfed in the next pair of strong arms.

"Damn, something smells good. Did my cooking lessons inspire that beef stew? I have taught you well, grasshopper." A series of appreciative sniffs followed the hugs as Roxy LaFollette sailed to the slow-cooker and lifted the lid. "I can't believe you used this contraption rather than a real pot on a real stove, but I might be able to forgive you." She opened a drawer and grabbed a spoon as if she lived there and scooped out a taste. Slurping it loudly, she said, "Oh yeah, baby, I can forgive you. Good job, girlfriend."

"Well thank the spirits for that. Here, sweetie, these are for you. Hothouse, I apologize. But daffodils will be coming in soon. Your aunt so loved those flowers." Tess Willowspring pushed a bouquet of mixed blooms into Angel's hands and gave her a kiss on each cheek. "You look pensive, dear. Is the gray weather getting to you?"

Angel shut her eyes and took the proffered hug. Where DK gave off impish mischief and Roxy spun with the controlled energy of a tightly-wound top, Tess exuded peace and calm like the soothing scent of the flowers she worked with. Peace and calm, just what she needed.

The chuck of a cork coming out of bottle had Roxy yelling 'opah' and DK countering with 'celebrate' as Tess stepped back and examined Angel's face with close attention. Angel forced her smile to brighten, thanking her for the flowers and using the excuse of searching for a vase in the lower cabinet as a reason to turn away.

Before she'd realized her life as an artist would be over today, she had invited her close friends to laugh and eat comfort food and drink wine. They would not approve of her killing her dream, especially since it had only been a year. She had to tell them, but for now, she would engage in good-hearted verbal hair-pulling with women who loved each other like sisters.

DK passed her a glass of a deep red wine and said, "So, I heard about what happened at the gallery today." She lifted her glass in a figurative salute.

Was her work that bad? Angel dipped her head. Evidently DK applauded her choice to remove her pedestrian scribbles from the co-op where they stood out, not because they were good, but because they were memorably bad.

"What happened at the gallery? Spill," Roxy demanded, passing around a tray of cold meats and cheeses with a bowl of olives in the center.

Better this came from her than being reported by DK. She struggled to force the reality around the hard lump blocking her breath. "I, ah, I decided to – "

Tess's words overran hers. "I heard about it too. Thomas couldn't wait to gossip. And congrats on selling that guitar piece, DK."

DK waved a dismissive hand. "I know, right? But that's not the important part. Did you hear the rest of it? Thomas called me right after and told me that – "

"Wait, you sold that guitar with the notes coming out of the top? That was an outrageously expensive hunk of metal. Did you get full price?" Roxy plopped down on the sofa and stuffed a slice of cheese in her mouth.

"Yes, I got full price. Do you think Thomas would allow anything else? That man does not bargain. Besides, the buyer didn't ask for any discounts. But anyway, that's not the part we need to drink to. Angel is going to – "

She couldn't take this any longer. "I'm taking my pieces out of the gallery. They aren't selling, they're all amateur crap, and I'm getting a regular job."

The room fell silent with her outburst. A sizzle of something wet hitting something hot sounded from the kitchen and the old grandfather clock against the far wall ticked like an ominous countdown to an explosion. Any moment now, it would come. They would sigh with relief and applaud her for coming to her senses. She was no painter. She could barely draw a decent stick figure. Her sense of color was bizarre. It was best to go back to what she knew, books and research.

Around the cheese, Roxy said, "Wait. What? You're giving up on your art? But why? I thought you really loved the painting stuff. How can you just quit? Your aunt would have a fit."

Angel sat up straighter, pushing her shoulders back and lifting her chin. "My aunt was a realist. Yes, I know she intended for me to try things until I found what I love to do, but I also don't think she'd like me to fritter away the money she saved with such determination for all those years. Look, I'll find something else to do."

Roxy didn't look convinced. Tess openly frowned at her, and Angel knew what was coming. Like almost any child who grew up in this town over the past few decades, Tess had been taught high school English by Angel's aunt, the famed Miss Jenny Reed. DK and Roxy were both transplants to Flynn's Crossing, but they too had heard the stories. No one doubted her aunt's determination or dedication, and Angel had wanted so badly to live up to her expectations.

"I don't understand. What do you mean? How can you do that, especially now?" Tess's frown deepened and she shook her head hard enough to cascade her black hair over the shoulder opposite her trademark white streak.

"I am. There is no point in it. Plus, once I get a real job, I won't be able to work in the co-op as I was before. It is the right decision. Let someone who can sell their work have a chance."

Tess turned to DK, who also shook her head. When DK looked back at Angel, her puzzled expression accented her confusion. "I don't understand either. How can you pull your pieces now when you've finally sold them all?"

"I told you. I should release the space to an artist who – wait. What did you say?" Angel felt her breath coming faster as DK's words sunk in.

"Didn't Thomas call you? The old rascal said he was going to. A man came in just as you were leaving yesterday and bought all your work. He picked up that guitar of mine too. Thomas said he called the credit company himself to make sure the card wasn't fake or stolen, because it was black. He'd never seen one before."

Roxy let out a low whistle. "A black card. That's like the primo of the primo. Unlimited credit, like the kind on which you could build a chain of restaurants if you want. The guy must be loaded. Who is he?"

Angel blinked, trying to process words that were not making sense. She had recognized the gallery phone number and left that call unanswered. Later, Thomas's number popped up, and again, she let it go to voicemail. He would only want to argue with her decision. She hadn't had the will to listen to either message.

The fates had decreed the decision out of her hands. Someone had purchased her paintings, the ones she slaved over and poured her heart and soul into. She remembered the tall man standing at the counter, wearing a shocked expression. Something in his eyes as he stared at her with dazed surprise made her heart jerk. The emotional wave he produced, added to the one from her argument with Thomas, was all too much for her to stay. She wasn't proud of her retreat.

"This is it, Angel. Your big break. We're all so delighted for you. Do we have anything bubbly?" Tess threw an arm around Angel's shoulders, bringing her back into the present with a hard hug.

Roxy came next. "I always knew you were made for bigger things, grasshopper. You show promise as a line cook, but this, well, this will be much, much better."

Angel shook her head, her mind grinding hard to process the news. "Ah, thank you, I think. I don't understand. Someone bought everything? I mean, everything? That's, that's, I can't even do the math in my head. I thought they were all over-priced, but now we sold them?" Angel clapped a startled hand over her mouth as she remembered the total price tag. It amounted to more than two months' wages as a librarian in the Los Angeles public system, and there, she had thought she was well paid.

DK gave her a quick dig in the ribs and said, "Told you. You had to wait for things to tick through the clock a few times, like all of us artists do. Overnight success is a myth. Perseverance, hard work, and dedication to your craft are what move you forward. I'm so happy for you, Angel, and I'm betting your aunt would be too."

Her aunt would have been over the moon, of that Angel was sure. An ugly thought raced in on the heels of her budding pleasure. "Can the man return them?"

DK shook her head. "No. We tell customers all sales are final, and they are. Trust me, you can spend your portion of the proceeds if you want. The gallery won't renege on the deal, and the man, or rather his credit card company, can't."

Angel sprang to her feet. "I should thank him. You know, because he really launched my career. I mean, he is my career at this point. I should be at the gallery when he picks them up and say thank you." She ran out of words about the same time she ran out of breath.

DK shook her head again. "He took them yesterday. Thomas offered to crate them up and deliver them, but the man was adamant. He wanted to take them home immediately. He put them in the back of a van and drove off before Thomas could even offer to secure them. They're gone, Angel. As of yesterday, your display space is empty, and you need to fill that up again, pronto."

Angel bit her lip. She would find a way to thank her mysterious benefactor. It couldn't be too hard to find out where he lived and send him a note. Better yet, she could drop in and thank him in person. Or maybe call and then stop by. Oh, dither. She wasn't sure what the protocol should be in a situation like this, because she'd never sold a piece of her art before.

She grabbed DK's arm when the other woman would have followed Roxy and Tess into the dining room. "Did Thomas say what the man's name is?"

DK's eyes closed to slits. "Let me think. Josiah something. Wait, Hammond? Harmon? Hold on, I've got it. Josiah Harmond. Doesn't ring any bells with me, but ask Tess. She's lived here forever."

Angel nodded her thanks. Josiah Harmond. Her first art sale, multiple sales, and her first customer, a real patron. Life was looking up.

>>>>>

It still felt out of the realm of possibility that someone would want all her paintings, but there it was. An empty expanse spanned the alcove wall. With a face-splitting grin on her face, Bettie handed Angel a check for her portion of the sale the following week.

"I hope you'll be able to fill that space up soon, Angel. I mean, now that you've sold out what we had, your popularity will undoubtedly skyrocket. You see that sign? I had to put it up because over the weekend, people were curious about the empty spot, and I told them a collector bought all of your work. I have a waiting list of people to call when you have new stuff. Imagine that, you now have a following, and all because some man we don't know purchased everything you had."

Angel's gaze shifted between the empty wall and the check clutched in her fingers with dazed shock. It still didn't seem real. "About that, Bettie. Do you have the man's contact information? I was thinking I could send him a thank you note. You know, to be polite."

Bettie nodded her head in eager bobs. "That would be a marvelous idea, dear, and something your dear aunt would have done too. Except, there's a problem. Thomas, the old idiot, is losing his marbles, and he didn't get anything from the man other than the credit card. No address or phone number. No email address for the mailing list. Nada. Honestly, I am not sure what to do with him."

"I heard that, you old biddy, and I am not losing my marbles." The roar of words came from the back office. Before another minute passed, Thomas lumbered out to the counter, his eyes lighting on Angel. "Hello, Ms. Reed. Beautiful day, isn't it? I hope you listen to Bettie, since this one time she's making sense, and bring us more work, pronto."

"Tell me, Thomas, why don't you ever call me Angel, or even Evangeline? You call everyone else by their first name."

The old man suddenly found his shoes of great interest. "Well, I was just being respectful, because of your aunt. That's all." He didn't raise his eyes.

Bettie leaned forward with a conspiratorial gleam in her eye and didn't bother lowering her voice when she confided, "I think he's sweet on you, Thomas, because of your aunt and all, I mean, not that young man who bought your work."

Thomas glared at Bettie. "Damn it, woman, you are as gossipy an old witch as I have ever met. Tell all my secrets, why don't you? Ms. Reed, your aunt Miss Reed was a wonderful lady. We passed the time occasionally, but I knew she was made for better than the likes of me."

The revelation had her looking at Thomas with new interest. What did passing the time occasionally mean? She wanted to know more, but Thomas changed the subject before she could ask. "Listen, I had that graphics youngster work up a poster for your display. It's not much, just a little story and a photo from when you did the open studio weekend at DK's place. Thought we could put it up where your pieces have been hanging and when you bring in more, we'll feature it as your artist information."

He turned over a large piece of cardboard on the counter. Angel remembered that weekend. DK had asked her to do a painting demonstration at her old barn studio, and at the time, Angel was convinced her friend was being kind when she said it would give people an opportunity to discover her work. It had been a blast to create and have people ask her questions about her methods and inspirations.

The picture wasn't what she would call flattering, though. The photographer, a friend of DK and her husband, had snapped candid shots, saying they conveyed more about the artist than a staged version would. She wasn't sure how she felt about the result, with hair pulled back in a tight ponytail and a baggy shirt to protect her clothes. Her uncertainty must have shown on her face.

"Look, I can get that kid to change this. But I like it. That babushka thingy on your head makes you look Bohemian and the angle gives you energy and such."

Bettie snorted and shook her head, already pulling the cardboard away. "Honestly, you must be getting senile, you old fool. That youngster you speak of is thirty-seven years old. It's a scarf, not a babushka, and why would Angel want a picture of herself with paint on her face?"

True, smudges of paint on Angel's face marked an effort to brush stray hairs back into the bandana. Bettie and Thomas continued to argue about it, and in the interest of making peace, Angel raised her voice and said, "I love it. Thank you, Thomas, for being so thoughtful to have this made."

The comment shut down the squabble with Bettie looking confused and Thomas, pleased. "So, does that mean you'll stay with us?"

Angel smiled at the dear old man and nodded. Bettie grinned too and clapped her hands. "Excellent. Now I should go. Angel, are you staying for a shift?"

Angel shook her head, a sudden eagerness to grab a brush overwhelming her. She gave a final glance at the large empty wall and couldn't resist a delighted shiver of anticipation. She had more work, old pieces and new ones, and she would decide soon what she would bring in. Thomas placed the new poster in the slot next to Bettie's handwritten note about 'more coming soon'. As she opened the front door, she heard Thomas say in a loud voice, "Now ya see? I told you the girl had sense."

Chapter 2

"Mate, you have to give us something to work with. The natives are getting restless and soon they'll fling spears. Anything, any decent words or tunes at all."

Kaane pressed his forehead into the steering wheel, muttering a chant of curses under his breath. His lead guitarist was the band's amazing song arranger. He took Kaane's lyrics and melody and turned them into multiple part harmony for both voices and instruments. What he couldn't do with a guitar or keyboard wasn't worth knowing.

"Kaane? Are you there, mate? Tell me you have a place for us to start, and I'll fly up tomorrow. We'll turn it into magic."

Kaane lifted his head and stared at the parking lot. The bar's old door was lit in a blue and red neon glow by the beer-logoed signs on either side of it. Above the door, another sign proclaimed the place as Mallory's. He was due to meet the guys twenty minutes ago, but this call with Rodney was far more important.

"Listen, man, I'm working on some sh-, I mean, stuff. It's just not there yet. Just not quite – " He fell silent. Who was he kidding? It not only wasn't ready. It wasn't there, period.

Rodney's silence was so complete that Kaane pulled the cell from his ear and looked at its display to make sure they were still connected. The call glowed in a bright green to complement the neon in front of him. He put the phone back to his ear and said, "Rod-man? You still with me, dude? I'm working it. I promise you, I am."

A heavy sigh sounded through the line. "You don't have jack-shit, do you?" Rodney Moukou rarely swore, and Kaane respected that about him, along with everything else. Eighteen years of working together in the cesspool that was rock star fame never once caused the man to lose his morals or his values. Or his mind, like Kaane did, and too often.

That made the single curse word a thousand times worse. Rodney continued, "Have you tried changing venues, mediums, or muses, such as listening to the iconic classics?"

Kaane massaged the bridge of his nose. "You mean like the Stones? Or Aerosmith?"

A chuckle rumbled like thunder. "No, think further back."

"Beach Boys?"

This time the hissing sound was pure exasperation. "No, I mean truly far back. The classics. Beethoven. Mozart. Brahms. Or the old masters of opera. Verdi. Puccini. Rossini. Other types of artistic expression. Or find inspiration in other sources. Have you tried walking in nature?"

No, he sure has hell had not, and what did nature have to do with rock'n'roll anyway? But then, Rodney, like his background, had always been a little on the weird side. If that was what made him create great arrangements and perform as the perfect guitarist for the band, Kaane would embrace it. Kaane Scott and Rebellion would not exist without Rodney 'Rod-man' Moukou and his sophisticated ways.

Besides, Kaane had tried the different art thing and it wasn't working for him. He thought bringing that girl's paintings home and hanging them around where he'd see them constantly would be enough, but it wasn't. The art stunned his senses in its simplicity, but it didn't move him like the memory of her face did. And that memory exited stage left as fast as the band's patience.

"Classics, my man, classics. I am going to force things. I'm going to schedule a trip and you better have something ready for us to work on. One month. I give you one month. I will see you on April first, and I am not fooling. Start writing, Kaane-oh, because I am buying that ticket as soon as we get off, and I will not change my reservation."

Rodney hung up without a goodbye, but even that simple act broadcasted his frustration. It should have been surprising but wasn't, given the circumstances. This break served many purposes. It gave band members a chance to record solo work or play different music styles with other groups. Fans worked themselves up into a frenzy of desire for a new album. Arenas got hungry to book them and new acts lined up to front for them.

And oh yeah, this hiatus was supposed to be time for Kaane to come up with new material. That was the primary purpose, and the only one that really mattered. Without new songs, they may as well be doing covers for the kinds of gigs they would get.

And that may be what happened, if he couldn't get his shit together. Rodney's advice this time was much more refined than when he'd found Kaane drunk, naked in bed with a pile of bimbos when he should have been writing music. His advice then held a ring of foreboding Kaane could not forget.

"Remember when the music flowed, mate, before the booze pickled your brain and the women stole your energy? You need to clean up your act, or we won't have an act to return to."

Kaane hadn't liked the message over a year ago, putting his fist through a wall in response. Rodney looked at the wall and back at him before walking out the door without another word. It took sobering up and a trip to the emergency room to have his hand stitched and a whole lot of soul-searching to convince Kaane his friend was right. He needed to embrace a new approach to his life or there would be no life as he knew it to return to.

Running a finger under his collar and adjusting his fake glasses, Kaane considered starting the van and heading in any direction that did not involve other people. He didn't feel like a party, a sensation he'd grown accustomed to over the last year or so. Time on his own didn't bring any great revelations, but it was certainly better than making an ass out of himself as he'd done too many times over the past few years. The answers wouldn't be found in the bottom of a bottle or anything he smoked or the body of some willing but empty partner. He sure as hell didn't want to be recognized, didn't want the mob scene and the craziness it would bring.

But as if he knew Kaane was ready to run, his buddy Mac Smythe texted at that second. *'Get out of the van and get in here. We're in the back. You won't be recognized.'*

Kaane stared at the phone, then the bar door. It opened on cue. A sheriff's deputy ambled out, approaching the van's driver side. He glanced at Kaane. With an absent nod, he passed by, got in his official vehicle, and drove off. Kaane wasn't sure if he should be happy or depressed by the lack of recognition.

The blare of noise hit him first, punctuated by a roar of disgust from patrons. The team playing on every screen in the room was one popular with the locals, though by the outcry, things weren't going their way that night. He pushed his way through the crowd and kept his head down, barely mumbling to excuse himself in case someone took note of his voice.

Breaking through on the other side of the masses thronging in tight, he paused to take a steadying breath. The side of the bar away from the televisions was quieter and almost empty. Almost, that was, except for the table in the corner surrounded by three men. They grinned at his approach.

Mac stood, quick with a man-hug and a back slap before he shook his head, his smile widening.

"That is the most ridiculous get-up you've come up with to date, man. Really. Is that a fishing hat?"

Kaane nodded, knowing it was probably a little too much, but he hadn't been sure how else to hide his hair. It was getting too long, and he was afraid to slip into a shop in town because then for sure, someone would recognize him.

A gangly man rose next, fist bumping and hand-slapping him before giving him a pound on the upper arm. Vince Cassidy smirked and said, "Black is your color."

The third man laughed outright. Nothing shifted on Powers Ashland's brush-cut hair as he shook hands with enough force to make Kaane wish he'd worked out this morning. Powers glanced at Vince, and the two burst into fresh laughter. He said, "Really, Kaane? A priest?"

He thought he carried it off well. Black slacks, long-sleeved black shirt with cleric collar showing white against it, nondescript windbreaker. It was probably the hat. The glasses slipped down his nose far enough for him to make a grab for them. He missed, and they slid off completely and landed in Mac's outstretched hand.

His friend sighed and closed his fingers around the cheap plastic. "You know this doesn't work. People recognize you. They are generally too polite and respectful of anyone's need for privacy to bother you."

Kaane shrugged and put his hand out for the glasses. When he tried to put them on his nose again, Mac waved him off. "Don't bother. You can sit with your back to the room. Of course, the combined reputations of everyone else at this table will now be called into question. What are we doing having beer with a priest?"

A pitcher appeared at his shoulder, and Kaane muttered his thanks to the aging waitress. She leaned in and said in a stage whisper, "No problem, father. Or should I say father of Rebellion?" Her cackle of laughter made Kaane sink his chin deeper into the collar. "A priest in a fishing hat. I have now officially seen it all and can retire in peace." She moved away, still chuckling.

Mac leaned in. "Disguises only make people notice you more, you know that, don't you? Like the vehicles you drive."

Kaane grinned in response. There was no way they knew what he drove. He picked up those rides at a funky used car lot in Sacramento, and the registration went through his ghost company run by his manager. The address was in Los Angeles. No one would know.

Mac continued, "Like that blue van you have tonight. Our deputy friend picked it out the minute he pulled in tonight. It was parked off Main Street the other day. Rumor has it you went shopping."

Kaane's grin morphed into a grimace. The deputy had acted nonchalant. It had to be the man's training.

Vince picked up the story. "And that racy sports car, which I think is more your speed, was reported puttering sedately down the South County road heading to your ranch. As in, like, really, really slow. You might want to ditch the heroics. They tend to stand out around here."

Powers slapped him on the back, hard enough to dislodge the clerical collar from its tenuous hold on the shirt. "And that pick-up truck is the worst, man. People see you coming in that, and they forget to take their turn at the stoplight. Seems it's a young chick magnet too, rusty or not. What is it about women and pick-ups?"

The general commentary offered varying points of view, and most of those were probably bullshit, but they had a point. If his disguises weren't working, why did people stay away?

He sunk further in the chair, gouging the clerical collar into his neck. The damned thing hurt like crazy. In frustration, he pulled it off and threw it on the table, releasing a fresh round of laughter. To accent his point, he grabbed the fishing hat and tossed that after the collar. The swing of heavy hair fell out of the disguise and he shook it free. If this brought on a stampede, it would prove his point to these idiots.

"Oh man, you are getting shaggy, aren't you? Is this a new look to go with some new music? That's the rumor going around, you know." Mac flicked a finger at the hair and circled it once.

"No, the hair is not a statement." Kaane glanced over his shoulder with extreme caution, expecting to see pointing fingers, giggling women, and sagely nodding men. Soon, his friends would see why disguises were necessary. Soon, the stampede would start, and then they'd be sorry. He peeked over the other shoulder in cautious expectation.

But he saw – nothing. Faces weren't turned in his direction. The few who randomly looked over weren't in the least bit interested in their table or those around it. Ignored. He was being ignored. Had he fallen that far in the public's memory?

"And now, gentlemen, he's pissed off that no one notices him." Vince raised his glass in a silent toast. "Knew the feeling, dealt with the anger, got over it."

Mac nodded in agreement as Powers and Vince exchanged a knowing glance. "What?" Kaane knew the menace in his tone was probably overreacting, but they were all in on the joke, and it was on him.

Vince leaned in as if expressing an extremely confidential secret. "When I came here, I thought people would recognize me. I thought some would play up to me because I could write about this place and either put it on the map or destroy it. I thought I had power. Little did I know that no one really cares."

That was so out of the realm of possibility, Kaane thumped back in reaction. Didn't they know what it was really like out there?

Mac nodded with even more vigor. "I came with the bright lights shining on me, directing a movie that would put Flynn's Crossing on the map. Then I decided to stay, and while people sometimes comment on a film I've been in or something I've directed or produced, they care more about the new seasonal menu at Roxy's than what I'm doing."

Kaane could completely understand that. Any food Mac's significant other produced at her restaurant or gourmet store was phenomenal, and dinners at their house made the high life cuisine he'd had around the world pale in comparison. But Mac had to be wrong. His attention had to be so distracted, he didn't realize people chased after him.

"Yeah, that sums it up nicely. Most folks focus on the things they care about for their daily lives, not glitz and glamour. Now, if you had a current hit record, they might say something about it when they see you at the bakery. By the way, their lemon blueberry scones are one of my favorites too. Anyway, most people do not pay attention."

The other men nodded at Powers' words, but Kaane slumped in his seat. If people didn't recognize him, it could be because they no longer cared if Kaane Scott and Rebellion ever had another hit. They might not care if they toured. All they would remember, if they recognized him at all, was that once upon a time, long ago, he had been someone.

"Hey, let's try this out. A construction guy, a movie star and a priest walk into a bar. The construction guy says – "

Vince's voice droned on, but Kaane couldn't listen. Maybe he was already a has-been and he didn't know it. Maybe Rodney was throwing him a bone, saying he would arrange the next batch of music. Maybe he knew the truth, that the once famous, panty-attracting Kaane Scott was now a page in rock-n-roll history books. A faded record marred by scratches that skipped across songs like they didn't matter. A tune no one downloaded any longer.

Something had to give, and it had to be him. He wasn't going to buy into the washed-up theory. He needed to prove his best songs weren't on some long-forgotten playlist.

The pale memory of the girl at the gallery whispered across his mind. She could be his muse if only he could get closer to her. He inhaled sharply with the realization. She would be the answer to his fucking prayers.

>>>>>

He felt different without a disguise, and since he'd changed his appearance, like himself, but not really like himself. Kaane let the hair salon door fall shut behind him with a clatter of closed metal blinds. No one in the vicinity swooned in response. When he caught sight of himself in the window's reflection, he stopped.

He hadn't had short hair for over a decade. He looked different, younger, even. Like he had when he started his music career, about the time he met Mac in LA. They had struggled in those early years, struggled to be noticed or heard, struggled to find day jobs that allowed them time to follow any audition or play any gig, struggled to pay the exorbitant rent on the crappy apartment they shared. That week when they both found gigs, stepping stones to hitting it big, had been magic.

Good times, the best. Kaane's discovery as a song writer, followed by a contract with a major label, put Kaane Scott and Rebellion at the top of the charts. He and the band had been filling arenas and stadiums around the world and stacking up a long list of major music awards ever since. Yeah, good times.

But those good times would be long over if he didn't get his shit together. Mac had always offered sound advice, so when his friend pulled him aside as their group broke up the night before, Kaane thought it would be wise to listen.

"I know what's been happening, Kaane. I hear things, and I know people. Word in the biz is that you have run into a dry spell in terms of creating new material."

Kaane had juggled the cleric collar in his restless fingers in imitation of a guitar riff. He shrugged, unwilling to confirm or deny. Mac closed a fist over his restless hand, making him focus on his friend's earnest face.

"I think you need to find a new sound. A new musical genre. A new voice. People love your old stuff, don't get me wrong, but if you step out in a new direction, you'll keep your old fans and attract a whole new set. It never hurts to diversify, which is why I'm producing and directing as well as acting. Roxy does it too, with the restaurant and the grocery store and the catering and the other pots she's stirring over the fire. Look around you. Diversification is the way to go these days."

He didn't know if that was possible. He'd always played rock from that first day in middle school when he'd picked up a guitar.

"And one more thing," Mac said. "Get a haircut. Maybe lose the facial hair too, since it's almost completely gray. You look like a shaggy old dog."

The youngish dude reflected in the glass shook his head. The shave and haircut did make him feel like a new man. If he was going to change, not only the melody but the refrain, he needed to commit to it completely. But he still needed to find his muse.

He glanced into the gallery, praying the angel with soft blonde curls would be working at the counter. Sunlight hit the window. With that glare, it was difficult to see inside, but Kaane thought he could make out a woman moving between display areas. He pushed the door open with a surge of hope, his eyes flicking to the alcove where the art he now owned had been hung.

"Good morning. Can I help you?" The cheery voice didn't hold the musical notes he'd hoped for, and as he turned away from the now-blank wall, an older woman smiled and rushed forward. "Lovely day, isn't it?"

"Yeah, and a terrific day to check out everything Flynn's Crossing offers," Kaane replied.

The woman responded with an enthusiastic exclamation and pointed out various items on display, barely taking a breath. Kaane smiled, hoping it didn't give him away, and nodded politely as she ran through names of various artists. She never mentioned the one he was impatient to hear. It took her a while to run out of steam, and he pounced on the pause to point to the empty wall. "When is this artist going to have new pieces on display?"

Her face lit up. "She will soon, I'm sure, but I don't know when. She's busy painting now. Someone bought out everything of hers we had, and we have a waiting list. Can I add your name? I tell you, we have never seen anything like it. It's like someone sprinkled fairy dust on our Angel."

His eyes fell on a black and white poster on a stand at the base of the blank area. He drew closer, his heart skipping a beat as he noticed its contents.

"How much?"

The woman bustled up next to him and flicked a confused gaze around the white space. "I'm sorry?"

"How much for the poster? This one, about this artist."

She fluttered her hands. "Oh my. Well, I guess when your star takes off, people will want anything they can get their hands on. I'm sorry, that's just a display about the artist until she can bring in more work."

Kaane turned to her and gave his best enticing grin, the one that used to make women of all ages beg. "I'll pay any amount. I really want the poster."

Her confusion seemed to grow to astronomical proportions. "I honestly don't understand why you'd want to spend good money on a poster when you can have some of her work in a week or two, I'm sure."

Kaane kept his smile in place. The woman's fluster faded into a calculating gleam. "Wait right here. Let me check with my business associate." She bustled off to the back, and Kaane turned once more to the photo.

Evangeline Reed. Her age was hard to gauge from the picture, but he'd guess her to be in her twenties. Was that a tattoo on her cheek? He leaned in closer, trying to tell. Her grin sang out about the joy she felt. Her hair was hidden and a nondescript shirt bagged over her body, but it didn't matter. It was her expression and spirit he needed to inspire him.

"Ya want to buy a poster, she says." The old man's grumbling voice matched the scrapes of his feet on the floor. Kaane did his best not to duck his face in response. The old man had seen him before and hadn't recognized him then, but today, he was without any disguise.

"Yes, I would like to buy this poster of Evangeline Reed."

The old man exchanged a disbelieving glance with the woman, then stared at the poster, and finally, at Kaane. He looked him up and down. "Ah, it's you again. Ya cleaned up nice. Did you do that special for coming into the gallery today?"

Kaane grinned, exhaling the tense breath he'd been holding. "Ah, no. You caught me on a bad day before."

The old man nodded as if he understood, then said, "Poster's not for sale."

The woman gave her associate a pointed look with raised eyebrows. She shifted back to Kaane with a smile. "Tell me, how much would you like to pay for this poster?"

The old man barked out, "It's not for sale. It's the only one I had that fool kid make up."

"You'll have to ask him to print up another one. It's not a big deal. Now, how much did you say you would like to pay?"

Kaane opened his mouth, but the man beat him to it. "Thousand bucks."

"What?" The woman's voice came out in a shriek.

"Sold," Kaane said, and she shifted her open-mouthed surprise to him.

The old man leaned over the shocked woman and didn't bother to lower his voice when he said, "Told you he was a fool about his money."

Kaane ignored the man's retreating back as he lifted the cardboard off its stand. He couldn't take his eyes off that joyful grin.

"One more thing. I'd like the address of the artist's studio."

The man didn't stop his retreat. "We don't give out that kind of information. Artists want people to know, they put it on their brochures."

"Do you have a brochure for Evangeline Reed?"

Both shook their heads.

"Is it possible to ask her if she'd sign the poster?"

The woman opened her mouth as if she planned to respond, but the man beat her to it. "When Evangeline Reed brings in her newest pieces, we'll have a gallery open house with cookies and wine and stuff. You can ask her yourself."

That was the perfect solution.

The woman shook her head as if she didn't believe what she was hearing, but her smile stayed firmly in place when she turned back to Kaane. "Now, if I could just have a method of payment and photo identification."

He slipped the cards on the counter, and she picked them up with care, her eyes going a little wide when they landed on the black credit card.

"I'll just have to call this in. It shouldn't take long. While you wait, would you like to sign up for our email list, Mr. Harmond? That way, you're sure to know about the event I didn't know we were planning for Evangeline."

Kaane grinned as his fingers tightened on the poster once more. He took the pen she offered. "I'd be absolutely delighted."

Chapter 3

"Ms. Reed, I hope you're painting."

"Yes, Thomas, I was just finishing up a – "

"Well, you better get painting faster, and paint a lot. That patron of yours came in again today, looking for more of your stuff. I told him you'd have more soon and sold him what we had."

Angel's brush boggled in a suddenly slippery hand. "But I didn't have anything else there."

Thomas grumbled something unintelligible, then said, "He bought the poster."

"The poster?" She switched the brush to her other hand and tried to rub the damp palm dry.

"Yup, the poster we put up in your space. Couldn't believe it. Fool paid a thousand dollars for it without so much as a blink. I guess his ranch or farm or whatever he's doing is going well. You'll get your usual percentage on that, by the way."

A thousand dollars. A thousand dollars for a poster? She blinked her eyes in confusion as Bettie's voice came on the line.

"Hello dear, and congratulations. You have quite the admirer, it seems. I wanted to tell you that Thomas also committed you to an event."

Mind spinning, Angel could only repeat, "An event."

"For the release of your new work, of course. You know, wine and finger food and the artist mingling with people in the gallery. Maybe we'll add some nice live music too. Never hurts to help other kinds of artists in the community, you know."

"New work," Angel parroted back.

"Yes, an event for your new work, like an exhibit. Are you all right, Angel? You sound a little funny."

Angel nodded, with a light-headed sense of joy washing over her. "Yes, Bettie, yes. I'm fine. Just stunned, that's all. I guess I'd better get painting then."

"Well I guess you better. What's that? Oh, Thomas said you should also think about putting your studio on the spring tour."

"But I don't have a studio."

"Well, I guess you'd better think about that too, dear. I'll leave you to it, then."

As Bettie began signing off, Angel jumped in with quick words. "Bettie? Did you get an address for my, ah, my collector?"

Rustling paper sounded in the background. "He gave us an email address, so that will have to do. I'll send it to you, dear, but would you mind a word of advice? Think carefully about what you say and what you agree to with this man, Angel. I wouldn't be true to your aunt's memory if I didn't say that. There's just something off about him, like he's hiding something. You know how strange some people can be."

Angel agreed, not that she planned to do anything more than thank her mysterious patron. She had painting to do, not socializing. She dashed back to the easel and had a brush in each hand, unable to control the burst of energy to create.

Three hours later, she hadn't even bothered with dinner. Euphoria made her giddy, though whether it was with her progress or because of her patron, as Thomas called him, was not something she was ready to contemplate. It was late when her hands complained with cramps and she set aside her palette. Only then did she allow herself to check her email for Bettie's message.

'Here is Josiah Harmond's email address. Now remember, you don't know anything about him. He might be married or crazy or both. Thomas is an old fool, but he does have a good nose for these kinds of things and he says the young man is suspicious. You be careful. You'll have a chance to meet him in public when we have your exhibit event. Just be patient.'

The email address seemed innocuous enough, JKSHarmond followed by numbers at a generic carrier. Angel hesitated, wondering what to say.

'Thank you' didn't seem like enough. What did one say to someone who bought work that might be less than buy-worthy? She deleted most of a message that made her sound like an empty-headed teenager in a fan rave. In the end, she'd typed out a simple thank you and reiterated the invitation to view her new pieces when they scheduled the event. She hit the send button before she could second-guess it further, and when a week passed with no reply, she tried not to let it get her down.

After another long but productive day, Angel blew the hair out of her eyes and put the brush down. She leaned back and heard a distinct crack as her spine realigned. She'd spent so much time on this stool or standing that her body felt frozen. But the results were worth it, she hoped. It remained to be seen what others would think.

She chewed her thumbnail as she walked from canvas to paper and back again. Watercolors dried propped on shelves that used to house the African violets her aunt had been so fond of. Canvasses lined the porch's perimeter and spilled over into the house interior. Chalk drawings were already in a portfolio for framing. The whole place smelled like a studio, and if she wasn't careful, it would all look like a messy one too. What would aunt have said about that?

As she picked up the brush and her palette of colors, the doorbell rang. She hadn't ordered any new supplies, but then she'd been so distracted, she might have done it and forgotten. With the brush still in hand, she rushed to the front door and pulled it open without looking.

Bright flashes of color grabbed her immediate attention and she grinned at the sight. The three women on her front porch wore serious expressions as they struck a designed pose.

The blonde said, "Charley needs a fourth angel. You in?" Roxy blew on cocked fingers held like an imaginary pistol.

To her right, Tess shook her head and rolled her eyes. "That is getting a little old, don't you think?" Her black hair swept over her shoulder as she turned to Angel, giving a wink.

"It is almost quitting time, right?" The redhead on the other side didn't even spare the others a glance, a smile lighting up her face. DK's eyes darted over Angel's shoulder to the collection of pieces drying in the living room. "Oh my, you've been busy."

Angel stepped aside for them to enter, returning each hug with care to avoid getting paint on someone else's clothes. "I'm sorry, I lost track of time. I should have set an alarm for tonight."

Tess shook her head as she linked arms with Angel. "I believe we all get like that when we're creating, and it's a glorious feeling. Powers says he could dump a truck of rocks next to me and I wouldn't notice when I'm in that mode."

From behind them, Roxy snorted. "Come on, you two. Slower than molasses in January, honestly."

Tess said, "What's your rush, Roxy? Did you leave something boiling on the stove?"

"No, this is my night off, remember? I don't get many of those anymore, and I want to make the most of it."

DK rounded the room, stopping in front of each piece and examining it with a serious expression. "I think it's more that you don't take the time off, which is, I fear, also a lesson for our young friend here. Tell me, have you slept at all?"

Angel's heart fell. DK was her role model. As a gifted metal artist, she'd battled her own odds to make her art her life's work, and she now made a successful living at it. Plus, she had an amazing husband who worshipped her in a goofy way more endearing than anything in a romance book. When Angel found her calling, she wanted her life to be as fulfilling and rewarding as DK's.

Except, it sounded like her friend had doubts. Just because she didn't want to read anything into it didn't make it easier for Angel to ignore the implication. Perhaps this was all trash, and she had been fooling herself. The gallery would have a party when she hung her new work, and no one would come. Except these three, of course. They'd probably have to drag along their significant others.

And Mr. Harmond. She hoped he'd come. Maybe it was just as well that he hadn't responded to her email. When he saw what her latest efforts produced, he'd probably laugh.

"Evangeline Reed, I asked you a question. You look downright forlorn and I hate that." DK gave her arms a shake, and Angel snapped to attention at the emphasis.

"Ah, sorry. Wool-gathering. What did you ask me again?"

DK examined her more closely. "You'll want to clean the brown off your face before we go to dinner. Is that oil paint? I asked you if you were painting around the clock. You have produced an amazing amount of work recently."

Angel avoided any response by turning to the mirror over the side table. Yes, paint on her face. Brown, along with some white she'd used for blending. Pushing the scarf off her hair, she shook out the annoying curls and stared back at blue eyes shining with somber self-doubt.

"What's wrong?"

Angel shrugged at Tess's reflection, lifting her palms and circling her hands to indicate the porch. "Is any of it any good? I mean, there might be a lot of it, but all of it could be crap."

"Crap? You think its crap?" Roxy shook her head as she crowded around Tess.

DK added, "Angel, you have a great sense of perspective, your brushstrokes and pencil work are bold and unique, and the variety of mediums means you have a larger potential audience for your work."

"But?"

Her friends stayed silent at her question. She fluttered her hands as her stomach dropped to the old plastic clogs on her feet. "I'm not sure I have time for dinner tonight. I still have more work to do." Clearly she did, like starting over with fresh everything and hoping for an artistic miracle.

DK glanced at the others and stepped forward, putting her hands over Angel's flaying fingers. "Everything I said about your work is true. You're good, and with a little something, you will be great."

Angel huffed out air. She somehow doubted that little bit was going to be something she could easily find. She was giving it all she had.

"I agree, and as DK will tell you, I know absolutely jack-shit about art, other than I know what like."

Tess shook her head. "Roxy, honestly, language. Angel, I agree with DK, and I'm looking at this from a floral perspective. Balance, structure, theme, variety, it's all there."

Angel asked, "Then what's missing?"

The three women glanced at each other as if in silent consultation. By the time they looked back, DK scrunched her face into a knot of gentle sympathy. "Is there a reason all of your colors are drab? I mean, you have other colors, right? Is this like Picasso's blue period or something? Angel's middle of winter motif?"

While the words were delivered with kindness and the motif comment held humor, Angel's spirits took a deep dive. She hadn't deliberately set out to select quiet, fading colors. But there they were, on nearly every piece of work around the room. She turned in a circle and identified the three pieces that held splashes of random brightness. The first three oils she had done back at the beginning of the week, as she anticipated an email response from Mr. Harmond, held a vibrancy the others lacked.

"I am a passionless dweeb of an artist, aren't I?"

"Why do you say you're passionless?"

"Well, look at them, DK," Angel said, aware her voice was rising. "Dull, safe, and boring. Let's face it, I haven't exactly had a lot of excitement in my life. For that matter, up until Aunt Jenny's unexpected legacy, there wasn't a lot of living in my life. My former job was all about keeping my nose in books, or databases, or other resource materials. I solved information puzzles in a cubicle, and while that can be fun, I am an empty vessel when it comes to life experience." She panted into the sudden silence.

"Oh man, I think we've heard this before," Roxy said. She gripped a hand on Angel's arm. "How about men?"

"I thought all men are scum," DK said.

Roxy's shoulders lifted and fell. "True, some guys are horn dogs, and that's insulting canines, but there are plenty of nice guys in the world. So tell us, Angel, have the guys you've dated all been scum, or have there been some good ones along the way too?"

She wasn't sure how she could respond to that. The silence could officially be called deafening as all three women watched her with a range of expectant expressions.

"I, ah, kind of have not dated a lot." Or at all.

"Define a lot," Tess said.

Angel pressed her lips tight.

Roxy dropped her arm and clapped her hands. "Ladies, we are staying in tonight. We clearly have work to do here. Luckily, I know just the place that delivers." Her cell phone was already dialing a series of beeps. "Hi, it's me. Listen, I need – " Her words faded as she walked back into the main part of the house.

Tess took Roxy's place at Angel's side, linking arms and closing the distance between them. "Back to the question. Define a lot."

Her voice dropped to a whisper, a flush of embarrassed heat warming her face. "I dated a few nice guys. They were quiet, studious types for the most part. I didn't have a lot of time to date. Commutes are brutal in LA and after work, I only wanted to go home and read." That made her sound twenty different kinds of boring.

DK came to her other side and linked fingers. "Has anyone ever lit your hair on fire?"

Angel stared at her in astonishment. "What? No. I mean, the fire part. I assume that was metaphorical."

Tess chuckled, "Yes, of course it was, dear. But none of them touched your heart, did they?"

Her cheeks heated as she nodded. She wished the porch would fall in and distract them from this line of questioning. She might as well toss the work around her, because she'd been following a fool's dream too. She was no artist. Artists felt passion. She had none.

Roxy reappeared, clapping her hands once more. "Food's about thirty minutes out, and I ordered wine too. And ice cream, because these talks always result in tears with only one solution. I think we are about to initiate an artistic break through."

Tess drew her into the living room. "Forget about the art. I think this is going to be a personal break through."

Angel tried to resist being pulled forward, but she also wasn't clear about what was happening. She wanted to go to bed and pull the blanket up and not come out until this whole art thing was forgotten by everyone. She finally moved to help DK pick up dried watercolors off the dining room table. "Um, I'm not sure what you're all talking about. And I'm not sure I'm in the mood for dinner. I think I have some cleaning up to do, and then I need to think about getting a real job. I don't think I have what it takes to be an artist, not the kind you think I can be."

Sorry, Mr. Harmond. She let the silent apology go out into the universe, hoping that if he ever remembered to check back at the gallery, whoever was working would be unfamiliar with her name. Her aunt hadn't gotten it right. She wasn't going to find her passion through this little sabbatical.

DK wrapped an arm around her shoulders and gave a squeeze. "Angel, have we ever told you the whole story about how Vince and I met?"

An hour later, Angel didn't bother to hide her sniff. It was such a lovely story. "Vince proposed to you that soon?"

DK grinned, though a mistiness clouded in her eyes. "Yes, only a month after I thought we were done forever. I tell you, that was the worst Thanksgiving on record, but every holiday since has been a keeper, just like my man."

Tess and Roxy nodded. Roxy added, "It took a while for me to be convinced he was good enough for her, because let's be honest, this is Vince we're talking about, and he only has two settings, cynic or goof, but we love him anyway. Just like Powers, bless his over-controlling heart, won us over when he supported Tess. And Mac came through when it counted, though he was the reason I believed all men were scum."

Angel stood to collect dishes, only to have Tess take the bowl from her and push her back into the couch. "Sit. You have things to learn yet. You tell us what kind of man you're looking for. We can vet possibilities for you. We've gotten kind of good at this sort of thing over the past few years."

Roxy snorted and shook her head. "I don't know. Remember when we tried to fix you up? Three blind dates on fast roads to dead ends, I think were your exact words."

Tess shrugged. "Yes, but that was eons ago. How many happy link-ups have we been a part of since then?"

The other two nodded seriously. Angel could only watch them with growing apprehension. "You're all being wonderful to worry about me like this, but you don't have to be. I'm happy as I am."

All three shook their heads. "Not buying it," Roxy said. "Now tell us. What do you like? You mentioned studious, like a professor or something? We could ask – "

"Yes," the two others cried in unison, before the rest of the words were even out of Roxy's mouth.

Angel rubbed her temples, trying to rid herself of the deliberate beat that had taken over in the last hour. "No, he doesn't have to be a professor. Listen – "

"I know," Roxy shouted as she jumped up. She flung an arm in Angel's direction. "You like a bad boy. You know, a walk on the wild side and all that."

"Roxy." Tess's single word carried a warning.

Roxy shrugged with her palms up. "What? We need to know. No point in matching her up with a serious guy wearing dorky glasses if she wants a stud muffin on a Harley where they're, you know, doing it."

Laughter followed the words, but Angel didn't join in. She looked from woman to woman as her depression hit a new low. "You're all so amazing. I have nothing that can compare."

"Angel, what are you talking about?" Tess frowned at her.

Angel waved an arm to highlight Tess from head to toe. "Look at you. Outside of the fact that you have that Native American spiritualism coolness going for you, you're tall and willowy and brave and smart. It's obvious why Powers is crazy about you. He'd be crazy not to be into you."

She turned to Roxy next. "And you. Everything you touch turns to gold. Look at the businesses you've built, and every one of them successful. And you revived a storybook romance with a guy who is admittedly one of the hottest guys on the planet. And I would kill for your hair."

Roxy boggled her water glass before saying, "Right back at ya, sister. I always wanted curls. But no, straight as a ruler."

As Angel turned to DK, she felt tears welling up in her eyes. She couldn't remember the last time she'd cried in front of anyone.

"DK, you are perfect too. You do this amazing art, hard art, stuff people pay big bucks to buy."

DK gave her an indulgent smile. "I've had years to learn my craft, Angel. You're only beginning. Trust me, you'll keep learning and evolving and someday, you'll look back at the early years with a certain fondness because then, you didn't think about all of the things that could go wrong."

Angel felt the tears run down her face and she sniffed. Roxy immediately shot out of her chair and said, "That's my cue to dish out the ice cream."

Where the words came from, Angel wasn't sure. She didn't mean to say anything. She certainly didn't mean to say this.

"I'm a virgin," she said, following the blurt of words with another loud sniff.

Stunned gasps echoed in the room. Roxy broke the silence. "Holy crap, I did not see this coming. Did you guys see this coming? I did not, not in a million years." She took a step forward, and Angel had the uncomfortable sensation of being examined like a weird insect on the head of a pin.

Tess cleared her throat and said, "I must admit, in today's times, that is a little unusual. Is it due to religious reasons?"

Angel hung her head lower and shook it with glum resignation.

DK leaned over from the other end of the couch. "There is absolutely nothing wrong with being a twenty-something-year-old virgin, Angel."

"Thirty-three," Angel hiccupped, willing the tears to stop. "Soon I'll be thirty-four."

Roxy shoved a box of tissues in front of her face, and she grabbed a handful without murmuring her thanks. Then her friend dropped to her knees and wrapped her hands over the ones clutching the tissues. "No worries, Angel. You are in the best of hands. Let's get you good and laid before that next set of birthday candles, and your creative problems will be solved."

Chapter 4

It was hopeless. Kaane couldn't string two notes together and his lyrics didn't make sense. There was no point in trying when nothing came. He turned to the poster in its place of honor, next to a printout of the single email. All it needed was candles to complete the altar. Running a finger over the face on the spot where a splotch marked the subject's cheek, he whispered aloud, "Angel, I need help."

Yeah, like talking to a picture was going to do it.

A rock melody sounded through the house. The doorbell his band had given him as a house-warming gag gift played their first big hit. He hated the thing every time it rang because it reminded him of what he no longer had. Words. Melody. Songwriting chops. Luckily, the bell didn't ring often.

The song played again, and he grabbed the poster and the email, sliding them behind sheet music. He didn't want anyone to know about his secret obsession. The art on the walls might give him away, but he could always say he liked the stuff. He straightened his shirt and ran a hand over the short hair he still wasn't used to before pulling the door open.

"Hey, about time. Love the doorbell, by the way. Retro." Mac crossed the threshold carrying a full paper bag and bumped shoulders with him.

Vince followed with a wicked grin on his face. "Was that your first hit? I remember hearing it way back when. You don't write songs like that anymore. Why is that?"

Yeah, he'd unplug that doorbell.

Powers came last, gesturing to Vince. "Sorry, this one tagged along. His woman ran off on a secret errand and he was at loose ends. What's this about another renovation?"

His glance at the prominent gap in drywall spoke louder than words would have. When work was underway on the house, Kaane had come upon Powers measuring the fist-sized hole. "I'll have the guys patch this. By the time we're done, you'll never know it happened." Curiosity about the cause lit his expression despite his business-like tone.

"Leave it. I want to keep it."

Kaane remembered quick shock on his friend's face before Powers frowned at him. "Really, it won't be any big deal. No cost to you, my treat."

When he had shaken his head and insisted the damage remain, he was greeted with a thoughtful considering look. Powers had never spoken of it since.

Kaane waved a hand to include the entry and main rooms. "It's great, Powers, and exactly what I wanted. You kept the bones of the old ranch while making this a modern showpiece. Not that many people see it, but if I was going to show it off, I wouldn't hesitate."

Apparently satisfied, Powers grinned. "Good, because I would hate to change a single thing. You must have remodel fever. It's a true condition, I swear. Don't worry, soon your new music studio will be more than bare bones and you'll be fine."

"Did I hear you say a music studio? Like your band playing here? Man, that will be so cool." Vince rejoined them, two glasses of amber liquid in his hands. "Here, time for a toast done right."

"Um, thanks, but I'm abstaining."

Vince's smile faded into disbelief. "What? Since when? And why? Wait, is there a woman involved?"

Mac appeared next with two more glasses, his eyes darting between Vince's expression of shock and Kaane's upraised hands. Shock didn't last long, and between the four of them, the wide hallway was filled with a dozen questions and bouncing words.

"No, no woman. I'm abstaining there too."

Stunned silence met that proclamation. Kaane wasn't sure what to say to follow up. He doubted any of them believed him, even a gawking Mac. But he'd made his mind up, and damn it, he was going for it.

Powers turned to the other two and gave a raised-eyebrows tilt of his head. As if suddenly coming to his senses, Mac shut his mouth and elbowed Vince. "Come on. We should ditch these."

Vince looked like he was ready to argue, but Kaane had to give it to him, he manned up quickly. His frown turned into a nod that grew stronger as he followed Mac back to the kitchen, but Kaane heard his words as they faded into the background. "What the hell? Kaane Scott, off women and booze?"

Powers' steady gaze didn't waver, and he didn't ask what was going on. He just waited. Over the past months, Kaane had come to appreciate three things about the man. He put his client's concerns first on projects. He came through when it counted and under the most difficult circumstances. And he was the soul of discretion.

But that wasn't enough for Kaane to take him into his confidence. Instead, he yelled, "Hey, we're going out to the barn." With an abrupt nod, he opened the door and Powers went through it.

The graveled crunch of their boots matched steps as they walked to the old structure. Kaane had fallen in love with it when he first viewed the house, and while he knew it was crazy, he swore happy ghosts lingered in the dusty interior. The small access door creaked on rusty hinges as he pushed it open. The larger hanging door that welcomed countless generations of large animals was harder to move, though someday, he hoped to have it in fine working order too.

"I want to make this into my personal music space."

Powers followed him inside, flicking on a small penlight and sweeping it up to follow the old rafters. The upper hayloft had seen better times, and the stalls on this level showed the price of neglect, but it remained an impressive building, one that weathered over a hundred years.

Walking back through what had been a breezeway between stalls, Powers ran his light over various joints and beams. Kaane didn't need to follow. He'd spent hours in this barn, hoping it would speak to him in words he could translate into a song. So far, nothing.

Powers clicked off the light, striding back in the darkness like he could see through it. Kaane bet he could. A contractor didn't face blinding stage lights and the flash of camera bulbs night after night like a performing musician did. Along with loss of hearing, light sensitivity was another of the afflictions he could claim from his career.

Career. Did he even have one of those anymore? Would he be better off fading away without a whimper? Fans would forget him. The band would find gigs, because they were great. No one really needed him.

As if he conjured her, the face on the poster floated in the darkness. His angel hovered in his vision as if she stood in front of him, encouraging him not to give up. He knew if he reached out to touch her, she'd disappear like smoke. That didn't keep him from wanting to run a hand through the curls hidden by the bandana.

Evangeline. Even her name sounded angelic, like a muse's should. The shy smile and her clear eyes inspired his confidence. She would know what he needed.

"Don't do it."

Powers sudden firm words made Kaane jump. He'd forgotten the man was there.

"Don't do what?"

Powers gestured to the barn's darker corners. "Don't try to change this. It's a beautiful old building. If I was going to do anything here, I'd repair what's broken and return it to a usable condition. But changing this into a music studio? It would cost much more than starting from scratch. The permitting process would take a year alone. And you'd lose this wonderful old space."

In a tone he knew was defensive, he said, "Mac renovated a barn, and Vince has one with DK. They use them. What's wrong with using this one?" Yes, he sounded like a pissy fan who lost a backstage pass, but he needed something to get going again.

Shaking his head, Powers advanced and turned them both toward the door. "DK uses hers as a studio, and she hasn't changed a thing inside other than adding removable lighting, winches, and platforms. Mac took his back from a garage, and that's where they keep the heritage animals they're raising. Still barns, both of them."

"I need a studio, one with character."

"And the one we're building out back, at no small expense and to your specifications, won't give you that?"

An adamant shake of his head was all Kaane could manage. None of it would work, a voice whispered inside his brain, without the essence of his muse.

Powers stopped a couple of strides ahead and turned to him. "What's wrong with the dining area we turned into a music room?"

Kaane shrugged, unwilling to give away his plans. Powers stayed quiet, watching and waiting. He'd probably stand like that until dark if Kaane didn't say something.

"I have new plans for that."

Powers lifted a shoulder as if to ask about those plans.

Trying to redirect the interest, Kaane said, "I need the space for something else."

Another shoulder, this time accompanied by crossed arms.

Sighing, Kaane caved. "That is going to become my social space. I have a grand piano arriving in two days, and I'll keep my guitar collection there as we had planned. I want to create my music here." He stomped his foot in the dust to emphasize his point.

Powers narrowed his eyes. He pushed the door shut behind them with a firm swing, as if to make his point. His arms fell to his sides once more, and he resumed the walk back to the house as if this had just been a momentary pause. Kaane shook his head, wondering what the man was thinking. Why didn't he ask about the new music?

The front door yawned open and framed Vince. "Good, you're back. Kaane, your phone's been ringing like crazy, and it lights up with the name Rodney. Mac thought you should know, since it doesn't stop."

He'd expected that. Rodney would want an update and then he'd want to rip Kaane a new one. As if on cue, the phone buzzed on the kitchen counter hard enough to jump in vibration, and all four men stared at it as if expecting it to explode. "I'm not going to answer it," Kaane said, as if that wasn't already obvious. As soon as the ringing stopped, he reached over and turned the phone off.

"Well, all right then," Mac said. He and Vince exchanged a pointed glance, before he swung the look to Powers. The man lifted his shoulders in a noncommittal shrug and nodded his head in Kaane's direction.

Mac bustled into action, shoving the bottles he'd arrayed on the counter back into the paper bag. "So, gentlemen, what's your pleasure? Soda or good old H-two-Oh?"

"I don't know. This is not the Kaane Scott we all grew to love and admire. I mean, you were a hard rocking, hard drinking kind of guy. And the women. You have a broad circle of male pupils, so labeled because of their willingness to learn from your skill with the ladies." Vince's hand hovered for a moment before he lifted a can of soda from the counter. Mac followed suit with a barely concealed sigh.

Kaane would not change his mind. He would not be swayed. He would stand firm. This was for his music. His muse demanded it. His celibacy, his virtue, his commitment. Then maybe she'd speak to him and show him the way.

Vince waved his soda in Kaane's direction and said, "Come on, man, throw us a bone. What's it like, living in a world where women throw panties at you all the time?"

It had been a long time since Kaane felt like he was on the receiving end of that kind of female adoration. In fact, the last few concerts, and they were a while ago, the women were older and rarely sent lingerie at the man behind the microphone. Not only was his fan base less enamored, they were aging before his very eyes. Soon, he could expect to hear his hit songs played as elevator music in department stores.

"Hey Powers, why don't you go check on that new construction out back and see if you have any more of your excellent ideas for it? And take Vince with you."

When Vince began to protest Mac's direction, Powers put a big arm around the arguing man's shoulders. "Come on, Cassidy, I need someone to hold the other end of my tape measure."

"I thought you had a laser thingie, you know, with the light thingie. Oh, oh, I get it. Yeah, I can do that. I know you need the help, man."

The two rustled out the door, leaving Kaane staring at anything but his friend of two decades, the one who would understand his current predicament and be supportive to the end. Despite that, he couldn't explain it, not to Mac, not to anyone. They would think he was crazy. Maybe he was.

Instead of saying anything, Mac motioned to the big front room of the house, the place Kaane had chosen for his man cave of a media room. The television filled a side wall, the windows had blackout curtains that lowered with a remote control, and the bar in the corner included a popcorn maker. When Mac sank into a deep lounge chair in the middle of the room, Kaane took the one next to him.

"Do you want to talk about it?"

Kaane shrugged, ready to tell Mac it was no big deal. He knew that Mac wouldn't push it. Then again, there was something about staring at a blank screen, side by side with someone who was not going to put you under a microscope, that made it easier to say.

"I can't write a damned thing." He'd been holding the words in so hard, they hurt to let go.

"You're in a little slump. Happens to all of us. Think of where my career was a couple of years ago. Bets were being taken including a line in Vegas about whether I'd collapse on the set of every movie I was working on."

Kaane remembered that time. Drinking too much, sick with something mysterious, and looking like he was twenty years older than his age, the world had written Mac off. It had seemed like a miracle when he recovered. Not only did he rise back to his former greatness, but if anything, his current work was the best of his life. And he owed it all to Roxy, something he underscored often and with pride.

Shaking his head, Kaane said, "It's a little bit more than a slump." He hesitated, not sure what to say past that.

Mac took a slow sip, his eyes traveling around the room. They paused on each picture on the wall, the collection of art now part of his shrine.

"Interesting art selections." Mac's gaze lingered on a set of watercolors over the bar. "They look familiar."

"Just some stuff I liked, you know, to dress up the place."

"They're dark, like the artist was in a funk." His friend's eyes traveled to an oil near the room's entrance. "Are they all from the same artist?"

Kaane gulped his water and stayed quiet. He didn't want to hint at how close he was to returning to the gallery and begging to learn an address where he could meet the artist in the flesh. Her brief email wasn't enough contact. His fingers still itched to respond, but what could he say without sounding obsessed?

He shot to his feet. "Come on," he said, grabbing Mac by the arm and giving him a yank hard enough to fizz carbonation. "I just had a brainstorm I want to share with Powers. I want you to hear it. Come on."

"But, I was – " Whatever Mac was going to say next was lost when another firm pull from Kaane had him spilling cola on his white shirt. "Damn, looks like I'm doing the laundry again."

That was interesting enough to give Kaane a reason to pause and look at his friend with wide eyes. Mac Smythe, doing laundry?

Mac wore a sheepish expression as he shook the folds of his shirt away from his body. "Yes, I know how that sounds, but Roxy and I have an agreement. If she can keep her chef's whites clean on an evening when the restaurant is slammed, and I can't keep a shirt clean sitting in an office, which seems to be something I have a problem with, I do the laundry. If she gets messed up, she does it. It's a fair arrangement."

Before Kaane could question it, Mac leaned closer with a conspiratorial look in his eyes. "And honestly, I don't mind. Sometimes I even put a stain on my shirt on purpose. That woman doesn't let me do much for her. She's so independent, like she doesn't want to rely on me for anything. I guess I haven't completely earned her trust after our problems years ago."

"Yeah, well, that was not a good scene for either one of you, but you're over it now. Two little lovebirds in their cozy nest," Kaane said, grimacing at how idiotic his wording sounded. Soon, he'd have a hard time carrying on a conversation.

Mac punched him in the arm. "Find a good woman, the one meant for you, and your world changes for the best."

"No women. Celibacy. I am on the straight and narrow. For as long as it takes."

Mac shook his head, his face grave. "Man, you are acting so out of character, it's like you're reading off a completely different script."

If only his friend knew.

It took Kaane two more hours to pile the men out the door. As soon as it swung closed and the sound of engines faded away, he reached into his hiding place and pulled out the poster and email, returning both to their places of honor. He re-read the message, the simple note so tastefully done. He read the brief artist biography on the poster, not that he didn't already know it by heart. He traced her cheek, realizing his finger shook.

He hadn't responded, and it was suddenly and abundantly clear to him that staying silent was a mistake. He would never be able to understand her role in his life until he met her in person, and to start down that path, he needed to connect with her.

But what to say? Words. He was losing any ability to use his words. He had to try.

Turning on the phone, he pounded his fingers on his thigh like a crazed drummer during a solo as he waited for the email app to load. He scrolled down, past the multiple posts from Rodney that undoubtedly held a litany of lectures, focused on moving to her message, but his finger froze and backtracked when it caught his eye.

A message from the gallery highlighted an event a week from Saturday night. A show introducing new work by a co-op member featured honored none other than Evangeline Reed. The artist would be in attendance and looking forward to sharing her new pieces.

Kaane's smile turned real for the first time in days.

Chapter 5

Protesting did no good when DK insisted she would drive. They buzzed down the freeway in a red convertible Angel had a hard time associating with her truck-centric friend.

"Was this the car?"

DK's smile turned dreamy and reminiscent. "Yes, it was. This is the one he drove to the winery's opening event, the one where my new sculpture was on display. I already knew something was wrong with it before he taunted me, but it took time to figure out what it was. Vince was how I fixed it." She ran a loving hand over the old dash.

Passion. It all came down to passion. Angel searched for it, reached for it, but so far, she didn't think she had made much progress.

"Okay, here we are. Ready to shop your heart out?"

Angel shied away from looking at the façade of the store, shaking her head. "No. Listen, this is very nice of you, but my clothes are fine. I can wear something from my closet."

DK gave her a pointed stare, her eyes flicking from the sweater set to the plaid skirt. "You look like a librarian."

Angel laughed without humor and said, "I am a librarian."

DK shook her head in fierce denial. "No, you are a painter, and you have a gallery event, your very first opening, in a week. You are not going to look like a librarian on that night if it kills me. If we aren't successful, Roxy and Tess will kill me, so we're finding something that turns you," she waved her hand up and down, "into an artist."

Angel was slower to leave the car, her hands wringing the purse strap in a high state of nerves. "DK, I can't afford this, not on a – " She bit off what she was going to say, on a librarian's salary. Her present circumstances with her one customer aside, her artist's earnings were even worse.

DK linked an arm through her elbow and urged her forward. "You're not a librarian anymore, and I think once we solve your little problem, you will reach that magical tipping point. You're going to find that your art is in high demand, and not just by one guy. Come on, this will be fun. We've taken up a collection."

Angel stopped them both on the sidewalk a few steps from the imposing glass doors. "A collection?"

Grinning widely now, DK nodded with enough vigor to dislodge the sunglasses on top of her red cap of hair. "Think of us as your sponsors. We, the girl tribe, are each sponsoring something to help you come out of your shell. The others were disappointed they couldn't be with us today, but I'll send them pictures as we shop."

When DK tugged again, Angel stayed in place on stubborn feet. "I cannot take charity from all of you."

In clear exasperation, DK began waving her arms. "It is not charity. Besides, it wasn't money we collected. It was style ideas and who gets to decide on what you buy. I get to pick out your gallery outfit. Tess is in charge of casual wear. Roxy, the brat, picked undies."

Undies? Her plain old cotton was fine. It wasn't like any man was going to see her in less. It would be a waste of money.

Yes, her aunt had left her more than enough to cover basic living expenses, but Angel had come to think of that as a safety net, emergency funds she didn't want to touch unless she couldn't find a job, when this charade of an attempt at art came to an end. Until then, she wanted to be able to survive on her savings.

"I can't afford this," she said again.

With gentle understanding in her expression, DK said, "Angel, you can't afford not to."

Which was why, on Saturday night when she'd usually be home reading, Angel smoothed her hand down the filmy pants, the ones DK convinced her to buy at the high-end store she would never have set foot in on her own. Despite the thin gauzy top, clammy sweat made the room feel overheated.

"Angel, are you ready? We've opened the doors."

The question, delivered by an eager Bettie, yanked her attention to the prominent display. She'd spent the past two days fussing and moving and changing out her pictures, until Thomas grumbled she was more restless than a room full of monkeys with no bananas. The saying was so like something her aunt would say, it made her giggle on a nervous exhale.

"Do you think everything looks all right?" She turned to Bettie, grabbing her hands and glancing once more at the fresh display.

"I think it looks amazing, dear. I love that use of new colors, almost as much as I love that new outfit."

The colors, new oils sent to her by a determined DK, splashed across her usual duller work in fierce defiance. Angel had nearly covered them more than once, but Tess stopped by the house and saw them and declared them keepers. Her friends were conspiring against her to make her into a brightly colored butterfly, like the ones taking nervous wing in her stomach.

She was saved from answering Bettie and her too-sharp questions when Tess, Roxy and DK came up to them, glasses of bubbly in hand. Roxy pushed one at Angel. "Here, you look like you need this."

"A toast," Tess said.

The three women raised their flutes, and Angel added hers with great hesitation. Tonight was either going to be a big bust, or she was going to have the shock of her life. She'd bet on the former.

"To Angel and her new adventures. May your art be the wave that carries your sex life forward," Roxy said.

"Roxy," Tess and DK admonished as one.

"What? Okay, okay, the wave that carries your passion forward. But let's be realistic. There needs to be some sex involved. You can't be the only one not getting any."

Tess added a wink. "You look absolutely stunning, sweetie. I love the new clothes. I love the new art. You are breaking out and breaking through. How does it feel?"

Angel released nervous chuckles, trying without success to keep color from flooding her face. She didn't feel like herself, not in these clothes, not being the center of attention, and not when she had no idea what came next. "I feel like an imposter," she admitted.

DK frowned. "But this is your night. Your art is drawing all sorts of good attention. Look, people are swarming the desk and putting their names on your items. You're a success, Angel, and you should celebrate it."

"It still doesn't feel like me."

Roxy threw an arm around her shoulders and leaned in as if she planned to whisper advice. When the words came out, though, they were loud enough to attract attention around them. "You know what I always say, don't you? Fake it 'til you make it. It works in everything. Well, almost everything. It isn't the best solution in the sack."

A gasp of dismay sounded from Tess and DK told Roxy to shush, but all three of them were laughing. Despite the implication, Angel laughed along too. Their ease was putting her at ease. Besides, it wasn't like she was going to meet anyone special tonight.

Except Mr. Harmond, hope whispered. Her feelings dashed between the outposts of excitement and panic when she considered the possibility she might soon meet him in person.

As if the women's shared laughter worked like a magnet, three men drew near. Their gazes settled on the faces of their women in heated degrees of doting love. Before Angel could feel left out, Roxy's Mac wrapped an arm around her shoulders and pulled her into their circle.

"The exhibit is great, Angel. Unique, and I like the slashes of brightness. Tell me, have you been painting like this for a long time?"

The torrent of questions about her inspirations and her techniques drew more people closer. Soon, her friends faded back with broad smiles on their faces as people Angel didn't know surged forward. Their enthusiasm became hers, wiping away her nerves. She even began to enjoy herself.

As she took a brief breather, she noticed a man standing alone to one side. Tinted glasses and a slouchy hat obscured his expression, but his gaze seemed to be stuck on her.

Was that him? She glanced around, trying to find Thomas or Bettie in the crowd. They were the only ones who knew what he looked like. Spotting Bettie on the other side of the room, Angel waved a hand. Bettie caught her signal and excused herself, but Angel couldn't wait. As the older woman crossed the crowd, Angel tried to point toward the mysterious man without drawing attention to her movement. Bettie frowned, shaking her head, but before she could make it to Angel, someone pulled her aside.

With a huff of frustration, Angel turned back to the shadowy man. He stood as still as a statue, and there was no doubt his face aimed in her direction. Intensity communicated across their divide, even though he leaned casually against the wall. Amazon-sized butterflies flapped hard enough in her stomach to cause a gale in China.

"This is a fantastic turnout, Angel. I can't believe we're going to sell out of your work again. Imagine, people on the waiting list have put their tags on your new pictures. And people are buying other artists' work too. It's a wonderful way to showcase our members."

Angel swung around to find Bettie finally next to her, already turning away to greet new arrivals. A young couple gushed over Angel's watercolors and the pottery belonging to another co-op artist, and shared their collecting experiences and the places they had visited to buy art. Angel smiled, answered their questions, and forced herself to stay still. She wanted to spin Bettie around and point at the man. Tapping her foot, she nearly screamed with joy when the effusive couple turned away.

She grabbed the woman's arm. "Bettie, is that him?"

"Is that him who, dear?" She fluttered her fingers at someone in the opposite direction.

Angel spun her around to face the corner. "Is that him? You know, the man who bought my work? Mr. Harmond?"

Bettie peered in the direction Angel pointed her. "I'm not sure who you mean, dear."

Realizing she was going to have to be strikingly obvious and hope it wasn't too embarrassing, Angel turned to the corner, aligning herself shoulder to shoulder with the older woman. "That man in the corner, right – "

Right there. He had been right there. Now, the corner stood empty. Josiah Harmond, if it had been him, had vanished.

>>>>>

Kaane lounged under the eaves of the bakery across the street, grateful its awning cast a shadow offering a place to blend in. His choice of dark clothing had been deliberate, and while some people noted his sunglasses with curiosity, it didn't matter. They couldn't place him, not with this new disguise.

The only people who really worried him were his friends. Lucky for him, though, Mac was occupied with Roxy and the others, and people felt bold enough to step forward for his individual attention. Vince's constantly darting glances scanned the room, as if he was afraid to overlook something. Powers, with a cool gaze that moved slowly over the crowd, missed little.

He understood how protective they were. Powers and Vince had women they treasured. Mac felt the same about Roxy, but as he laughingly stated more than once, the woman knew her way around a meat cleaver and wasn't afraid to use it. It might be more likely Roxy would be the bodyguard in their relationship, but that didn't lessen Mac's watchfulness either.

An unfamiliar sense of longing washed over Kaane. His friends, old and new, found peace in their lives. They tackled challenges with strong partners at their sides. While he told himself settled was not something he wanted to be, perhaps if he had someone to watch over, he'd feel less like a failure and could enjoy that well of inspiration others seemed to find.

A tone sounded, low and persistent, outing his hiding place. His phone vibrated in his pocket as the tone sounded again, and he fished it out and triggered the call before it drew attention.

"Hello?"

Noise of a happy crowd came through the phone. "Hey, Kaane, I thought you were going to join us tonight."

Shifting to muffle his words, Kaane said, "Sorry, Mac. Something came up. How's the gig?"

Not that the response mattered. He could see how it was. The ethereal vision of Evangeline Reed held him in thrall. Her hair cascaded in long curls halfway down her back, making him fist his hands to keep from reaching out to caress their softness. Floaty fabric in a rainbow of colors whispered around her body as she moved, shaking hands, laughing, glancing around the gallery as if she knew she owned the room. When her gaze landed on him, her lips rounded in a circle of surprise, and her eyes, stunning blue and intense, widened in expectant excitement.

He couldn't move his feet, couldn't step closer, and while she stared at him, couldn't glance away. He wanted to murmur hello, take her delicate hand in his, and say in his best seductive voice that he was delighted to finally meet her in person. When people stepped in his line of vision, he fought the urge to toss them to the side because he needed that unimpeded view of his muse more than he needed to breathe.

What held him back? He wanted to whisk her away and place her in a castle tower accessible only to him. Obsession. He wanted to beg her to be his muse. What if she said no? What if she laughed at him? Doubt swarmed over him like a million ants on his skin. What if she said yes? That was the most frightening thought of all.

Kaane shook himself back to the cold reality of the street as he realized Mac had asked him a question.

"Hey, sorry Mac. Our connection must be fading in and out. What did you ask me?" He ducked into deeper darkness when the gallery door opened and music and voices spilled out into the street.

"I said, where did you say you bought that new art in your house? Because I must say, man, I think you'd like this artist's work. She's good, with the same serious undertones but spots of color in the foreground that catch your attention. You're really missing out."

"I guess I'll have to check it out sometime," Kaane said. He'd seen Angel's new work, and its shift from darker themes to bold strokes intrigued him. He'd almost walked up to the counter and claimed them all. But that would have achieved nothing. He needed Angel.

"That will be tough. It looks like every painting has a sold sign on it. She doesn't seem very excited by that, though. She's acting distracted, like she's looking for someone. Do you want me to ask her if – "

Restless twitches roamed over Kaane's body. "No, Mac, I don't want you to ask her anything. I'm glad you're having a good time. I need to split, man." He clicked off as Mac tried to get in a final encouragement to join them.

No, if the time came, he'd ask what he wanted of Angel himself. He'd invite her to become his muse. Maybe someday, he'd be able to speak to her. But not tonight.

"Are you sure he wasn't here?"

Thomas shook his head in response to Angel's question. "I didn't see him. Hell, I would have made sure you met him. Maybe he didn't get the invite, or maybe he had something else to do. Or maybe he can't afford to buy anything more and he's too embarrassed."

"But you should be celebrating, dear. Look, almost everything you brought in for tonight was sold." Bettie shuffled through a stack of receipts and waved the bundle in Angel's face.

The wonder of it wouldn't get old, not any time soon. People liked her work, though why, she didn't completely understand. She was certain there was still something missing.

Passion.

"You run along, dear. You must be pooped, what with talking to all of those people." Bettie made a shooing motion with her hands.

"Now wait a minute. It's late. Just you wait a few minutes and I'll drive you up."

Angel shook her head. "No, Thomas, but thank you. I like the walk. It's not far and it clears my head. Like Bettie said, I've been talking to a lot of people tonight, and the peace and quiet will do me good. Are you sure I can't help you straighten up?"

Thomas argued with her about walking, and Bettie demurred any need of assistance, right before she grabbed Thomas by the sleeve and directed him toward the area they had set up as a wine bar with instructions to take it apart. He grumbled as he moved away.

Once he was out of earshot, Bettie turned back to her. "Are you sure you're all right walking by yourself? I am so sorry your young man didn't come in tonight."

Angel had come to realize that anyone under the age of fifty was probably considered young by these two. And she didn't have any man. She had, or hoped she still had, a patron, but since he hadn't made an appearance, he might no longer be interested.

"I'll be fine, Bettie, honestly." She flung the thick shawl around her shoulders and draped it across as DK had shown her. She'd never had clothes like this. Glamorous material and bright colors drew attention, and that had never been her goal. Even tonight, she felt like she had landed in a dress-up game.

But then, there had been that single instant that made it all worthwhile. The man in the corner had stared at her, she was sure of it. Or rather, that's the story she decided to tell herself. Even if he wasn't her patron, his air of mystery drew her in. The words of her friends echoed in her mind.

"You are a beautiful and engaging woman, Angel. If you open yourself up to the possibilities, who knows who you'll meet?" Tess had wrapped that opinion up in a convincing hug that had Angel believing it too.

DK followed. "Life is about living in primary colors, kiddo. This work you've been doing is good, and you can make it great. Open your heart and do something you'd usually be afraid to try. We artists can't be emotional hermits. When we are, it comes through in our work." Her gaze had flicked to the washed out paled blues and grays in an array of watercolors.

Instead of talking about art or emotions, Roxy had taken a different tact. "Some men are scum, and some are worth the effort. If you need advice, when you do, come to me. I can tell you all about it." DK's snort of disagreement from a good eight feet away only made Roxy wink.

But that was then, and this was now. Angel juggled twin emotions. Elation that her new pieces sold had her drifting down the street like her feet weren't touching the sidewalk. Reality dragged her along like the ballast on a hot air balloon, reminding her the one person she truly wanted to thank hadn't shown up tonight.

Her patron would have introduced himself if he had come. He would have said hello, and he might have complimented her on the new paintings. Or maybe he would have discussed the ones he already owned. They would talk. He would be charming and charmed by their repartee. Angel would not have been tongue-tied. Delighted, he would invite her to dinner, and a wonderful friendship and maybe more would begin.

Who was she kidding? She shook her head, thinking that silly talk about passion and art and men had gone to her head along with the glasses of bubbly. She would no more meet a man who would change her life than she would flap her arms and fly to the top of that bell tower.

Her feet stopped of their own volition and she looked up at the old structure. A half-moon hung behind it, shrouded on the edges by filaments of clouds. It would be a wonderful thing to paint, perhaps in the watercolors she had promised to brighten up. But this scene lent itself to muted shades and shadows.

"It's a beautiful night, isn't it?"

The man's voice made her jump, and she peered around at the buildings to identify his location. Main Street was well-lit with old-fashioned streetlamps, but the shapes of buildings created darker zones. Who knew what lurked in those corners?

But she saw no one. There were no strange shadows and no sign of anyone walking away. Deciding she must have been making up the words from her over-active imagination, Angel resumed walking with more purpose in her step. She was tired, and she was hearing things.

"Wait, please. I'm sorry I frightened you." The voice sounded mildly panicked.

Angel walked faster, with the click of her unaccustomed heels echoing with each step. She could have left with her friends, any of whom were happy to drop her off. She should have taken Thomas up on his offer of a ride. Fingering her keys into position, she ran through the lessons of every self-defense class she ever took. She just never believed the first time she'd have to use them was in safe little Flynn's Crossing.

She felt the hand close on her upper arm, winding into the material of her wrap as it did so. Looking down, she stared in disbelief at the broad fingers with flattened ends. This wasn't her first incident with unwelcomed attention. Working in Flynn's Crossing was a huge step up from the inner-city library in Los Angeles where they had metal detectors out front. Not to see if anyone snuck out a book without checking it out, mind you, but to make sure no one tried to smuggle in a gun or a knife. The place in Texas was mild in comparison, up until that extremist minister came in cursing her and saying she was the spawn of the evil because he thought all books were filled with the devil's preaching.

But this was different. Walking home on the quiet street she now noted was deserted had always felt safe to her. She tried to think quickly. What would her self-defense instructor advise? Or better yet, how would Roxy kick this guy's ass?

She spun around and lifted her foot, ready to plant the spikey heel in the man's instep, but teetered precariously. She didn't usually wear heels. Another hand came to hold her opposite arm, and the man took advantage of her momentum to pull her forward.

"Hey, be careful. This sidewalk is uneven and you have those stilts on. You don't want to trip and fall."

The voice, melodic and mesmerizing, came from the shadows once more, though this shadow was right in front of her. The slouchy hat. Tinted glasses. Dark clothing. The man from the gallery.

Despite what she knew should be sounder judgment, Angel felt a burst of electric excitement run up her arms from where his hands rested. Even through the layers of clothing, those hands were warm and pulsing with life. While his face remained hidden, she had no doubt his attention was completely on her now, as it had been in the gallery.

"You came to my opening," she said, wishing the pathetic breathiness in her voice was something she could hide.

The man nodded. "Yes. And you noticed." His words sounded strained to her ears, as if the idea that she did pained him.

"Of course. Did you like the new pieces?"

He nodded once more.

The sense of elation had her thinking the high heels had nothing to do with the spinning feeling she had now. How would he know they were new works unless he was familiar with what she had before?

A car drove by them at a slow rate of speed. Angel ignored it, but the man did not. He dropped his hands abruptly and stepped back, watching the disappearing taillights.

Not wanting the moment to end, Angel paced after him. "What about the changes?"

His attention snapped back to her. She wished she had the courage to pull him into better light and rip off his sunglasses. She wondered what he looked like, without the hat to hide his features.

"Tell me about the color."

He had noticed.

Another vehicle, this time an old pick-up truck, slowed with deliberate intention as it drew next to them. With a quick glance at it, the man linked their arms and put her between him and the truck, and continued them up the street in the direction she had been heading. The truck kept pace.

"Listen, I have to go. Can I meet you someplace Monday so we can talk?"

Urgency in his tone communicated more clearly than his words how important this was to him, and Angel bit back the giggle of delight on a new surge of self-confidence.

"How about Roxy's Grocery, at the coffee bar?"

The man shook his head with marked vehemence. "The diner out on the old stagecoach road."

South County. Thomas said he was a rancher, so that must be near his place. She had only visited that diner a couple of times, but it seemed like a safe public location.

She nodded, but he wasn't looking at her. His eyes darted from the street and their cruising company to the path in front of them. Breathless again from an overdose of glee, she said, "Ten o'clock?"

A panicked hiss marked his words. "No. Two. The afternoon is quieter there."

He dropped her arm without waiting for a reply and slipped into the narrow walkway between two old brick buildings. Angel halted and was ready to call after him to confirm their meeting when a gruff voice sounded behind her.

"Ms. Reed? Everything okay? I don't like you walking this late by yourself."

She continued to stare at the space where the man had disappeared. An instant later, his silhouette was outlined against the alley lights at the end of the buildings. He stopped and looked back at her, lifting a hand in a wave. Then he was gone.

"Ms. Reed?"

She should be frightened of their strange exchange. She should be worried or angry about his odd behavior. But Angel was none of those things. She smiled, wondering how she could make the next day and a half go by any faster.

Turning around, she walked to the truck with a decided spring in her step. "Thank you, Thomas. I think I'll take you up on your kind offer. These heels aren't meant for a stroll."

Chapter 6

His palms stayed cramped in tight fists for hours. His heart raced too fast, like that time he'd gotten some bad speed and mixed it with bourbon, but he hadn't taken a damned thing. He sat transfixed, unable to swing his eyes away from the poster. He had gripped his muse in his hands. As if in recognition of the importance of this, his fingers throbbed.

If only he could say their meeting brought on a wave of inspiration. If only the words had flowed and then bounced to a hit-worthy tune. If only he'd done a better job of introducing himself.

He didn't even have her phone number. His plan to walk her wherever she was going had failed, brought to an abrupt end by the watchful presence of the old man from the gallery. He needed to spend time with Angel, needed to tap her energy as his muse. He needed that more than life. His future depended on it. Why he was so sure of that, he didn't know.

The hole in the wall mocked him, gaping next to the beauty of the poster. He should have taken pictures of her during the opening. Angel, laughing off someone's compliment. Angel, intent and serious as she discussed the finer points of a painting, undoubtedly something deeply artistic. Angel, her eyes sparkling in the downward glow of the century-old styled lighting as they stood face to face last night.

He'd hardly slept, forgotten to eat, and surged between pent-up energy and debilitating low spirits, making him glad he had a commitment tonight. Mac and Roxy. Sunday dinner at their house, Roxy cooking. He almost cancelled, but going would make the time pass faster. Time until he could again breathe the same air as his Angel. Their date at the diner seemed to yawn across a chasm too wide to see the other side.

He was out of control obsessed. If it showed on his face, Mac would see it. If Mac saw it, he would question it, and he would not leave it alone until Kaane admitted it all. He'd seen Mac giving Angel a peck on the cheek and a broad smile of greeting. He knew it was only the meeting between good friends, but the jealousy he experienced when he saw the display overwhelmed his senses.

The alarm in his smartphone sounded with a quick chord of noise. Mac had insisted he set it. His friend knew him too well.

The drive wasn't long, but every minute until tomorrow seemed to last an hour. Kaane tried to imagine what it would be like to take a drive like this with Angel at his side. Instead of this old pick-up, he'd have his sports car. Angel would have a scarf around her hair against the wind streaming over them from the convertible top, and her curls would unfurl behind them in a magic carpet. She would be laughing, a throaty breathless sound that would make the day perfect no matter what the destination. It was too bad he couldn't translate the pictures in his head into lyrics on a score.

"Hey, you made it, and on time too." Mac covered the porch steps with a jaunty leap. The punch and man-hug had a bit more enthusiasm than Kaane expected, and he nearly face-planted into bushes by the walk.

"What the hell? Are you that surprised to see me? I told you I wouldn't miss any dinner cooked by Roxy, not for anything in the world."

Mac laughed and pulled open the front door, yelling out in an exaggerated voice, "Woman of the house, I have brought the brother home for supper."

A single curse greeted the statement, and the emphasis behind the word made Kaane's smile widen. He appreciated the heartfelt message. Here, he was accepted as he was. That knowledge uncurled an edge on his tension.

Roxy appeared in the central hall with a towel over her shoulder and a big spoon in her hand. "Mac, I keep telling you your John Wayne imitation needs work. Hi Kaane. Glad you could make it." She disappeared after accepting a fast kiss on the cheek.

"I'm sorry for making Roxy cook on a night off," Kaane said, even though he wasn't exactly feeling it.

"I'm not," Mac replied. He waved them toward the kitchen.

"I heard that," Roxy said, stirring something in a large pot on the stove. "Just for that, Mac Smythe, you will be my sous chef. Chop those carrots. I want them matchstick size."

"Can I chop something?"

"No," Mac and Roxy said in unison. Roxy gave Kaane a stern glance. "I do not want to be responsible for the great Kaane Scott cutting off a digit and being unable to play. Mac can do it. Actors don't need all of their fingers."

While he laughed with them, Kaane had that heart-sinking feeling missing a finger wouldn't matter.

Roxy picked up an open wine bottle and an empty glass and gestured to Kaane. He shook his head. In case there was any question, he said, "Abstaining."

She watched him for a moment with narrowed eyes before pushing a bottle of sparkling water toward him.

"You missed a great time last night. The gallery was packed, and the new displays were terrific. I wish you'd come." Mac chopped with apparent gusto along with his words, drawing Roxy's supervision with an exaggerated roll of eyes.

"Matchsticks, Mac. Little bitty logs. Honestly, it is so hard to find good help these days."

"Yes, my love. Kaane, did you have a date?" Mac left the question hanging.

"Celibate," Kaane said, firm in his belief that his date at the diner did not count. How would he explain what he needed? Would Angel agree? Could he safely tell her who he was without an overreaction?

He didn't realize the room had fallen silent and activity ceased. It was only when he capped the fizzy water that he noticed both were staring. Mac, at Roxy, with a meaningful expression. And Roxy, at Kaane, stunned.

"Shit. You told me and I didn't believe it. It's real." She shook her head.

Shifting on the stool, Kaane took a larger gulp of the water to avoid speaking, and bubbles roared up into his nose. He began coughing, earning him slaps from both the chef and his friend until the fit subsided. Roxy was still muttering when she returned to the stove. "I just do not believe it. Wait until I tell the girls. They will be stunned."

"You can't tell anyone." Kaane couldn't keep the panic out of his voice.

"Okay," Roxy said, drawing out the two syllables until they seemed to be four.

Of course, if he was found out, there would be no expectations. He'd be Kaane Scott, former front man for Rebellion, accent on former.

Mac dropped the big knife on the counter and rubbed his hands in his jeans. Roxy raised her eyes to the ceiling and muttered something about good help again, but moved to the cutting board herself and chopped with strokes that sounded a machine-gun staccato on the plastic surface.

"I know it's been a tough time for you, but you will get back in your groove. You need a distraction, and I know just the thing. I had hoped you'd come on Saturday night because I, that is, we, Roxy and I, wanted you to meet someone."

Roxy's head popped up at Mac's statement, but the chopping continued. Unable to look away, Kaane waited for the blade to fall on her fingers. Miracle of miracles, it never did.

"Who are you talking about?" She kept her eyes on Mac.

The man's face split into a sheepish smile. "Who is the only single woman in your girl tribe?"

Her mouth dropped open and the knife came up to stab at the empty air between them. "No. Mac, not only no, but hell no. I will spit in every dish I put in front of you if you so much as dare."

>>>>>

"Thank you for letting me use your shop today. I needed a change of venue, and it's too rainy to work outside." And she had hours to kill until her meeting.

Angel adjusted the easel and moved around it to fiddle with the vase of flowers. She couldn't get it situated to her liking. The light, the shapes, the artful droops. Who was she kidding? The bright, airy colors threw her off.

"It's not an imposition. The shop is always closed on Monday unless it's an important holiday, and by important, I mean one when people must have their flowers. I use this time to put my orders together, design new arrangements, and straighten up." Tess flipped a page in her binder and consulted something on the computer screen with a pointing finger without ever looking her way.

Which was just as well. Her too-perceptive friend would have noticed Angel's nerves, the nearly toppled cup of water, the restless shift of watercolor paper and brushes.

"I promise I'll be out of your way no later than noon. I have a, ah, a meeting this afternoon." Her heart skipped two beats at the thought. She should be used to the concept by now, but it still made her giddy. As if to accent her excitement, the brush flipped out of her fingers and landed with a tinkling noise on the floor.

Tess glanced up and her gaze sharpened. "An appointment? Is it something you want to talk about? It appears to have you somewhat on edge."

If her friend only knew, she would be shocked. Angel Reed, meeting a man she did not really know.

"Are you worried about this meeting?" Tess put her glasses to the side and closed the laptop's lid. Folding her hands on its surface, her focus landed fully on Angel, and under that scrutiny, the tension increased.

"I am a little uncertain about it," Angel admitted, pretending to be fully absorbed in her brushstrokes.

"Without uncertainties, there are no possibilities," Tess intoned with a serious voice. Then she grinned. "It's part of what makes life interesting."

Angel abandoned the appearance of work and set her brushes and watercolors to the side. "But what if that uncertainty means something? What I'm trying to say is, what if someone should be certain before they do something?"

Her questions clearly sparked Tess's interest, as the woman walked across the room to take a seat on the vacant stool next to the worktable. "Perhaps you can give me a little background. I do better with specifics."

Angel flopped on to the adjoining stool and toyed with the leaves on a fragrant peony. "I met a man."

Eyebrows raised, Tess leaned in. "Details, please."

"At the event. We talked afterwards. He's – " She tried to find the appropriate word, then settled on, " – interesting."

Tess smiled in sudden understanding. "Ah, that would explain it."

Flashing her gaze up, Angel asked, "Explain what?"

Tess chuckled and shook her head. "You didn't even hear yourself, did you? You've been singing under your breath, that is, when you weren't mumbling. It sounds like you're on a rollercoaster, elated one minute, worried the next. How can I help?"

"I, ah, I – " Angel fumbled with words. "It's just pre-date jitters."

Tess examined Angels' face closely as if seeking confirmation. "Do we know him?"

Angel shook her head, pretending interest in the shape of the peony's petals. The unknown was what made meeting him on the outskirts of town more thrilling. Doing something daring, something her old self would never had tried, whetted an appetite she didn't know she had.

In a hesitant tone, Tess said, "Well, this can't be any worse than what Mac had planned."

"What did Mac have planned?"

Tess waved a hand and stood, crossing to a display of vases and straightening things that were already straight. "Don't worry. Roxy put a nix on it."

"Okay, now you have my full attention. What could be so bad?"

Pacing back and forth in obvious discomfort, Tess said, "He was going to fix you up with a friend of his."

The notion of anyone setting her up was so foreign, she wasn't sure how to respond. "That was nice of him. Why did Roxy think it was a bad idea?"

Tess stopped and looked at her as if uncertain whether to respond.

"Come on, Tess, now you have to tell me. I'll ask Roxy if you don't, and we both know what kind of tirade that will generate if she doesn't approve of the guy."

Tess grinned as if it was against her better judgment, before replying, "He's a rock star." She must have noticed Angel's puzzled look, because she clarified things. "The kind that plays a guitar in a band."

Angel gaped at her. "A rock star? As in, a rock musician? What was Mac thinking?"

Tess shrugged as if she had no clue but agreed with the sentiment.

"I'll have to tell Mac I appreciate the consideration, but I'm more of a foreign film with subtitles kind of gal. I can say without any doubt that I have never been to a rock concert. What's his name, out of curiosity?"

A sly smile came over Tess's face with slow changes. "You would research him, wouldn't you?"

Angel lifted a shoulder. "Of course I would. Wouldn't you?"

A chuckle accompanied a shake of her friend's head. "And what about the man you're meeting? Have you researched him?"

It was Angel's turn to bolt up and pace. She had, but nothing specific surfaced. There was nothing in the county's public land records about Josiah Harmond owning a ranch. She'd even used a couple of not-so-public databases, but those similarly offered no illumination.

"I can tell by your face that you either didn't like what you learned or didn't learn anything. I think I should call our sheriff friend. At least he can tell us if the man has a record. He could follow you to your meeting, too. Where did you say it was?"

Angel pursed her lips and pulled an imaginary zipper across them, earning her a glare.

"I'm suggesting this for your protection, Angel. I would do the same for any of our girl tribe."

But she was the only who's single. That was why they heaped such attention on her love life, or lack thereof. That was why people wanted to fix her up, because they wanted everyone to be in a relationship. And this was why she wasn't going to say anything else, one way or the other, until she decided if she liked this guy or not. And if he liked her.

Angel began packing her paints and supplies, waving a dismissive hand. "Don't worry. I am a grown woman, and I've dealt with far crazier things as a librarian, believe me. Gangs coming in with guns. Homeless people camping in the nonfiction section. Fanatics threatening to burn the library down with people inside. I think I can handle one man in a public place with other people around."

Or at least, she hoped she could.

Chapter 7

Kaane hunched low, tapping the steering wheel in a loop of indecision. Go inside and find the table offering the greatest privacy? Stay here in the far corner of the parking lot and intercept her when she got out of her car? Wait for her to get settled inside and then follow as casually as possible? It didn't help that he'd left so early, he had almost half an hour to kill.

Sweat rolled down his neck with the fear of uncertainty. What if his Angel said no to his proposal? Calling Rod-man might steady his nerves.

"You have good news, I hope," Rodney said, over strains of Hawaiian guitar music. A giggling female voice faded, then the pound of waves on a beach filled the background.

"Sounds like you're working hard."

"I am using this time wisely and extending my musical reach. Did you know Hawaiian slack-key originated with Mexican cowboys two centuries ago? Fascinating technique, and more difficult to learn than you might think. Detuning the guitar so it sounds appropriate requires skill, and I am learning it."

The background noise returned to the splash of large rollers, stretching into a full minute. Rodney's patience wore out before Kaane had a chance to come up with something to say.

"And how are the songs coming?" More waves broke through the connection.

He hesitated, trying to be honest without admitting reality. "Progressing. I have a lead-in on a couple of tunes, and the lyrics are floating out there, and I hope to have some usable working pieces soon."

The answering pause left him hanging longer. "Which means you have jack-shit. I know you, Kaane-gent. If you had anything decent, anything at all, you'd be bouncing off the walls and screaming about it."

The use of their old shit-names for each other, the 'gent' to Rod's 'man', forced honesty.

"You're right. I have nothing. I keep thinking I have something, like it's just out of reach, and then I close my hand over it and it flies away like an old fart." Which is what he would be by the time he had even one song that worked, unless he could work his convincing magic today. Having Angel by his side would be the key to having songs once more.

The gusty exhale on the other end was a cross between a sigh and growl. "Stop the partying and the whoring and write some music."

Defensive urges struck the wrong chord. "I am both abstinent and celibate. I am worshiping at the altar of the muse."

Dead silence greeted his pronouncement, as if the thought of his becoming a monk even stopped the ocean from moving. Then, "Dude, really? Has that ever happened before?"

Kaane shook his head at the incredulous tone. "No. It proves I'm trying different things. And I wasn't kidding. I am breaking bread with my muse today. Things will change. I promise you they will." And if they didn't, Kaane planned to change his name, have reconstructive surgery, and live in obscurity.

Rod-man's tone was thoughtful. "Well good for you. Good luck, dude."

Kaane hesitated, wondering how much Rodney would read into the silences. As they signed off, his eyes flipped to the time. Fifteen minutes to go. Rain drummed on the windows and he ran the wipers to clear his view. Concentrating on the sounds around him, he tried out a mental harmony, hoping a tune would take hold in his brain. It drifted off without the stirring recognition of a melody in the making.

Words. He should begin with words. Glancing around the truck cab, he realized he had nothing to write on. He picked up his phone and ran a finger over the apps, finally locating the one he needed. Typing quickly, he tried to capture a description of the sound of the rain, the isolation of an empty parking lot, and the gray landscape. The tapping staccato filled the cab until he ran out of phrases and metaphors and ideas. Staring at the jumble, he nearly threw the phone across the front seat.

Feeling. Sensation. Emotion. He'd always ridden those to successful inspiration. Ask his millions of fans. Kaane Scott knew how to put passions into words and those words to music that people said expressed their lives. But not anymore. The only refrain he had was a loud groan. She had to help him. He had no other chance.

He peeled his eyes opened and took inventory of the vehicles around him. While he hadn't been paying attention, a small foreign sedan had pulled in near the diner door. Its headlights reflected in the bank of windows before going dark. The driver door pushed open. The person carted a large brown tote and ran inside without looking around. A quick flash was all he had, but it was enough to make his heart pound a faster drumbeat.

She was here. Bundled into a raincoat and a wide hat, her hair was almost hidden except for a stray curl winding down her back. His door was open before the diner door swung shut. A sudden lightheadedness made the pounding in his ears more pronounced. His salvation had arrived, and he couldn't afford to keep her waiting.

Sprinting across the parking lot with as much energy as he put into racing across a performance stage, he didn't notice the puddle until his feet landed in it. Water seeped in the sides of his boots, intended more for show than protection. Rain ran down the back of his neck, but its chill did nothing to cool the heat he was feeling. Everything hung on these next few minutes, absolutely everything. He could not fail. That chant ran through his mind as loudly as a crowd of cheering fans. His fingers closed on the diner door's handle and yanked it open.

"Thank you."

Her simple words transfixed him. Her voice sang through the room like a forgotten melody. The hat was gone, and curls pulled snug below a band trapping them at her collar. She slid into a window table in plain view of the room, and Kaane didn't care.

"Seat yourself," a brusque male voice called out, followed by the clang of metal on metal and the ceramic slide of plate on counter. Beef-filled aroma clouded the air, but over it, Kaane swore he could detect flowers. Pretty flowers had to be coming from Angel. Moving forward made the scent more pronounced, along with the loud squish of his waterlogged boots.

"You need something?" The man's voice was closer this time. A big white apron stained with something brown blocked Kaane's view. The man was as meaty as the food he cooked, and he eyed Kaane with crossed arms and a tapping foot.

"I'm, ah, meeting someone." Only now that he stood here, feet away from his muse, he didn't know what he'd say. 'Hello' seemed inadequate. 'I need you' would send her screaming for the door. While trying so hard to find a way to spend time with her, he never thought past what would happen once it became a reality.

The cook shook his head and waved at the room. "Like I said, seat yourself. Poopsie will be with you when she gets with you." He turned away in dismissal and rounded the counter grousing.

"Oh, I, I mean we, need a second menu. I'm meeting someone." Her voice rose and fell an octave, breathless and seductive. The cherub's face drew attention to the bow of her lips. He knew from watching her at the gallery that the coat she still wore hid an hourglass figure. So not his type, but that was fine. He wasn't here to get laid.

A waitress in a checkered diner uniform that belonged in decades past stopped at his side. "You can sit at the counter. Or a table. You pick. Plenty of space, as you can see. You from around here?" She popped gum to accent the end of her question as she scanned his clothes.

"I'm meeting someone," he repeated, never taking his eyes off Angel.

"Oh, well then. Sit wherever." The waitress moved out of his peripheral vision. His eyes stayed glued on his target, as Angel struggled to pull an arm out of her coat without rising.

His noisy feet carried him forward without instruction. His hands reached out before his mind formed the words, and his fingers closed on the sleeve and tugged as she turned her face up to him.

"Thank you, but I don't need any – " Her protest died off as she stared at him, her eyes growing huge and red lips parting in a perfect circle. "Oh, it's you." The tentative smile lifting corners of that sensuous mouth made it impossible for him to think.

Angel, his angel, his road back to fame and fortune and whatever else there was on that path. Kaane hadn't a clue what that was, and he didn't care. Her smile faded, and he'd do anything to bring it back.

"Um, my coat?" She wiggled, doing interesting things to the sweater she wore beneath the raincoat. A tug let his fingers know they still clutched the material. He tilted his head down and released it, intent on hiding his face until he could sit down, make his case, and hope for her discretion. Why the hell hadn't he planned this part out?

He knew why. In some dark place inside him, he was convinced she wouldn't show. She'd think the better of it, or someone would talk common sense into her, or the torrential rain would force her to stay home.

"Thank you. My, it is raining hard out there. Would you like to sit down?"

His gaze flicked up to find her watching him with an expression that held both welcome and reservations. She had to know who was about to sit down across from her. Any moment now, she'd say it. In the light of day, it would be impossible for her not to know, disguised or not.

On so many levels, he was fucked. He did the only thing he knew how, under the circumstances. He went on the offensive, sliding into the bench opposite hers and settling low. The arm he extended along the back touched the cold window, where he could feel the impact of large drops against the glass. Dropping his lids to half-mast, the move he used as he sang the low notes designed to make women cream in their jeans, he gave a half-smile as if it didn't matter. He waited for her to say it.

She leaned forward, eagerness brushing away every other emotion on her face. "Thank you for meeting with me. I've been so excited. This means a lot to me, more than I can ever tell you. What you've done means so much to me. Thank you."

Okay, so she was a big fan with a capital B-I-G. At least she hadn't blurted out his name loud enough for the back tables to hear it. He'd quiet her down, give her autograph, and head out before too much longer. She was no more his muse than the salt shaker.

Why the hell had he thought this would be a good idea?

Angel's eyes dropped into a dreamy glaze, and he recognized the look. It was the same one women got right before they swooned over meeting him. Right before they offered up their panties, their bodies, and their night to him. The sense of the inevitable about to happen clanged louder than a rapid tattoo on cymbals.

"I'm sorry, I haven't introduced myself properly. I'm Evangeline Reed." A hand stretched across the table. He didn't usually shake hands, believing with a guitarist's paranoia that someday, someone would squeeze too hard and break his fingers, but she looked safe enough. He lifted his arm from the back of the seat in as lazy a move as he could manage and brushed fingers with her.

The zap of power hit him harder than the current had, that time he plugged in his old amp and the frayed cord shot electricity hot enough to straighten his hair. It was just fingertips touching, and yet he could not move away. The sounds of the diner turned into fuzzy white noise as his ears rang. He yanked his hand back, shaking it to dissipate the sting.

Angel's hand retracted too, and she cradled it in the other one on her folded paper napkin. Those hands looked so small and defenseless, and he fought the urge to lean across and wrap both of hers in his. A cramp in his spine let him know he was sitting as straight as a drumstick and his feet tapped impatiently, looking for piano pedals.

"What can I get for you two?" The snap of gum made Kaane blink. Another snap, and Angel blinked too. She gave a sudden shy smile, and Kaane remembered all over again why he needed to do this more than he needed to breathe.

"You guys ready or what?" The waitress bit her gum in renewed impatience.

"Un, no, we haven't even looked yet. Give us a minute, okay?"

His eyes dropped to the menus in front of them, and he slid one toward her and opened his own. He linked his fingers under the brim of his ball cap to block any view of his face. He needed the woman across from him, or his career was finished. Tension like a wall erected between them grew thicker, and Kaane was at a loss about what to do about it.

The woman across the table flipped the laminated page with a nonchalance he wished he could match. She said, "I know who you are, so you don't need to return the introduction."

His head reared back in shock. *Here it comes.* She'd not only broadcast his name to the world, but she'd laugh when she knew what he wanted. Panic set in, making him half-rise in anticipation of a fast escape.

She dropped the menu and lunged across the table with her hands outstretched. "I'm sorry. I know I'm acting like a crazy woman, but this has never happened to me before. I'm trying to get myself under control."

He dropped his eyes once more, willing his body to come down off high alert. It paid to be cool under these kinds of conditions. Angel withdrew her fingers and they disappeared under the table into her lap.

"I really am sorry. I understand if you're having second thoughts, Mr. Harmond. My work isn't very good, at least not yet, and you did spend a lot of money on it. I can buy it back from you if that helps." Her gaze flicked over his clothes, the worn military jacket with its holes.

At first, he wasn't sure he'd heard her right. Pieces clicked into place, but in a slow rhythm. She was talking about her art. Understanding helped him calm the jitters and his shoulders relaxed. He glanced around the diner to see if anyone noticed their strange interchange or stared with that wide-eyed look people get when they recognized a celebrity.

Satisfied no one seemed to care, he picked up the menu. He ran his finger down the page and stopped on a picture, not focused on what the item was. It didn't matter. He snapped the menu shut and pushed it to the outer edge of the table, his ill-ease returning. He looked around, at the diner, outside the window, at the ceiling. Anywhere but at her. She had to say yes. He was afraid she would say yes.

"So, you decided, hon?" Snap, pop.

Angel rattled off something, which only agitated him further. How would he ask? When could he ask? A sudden silence made him realize his muse had finished ordering and he'd said nothing.

Kaane opened the menu at random and pointed to a picture of a hamburger overflowing with toppings. "I'll have one of these."

"And for your sides?" The waitress's pencil hovered over her pad.

"What do you have?"

She tapped the top of the pad in time to her snaps of gum. "You can read it right here. You get to pick three, like it says. So, what are you having?"

Kaane shifted in discomfort, frantic in trying to focus on the words. What if she didn't want to help him? But what if she did?

He tried to smile at the waitress, though based on her expression, it had zero effect. "Poopsie, is it? Why don't you pick for me? You know what's best with that burger."

If the waitress thought this was a strange request, she didn't show it. "Fries and coleslaw and jello it is."

Jello? Shit. He hadn't had that since he was a kid. Yuck.

The waitress wandered off yelling 'order' as she headed for the counter, and panic raised an octave. His focus sharpened on Angel's face as he tried to decide how to ask for what he craved. Leaning forward and folding his hands hid their shaking.

Angel leaned in too. "Mr. Harmond, I am sorry. I don't know why I'm acting like this. I should know better. After all, I have a responsible job." She paused, looking uncertain. "Well, I had a responsible job. I was a librarian, you see. I'm new to the art world, but then, you can probably tell that from my work." Her laugh came out in a breathless gasp, and the color rose in her cheeks. With her wide blue eyes and that cascade of curls, she was beyond stunning. Not that how she looked should matter to him, but he wouldn't be a guy if he didn't notice.

His fingers twitched, looking for a chord that fit. The smile lifting his lips wasn't something he could control. He tried to lean closer, smelling those wildflowers again. She was utterly captivating, and he couldn't move away. In a whisper, he said, "It's Josiah."

Angel shook her head as if she didn't understand.

"It's Josiah, my name. Please, when you call me Mr. Harmond, it makes me feel old." He glanced around the diner to see if they were overheard.

"Josiah. Thank you, Josiah, and thank you for buying my work. I know you spent a lot of money and I'm very, very grateful that you took a chance on me."

Josiah glanced around in embarrassment. She was thanking him, when he should be the one on his knees in grateful adoration. That is, if she would agree. How did one ask a woman to become your muse? He'd never even had a woman as a close friend.

Angel's expression dropped from hope to dismay, as if his silence in this conversation mortified her. That was the last thing he wanted her feeling. He jumped in with a quick assurance. "I was happy to do it. I like the pictures." He paused, unsure how to continue. His gaze traveled up to meet hers, and he couldn't keep back the jerk of shock.

Something in her look made him shiver, starting at his toes and ending in the roots of his hair lifting like they were on fire. He wasn't sure he could blink, and then it didn't matter. Air didn't seem to be getting into his lungs and breathing didn't matter either. Nothing mattered, as long as she kept looking at him with eyes gone too wide, like deep blue depths of the ocean.

His words came slowly, or maybe his hearing had gone haywire. "I have a favor to ask you."

She nodded, and a knot tightened around his vocal chords.

"I have a secret, and I need you to help me with it."

He read the uncertainty, and perhaps a bit of fear. He knew this wasn't the best approach, but the words blurted out without his conscious thought. The merest twitch of her head seemed a precursor to a more definite decline of whatever he asked.

"Please?" The pleading tone would only be the beginning. He'd beg, if he had to, and on bended knee on the questionable diner floor.

"Please, Ms. Reed?"

She took a deep breath and blew it out, the nervous clutch of her hands unfolding on the table. He didn't think about a way to cajole her. He flipped his hands over and grasp on to hers with a force that seemed to surprise her, but she didn't pull away. She stared at their joined hands for long enough for his soaring heart to plummet once more. Forever might have passed before she spoke.

"Tell me what you need, Josiah," she whispered.

>>>>>

"What the fuck have I gotten myself into?" He shouted the words loud enough to make them reverberate in the piano's sound board. If he didn't hope he would need his hand for music, he would create a matching hole in this wall with a quick fist and take the consequences.

He couldn't believe the lies he had told. He'd tried to justify it to himself, but all he could claim was being crazy. How else could he explain why he'd told her what he did?

"I can't read, and I'd like you to help me learn."

Angel's eyes had gone wide with understanding and empathy, and there and then, he knew he had to find a way to keep her looking at him. Even if it meant he had to live that lie, he knew it was the right thing to do for his career. Their food arrived, and between bites, she'd begun with the basics. Her sincerity and gentle way of explaining things only made him feel worse.

He could win an acting award for the way he played it. If only he didn't feel so damned lousy about it. Lying never sat well with him, and to lie to someone so perfect, so angelic, bordered on lunacy. But he could justify it for his music. At least, he thought he could.

In his saner moments since then, he considered coming clean, admitting who he was and what he really needed. He even played the verse over in his head.

'Angel, I'm not what and who I've led you to believe I am. I'm actually a washed-up rock star who's lost his music. I need you to help me find it again. I need you to be my muse.'

Yeah, like that didn't sound even crazier.

He flopped on to the piano bench and ran his right fingers over the keys in ascending chords. Anything for his music. He ran the chords again, faster this time. He added his other hand and played in unison two octaves apart. Faster again. And again. He kept at it until he was panting and a cramp curled his left hand.

Anything for music. His verse of honesty ran through his mind again, and with it, a tinge of guilt rang too. He was not the guy she thought he was.

He'd asked with as much sincerity as he could muster, and she had agreed with quick reassurances. Tell no one why he needed to meet with her. Him being unable to read must go against everything Angel the librarian believed in. She wasted no time in beginning their first lesson, using the dessert menu stuck in the stand holding sugar packets.

"Oh, so that's what those letters say. I always wondered, but they didn't make sense to me." He'd laughed with what he hoped was a self-deprecating grin, not the layers of self-condemnation swamping him.

Every time he touched her hand, which he found he needed to do a lot, he felt the quivers of something he didn't recognize. Her cheeks colored a pale pink, reinforcing the vision of a cherub. His Angel. He was afraid he'd spook her.

"I'm fascinated by your creative process. After I read your poster, I had to get to know you better."

She'd frowned at his admission, and he gave himself a mental kick for the slip.

"How did you read that?"

He shifted again, trying to cover things up quickly. "I asked a friend to read it out loud while I was doing something else. Made him think I wanted to hear it all again because I enjoyed it so much." He lowered his eyes with the lie, focusing on the clench of his hands on the tabletop.

Angel wrapped hers over them. "I can't imagine how hard it must have been for you. Didn't your parents or your teachers ever notice?"

He shrugged and tried to pull his hands back, but she tightened hers. Her face shifted into a solemn expression. "Josiah, were you ever tested for a learning disability? You know, sometimes brain wiring short-circuits and with training, we can work around it. It would be good to know."

He shook his head hard enough to make his ballcap bob. These lies were piling up so fast, he could barely see over the top of them. He changed the subject to talking about his ranch. As if she sensed his discomfort and felt sorry for him, she played along.

He made up shit at a rate that he wished was the same speed he used to write lyrics. Fast, deep, and without thinking. Angel only interrupted his running commentary with occasional questions, her eyes shining across the table with a mix of compassion and curiosity.

"How did you manage the contracts and orders and things? You now, the legal part? Do you have someone you can trust to help you with that?"

He'd shrugged, dipped his head, and mumbled he did. Oh yeah, someone he could trust. Guilt made the loaded burger roll in his stomach.

"I can pay you for your lessons."

A fry dipped in ketchup stopped halfway to Angel's mouth. She shook her head and returned the food to the plate. Her troubled eyes carried heartfelt sincerity.

"No, that's not necessary. I'm a librarian."

"You're an artist."

Her face colored again, a pink deeper this time. "What I mean to say is, I used to work in a library. We could meet there, at the library, for your lessons, I mean."

He inhaled sharply. Being in town, in public, every day? Because he wanted to meet with his Angel every day. He needed the muse like a junkie needed his daily fix.

Trying to think quickly didn't seem to work for him around this woman, a fact he was slowly coming to realize. He ran his fingers over the piano keys again, a race of a melody running through the center of the bridge. Just as quickly, it was gone. Yes, he needed a hit of his muse every day. Oh yeah, he knew. He was desperate.

"I could meet you at your studio."

"I, ah, don't have a studio."

He sighed now as he had then. His fingers trembled on the keys. He could do this. He had no other choice.

"You could come to the ranch, that is, if it isn't too inconvenient for you. Maybe you could paint there too."

She opened her mouth, then let it drift closed. There was no mistaking the uncertainty in her face. "I'd, ah, have to think about it."

The warning bell in his brain told him not to push it, and he tried to listen to it and let her have the time she needed. Poopsie's timely arrival with the check hadn't been long enough. Neither was the walk through the puddles in the parking lot. He didn't have far to go to escort her to her car, and he wished with newfound desperation that the pouring rain still fell or her car didn't start.

But the rain didn't materialize, and before he knew it, he'd closed her car door with a joyless smile. She'd disappear, poof, and with her, his last chance. He was ready to slap his hands on the hood of her sedan and cling to the edge, hanging on for as long as it took to convince her, as her motor fired up. He lifted on the balls of his feet, ready to launch himself before she put the car in reverse, when she rolled down the window.

Her words came out rough and uneasy. "How about in the mornings?"

He nodded, unable to speak around the block in his throat.

"That is, if it's the best time for you with the ranch and all."

He nodded once more, struggling to order his voice to work. "Tomorrow, then?"

She nodded, a stunned expression taking over her face. "Tell me the address."

He wasn't sure how he drove home. He wasn't sure how he passed the rest of the day and deep into the night. The daze of creative energy burned through him, until the effect of being in Angel's company for those few hours snuffed out. But when it did, he smiled at what it left behind.

'I know I'm a long shot, not the man you think I am.

I'm not who and what I've led you to believe.

But darlin', this washed up shell could be so much more,

so much more,

If you would only believe

in me.'

Chapter 8

She'd been reading too many romance novels of late, she feared.

Josiah Harmond had walked her to her car after lunch, his eyes on the ground as they covered the short distance of potholed gravel. He put a hand under her elbow as if to guide her around puddles, and with each touch, she grew more confused. He said little, but his eyes were bright when they met hers, as if he was pleased they had this time together.

It was only when they reached her car that his apparent hope seemed to fade. He'd ducked his head as if she embarrassed him. His shuffle of feet as he waited for her to start her car made her regret her dithering.

He was a nice man, a hardworking man by the look of it. He wanted to learn to read, and if there was one thing she loved above painting, it was helping people discover the joy of words. She tried not to muse over why the man seemed like such a puzzle.

And not only the man, but her attraction to him confounded her. That was something she did not understand, and she wished she could talk to her girl tribe friends about it before she decided. That was a conversation bound to raise embarrassment to new heights. Maybe she could find the answer in a book.

Her aunt's words flooded back to her with unexpected clarity.

'Everything there is to learn in life cannot be learned from books or research. Experiences are often our best

learning opportunities. Try things that challenge you, and you may learn as much about yourself as you will about the topic. I know this from my own life's lessons. Learn this lesson early, and you will live your years with fewer regrets and greater happiness.'

Experiences were learning tools, just as books were. Funny how she had so much of one, and Josiah must have an excess of the other. Closing her eyes, she tried to imagine what it would be like to have no words. The feeling, she was sure, would be devastating. She tried to be logical and tell herself she would give her decision time, but she knew it was already made.

When her motor caught, she rolled down the window and tried to get Josiah to meet her gaze. After a time, he raised troubled eyes to meet hers. She wished she knew the right words to reassure him he had nothing to be ashamed about. The poor man had opened himself up to her, while she owed him her gratitude and thanks. He looked like he couldn't wait to bolt away.

Her throat felt tight as she choked out the words. "How about in the mornings?"

He nodded, uncertainty clouding his gaze.

She released the breath she'd been holding. They would make this work. In a firmer tone, she said, "That is, if it's the best time for you with the ranch and all."

He nodded once more. "Tomorrow, then?" His strangled voice recited directions. She wrote them down, refusing to acknowledge the fingers that shook as she did so. Yes, tomorrow would do just fine. Tomorrow, she'd help him begin his journey to find reading and words and books as the same beautiful escape she did. And maybe in the process, she'd learn something about herself too.

But that was yesterday's confidence, and this was today. She'd never done anything remotely like this before. Last night, she'd thought about calling one of her friends and asking their advice, but how could she put it? She didn't want to reveal Josiah's secret, and whoever she called was bound to want to talk her out of this.

She wasn't being foolish or foolhardy, she assured herself. Josiah was safe. The man wouldn't be an ax murderer. He was a rancher, and this was Flynn's Crossing.

Her mind flicked over what she knew about him, and the memory of the black credit card flashed back to her. People with black cards couldn't be murderers, could they? It was too late to research that now, as she punched in the security code on an impressive looking wrought iron gate. This was the kind of place only money could buy. Why hadn't he tried to find help before?

Scanning neat fences lining empty pastures, she thought she might have a clue. Pride in what he had achieved probably warred with embarrassment that he hadn't learned to read before now. That was the point, though. Look at all he accomplished without the benefit of writing ability. How much more could he do once he had the tools most people took for granted?

A barn stood to one side, stately and grounded as if it had been part of this landscape for eons. The ranch house looked old but well-kept, reminding her of Roxy and Mac's place. The gate code must have triggered a doorbell, because Josiah paced the wide porch with impatient footsteps, faster than most people took any casual walk. When he spotted her car, he stopped, his eyes seeming to search for hers.

And despite all her lectures to herself about maintaining objectivity and returning his kindness about her art with understanding about his need to learn, her heart kicked up to a new speed. The intensity in his gaze, even thirty feet apart, made her suck in a harsh breath. Like the electricity when they touched, the shock of it arced across the distance.

He was the first to break the spell, bounding down the steps to her driver door before she had the chance to turn off the engine. His smile dazzled her, making the cloudy sky brighten like the midday sun. She was sure she stared and double-checked to make sure she wasn't gaping at him like an idiot. So much for poise and professionalism.

"You came," he said, his hand reaching in to help her out of the car.

"Of course." Did he really think she wouldn't keep her end of their bargain? "Or is this a bad time now?"

He shook his head in rapid twists, with enough force to make his neck sound an audible crack. "You couldn't come at a bad time, Angel."

Their hands were still engaged, and this time, the power between them was more like a continuous current, pulsing with life and energy. Angel tried to pull her hand back, and he tightened his fingers. That alone should frighten her, but it felt strangely comforting. It was nice to feel this connected to a man, even if she barely knew him.

"Um, my hand? I need to get my briefcase." She hated that sound in her voice, the quality all weak and airy, but it was the best she could do.

His wide eyes dipped to their joined fingers, and he dropped her hand like it burned him. So much for their connection. It had to be one-sided. Yes, too many romance novels. Of course, if she'd been reading mysteries or thrillers, she would not be here.

Her palm slipped on the handle of the leather bag, moist with nervous sweat. He didn't seem to notice how she almost dropped it. His attention focused on the old barn, and in profile, his aristocratic nose and sharp features took on a stunning beauty. He looked like one of those statues of Greeks preparing for battle. That was probably what this was for him. A battle for improvement, for learning, for knowledge.

That idea forced her to straighten her shoulders. She was here for a reason. This nice man bought her paintings. The least she could do was give him the ability to read.

"Where will we be working? I'd like to get set up."

Her words drew his focus back to her, and that intensity flooded her senses once more. She'd have to ask her friends about this thing, this zinging around in her belly and making her feel too hot and tight in her own skin. Something had to be wrong.

Josiah reached out as if he planned to take her arm, and she stepped back. The light in his eyes dimmed as if she'd hurt his feelings. Distance. They needed space between them if they were going to get anything done. Scratch that. If she was going to be able to concentrate, she needed deep space, maybe light years, to maintain it.

It was hard to capture any impressions from her brief glimpse of the interior of his house. The touches were modern, but the feel of the place was old. When her eyes lighted on her pictures, hung throughout the rooms, delight bubbled to the surface.

"I never imagined how they would look, hanging in someone's home."

Josiah shot her a curious expression, chased by a narrowing of his eyes and a faint smile that said her words pleased him. He said nothing about it, waving her to a dining table that looked barely used. She forced herself to focus on the task at hand, pulling out books and papers. When he pulled up a chair next to hers and dropped his chin into his hands with apparent concentration, she tried to block out the way his hair dipped across his forehead and the itchy need to brush it back with her fingertips.

Two hours later, she'd forgotten about the urges. He knew more than he thought, and while his hesitancy indicated his insecurity, Angel was sure that with a little work, his confidence would match his growing capabilities.

She stood, glancing at her watch. "I am so happy you asked me for help, Josiah. I had forgotten how much I enjoy tutoring people who are eager to learn to read. I'm so excited for you, and for the world that will now be opened to you. You can read much more than you think."

Josiah rose from his chair and stretched, and Angel's eyes strayed to the little bit of skin showing above the waistband of his jeans. It looked smooth and soft, unexpected in someone who, she suspected, worked outside for long hours each day. She tapped the pages of worksheets into alignment with more power than required, reminding herself she was here to do a job. Josiah Harmond had supported her when it counted, and she would do the same for him.

"You know, it's hard, sometimes, to ask for help." He scuffed his feet like the thought bothered him.

She gave a sigh and shook her head. "No, I have often asked for assistance. Like with my art. I'm only starting out, and my friends have been so helpful. I knew something was missing, but I couldn't put my finger on it."

Surprise rippled through her when Josiah took her hand and pressed their fingers into linking. "Can I help you with it, whatever it is? I mean, you're doing me such a favor, and I'd like to return it."

Do her a favor? He'd already done her the ultimate favor, buying and even hanging the art she knew was lacking. Could he help her? The open sincerity in his expression, as if her success meant something to him, made her heart skip like little kids on a playground. His eyes flashed as he moved back in a sudden jerk, an explosion of air leaving him and settling a breeze around her. He raised his arms over his head in a position of surrender.

"You've got me. For whatever you need, you've got me. I'll learn to read or carry your paints or any damn thing you want, Angel."

A gasp of awareness sizzled through her. If he was willing to do anything, they could both win. He would have the gift of reading. She could have the passion and understanding she needed to take her work to the next level.

She realized with a start that Josiah watched her with an intent stare that made her nervous. She didn't recognize the expression, and she dropped her eyes to the books in front of them, running her hands over them in rapid movements as if they would provide the answer to a question she couldn't even define.

"Angel? What's wrong?"

Her mother always said her face was an open book about what she was feeling. Over the years, she'd struggled to overcome what she thought of as a shortcoming. She kept her eyes down and grabbed for her teaching notes, though she had no clue what she was looking at.

"Your face is so expressive. I hate seeing you so worried. Is it something I said? I promise I'll work hard and try not to let you down."

She'd love to read many, many things into his words.

"I know you'll try hard," she replied, sorting through the pages in the folder with blind eyes. Her face felt hot and her body buzzed with an energy that left her restless.

"I hate for you to leave, but I know you need to paint and I guess I should get outside. I feel like I've learned a lot already. What do you think, Angel? Is there hope for me?"

He flashed her a high-wattage smile, and she inhaled sharp enough to bring in his earthy aroma. A fresh scent, one she associated with being outdoors. The scent distracted her with its persistence and depth. It was like diving into a forest floor. She had to get out of there before she said something stupid, or worse.

She pushed a couple of children's books toward him. "Here's something for you to study tonight."

He took the books from her outstretched hand, and their fingers brushed ever-so-slightly. Hers quivered in response, and her eyes shot up to see if he noticed. He wore that same shell-shocked look she'd encountered earlier this morning. Without saying another word, Josiah spun for the door and was out of view before she could think of what to say.

Chapter 9

Kaane threw his pencil across the room, liking the dull thud of it against the far wall. Words escaped him. He found that faking his lack of understanding was easy when his mind was completely focused on the woman sitting next to him. He tried to capture the memory of Angel's face, intent on his lesson, and her smile when he sounded out the words.

She'd declared him a star pupil today. He'd let enough words slip to have Angel saying he read well into the grammar school level. The congratulations made him nervous. He was living a lie, and it sickened him.

If their first lesson didn't warn him he was in deep trouble, his reaction should have given him a clue. He'd convinced himself she would not come, so when he saw her car pausing at the main road to open the gate, he shot out of off the piano bench to hide the poster. It seemed inappropriate for it to be sitting on a shrine when the real thing was about to walk in his front door.

She drove up slowly as he paced the porch in indecision. Tell her the truth? Now would be a good time, before this charade went any further. Then she smiled at him before she'd even gotten out of the car, and the coffee in his guilty gut churned in the face of her joy. When she settled at the table, placing one palm on a folder with pages sticking out and the other on a small stack of books as if making a pledge, he could only freeze in the doorway and stare.

He swore there was a halo around her head, but it had to be a trick of the light. Was she real? Had she been sent from some other universe to both help him and torment him?

When he stayed standing in the room's entry, she patted the chair next to her with an encouraging smile. "Come on, sit here. I won't bite, and I promise, this will be painless. In fact, I think you'll have fun. I used to be pretty good at tutoring, and I don't think my skills have faded with time."

Unlike his. The words he'd written last night that had been bouncing through his brain in a constant happy refrain disappeared in a poof of shot neurons. What were they again? Why did he think they were any good?

"I don't think I can do this." His voice was rough and gravely, like he'd been shouting over a noisy crowd for hours. Stage fright, a feeling he hadn't registered in years, made his muscles shake.

Angel's smile fell. "What's wrong? Have you tried to learn before and it didn't go as you hoped?" She shifted as if she too was suddenly nervous. "I know this is difficult. It's hard to ask for help. Success can seem like it's so far away, you can't even see a shimmer of it in the distance."

She had a way with words. He'd have to remember this phrase. *'Success can seem so far away, it's only a shimmer in the distance.'*

"I bet you never had to ask for much help with anything. I bet you are the smart girl, the one everyone turns to for help." Once he said the belief out loud, he knew it had to be true. When she began his lessons without responding, he wished he could wipe away the sadness in her eyes. He attacked his fake studies with an enthusiasm he didn't have to force. Anything to bring the light of joy back into those huge cornflower blues.

It wasn't until later, when they were through for the day and he rose to stretch, that he caught her looking at him with a stunned expression. Oh shit. She just made him for his public persona, and he expected a squeal or more likely, a lecture. But instead, her eyes shifted away and she looked mournful once more.

"You know, it's hard, sometimes to ask for help." He attempted to lock his feet to the floor where he stood, because the need to scoop her up in his arms and comfort her overwhelmed him.

She gave a sigh and shook her head. "No, I have often asked for assistance. Like with my art. I'm only starting out, and my friends have been so helpful. I knew something was missing, but I couldn't put my finger on it."

Thinking of the work adorning his house, he frowned. He was no expert, but the work appealed to him and not only because the artist in front of him conceived it. She traced the edge of a children's book, one he'd forced himself to read with slow uncertainty. Angel looked so forlorn, and he took her hand because her comfort consumed him. "Can I help you with it, whatever it is? I mean, you're doing me such a favor, and I'd like to return it."

Her face turned up, and with the movement, that aroma of flowers in bloom washed over him. The tremulous quiver of her lips, as if his declaration affected her deeply, made him pull closer. If he could paint, he'd paint this perfect moment.

'If I could paint, I'd paint this perfect moment with you.'

Words, more words. His shoulder brushed hers, and with the simple touch, another stanza flashed through his brain. It froze him in place, breathing the same air as his muse, as she watched him with eyes too large and a stunned expression. He dropped her hand and spun away, desperate to escape the room before he did something profoundly stupid.

In the five days since, he'd made every effort to be on his best behavior, showing her progress with each passing lesson. He tried not to sit too close, only to find his chair butted up against hers, their thighs pressed together. Each time, he sprung back, reminding himself these hot thoughts were not the kind he should be having, not if he wanted Angel as his muse.

Never had he expected this charge of interest, this need to know everything about her. Each day, he asked a few personal questions, and Angel didn't seem to appreciate the attention. She might answer his query, or she might not. In either case, it wouldn't be long before she set him back on a straight and narrow study path. She never asked to see more of the house, though her eyes lingered on her paintings with open curiosity, like she might be taking inventory and wondering where the rest might hang.

It wasn't until the end of their Friday lesson that she allowed something personal to creep into their conversation. "I never asked you. What kind of rancher are you?"

He hadn't thought that through. The first thing that popped into his head came out of his mouth. "Pigs. I ranch pigs."

Her gaze up at him in surprise. "Pigs? I thought pigs were farmed, not ranched, but then, I don't know much about that."

Not sure how to proceed, he flubbed along in a big way. "Oh, well, I guess that depends on where you learn about it. I have been learning about it from an Australian, and down there, they call it pig ranching, so that's stuck with me."

She still stared at him with questions in her expression. Those warm eyes with the hint of dusky purple edging the brighter blue would be the death of him yet. He couldn't find a way to describe them that did them justice. In his discomfort, he kept up the chattering nonsense. "I haven't actually gotten my own herd yet." Hell, even he knew a group of pigs wasn't a herd, but he stumbled on. "I'm going to begin later in the spring. You know, when it gets warmer outside and they can run around in their outside pens." At least he thought he got that last part right.

"Could you show me around your ranch sometime? That is, if I wouldn't be in the way."

The hopeful expression, accompanied by a little bite of her lower lip that made him forget it would next to impossible to hide the guitars and piano and other accouterments of a musician's life in his house, overwhelmed him. "Of course, I'd be honored."

She nodded once with a satisfied smile and said, "How about tomorrow? I've finished up my next round of paintings, so I'm taking a breather. No lesson required. I'd like to fill my creative well, so to speak."

Saturday. As in a few hours from now, Saturday. He hadn't figured out how to hide the piano, so he came up with a story about it, that it belonged to his parents and he'd inherited it.

Running his hands through his hair, he pulled hard. Why had he done this? He should have just come clean at the beginning and taken his chances. Now that he could spend time every day with Angel, he found the words still wouldn't came with any regularity, probably blocked by his lies.

His phone rang on the counter, and he welcomed its noisy distraction. "Hello."

"Hey Kaane, it's Mac. Listen, is it okay if I come over in a little while? I have something I need to discuss with you."

A glance at the clock surprised him. He'd been working through the night, and while he thought he'd slept with his forehead on the table for a few hours, the passage of time had still gotten away from him. Angel arrived in five hours, and he still had things to hide. Could he pull this off?

"Kaane, you there?"

He jumped at the sound of Mac's voice in his ear. "Yeah, man. What did you need?"

His friend fell silent. It was uncharacteristic of Mac to be without words. He didn't call unless he had a purpose and he rarely shut up.

"Mac?" His voice was sharper than he intended, but he would not have time to shoot the breeze and still make his deadline. He needed to come up with something, any snippet of a song, to prove his worth. Then he could tell her the truth.

"I'll be by in half an hour."

The abrupt sound of dead air marked Mac's hang-up. Kaane didn't even have time to refuse, which is probably what Mac counted on. Half an hour, just enough time to make himself a cup of coffee and get his shit together. Mac's tone wasn't exactly warm and friendly.

The smell of java rejuvenated him ten minutes later as he toweled his hair and lifted the cup. The shower had helped, but with each passing minute, Angel's arrival drew closer, and he still didn't have his story straight.

'Angel, I have to tell you the truth. I'm not a pig rancher. I'm a musician, and I used to be a rock star. But lately, I've had a hard time writing new songs and I've needed a muse. You are that muse, Angel.'

Yeah, like that didn't make him sound like a nutcase. She'd fly out the door and he'd never see her again.

'Angel, I have to be honest with you. I can read just fine. I'm a washed-up songwriter and I've been searching for my muse. I think that muse is you, Angel, and I've thought that from that first day I caught a glimpse of you at the gallery before I bought all your work.'

Add asshole to nutcase for not confessing this sooner and for lying to her in the first place. He was the one who said he couldn't read, after all. How could that not be classified as an outright lie? The sip of coffee burned his tongue as he tried again.

'Angel, I have to be honest with you. You have something I need, an energy and light about you that is special. I would do anything to spend more time with you, anything at all, anything you want. I even made up the story

about not knowing how to read, once I learned you had been a librarian. Will you help me, Angel? Would you be my musical muse?"

He thought this was marginally better. If he played it as humble and sorry and embarrassed, perhaps she would overlook the lie and forgive him and shine some of her special light on him.

The rock song rang out through the house, followed by the rough rap of knuckles on the front door. As if that wasn't enough of a warning, Mac yelled, "Kaane, open up. We have to talk."

He flashed a glance at his watch, surprised to see he'd spent his available scant minutes trying to figure out his words for this afternoon. Mac kept his finger on the doorbell and the other hand slammed the door in a beat to match. Kaane jogged through the house, hands on his ears. As soon as Mac left, he was going to disconnect that damned thing.

He pulled open the door and nearly got knocked in the nose by a fist. If he'd surprised Mac, the man didn't show it. His face looked like thunder and he pushed by Kaane with enough force to splash coffee out of the cup.

"Why are you doing this?"

Kaane stopped in the act of closing the door, and turned to regard his buddy. "Doing? Doing what?"

Mac waved his arms and ran his fingers through hair that looked like it had suffered this abuse a few times this morning. "Doing what you agreed you wouldn't do. Come on, man, you promised, and I'm getting grief for it."

He drank down the remaining coffee, thinking that any moment now, the caffeine would kick in and he'd have a clue what Mac was talking about.

He stared at Mac, waiting for an epiphany. Mac stared back, sheer frustration written on his features. They stood like that for at least a minute before Mac threw his arms up in the air.

"Angel. Seeing Angel. You promised Roxy you wouldn't go after her."

Kaane opened his mouth, then snapped it shut. Mac froze in place and his expression became grave. "Oh man, you are, aren't you? I told Roxy she had to be mistaken, but now you're going to prove me wrong. Shit, man, Angel's just a kid, and Roxy is going to come after you with a carving knife."

Closing his eyes didn't block the vision of Roxy on the warpath, and while Kaane didn't think she'd do him bodily harm, he wasn't sure.

He heard the squeaky crunch of leather compressing and opened his eyes to see Mac on the couch, his face in his hands, shaking his head. "No, man, tell me you didn't. Roxy's going to kill us both."

Kaane leaned his butt against the back of a chair and regarded the bottom of the empty mug. "I take full responsibility. None of this is your fault, Mac. I'll tell Roxy that. She can't blame you." Or at least he hoped she didn't. He didn't have many good friends, and he couldn't afford to lose one to death by cleaver.

Mac's face emerged and his eyes were thoughtful as he stared at Kaane without blinking. His chin landed on his clasp hands and he continued to stare. "She doesn't know, does she?"

Kaane looked up in confusion. "Huh?"

Mac shook his head, standing too. "Angel doesn't know who you are, does she? Because she still calls you Josiah."

Kaane whirled and headed for the kitchen. He could not have this discussion without a stimulant. He heard boots on wood as Mac followed, and after filling his mug, he pushed an empty one to Mac. He didn't wait to see what his friend did with it, turning to the window and staring out at the spring landscape to turn green.

Liquid splashed and soon Mac joined him, standing an arm's length away and staring too. He sipped. Kaane sipped. They stood like that for perhaps half a cup before Mac said, "Man, I could use something in this."

Kaane shook his head. "Help yourself."

Instead of moving to the liquor cabinet, Mac turned to the side. Kaane felt the man's heavy stare. "You're serious about this abstinence thing, aren't you?"

Kaane nodded, taking another sip of coffee. "No women, no booze."

"Is it helping?"

Kaane shook his head, unable to speak past the knot in his throat. Words and music came to him as he sat next to Angel, as he listened to her voice, her laugh, her teasing tone as she tutored him. Little did she know he was using her for his own purposes. She wouldn't gift him with her angelic smile once she knew.

"Well, at least I can tell Roxy she doesn't need to worry about that part."

"What part?" Kaane didn't meet Mac's gaze, but turned for the living room and the piano bench.

Mac followed and settled on a chair to the side. "How do I put this tactfully? Roxy is blazing mad you've gotten your screw-'em-and-forget-'em clutches in Angel and you're taking advantage of her."

Kaane sniffed, unable to form a response. Mac continued in the same contemplative tone.

"But since you're celibate and not taking advantage of Angel, what's in it for you?"

Snapping the lid over the piano keys, Kaane dropped his head to the top and banged a couple of times. The sound echoed in the instrument like the bell of doom. "She's my muse."

The only sound after his words was a slurp of liquid. "So, how's it going for you?"

Kaane shook his head, not raising it from the piano.

"Well then," Mac said, sounding perplexed.

Kaane bounced up, unable to explain, but willing to try. "I mean, it works as long as I'm next to her, but as soon as she leaves, I can't find the words again. I can't even remember them. And the killer part of this is, I have misled her."

"What did you do?" Mac sounded resigned, as if he expected the worst.

"I told her I couldn't read, and I asked her to teach me. So that's what she's doing, tutoring me. Every day this week, she came here and I've pretended I don't know how to read very well and she tries to teach me. I tell you, every day I sweat bullets that I'm going to screw up and skip ahead and she'll figure it out and she'll have nothing to do with me. Not that it matters, anyway. If I can't hold on to the words in my head, I'd have to write them down when we're together, and then she'll know it was all a lie."

Mac stared at his hands as if processing this. Finally, he looked up with a troubled frown. "That's not all you're lying about to her, is it?"

In the path of Mac's steady gaze, Kaane felt like he did when the sound system didn't work and the roadies couldn't figure out why. The risk of failure loomed large.

Mac waited as if he expected an admission in return, but Kane couldn't say it. Minutes passed and the stare-down grew heavy with the air of a dare. Finally, Kaane threw his hands up and submitted.

"Fine, yes. She doesn't know I'm Kaane Scott. She thinks I'm Josiah Harmond, and she doesn't recognize the name. She thinks I'm a pig rancher."

That brought a guffaw of laughter from Mac. "A pig rancher? Pigs don't get ranched. They're farmed." His laugh boomed through the excellent acoustics of the room.

Kaane grumped in response. "I know that. She knows that too, but I made up a story about learning about it in another country and there they call it pig ranching. I think she believed me."

"You are an idiot, Scott. An idiot and an asshole. Maybe I should let Roxy come over here and set you straight, but lucky for you, she had someplace else to be this morning."

Kaane shuffled from one corner of the room to the other and back again. "How did you find out, anyway?"

Mac leaned back and put his arms out, the picture of sudden ease as if he was enjoying this. "Angel called Roxy this morning, and from the side of the conversation I heard, Angel was gushing about her new friend, Josiah. Roxy asked her about this Josiah, all the while sending daggers my way, because you know, she does remember that's your given name. I left the room while she was still occupied on the call and before those daggers turned into her newly-sharpened knives. But I gathered was trying to talk Angel out of seeing you anymore."

He expected this would all blow up in his face someday, but somehow, he'd hoped he'd salvage a friendship with Angel out of the explosion. Once she knew who he was and how much he'd lied to her, he was certain she'd have nothing more to do with him. If she heard the truth from Roxy, he was doomed.

"Promise me you'll tell her who you really are, Kaane. You can't take advantage of Angel. Promise me you won't."

Kaane nodded. "Celibacy, remember? Besides, you don't screw your muse, or she can't be your muse anymore."

>>>>>

Angel splashed a streak of bright blue across the yellow already marking her canvas. She didn't know why she felt this urgent need to paint something colorful and bold, but she could see the difference in her work already.

Energy. She had so much of it, she wasn't sure how to spend it all. She'd made up her mind, and she didn't intend to go back. She was going to learn all there was about sex in exchange for teaching a man all about words. Josiah looked like he knew the way around a woman, from that loose-hipped swagger to the way he touched her and then held her gaze as if memorizing her face.

Unless she'd read him wrong. This wasn't her expertise. When she called Roxy for advice this morning, her friend had listened to the basics, swore with as much color as the paints on this canvas, and said she'd be right over.

The bang against the front door came only once, but it was enough for Angel to stand and set aside the brush. She could come back to this. She'd thought it was finished, until she'd bubbled over with new ideas, and she knew why.

She was going to take the next step today. A social visit with Josiah at his ranch would take things to the next level. And if he didn't make the first move, she would.

Another bang reminded her to unlock the door, and Roxy stood with an arm propped above her head on the jamb, wearing a serious expression. She pushed past Angel and headed for the little kitchen without a greeting. Pulling open the fridge, she stuck her head inside and stayed there.

"Well, hello to you too. I would have thought you'd have food at your house, you being a chef and all, but feel free to help yourself. I've already eaten."

Roxy's head popped up and she slammed the fridge shut. "I wasn't looking for breakfast. I wanted to see if there was any sign of the psychedelic mushrooms you must have eaten. Are you crazy?"

Angel bit off the laugh. "I'm just helping a man with his words. He isn't as bad off as he thinks. I think it's more a matter of self-confidence than not being able to read. He's kind of sweet about it. And Rox, he's cute."

Her friend threw her hands in the air and examined the ceiling. "I cannot believe this is happening. Tell me you haven't acted on this craziness."

Angel frowned and busied herself straightening cushions in the living room. No, she hadn't, because she didn't know how to act and she didn't know how to seduce him. She'd hoped Roxy would help with that.

"Oh my god. Shit, you have, haven't you? And what did he do?" Roxy sank into the opposite chair and took Angel's hands in hers, stilling the busy flutter.

"I haven't done anything, not yet. But he's so sweet and nice to me, and he said he'd help me with anything I needed. He's so grateful I'm helping him, and I'm going to take him up on his offer. I'll help him read, and he can help me do it."

"Do it," Roxy repeated slowly.

Angel met her eyes with a defiant lift of her chin. She was not going to apologize for this. She was going to own it, just like she'd owned her virginity for too many years. She was a grown woman and an artist, and she needed to explore her emotions and passions. "I am going to ask him to help me lose my virginity, and I'm going to do it today."

Roxy dropped her hands and used them to cover her eyes. "Oh fuck. Fuck. Fuck, and I'm not going to apologize for the word. No, Angel. Don't do this. This is wrong in so many ways. I'm going to kill him. I'm going to kill them both." She flayed her hands around like she was a giant mixer set on high.

Angel tried to follow the words, but saying her intention out loud had brought on a fresh spat of nerves. What if he said no? What if he laughed at her? How many almost-thirty-four virgins could there be in the country?

Roxy uncovered her eyes. "Let me think. Let me figure this out, and then I'll kill them."

Her words finally registered. "Kill who?"

Roxy lifted a finger to have her hold the question, and Angel had nothing to distract her again but the nerves. How did you ask a man to pop your cherry? Her experience in the deflowering department was limited to reading about it, and she doubted she'd find much on the subject in her usual research resources.

"I've got it." Roxy clapped her hands and sat forward, grabbing Angel again. "You can't just come out and ask him to do you, you know."

"Give me some credit. I wasn't going to ask him like that. I was going to work up to it." Though how, she didn't really know.

"Good idea, great, actually. But instead of asking him to do it, you could ask him for his help with another guy. You know, like you're interested in someone else and you need Josiah – " Roxy stopped as if the name choked her. Taking a deep breath, a decidedly evil gleam came into her eye. She continued on, "You need Josiah's help in learning how to seduce a man. You don't have to explain about your, ah, status. Just make him help you learn the ropes, so to speak."

Angel listened with half an ear, as worry made it difficult to concentrate. Then she popped to attention. "Roxy, that is perfect! I can pretend someone is interested in me, except then the guy can leave town or something. Then Josiah will want to date me and things will take their natural course. Plus, he's already a fan of my work, so I'm sure that if I let it slip this will help, he'd be happy to do it. He's such a nice man, Roxy."

Her friend's eyes narrowed. "Yes, I'm sure he is," she said, but her voice sounded ragged. Her smirk was hard to miss, though. "Yes, it might be a little hard for him to resist you, and that is just what he deserves."

"Deserves? You think he deserves me?"

Roxy stood and paced to the door, smiling a wide evil grin. "Yes, yes he does." Angel didn't want to press her to find out what had her looking like she'd just won Iron Chef.

Yes, Josiah deserved her, and she deserved to learn more about passion from him. Angel let the thrill of a new adventure, adventures she never imagined, run through her.

Opening the fridge once more, Roxy paused and met her eyes. The broad smile grew even bigger as she said, "So Angel, remember, you need to ask him how to make yourself irresistible. But don't go too far. Play it a little coy. A little trampy too. Make it impossible for him to tell you no."

Angel nodded, thinking those romance novels she'd spent years reading as a substitute for the real thing might come in handy.

"But when the time comes, you need to tell him no, get me? You absolutely cannot go through with this. It's, ah, too early in your relationship to have sex. Make him wait. Promise me you'll do that. Promise me. You won't go through with the act until you talk to me first."

The vehemence in her tone had Angel nodding in agreement. As her friend watched her carefully, Angel lifted her chin and cast her a sultry look. Roxy laughed in deep guffaws. "Oh hell yes. This is going to be so much fun, and just what your friend deserves."

Chapter 10

He swayed between bizarre elation and abnormal nerves in the downbeat hours before Angel's visit. Kaane had been hiding things. The Grammy plaques and other awards. Reams of score paper where he'd scribbled, erased, scribbled again and ultimately crossed out with a heavy pencil until the pages tore. Scraps of notes with random phrases he hoped would someday organize themselves into lyrics. Things he wasn't ready to explain.

He'd lost track of time in the deep concentration of making things right, so when a car door slammed outside, he didn't have time to prepare. It was like that time in London when he was still an opening act. He flubbed the first song so badly, he thought he'd get thrown off the tour. He'd sworn he would never hit the first note without settling inside his head since then.

Except for now. Here he was, throwing open the front door in time to see the woman he couldn't stop obsessing about pause a few feet away. What he saw made him gulp. Gone was the sweet, shy librarian, the one who spoke with confidence about books and reading but seemed so unsure of herself otherwise. In her place stood a siren who ran a hand down her jeans, drawing attention to exactly what they did to that delectable lush body. Bright blue high beams pinned him in place like the proverbial deer in the headlights, and he wouldn't have been able to speak, even on pain of death. He sucked in air, searching for a sense of survival. This must be what drowning felt like.

Each step she took closer brought a sway to the torrent of curls cascading over the collar of a denim jacket designed for temptation. The big grin she wore with as much assurance as the rocker chick clothes didn't falter as she put a boot on the bottom step and lifted nearer. The middle stair creaked as if to warn him, but it was already too late. He was in a hole so deep, he couldn't even see daylight. His muse shined her ever-loving light and he couldn't see anything else.

Her voice sailed on the breeze in a throaty whisper. "Hello. Does today still work?"

Today? He had no clue what day it was. He'd find it impossible to remember his own name.

Her smile seemed to waver and the glow of amusement faded from her eyes. Uncertainty rapidly took its place, and Angel looked like she'd step back at any moment. Kaane willed his voice to function and took a step forward.

"Sorry, I'm sorry. I was, ah, working, and you caught me in a distracted moment. Please, come in, Angel."

He stepped aside and waved her in the door. Her passage carried that scent of wildflowers, an instant turn-on. As if she was the hottest ticket in town, blood drained from his head and hardened on the way down. Angling his body so Angel couldn't see the effect she had on him, he let his eyes roam the room in desperation. Tenting his jeans in a painful way was no way to respect his muse.

"What were you working on?" Her musical tone matched a nonchalant, hip-swaying stroll into the living room. Her gaze traveled across the walls. The minutes she spent in silent examination offered him plenty of time for him to contemplate something too. The incredible job those jeans did in cupping her perfectly excellent behind grabbed his full attention. He envied the denim, even as he reminded himself he wasn't doing anything about those urges. Of course, he hadn't had those urges in a long time, and now was a hell of a time for them to reappear.

She caught him staring when she turned. The smile she'd been wearing faltered as if she recognized his hungry gaze. Her breathless words sounded shaky. "I had something I was going to discuss with you, but I think it's the wrong time. I should go."

She spun toward the door in a pirouette, fast enough to tangle the rug around her boots. Kaane couldn't think about the consequences. His feet made fast work of the distance and he grabbed her, turning her into his chest to take the brunt of their combined fall. His arms banded around her as the pillows of her body slammed into the hardness of his. They both let out a gust of shocked air as they crashed into the floor.

Sweet torture sang in every inch where they touched. The rise and fall of her chest matched the tempo of his, and damned if that only made things worse. If he shifted, she'd feel what she did to him, and that was the last thing he wanted. Everyone knew a muse belonged on a pedestal, not where his mind now wanted to drag Angel, to the heat of his bed. Her eyelids lowered, and she didn't lift her chin to meet his gaze.

He cleared his panting throat. "Are you all right?" The panic in his tone didn't even begin to match what he felt.

She nodded, but the moan she gave contradicted that as she pushed hard on his chest. He hesitated, unwilling to let her go, and she shoved again, averting her face as if their situation embarrassed her. He pinned his arms to the floor as she clambered to her feet, because he didn't trust himself not to grab for her once more. When she finally glanced down at him, the shy blush on her cheeks emphasized the porcelain glow of her skin.

He could not look away. God help him, that smile, those luxurious curves, her wide eyes. He recognized the innocent look, though it had been years since he'd been this close to a woman wearing it. She had no damned idea what she was doing to him, and it had only been minutes since she walked in.

"I'm sorry." Her blush deepened.

"It's nothing." Was that growling his voice? He couldn't think of anything more to say as he rose to wavering feet.

The rose marking her cheeks faded to a ghostly pale, and light sunk out of her eyes. There was no mistaking the embarrassment taking up residence now. Her eyes dropped from his and roamed the room in a random pattern. She paced the perimeter from painting to painting. They brought the only lightness to the otherwise sterile rooms.

"I never expected to have anyone display them." She paused in front of the one he'd hung over the fireplace, 'Contemplation', and her hands dug into the back pockets of her jeans. The pose did amazing things for the pull of knit fabric under that denim jacket. He really wished she didn't do that, even while other parts of him were more than delighted she did.

When Angel finally spoke, her voice sounded over-bright and forced. "My friends will be so excited to know you're displaying these. I told them I would get a tour of your ranch today, and they want to hear all about it. You know DK, or at least about her, since you bought her guitar sculpture. What about Tess and Roxy? Do you know them?"

Pig farmer Josiah would not, he decided. "No, I don't. Are they artists too?"

Angel seemed to relax into her answer. Tess owned the flower shop on Main – if he ever got a chance, he should check out the amazing displays. "And everyone knows Roxy."

She looked around the room again, uncertainty and silence back where effusiveness had been moments ago. Her expression grew pensive as they settled on 'Contemplation', and it sliced him like sharp metal.

"I'm not very good, am I? My art, I mean. Not like DK, that's for sure. Not like Roxy and her food or Tess with her flowers. My work is mediocre in comparison." Her whole body deflated in apparent grief.

The feel of her arms in his hands from her near-fall made his palms tingle still. The warmth of pressing her softness against every hard edge of his body made heat renew its impression against the zipper of his jeans. Eyes he never wanted to see sad settled on him with barely controlled tears. Despite his better judgment screaming he had to keep away, Kaane stepped close and raised a shaking finger to brush a droplet from her cheek.

"Your work is amazing." He cleared the lump in his throat, the one making it hard to speak above a mutter. "I am sure your friends would tell you that it took them years to reach the places they are now in their art. No one becomes great without hard work and dedication. Artists need to recreate themselves and their work all the time. The concept of an overnight success is a misnomer." He wanted to keep his fingers on her face, tracing the fine bones and overlying softness, but he withdrew his hand while he still could.

Angel looked confused. "Where did you learn that word? Misnomer?"

Kaane inhaled sharply, chiding himself for the slip. He shrugged and scratched his head, as he imagined a semi-literate ranch dude would do. "Not sure. I must have heard it somewhere. Is it the right word to use?" He pushed uncertainty into his expression.

Angel smiled, though it didn't make her eyes light up. She took his hand in hers. "Yes, it's the correct word. I'm proud of you, Josiah. Even when you aren't sure, you're trying, and that's what will make you successful. You'll be reading complex books in no time."

She clasped his fingers tighter, and he swore she was about to move their joined digits to her chest. He would not survive it. And yet, he could not yank his hand away. He stayed where he was and didn't move, hoping she would act on her desire, and afraid she would.

Angel smiled but didn't look up at him, absorbed instead by looking at their joined hands. Confusion scrambled his brain as he waited for her to look up. When she didn't he followed her gaze.

She traced the ends of his fingers. Imagining that tender motion on another part of his over-stimulated body only made things worse. He tightened his fingers so she couldn't continue, and her surprised gaze shot up to meet his.

"Your fingers are different."

Josiah blinked a few times and looked down. His hands, the broad fingers on his left hand and the side callouses on his right, provided a welcomed distraction. "Uh, yeah. Work, you know. Different hands, doing different things, and things change, I guess. Here, let me look at yours."

He turned her palms face up. The rough texture of his fingertips gliding over her smooth skin made the pads of his digits burn. She sighed as if the gestures pleased her, and guilt over his deceit swamped him again. Then she curled her fingers and ran her short nails over his palms, and he gulped in shock at the sensation. He dropped her hands and reeled away, unable to stay that close to her without making a move so off tune, it was off the charts.

"So, let me show you around. I've been working on the house, but haven't done much else to the property. I guess I should begin getting it ready, for the pigs, you know. I have a friend who's building me a room – I mean, a barn. It's behind that barn you saw as you came in. The old barn is original to the old ranch. This house came later. My contractor said it was built on the foundation of what must have been the original house, and it looked like it burned down. There isn't any written history about the place, just stories."

His words came out in a rush, making his nerves obvious. But then, she was his muse. Having this surge of feelings for the woman he should worship flipped his emotions between failure and anger. If only he could get his pounding blood to settle, he might be able to think. Anything to get out in the open and cool the heat making his hands burn to touch her skin once more.

"Let's take a walk," he said with sudden inspiration. "I have something I'd like to show you." He was strides ahead of her, down the porch and crunching on gravel, by the time she followed.

She glanced at her car as she passed it and paused. "Do I need to lock this?"

Kaane stopped too, frozen by the vulnerability and doubt in her expression. "You don't need to lock it. You're safe here, Angel. Nothing and no one will hurt you."

Except for him. This had been a bad idea. Kaane kept reminding himself it was for his art, for his music, that he needed Angel in his sights, but it wasn't doing much for him.

But if he could keep her close by every day, not under the ruse of learning to read but instead, encouraging her art, would that work? She had no studio. He had nothing but space. Offering it to her would keep her close, close enough, he hoped, to allow his muse to do her magic.

Her wide eyes shined up at him with such genuineness. The denim clothes accented her beauty when they should have muted attention. The soft touch of her hands left a sensation that made him wonder what they would feel like running over him everywhere.

He was not going to hit on her. His muse deserved, no, required respect. In her pristine state, she was his conduit to success. Or so he kept repeating to himself. He raced on, trying not to think about the woman hurrying behind him, but it was a useless repetition. Every cell in him beat with rock hard awareness about every cell in her. His feet only stopped when the new construction came into view.

"Wow, that is a pretty impressive building. Those pigs are going to think they landed in hog heaven." She giggled, but to his ear, it sounded nervous.

And who could blame her? The building didn't look like a pig barn, or sty, or whatever he was supposed to call it. How could he explain the large central space and the smaller ones to the sides? And the foundation. Why would pigs need a nice floor and thick walls and tall ceilings?

But Angel seemed unaware of his predicament. She walked forward slowly, careful of the pile of scrap boards and odd bits of leftover concrete. She paced around the structure and stopped at exactly where he planned to place the entry door. Glancing over at him, she smiled and dazzled him with the simple move.

"I always thought about them wallowing in muddy outside pens. This is like the Ritz of pig ranches. Tell me, where will the mama pigs have their babies?"

He opened his mouth, planning to say he knew not what. True confessions? Telling her he wasn't a pig rancher but a musician and needed her to write his songs? As if that didn't make him sound like a stalker and a greater danger to her.

"I've learned I should be saying pig farmer and not rancher," he said, giving himself a mental kick about what came out.

"Oh, I thought it was farmer, but I don't know much about it without research. I've lived in cities most of my life, and even when I visited my aunt here in Flynn's Crossing, I stayed close to home. What I know of country living, I've learned from books."

He grabbed on to that lifeline with both hands. "Tell me about your aunt."

Angel shrugged, and a sad cloud crossed her face. She ran a tentative hand over the frame where the door to the sound room would be one day. If she noticed the extra thickness of the boards between these walls, she didn't mention it.

"My aunt lived here for most of her adult life. She taught high school English to multiple generations in this town. Mothers and fathers said they were always pleased their children would learn from the same dedicated teacher they had growing up. No one had a bad word to say about her."

Kaane took her elbow to make sure she didn't trip over an area of the floor still open for electrical work. The minute his fingers touched her jacket and closed on the muscle and bone underneath, he knew it was a mistake. The audible gasp she gave matched the catch in his own breathing. As soon as they passed the hole, he dropped her arm. That didn't keep him from rubbing his fingers together to hold on to the sensation, though. He said, "You two must have been very close."

Angel faced the main jam room, though her gaze seemed far away. "She was my dad's only sibling. During summer breaks, she'd come to stay with us for a while, wherever we were. Mom and I followed Dad to as many of his job sites as we could. Construction zones, for the most part. The jobs were manual labor and never paid very much. Mom always emphasized the need for a good education, even while she herself only finished high school and then while she was pregnant with me."

"She's a young woman, then," Kaane said, drawn into the story despite his misgivings about getting too close.

A sad smile came to Angel's face as she kicked a rock with her boot. He winced. The boots looked brand new. "Yes, she was. When Dad took a job on fishing boats off the Oregon coast, Mom put her foot down. She settled us in Portland, where I could attend a good school for longer than a semester and she could get a steady job. I was twelve, and so happy to be able to make friends and stay in one place. Dad didn't come home often, though."

Letting out a whoosh of air, Kaane thought he might have made a mistake going down this path. What did he know of families? Something told him this story wasn't going to turn out well.

Angel walked on as if blind to her surroundings. "Four days into my sophomore year of high school, I came home to find a very nice police officer waiting by our apartment's front door. The neighbor had heard Mom screaming for help, and by the time the super came to open the door, it was too late. She died of a brain hemorrhage."

Without thinking, Kaane put an arm around her shoulders. He felt the tremble run through her body. Even after all this time, the loss clearly cut at her. He would do anything to take her pain away.

"What happened to you then?"

Angel shrugged. "I was fifteen, and I had a remaining parent. Dad came home to make arrangements. I could live alone, he said, because I was mature for my age. He headed back to the ocean, out of Alaska this time. It was hard and risky work, but I knew why he did it. Without Mom, he had nothing to stay home for."

"He had you," Kaane barked with an outrage in his voice he could not control.

She looked up at him with a brave smile as if she was happy someone took her side. "That's just it. The link was Dad and Mom, or Mom and me, but never Dad and me."

That cut through him like a sharp note. No man should treat his daughter that way, and especially not someone as special as Angel Reed.

She resumed walking, approaching the split rail fence separating the maintained area around the house from the wilderness beyond. She leaned on the top rail and tucked her chin in her hands. The posture brought her head low and her rear end out. One hip canted higher than the other, and Kaane halted in shock at the sheer perfection of the view.

"This is wonderful view," she said.

"Damn right it is," he muttered.

She looked back over her shoulder. "What did you say?"

Kaane cleared his throat and tried to concentrate on her eyes. In this light, they shown in gray-blue storminess, the color odes should be written to. Too bad he couldn't think of a single phrase. "I said, I agree, it is. I plan to keep as much of the land natural as possible."

She nodded as if the idea pleased her and resumed her examination of the open field. He leaned on the fence too, putting a boot up on the lowest split rail. She did the same, rocking as if she heard an inner rhythm.

He wished he could hear it. He wished he could demand she hum it for him so he could capture it. He'd find the words, if she stayed beside him.

He tried to get his mind thinking about anything normal. "Where is your father now?"

Angel shrugged. "He died on a halibut boat when I was in college. By then, I rarely saw him. The last time, he couldn't even meet my eyes. All he said was that I did good not to follow in either one of their footsteps." She straightened and turned toward him, her face pained. "Do you mind if we discuss something else?"

He nodded, then shook his head. "One more question, and then I promise we can talk about whatever you want. Where is your aunt now?"

The sadness in her expression made his heart break for her. She put a brave face on things with a quick smile that didn't reach her eyes, then said, "Aunt Jenny was run down two summers ago on Main Street. The kid who hit her was high and had stolen his parents' car. Those parents claimed he didn't know what he was doing because he was wealthy and had no sense of responsibility. I ask you, who's responsibility was that?" Anger made her words harsh. "But karma is, well, you know. The parents were charged as accessories, because the drugs were theirs, and the kid went to rehab and then to juvenile detention. None of that, though, brought my aunt back. And now, I really want to talk about something else."

The determination in her tone had him dropping the litany of comments and questions he wanted to follow. Without thinking, he pressed a hand into her lower back and led her toward the old barn. Even separated by thick cotton and the layers underneath, his palm burned in that proximity to her skin.

Angel paused and seemed to take in the old wood and worn siding. When she put a hand on the door handle, he took over. The door gave its unforgiving creak as he hauled it open and strode into its darkness. It wasn't clean or pleasant or beautiful by any stretch of the imagination, and it was only because of Powers' insistence that the place still stood.

"What a wonderful place. Did you know my friend DK has her studio in an old barn? I envied it from the first time I saw it. I'd love to have somewhere like that to paint."

Kaane spun in a fast circle, yanking on the chain from a bare lightbulb hanging from a beam overhead. It didn't do much to pierce the darkness around them, but it lit Angel's upturned face with its warm glow.

His heart let hope bleed into his emotions and his voice. "You could work here. I don't use this space, and you'll have all the privacy you need." He trailed off, biting off the rest of what he wanted to say. If she worked here, he could worship with his muse every day.

A clap like thunder sounded in the room as Angel slammed her hands together and gave him a brilliant smile. The second clap accompanied a small jump, as if she couldn't contain her enthusiasm.

"Really? You wouldn't mind? I wouldn't be in your way? I would love that. I paint on the porch at the house, and quarters are tight. It would be such a help to me to have this kind of space."

"You would be doing me a big favor. This barn deserves some love, and I think your painting here is the solution. As long as you don't mind me hanging over your shoulder every once in a while." All the time, he thought silently. "And we could still have our reading lessons." So I can sit close to you for a time each day and pretend it's real.

Awareness hit him as hard as a light bar falling from scaffolding overhead. He needed to be next to her in any way possible for as long as it took. Already, new words and notes played in his head, and all he had to do was watch her for this tap to run.

"When can I start?"

Her question didn't register, not when that floral scent suddenly enveloped him and her shining eyes lit his world up.

"Josiah?"

As long as he behaved himself with Angel. That was part of his pledge, and he didn't plan to break it. Even so, keeping his promise was going to be so damned hard.

Chapter 11

She usually didn't talk about her family, not about Mom and Dad, and only a little about Aunt Jenny. But with Josiah, the conversation and its hard explanations were painless. The anger in his eyes, she suspected, was on her behalf.

It wasn't until later, when they'd come to an agreement on the barn and he'd insisted she stay for dinner, that she had a chance to ask things of him.

"What about your family?"

Josiah's hands paused over the dish, seasoning pinched in his fingers and his face in a frown. He gave a small nod, adding words as his movements resumed. "My family does not approve of my chosen profession."

The sadness wasn't hard to miss. Who wouldn't approve of a man who worked hard off the land? The thought puzzled her beyond reason.

He continued, "I have three brothers, and they all have fine, upstanding jobs. I didn't want to be a doctor or a lawyer, though."

"A farmer is a noble and necessary profession too. How much land do you have here?"

His feet shuffled as if answering embarrassed him. His lips pressed in a firm line, and she fought the urge to run a thumb over them to release it. She feared he'd jump out of his skin if she did.

"Two hundred acres," popped out of his mouth like a series of guttural grunts.

"Wow, that's a lot to be responsible for."

Josiah shrugged as if it was nothing and lifted the plate carrying two steaks. "I'm going to put these on the grill."

He disappeared out the kitchen's back door and into the ring of outdoor light. The halo glowed on his blond hair, reminding her of a man in a spotlight. How could she ask him for what she wanted? Lying to him about some other man didn't seem right. It was bad enough using him without complicating matters.

Josiah returned, putting the plate in the sink. His open face rose to meet her gaze and he smiled in the way that sent a sharp fire through her. "Want to come outside while I cook the meat?"

She'd nodded, unable to speak. When she pushed out the door and sat at a table near the grill, he turned their conversation to other topics, and three hours later, she wondered where the evening had gone. Her thoughts lingered on their time together every time she woke during that long night.

Today, an unpleasant task like cleaning an old barn had been fun because of the man helping her. This morning's conversation, between cough-inducing sweeps of dust, centered on things they favored. She admitted to a classical music addiction, fostered by her aunt. He said he liked classic rock and new country and sometimes, jazz. She carefully navigated around the next usual topic, books, because she didn't want him to feel bad.

"What made you get into art?" He asked the question as he bravely swept down cobwebs gray with accumulated silt, as if the spiders who built them were no big deal. She shivered every time he did it and made sure to stay far away.

"I, ah, I like to make something out of my imagination. You know, be creative. Research is like that, for a librarian, solving a puzzle or a mystery. But making something that comes from inside you is a treasure unlike anything else." She blushed with the words. She rarely talked about her art like this, because even to her own ears, it sounded childish and silly.

Josiah stopped his sweeping and stared at her as if he didn't believe what he heard. He even took a step forward before halting and shaking his head as if to clear it. His smile grew slowly. "I know exactly what you mean."

She was ready to ask him how he knew when she saw it. A big, hairy, black something crawled on his shoulder, heading down his arm. Angel couldn't help the scream that echoed off the rafters, and ran for the big open barn door like a devil chased her.

"Angel? What's wrong? What did I – oh shit!"

The crash, bang and cursing that followed made her giggle with nerves. The noise ended abruptly, and silence stretched long enough for her feet to hurry her forward.

The darkness inside the barn yawned before her and she raced inside, willing herself to face it. "Josiah, are you – " Her words came out in a shriek, though whether it was for him or her own fear, she wasn't sure.

He stood in the circle of light with dust rising around him. The broom's fuzzy end was propped on the floor, and he held the handle away from him. His other hand hovered near his face, and in it, he held something she didn't want to contemplate.

"Ugh. Is that the thing?" Despite her desire to be strong, she backed away.

"I think it's a tarantula. I didn't know they lived around here. I'll need to check the corners, Angel. I don't want these monsters near you."

He met her eyes, and that stirring of energy teased her. She took a tentative step forward, trying to ignore the large spider in his hand, drawn to the fierceness in his expression.

"Is it dead?"

He nodded.

"Good." She couldn't stop the shudder of revulsion.

"I take it you're not a fan of spiders."

She shook her head hard enough to make her hair bandana fall to cover her eyes. When she lifted it, she found him grinding his boot heel into the gravel outside.

She ran to him on impulse this morning, reaching up and kissing his cheek. His expression, shocked and amazed, had her dancing back. Her knight wore an old coat that had seen better days a decade ago and worn dusty boots. Even now, the sight of his pleased surprise had her heating with reaction. Even now, she couldn't hold back the mirth as she thought of –

"Angel? Why are you giggling? You sound quite pleased with something."

Her eyes popped open to stare into Roxy's curious face. "Ah, I was just laughing at what you said."

Her friend turned to give the man across the massive kitchen cocked eyebrows. Angel turned too, noticing the worry on Mac's face as he gave a deep sigh and focused on the grill.

Grill. She was at Roxy and Mac's house, surrounded by her friends, but her mind was on Josiah and the fun they had kicking up dust and bugs and the refuse of years of neglect.

"All right, the cold food is set up on the covered patio and according to Powers, the heaters are ready to light. All we need are the meats and veggies and we're set." Tess glanced around room, silent except for sizzling. "What's going on in here?"

Roxy cackled a strange laugh, and Tess made a rude sound. "Is Roxy giving Mac a bad time? Ignore her. She gets this way whenever he grills something, like she's the only one qualified to cook. Mac does a great job on meat, when he doesn't burn it, and I think it's safe to say she has him well in hand. Come on, let's get some wine and relax outside."

She pulled Angel out the side door, shushing Roxy when she would have argued. The kitchen in this old farm house was huge enough to host forty people, she guessed, and she suspected Roxy used every inch of it. By comparison, Josiah's kitchen was tiny.

But he did a great job fixing dinner last night. She wouldn't mind getting her hands on the big gas range and pots and pans that looked barely used. But then, Josiah was a man living alone and by his own admission, he rarely had company.

"Did you hear what happened in town today?" Tess waved a hand in front of Angel's face. "Angel, what's wrong?"

"Nothing, Tess. Sorry, I was thinking about my student, the one I'm tutoring to learn to read. He's such a nice man, and I was just thinking how lonely he must be."

"Do tell." Curiosity danced across her friend's expression. "Details, my dear. Is he a nice single man? Why do you think he's lonely?"

"He is single. I invited him to come tonight, but he said no. I think he's kind of shy, like me. That's why I think it's a good idea for him to be – "

"Who wants appetizers?" A plate laden with bits and bites appeared in front of their faces. Roxy gave Tess a hard stare and mouthed what looked to be 'not now'.

Tess shot Roxy an amused look, ignoring the platter and finishing her pour of their wines. She handed Angel a glass and said, "Fine. I guess she wants to wait to hear your story too. I told her about this already, so no harm. As I was saying, did you hear about what happened in town today?"

Before Angel had a chance to answer, Roxy yelled, "Mac!"

"I am right here, woman. Hold it down. I'm going to pull the meat off. Are you ready with the rest?"

Another voice joined the melee. "Is it about time to eat? The natives are getting restless out there. Say, did you hear about what happened in town today? Some guy was asking about famous people who live around here, and specifically, he was asking about – "

"DK, great. Here, take this." Roxy shoved a plate filled with roasted vegetables into her arms, spinning her and giving her a push. "Come on, everyone, it's time to eat. Boy, I'm starving. How about you, Angel? Tell us about how the painting is going. You haven't given us an update in a while."

Roxy pulled her along so fast, Angel had to skip to keep up. "The painting is going great." A whoosh swallowed the rest of her possible words when Roxy gave her a push and her butt hit a chair.

Her friend did a fast swirl. "Good, sweetie, that's good. We can't wait to hear about it. Let's let everyone get their food and then we can talk about it." Her volume increased to a yell. "Mac, where the hell are you with that meat?"

DK looked at the others quizzically. "What is going on with her? Anyway, today, this guy was on Main Street, asking about famous people who live in the area, and guess who he mentioned by name? Anyone?"

"Here he is. I swear, this man's speed makes a snail look like a cheetah. Who wants meat?" Roxy rushed between their chairs, talking a mile a minute and dishing up huge portions.

Angel looked down at the pork chop large enough to feed a small army. She would never be able to finish it, but she didn't get a chance to ask for something smaller as the tornado that was Roxy buzzed around the patio.

Vince must have noticed her dismay. "Don't worry. If you can't finish it, I've got you covered."

DK poked her head around her husband and said, "Don't let him con you into that chop. The man has two hollow legs and he'll eat the meal right off your plate. Protect your food, Angel. I find a sharp fork is a necessary defense."

Angel giggled at the affronted expression on Vince's face. When his eyes settled on his wife, though, love shined like a beacon. Angel sighed inside. Someday, she wanted to be the center of that kind of emotion.

"Anyway, I really want to tell you about today. I was at the gallery, and this guy comes in, and – "

"Hold that thought," Roxy said over DK's words, leaping up right after she sat down and rounding the outdoor table, nearly running into a propane heater in her hurry. She grabbed Mac's arm and yanked, but the man didn't move. Like everyone else, Angel fell silent.

"Roxy, sit down. Eat your food. Let everyone tell their stories." Mac batted off Roxy's fingers so many times, they looked like hummingbirds in flight.

"Fine. Fine, just fine." Roxy's feet hit the deck hard enough to make things shake on the table and flopped back into her seat.

"Angel, please ignore my maniacal other half and tell us about your progress on new work," Mac said, sedately cutting into his meat in what had to be slow motion.

Setting down her fork, Angel couldn't keep the grin out her voice or off her face. "I'm going to have a studio, in a barn, no less. I spent today cleaning it out. I can't wait to have that kind of space to paint."

"That is wonderful. You can be part of the studio tours now. Where is it?" The words tumbled out of DK at a fast clip.

Angel grinned back. "It's actually not too far from here, in South County. And I can't wait to be part of the studio tour, but it might not be that pleasant for visitors once the farm is up and running."

"It's on a working farm? That sounds excellent. Maybe it can be included somehow. What are they farming?" Tess put a bite of food in her mouth.

"Pigs. He's a pig farmer."

Beside her, Vince choked on his pork chop. "Pigs? Man, that is going to be some fragrant location."

"Vince." DK's warning tone somehow made the single syllable into three. "Ignore him, Angel. What's the farmer's name?"

Angel chewed her food and swallowed. "Josiah. Josiah Harmond."

"Boy, that name sounds familiar. Maybe we've met him. Tess, does it ring a bell with you?" Powers tapped his finger to his lips.

"Who wants dessert?" Roxy shot out of her seat. A chorus of voices told her to relax, and she sank back down and reached for the wine.

Recognition brought delight to DK's face. "That's the man who bought your pieces at the gallery, isn't it? And now he's going to rent you creative space. That's fabulous. Vince, isn't that great?"

But Vince didn't seem to hear the question. He stared at Mac, his scowl a picture of confusion. Finally, the confusion cleared and his eyes narrowed further. He said, "DK, my love, why don't you tell the others about the gallery incident today?"

DK sat forward, excitement on her face. "This guy had to be a reporter, or maybe a paparazzi. He asked about famous people in town, and said he'd heard that Mac Smythe lived around here. I neither confirmed or denied, but he seemed to already know."

Angel turned to Roxy, now realizing what had her friend so worried. "Oh, Roxy, I'm sorry. Have they figured out where you and Mac live? It must be so hard to enjoy your privacy when people are poking into your business."

Roxy waved the hand not clutching her wine glass in a dismissive arc.

"I don't think it was Mac he was really after. I think he wanted to know about someone else. He asked specifically about Kaane Scott. You know, the rocker who's your friend, Mac. I didn't know he lives around here. Or does he?" DK shot her glance between Mac and Roxy with a question on her face.

The celebrity's name didn't mean anything to Angel, but the others seemed excited. Vince paused in the act of shoveling his food into his face and lifted his fork like a baton. "Hey, isn't Kaane's real – "

"Shut up, Vince," Mac and Roxy said in unison.

Across the table, Powers suddenly frowned at his plate. He set his silverware down with so much care, Angel thought he was about to say something was wrong with his food. Then he gave Mac a hard look. "So," he said.

Mac shook his head.

Roxy leaped up, grabbing plates and stacking everyone's on her arm. She had Angel's before Angel had a chance to set down her knife next to her partially eaten meat. "Well, this has been great, just great. I'm so glad we could get together, but I'm sure you're all dying to get moving. Late night, early mornings, all that. Wonderful to see you all."

She raced back into the house, leaving the group staring after her. Angel said, "What's gotten into her, Mac?"

She looked down the table at their host, but he wasn't paying attention. He pinched the bridge of his nose with one hand and rubbed his temple with the other, mumbling all the while, "This is not going to be good."

Chapter 12

"I don't know what you're talking about." Kaane toed off his boots and switched the side where he cradled the cell phone. The wet towel he rubbed over his face came away gray with grime, like the rest of him. He'd promised Angel he would get the barn cleaned up, and he'd spent the rest of the day doing just that. Now he wanted a shower, food, and the piano, and he was running out of patience to keep things in that order.

All afternoon as he swept and dumped and swept again, he thought about Angel's face, delighted with the light once the big doors were opened. Her shriek made him want to sweep her into his arms and make her monsters disappear. Words and notes floated around in his head in a litany that was turning, albeit slowly, into a song. If only he could capture it before it spun away.

Mac spoke in a quiet but heated tone. "Scott? I'm warning you. Angel Reed is a nice young woman and Roxy and the others are very protective of her."

Kaane blew out a frustrated sigh. "She is nice, and she thinks she's helping me, and she is. Just not in the way she thinks." He tossed the used towel in the general direction of the laundry room, missing the door completely. It hit the white wall and left a dark streak as it slid down.

Like a dark mark on his soul. He needed Angel. Her invitation to come to dinner with her friends would have resulted in disaster. The men knew who he was.

Mac continued, "Treat her with respect. Somehow, your identity will be revealed, and it would be better if Angel learned it from you. And while you're at it, you'll want to think about this. It appears a paparazzi was in town asking about you. Do you really want to bring an innocent young woman into that craziness?"

Kaane froze in place. Someone was looking for him, and where one shark circled, others soon followed as soon as there was a hint of blood in the water. But he could protect Angel from it. She didn't know him as Kaane Scott. To her, he was a pig farmer named Josiah who couldn't read.

"Kaane, please, I'm begging you. For our friendship and in the hope that I still have a loving relationship, and if you value not being carved up like a Thanksgiving turkey by my chef half, leave Angel alone."

"No can do, man. Sorry, but no. Angel is everything to me, Mac. I mean, everything." Kaane glanced down at the filthy jeans he would probably have to burn and the ground-in dirt under his fingernails. Yes, he'd do pretty much anything for that woman.

Mac hung up the phone without responding.

Kaane spent little time thinking about Mac's warnings overnight, exhausted by the manual labor he wasn't used to. Hours after Angel left, he stayed at it, adding lights he was sure she would want to replace but which could work for now. The big door moved on a well-greased rack, and he'd washed down the interior walls to remove their grime. He even moved in benches and platforms he figured she could use for her supplies or something.

To avoid pacing the floor bare as he waited for her to arrive, he tinkled the piano keys, waiting for inspiration. He tried out a stanza, an Angel-inspired mix of vibrant notes. His phone rang, and he halted the movement of his right hand long enough to register the rock chords marking Rodney's number. He continued playing over the insistent blare, and after two runs, the phone fell silent.

What was it about Angel that was so special? If he knew, he could imitate those creative triggers and his reliance on her would end. But would it? Would that be enough? He didn't want it to end, not even as he knew their relationship had only one purpose, his musical resurrection, and it was built on a shaky beat, his error of omission.

Rock melody screamed again, as if Rod-man knew Kaane avoided him. He closed his eyes, willing the noise to cease. When the phone fell quiet, his touch returned to the keyboard.

Why had Mac warned him to stay away from Angel? Why was he warning him away from the woman who made his juices flow? If he didn't see her every day, Kaane was sure the sun wouldn't rise in the morning.

There it was. It was more than creativity he found when he was with her. Angel brought him joy and fun and an ease he hadn't felt in decades. The rush of the next concert, the next recording session, the next jam, faded in importance when she was near. With Angel, he lived in the now, a place he hadn't been comfortable for a very long time.

A plain buzz sounded from his phone now, and he leaped up to get it. It could be Angel. She could be in trouble and needed him. As soon as he registered the thought, he realized how silly it sounded. The reality of that made him pause, picking up the phone to check the number. It was not one he recognized, and he tossed it back on the counter unanswered.

He was being an ass. Angel was an accomplished, adult woman, and the only thing she needed him for was killing spiders. He forced himself back to the piano, turning to the classical music Angel loved. It was better than staring like a lonesome puppy out the front window. Angel would arrive when she did, and until then, he needed an escape.

He wasn't sure how long he played, first through one sonata, then another. They were both full of misplaced notes and he knew he flubbed more than one run, but the pleasure was still his to enjoy. He reached the end with a flourish that would have made old Beethoven proud, when the words to a new stanza came to him.

You wake beside me, tousled and dreamy from sleep,

Your hair wraps around me like it's me you want to keep.

And I pray that it's true, that you want me for your own.

There is no place on earth I would rather call my home.

It wasn't poetry, but it was better than a blank piece of paper. As he jotted the words in his notebook, he wondered what Angel would look like, newly awake and finding him next to her. Would there be joy in her eyes? Would she want to keep him around? He was beginning to fear that the answer to that was more important to him than the words of a song.

He launched into a new melody, Chopin this time, and played only the first few bars. He dropped his hands into his lap. The song was so sad, about missed love and lost dreams if he remembered right, and he didn't want that coloring his day. He wanted, needed, joy, and joy was Angel.

"Oh please, can you play the rest? I love that piece."

He spun on the bench, shocked to find Angel standing in the archway from the front door. Her cheeks were pink and her eyes sparkled, and he knew he'd never seen anyone so beautiful.

"And what were you writing?" She took a step forward, pulling off gloves missing the ends of their fingers.

"Um, nothing. I didn't hear you drive up."

She leaned in closer to the notebook. He slapped the cover closed with what he was sure was a guilty look. She stepped back and her smile faded.

"I'm sorry, I guess I was prying. I just wanted to see what you were writing. You must be studying hard when I'm not around." She said the words with a forced happy note, but the smile didn't reach her eyes.

"I, ah, yes, I have. I want to be your star pupil."

That seemed to please her, and she pushed the gloves into a coat pocket and reached for the buttons. Her hand paused as if uncertain of her welcome, and he jumped up from the bench. "Please, stay for a while. I know you want to get to work, but I'd really love a lesson, if you have time."

She smiled again, the sunny beatification of it making him warm in her light. But she shook her head. "I actually came in to tell you I was here. I parked by the barn. I brought supplies over, but I was going to finish cleaning the place first."

He reached for a coat on a hook by the door and shoved his arms into it. Looking down, he realized his stocking feet wouldn't make it far on the gravel, and he glanced around for his boots. "Be right back," he said, lifting a finger and racing for his back door. They would still be wet from their wash off last night, but it didn't matter. He wanted to see Angel's face when she found her studio ready for occupation.

By the time he wrestled into wet leather, Angel no longer waited by the front. He spun toward the open door but didn't see her. A sound drew his attention to the piano. She stood beside it and read over the words he'd just written, genuine surprise on her face. She must have heard his squishy approach, because she turned to him with a big grin.

"This is good, Josiah. I'm impressed. You're using words that make well-read people stumble in their spelling. If I didn't know better, I'd say you know how to read already." A wink and a quirk of her eyebrows accompanied her teasing tone.

What would she say if he came clean now?

"I clearly need to revamp my tutoring plan for you. You've been hiding your true skill when we've been together. No session today, my friend, because I need to accelerate our program to a more challenging level. Tell me, when did you start writing poetry?"

And there, he had it. An opening he could use while not explaining the reason he needed her near.

"Off and on for a long time." He dropped his eyes at the fabrication. It wasn't a lie, exactly.

"Well I think this shows promise. I'm going to find a way to incorporate this into our lessons. But for now, I have a studio to clean." She smiled again, placing a hand on his arm as she passed. When they touched, she froze and looked down at their connection.

He felt it too. I came on like a fast glissando up the scale and back down, making the hairs on the back of his neck stand up as they did when the guitar riff hit the perfect balance of crazy and serene. Without thinking, he put his hand over hers and squeezed.

Her eyes shot up to him, shock making her lips a perfect circle. He heard the deep breath she drew, and he followed her down that path too. The truth was, he wanted to follow her everywhere.

She opened her mouth as if she intended to speak, then closed her eyes and shook her head. Withdrawing her hand, she spoke without looking at him. "I should get going. Thank you for the studio space, Josiah. Clearly, I'm going to need to pay you for it. You don't need my reading lessons. I'll, ah, I'll be working for a while today. Lots to do." She said the last words in a flip tone, her eyes on the door.

Quick steps later, she was gone, and his arm extended with his fingers still curled as if he held her hand.

>>>>>

Retreat. That was the perfect word for it. By official definition, it meant the act of withdrawing, usually from something unpleasant. Josiah's touch had been anything but, yet that was what she was doing, running as fast as her boots could take her over the uneven drive.

She needed to concentrate on work. Clean the space, and add the fresh supplies. Maybe in a couple of days, the place would be in good enough condition for her to paint. Paint anything that came to her mind, but now, the only thing she could think of was Josiah's face.

His transported expression as he played the piano fixed on something she could not see. Perhaps it was the same feeling that came over her when, brush in hand, she thought of nothing, and the painting Zen took over. Where had Josiah learned to play so well?

His poetry was interesting too. It sounded like he was working on a love poem, and she was a sucker for nice cadence. She couldn't understand why he'd hidden his talent from her, unless it embarrassed him as much as his struggles with reading did. He was gifted, but she wasn't sure she should tell him that. There had to be a reason he hid his talents behind a farmer's façade, and far be it from her to tear away those shields away.

She reached for the large barn door, ready to heave it open in her excitement to get to work. Big things would come from working here, of that, she felt sure.

"Hold on, Angel." Josiah put a hand over hers on the edge of the door. "I thought you might want to lock up when you're done. I know this is the country, but you never know who might be poking around." He handed her a lock and key set, and another key, shiny and brand new, shown on a ring in the palm of his hand.

She stared down at the items, unsure how to tell him thanks for something she should have thought of herself. "I'll pay you for them," she said, reaching out slowly.

When her fingers grasped the keys, his fingers closed around them. Her heart sped up and her eyes lifted to his. "No need, Angel. I want you to feel safe and secure here. Come and go anytime, and I hope when you're here, you'll treat my house as yours too. I leave the door unlocked when I'm here. I'll make you a key for when I'm not."

He released her hand, and cold loss bit into her skin. She nodded, not able to express her thanks in any words. He took a single pace backwards, his eyes staying on her, and she did the only thing her confused brain could managed. She stepped forward, lifted on her toes, and placed a whisper of a kiss on his lips.

The contact lit her up, dazzling like a string of holiday lights. She swore her bones melted into muscles gone slack. Jumping back did no good. Pressing a hand to her lips, she was unwilling to let the feeling go, even as she stepped back once more.

Now what could she say? She was almost afraid to look at him, embarrassed by her gesture. What would he think of her? They were barely acquaintances, and yet she'd kissed him. "I'm sorry," she said, "I have no idea what came over me."

When he didn't reply, she looked up. His expression, astonished with his mouth open, would have been comical, except she was sure the flush she felt on her cheeks echoed the same surprise. With a nervous giggle, she tried out a smile to ease the moment.

His face changed, the shock fading into determination. As if she'd thrown a switch, he moved with sudden speed and wrapped his arms around her. She didn't have a chance to register a new feeing before he lowered his face and kissed her.

His lips were soft, scorching, hard, seductive. The contrasts came in rapid succession with a speed her mind couldn't process. He deepened the kiss, as if he was a dying man and she was the water to refresh him. She couldn't back away, and she didn't want to, not when it felt so heavenly being clutched in a way that assured her he felt as crazed as she did.

A hand dug under the braid of hair down her back, finding her neck and holding her tight. Fingers massaged a knot of tension she hadn't been aware was there, not until he touched it and it evaporated like a puff of smoke. How her arms got around his neck, she wasn't sure. All she wanted was this amazing kiss to last as long as she had breath.

How long they'd been knotted up like that, she wasn't sure, but it wasn't long enough. The pressure lessened too quickly. Josiah lifted his mouth but rested his chin against the top of her head. She wanted to lean back and see what was in his eyes, but she didn't want to leave the warmth of his arms. She wiggled in closer, which evidently was the wrong thing to do. He released her immediately, but grabbed her arms and lowered his face until they were staring eye to eye.

His expression was solemn and he didn't blink. He examined her face as if searching for answers. His voice came out in an uneven gravelly tone when he said, "There are many things I need to say I'm sorry for, but I'm not going to apologize for that."

He dropped his hold on her and spun fast enough to kick up dirt. He strode to the house on rapid feet, pausing at the top of the stairs before rounding the porch out of sight. He never looked back.

She wasn't sure what to do. Follow him? And do what? If he wasn't going to apologize, then he must have liked that kiss. She certainly did, and was it wrong to immediately want more of them? Like a whole lot more. She kept staring at the place he'd disappeared, willing him to return. He didn't, and it wasn't until a gust of wind blew her coat open that she realized she'd become cold.

This must be passion, at least the stirrings of it. There was nothing to do but work. The sooner she cleaned her studio, the sooner she could funnel the emotions racing through her into new pieces. The big barn beckoned, and she hurried to the smaller door to pull that open. It swung without the screaming creak she had expected, making her pause. Inside, she could make out the dim outline of the overhead light. When she pulled the string, she gasped at what it revealed.

The barn was clean. Not just clean, but polished and washed and fresh. The stone and concrete floor shown, and where there was only dirt, any loose debris had been swept down to packed earth. New lights hung in corners to add interior illumination, and in one of the old stalls, a desk and chair stood with a smaller unlit lamp.

He must have been up all night to get this much done. There was nothing left for her to clean. All she had to do was bring in her supplies and set up her work stations. This was where she would create, and having the room to do it was such a gift.

Anticipation brought a tingling to her fingertips, the same kind of energy she felt when she touched Josiah, but different too. She wanted to follow him and offer her thanks. If he allowed it, she wanted another of those amazing kisses. Even if he didn't, she might take one on her own.

Inspiration brought a grin to her face, and she raced out to the car and pulled at the back door. Loaded down with easel and bags holding new tubes of oils and trays of watercolors, she couldn't wait to set up shop and begin. She knew exactly what, or rather, who, she wanted to paint first.

Chapter 13

Kaane glanced neither left nor right as he pounded across the porch. He wasn't sure what he was running away from, that stunning kiss and the woman he shared it with, or the reality that he was a lying SOB. In either case, he needed to get away and stay away. This had been a terrible idea, and even the necessity of his craft wouldn't offset the price Angel might pay.

His feet brought him to the unfinished studio, though it was not unoccupied. Two Ashland Construction trucks were parked to the side, and Powers leaned against one, a cell phone pressed to his ear. When he glanced up, he raised a finger before Kaane could escape.

He'd forgotten all about the crew working here today. He'd forgotten about everything except Angel and his need to see her. Now he had more explanations and fabrications to come up with. Powers knew Angel, and Powers knew Kaane. Kaane wasn't sure what else Powers knew, but he needed to set the record straight before Angel saw the construction crew.

Pocketing his phone, Powers leaned further into the truck's fender and crossed his arms on his chest. Sunglasses unnecessary on this cloudy day stayed on his face, so Kaane couldn't read his expression. He just hoped Powers was willing to help him, because at this point, the truth would ruin everything.

Kaane reached out a hand for a shake and said, "Powers, it looks like you're making great progress here. This is coming along faster than I expected. That's exciting."

The grip of the handshake was harder than usual, and when the glasses finally came off, the assessing frown made the man's face even more forbidding. When they pumped a couple of times, Kaane tried to pull back, but Powers wouldn't let go.

"What the hell do you think you're doing, going after Angel?"

Kaane yanked his hand free and shook it to restore circulation. He didn't blame his friend for being angry. If it had been him on the outside and someone was messing with a sweet woman like Angel, he would have been pissed too. But he wasn't messing with her. If anything, she was destroying him.

"Listen, Kaane, you have to stay away from her. The women are worried, Roxy in particular. Once they find out what you're doing, you don't stand a chance of running far enough or fast enough."

Kaane raised a hand to stop the venting words. "I've already received a call from Mac, and since I value all of my body parts, I will not risk them for no reason where those big chef knives are concerned. But Powers, Angel is important."

Powers narrowed his eyes and canted forward as if to peer harder. "Important in what way?"

Lifting a shoulder seemed an inadequate explanation, and he sensed that the man in front of him wouldn't accept it either. Staring at his feet, he kicked a piece of wood and felt rewarded by the loud clatter it made. Nail guns inside the unfinished building paused for a moment, then resumed like a firing squad. The wind bit into his hair and raised a ghost's touch on his neck.

A tentative touch, like her fingers, as if she wasn't sure if it pleased him. A spiritual touch, like a christening. His muse, granting him permission to create good words, good notes, from her inspiration. His Angel, that saving being in so many ways.

Powers would think he was crazy.

"Try me."

Kaane snapped his attention to the man in front of him. How much of that had he said out loud?

"You said enough for me to get it. Being with Angel is more than a quick lay. But what do you get out of it, besides the temporary friendship of a nice woman? You'll be gone soon, hitting the road like you musicians do, with groupies to enjoy in every city. Why are you toying with her?"

"You've got it wrong, man. I'm not playing around, not when this woman is so important. I can't afford to."

Now Powers looked curious, as if he had no idea where the conversation was headed but he wasn't going to walk away without answers. "You keep using that same word, important. Tell me how."

Kaane looked away, his eyes following the frame of the studio housing his next music endeavor. But there would be nothing to arrange and nothing to record if he didn't find the notes.

"Angel is my muse," he said, not wanting to see Powers' reaction.

"Muse? As in creative muse? Isn't that a kind of spiritual thing?"

Kaane exhaled and nodded, happy he wasn't being laughed at or worse. "Yeah, some people call it spiritual. For me, it's practical. I can't find the words or the notes on my own. I'm better at it when she's around."

Powers shook his head and took his turn kicking the board. "I get that. Sometimes, it takes two halves to make a whole, and you stand no chance of being whole without that other person. I get what you mean."

It was Kaane's turn to stare with sharper interest. Powers didn't fill the air with words for the sake of talking the way Mac did. He was serious, but not the cynic Vince could be. He didn't strike Kaane like a man who believed in the spirit side of anything.

But he had to take a chance and hope Powers would keep his secret. At some point, he'd have to tell Angel the truth, but he liked the fact that she thought of him as nothing more than a farmer who wrote poetry on the side. Few people saw past his fame to the man he was inside, and he knew she could.

"Listen, Powers, I need you to keep my secret."

Powers looked up with a half grin. "That she's your muse? I think she'd be thrilled. How many women would jump at the chance to be the great Kaane Scott's muse?"

"That's just it. She doesn't know me as Kaane. She thinks I'm Josiah Harmond, and she thinks she's helping me learn how to read, except that kind of fell apart this morning. So, I'm Josiah, okay?"

Powers looked around, his eyes traveling over the half-built studio and the surrounding empty dirt and scrub plants. He frowned and looked back at Kaane. "What kind of building did you tell her this was supposed to be?"

Kaane opened his mouth, realizing his badly planned cover story was about to sound truly stupid. He mumbled the words in the hope that Powers would drop the subject. "A pig barn."

Evidently Powers had excellent hearing, no doubt because he hadn't spent his adult years as the front man for a rock band. He chuckled, then guffawed. "A pig barn. Oh man, that is richer than a pig in, well, you know. I heard you had a new gig, but this takes the cake."

His laughter boomed again, and he even slapped his truck's hood. Powers kept laughing, and the sound only died down when his eyes traveled over Kaane's shoulder. Kaane turned too and watched an excited Angel take quick steps across the work area. She glanced at the construction trucks and back to the building, then her eyes landed on Powers. As her grin widened, Kaane cursed the fact that he hadn't extracted a promise from the man who'd straightened with a warm smile.

"Powers, hello. I didn't know you're building Josiah's barn. I'm not sure the design is quite right, but I trust you two know what you're doing." She reached up for a cheek bus which Powers seemed happy to provide.

With a serious expression, Powers nodded. "It's an innovative design. Our friend Josiah," he didn't trip over the name, though it looked like he was about to laugh again, "is experimenting with a new method of animal husbandry. Did you know pigs like to be clean? Those mud baths are for sanitary reasons."

Angel shook her head and linked her arm through Kaane's. He forgot to breathe as the floral scent drifted up to him, making him ignore the stack of lies piling up higher than a gel light catwalk. He wanted to hold the heady scent in him forever, but oxygen won out and he exhaled on a gasp.

She didn't seem to notice, with her attention still on Powers. "I didn't know that. I'll need to research it further. It's nice to know you two are already acquainted. You see, Josiah? You can come to those dinners with me. You know Powers, and you'll find the others are just as friendly. Next time, right Powers?"

The man nodded with an urgency Kaane thought excessive. "Thanks for bringing that up, Angel. Tess was going to call you and set up the next dinner. At our place this time, in a couple of weeks." His eyebrow lifted with the statement as his eyes bored holes in Kaane.

Kaane got the message. Time was running out. If he didn't tell her who he really was soon, others were bound to leak the information. And once Angel knew she'd been lied to, Kaane doubted his muse would be around, free studio or not.

When he gave a nod in return, the big man across from him smiled in grim satisfaction.

"That would be great, Powers. I'll call Tess and see what we can bring. You are coming, right, Josiah?"

She squeezed his arm, and he felt the charge of electric current through his coat. Her big eyes watched him with what he feared might be delight. Would she look at him the same way when she knew why a man like Josiah wanted her close? Maybe. But she surely wouldn't once she knew him as an empty shell of a rock star with no business keeping company with someone so sweet.

He found himself saying words he didn't expect, as if her presence alone pulled them out and he had no control over them. "Sure, Angel, I'd love to come to dinner and meet more of your friends."

The light from her eyes nearly blinded him, stunning him into a speechless state. When she gave a little jump of joy and reached up, he lowered his face on autopilot, and she wrapped a hand around his neck to pull him closer.

"Thank you for finishing our project. It's amazing." Her whisper felt like a tropical breeze on his cheek. Her lips were the kiss of a perfect sunset, the kind that lasted only a moment and then was gone. Like she was, giving his arm a quick squeeze and spinning back the way she came. Kaane couldn't take his eyes off her as she rounded the corner.

"Oh man, you've got this bad, don't you?"

Kaane could only nod bleakly in response.

Hours later, he was still shaking his head at Powers' insight. He'd fiddled with some lyrics, and they were kind of good, but not enough to complete a song. He walked to the window and gawked at the barn more times than he could count. Angel's car stayed where it was, and other than coming in the house to fill a big water bottle and use the facilities, she'd been out of sight. He nearly walked down there to see what she worked on with such dedication, but chickened out.

What if he told her now? Maybe not the whole thing, but at least the muse part. How would she take it? And how would he explain what he'd called his poetry? There was no good reason for a farmer to need a muse to write poetry.

And then there was that attraction happening. He had never been a monk, and while he'd only begun this celibacy thing to serve his work, it seemed important to be able to tell Angel he could be devoted to her. Honest and open, that's what she was. He doubted she held anything back. Secrets? No, he was the only one with those.

As the sky grew dimmer with a false sense of dusk on the cloudy day, his phone rang with the rock melody, and he picked it up. Listening to Rodney bitch at him would be better than pondering his misguided thoughts.

"About time." The deep voice boomed through the connection as if he was in the same room.

"Rod-man, sorry, it's been a busy day."

The background wasn't the noisy mess it had been the last time they talked. No waves washed on a distant shore. It was hard to read Rodney's mood from his abrupt greeting.

"I hope that means you're writing like a crazed rocker and not moaning about losing your tunes, dude. Because I should tell you, we have to come up with a new spread for the band or we won't have them any longer."

Rodney relayed the rest of the news. Their drummer wallowed in offers from other groups, both rock and country, and he was giving them serious consideration. One of their back-up singers decided to quit on the news that she was pregnant. Their manager said they needed to book a tour and pronto because the good venues were filling up. "And our public, my man, has somehow grabbed on to the notion that Rebellion is dead and will never play again. If we want to fade into oblivion, say the word and I'll tell the others. But if you want a fresh start, I hope you're writing."

Kaane fell silent with that flood of news. He gravitated to the front window and its barn view, watching as one by one, the lights inside went out. Angel must be quitting for the day. He couldn't let her leave. If he asked her to stay for dinner, at least he'd have a couple of hours of her undivided attention.

"Listen, dude, I have to go. I just got another shot of inspiration. I'll call you tomorrow, okay?"

He disconnected the call over Rodney's sputtering, dropping the phone on the entry table where it began to beat the ring melody almost immediately. He grabbed his coat from the hook and headed out before any plan other than getting close to Angel for a while formed in his mind.

She pulled the small door closed and slipped the lock on its hook as he walked up. "Hey, how did it go today?"

She glanced over her shoulder at him without surprise, as if she sensed he was there. Her smile held triumph and exhaustion. "It was great, really great. There's something about this space. I feel, I don't know, inspired. Like there's good energy here and it all flows into my brush."

Her smile faded into embarrassment, and as she turned away, he swore she blushed. It was hard to tell in the fading light, but her face was composed when she turned back. "Thank you again for letting me use this space. We still need to work out payment. You don't need me to teach you to read. On that, I'm clear. I can't impose on you. You have a farm to build."

It was an opening, and he decided to take it. He opened his mouth, the part-truth hovering on the tip of his tongue.

And her phone rang in the large tote bag over her shoulder. She held up a finger to set him on pause and fished it out, sliding a finger across the screen while looking up at him.

"Hi, yes, I know, I'm running late. I'm just leaving the studio. Yes, the studio, my studio. I still can't believe it. I had the most amazing day, and I can't wait to tell you about it." She smiled wider and turned away, her attention off him and on to the call.

Who was she talking to? A boyfriend? He'd never thought to ask.

"Yes, I'll be right there, honest. Fifteen minutes, tops." She hung up and shook her head. "I'm late. I got so involved in my work, I lost track of time. Do you know what an amazing feeling that is?"

She searched his face for a moment, and he nearly told her that yes, he did know what that was like. To play all night because the tunes were flowing. To write until his eyes blurred because he couldn't stop. To put it all together in a way that set people on fire. Yes, he knew.

But he couldn't say the words, not without telling her everything.

She probably should have stopped at home and washed off whatever paint was undoubtedly on her face. It wouldn't have hurt to change her clothes either. But Angel was good and truly late and stopping would hold up everyone else.

The girl tribe celebrated together in full numbers tonight, including women she rarely got to see. She rushed the drive back into town, on a sprint by the time she parked at Mallory's and headed for its back room.

Around the big table, women clapped when she arrived, teasing her about the streak of yellow pain on her cheek and the spray of red down her knee. She slipped into her seat between DK and Tess, and received a finger poke in the ribs from Roxy on Tess's other side.

"So, how did it go today? Did you have a successful day?"

The way Roxy asked the question, it seemed that she expected a specific answer. Tess hushed her and pushed her hand away. DK looked between them and back at Angel.

"Ignore them. They've been bickering like a couple of old biddies since they sat down, but they won't say what it's about. I can tell you had a great day. There's a glow in your eyes that I recognize. Tell me about the painting high."

And Angel did. She told DK and an eventually attentive Tess and Roxy about how Josiah cleaned out the barn. And how wonderful Josiah was being in offering her the space. And how wonderful it felt to be on that creative high, where it seemed every time she picked up a brush or even thought about painting, she had more ideas than she could possibly get done in a month.

What she didn't tell them was that she'd kissed him.

Chapter 14

Angel's car still stood outside the barn, but she'd been strangely absent in the house that day. The one time they'd crossed paths, she seemed almost embarrassed to see him. But Kaane thought he caught a hint of a glimmer of interest in her eyes, and it spurred him to make the offer.

"Can you stay for dinner tonight? Nothing fancy. I picked up frozen pizzas and I can pop those in the oven whenever. We can hang out."

She'd stopped then, the surprise on her face changing to something unreadable. Maybe he did need those reading lessons, lessons in reading Angel.

"Yes, that would be great." She scurried off before he could extend the conversation.

That ended up being all right, though. He'd found words today, lots of words, and while they weren't exactly poetry, it was enough of a start to fuel him for the afternoon. Pizza with Angel would be just what he needed to continue the trend tomorrow.

By the time his corner of the valley fell silent, the sun was near setting and still, Angel worked on. He was wondering if she'd fallen asleep in there and was about to check on her. As he stepped into his boots, the lights in the barn went out and she emerged, locking the door behind her. Over her shoulder, she carried that big brown satchel and her steps were slow with her head down.

He threw open the door and only avoided grabbing her in greeting because she shuffled sideways and didn't meet his eyes. "I'd like to freshen up, if I could."

"Of course." He waved her in the bathroom's direction, puzzled over her serious demeanor. Maybe her day hadn't gone well. He knew what it was like when the muse didn't cooperate. In contrast, his day was great. He pulled a bottle of white wine from the fridge. Today was cause for celebration. He poured her a generous glass. The pizzas wouldn't take long, and he didn't want to rush things by setting a timer that dinged as soon as they fell into serious conversation.

Because it would be serious. He was going to tell her. He was going to say that for better or worse, she was his muse and he needed her in his life to write. What's more, he wanted her close by so he could get to know her better and better.

And he was going to tell her he wasn't a pig farmer. He wasn't sure how much courage he'd need to tell her the full truth. It might take more than a few slices of Hawaiian-style pizza to make that come out. The longer he waited, the faster his fear grew. What would she say?

About the time he was going to knock and ask if she was okay, he heard the doorknob turn. She emerged in hesitant steps, and when his eyes settled on her, they nearly popped out of his head.

Freshen up wouldn't even begin to describe it. The hair she'd held back in a braid was down, curling in lush waves around her face and glancing off one shoulder. Whatever she'd worn to paint in was gone. At least, he didn't think the little straps and naked shoulders counted as painting attire on a cold spring day. In his rush to let her in before, he hadn't noticed the slim-fitting jeans hidden by her coat. They hugged her curves in all the right places, and above the denim, the camisole did the rest.

Dark coloring around her eyes made them seem larger as they rested on him. She gave a small smile, the kind designed to drive men wild. It certainly did it for him.

"Thanks. I was feeling a little grungy and in need of a pick-me-up after today. Is this okay for a pizza night?" She ran a hand down from waist to mid-thigh, and angels swore at the devils in his head. She smiled as if his dumbfounded gape was a good enough answer by itself.

Then he remembered his promise. He was going to tell her as much as he could get out, and hope for the best. And he'd do it before he'd do anything else, like kiss her senseless.

"Is it warm in here? I'm feeling a little – hot." She fanned herself and lifted her hair off her neck, and despite his best intentions, he found his jeans getting tight as his heart raced. This could not be happening.

"No, I mean yes, it could be warm in here. I didn't notice until you mentioned it. Let's cool it off, shall we?" He raced to the front door and threw it open, waving it back and forth. It didn't seem to do anything for her, and if a load of ice had dropped down his neck, he doubted he'd feel it. An immediate meltdown would be more likely.

"You know what, Josiah?" She walked toward him in slow, measured steps, as if each one was a statement.

"No, what?" He stammered the words like an idiot, and he could not keep a single thought in his brain when she stalked toward him with that swing in her hips.

"I don't want to drive back to town tonight." She leaned on the kitchen counter and glanced back at him over her shoulder. The grin on her face had him slamming the door and racing back to the kitchen.

"I can drive you," he said, then nearly kicked himself. That was the last thing he wanted to do.

Angel looked momentarily stunned and perplexed by that statement, then recovered. "What if I don't want you to drive me?"

"Um."

She reached for the wine glass and downed a big gulp, closing her eyes as if the taste relieved her. When she opened them again, she focused on him with a seductive smile. "Never mind. We'll work it out. Why don't we sit down and talk for a while?"

Talk. He thought he could still talk, if he got his tongue out of his throat. Out of his throat and down hers.

He clapped his hands to keep them from closing around her waist and pulling her close. "So, pizza. What kind do you like? I have Hawaiian, and Marguerite, and meat-lovers and there's one more. Let me see, what is it?"

The yank of the fridge double doors obscured his face from her view and gave him time to swear silently. He couldn't stay in here forever, and each minute that ticked by marked another segment of time when he lied. He was ready to tell her everything, confess his sins and hope for her absolution, when he looked back at her. She leaned against the counter, watching him with hungry eyes, running her fingers up and down the glass. What would those fingers feel like on him?

"What's happening here?" His voice sounded strangled to his ears.

She lifted a bare shoulder and gave a casual shrug. "I thought we were going to share pizza and get to know one another better. You seem like a nice man, Josiah, and I haven't had many nice men as good friends in my life."

"Friends. You want to be friends."

They studied each other, her drinking wine at a clip guaranteed to make sure she couldn't drive herself anywhere. His eyes darted down to her cleavage, which took advantage of her position to entice him further. Music or mayhem? He wasn't sure what he wanted more.

How long their staring contest lasted, he wasn't sure. He kept reminding himself he couldn't act without explaining first. They needed distance, and he needed anything to take his mind off how her smile faded into seriousness and he wanted more than anything to put the grin back into her expression.

Kaane whirled away to punch buttons on the stove. "So, pizza, coming right up."

She said nothing. When he looked back at her, he lifted a frozen pizza in salute. "So, friends?"

He thought he noted disappointment on her face as Angel lifted her wine glass in return. "To friends."

>>>>>>

Kaane banged his head on the piano, happy the emptiness he felt inside echoed with a similar tone in the instrument. The tune would not come, no matter how hard he tried to force it. The words sounded like a sappy country song, not a hard rock ballad. What was Rodney going to think?

Because like an impending force of nature, Rodney would arrive. He would read this, and he would either laugh or send Kaane to a shrink. Something had scrambled his brain and no matter how hard he searched, he couldn't find a way out.

He paced the living room, ending up at the front window, examining the empty spot where Angel usually parked. Two nights ago, their uneasy truce over drinks and pizza had turned into a fun night of sharing about their lives. The more he knew about her, the more he liked her. That just made him feel like more of a shit.

Last night, it was a quick crackers and cheese plate, because she needed to be at the library to teach an English class to native Spanish speakers. She impressed him when she rolled off a fluent explanation of the class in Spanish, with a rapid-fire sureness he knew would be a hit with her students.

Today, she hadn't shown, and it was almost three, which meant she might not come at all. The bitter breeze was a contrast to the warmer temps promised over the coming weekend. Spring, when a young man's fancy turned to love.

What the hell was the matter with him? He couldn't even come up with good lines that other people wrote. He threw the pencil at the far wall and contemplated the hole he uncovered as a reminder to behave.

In addition to all of this, he'd agreed to dinner with Tess and Powers and who knows who else on Saturday night, with Angel by his side. He still wasn't sure how that was going to work out. He had to come clean beforehand. The tension of hiding a secret this big around a woman he admired and cared more about each day was killing him like a slow dance.

His hands rested on the piano keys, but he didn't see the black and white. Instead, his mind rested on that scorching kiss. He replayed so many times, if it had been a vinyl record, he would have worn it out. Skips and scratches, wobbles and weeps, the needle would dance across its black surface, like his lie danced across his dark heart. He'd admit it. His vow of celibacy aside, he wanted her. That kiss was just the first chord in a complicated arrangement and he craved the refrain, as long as he sang in harmony with Angel.

The crunch of tires on gravel yanked him out of his misery and to the front window like a rope pulled him there. He hissed out a sigh of relief as he recognized the only car that mattered. She parked next to the barn and his ears picked up the quieting of the motor, but she didn't get out. He stood there, watching, and she sat in the driver's seat, waiting. He couldn't tell what she was doing, and he was about to grab a coat and pace out to her when she threw the door open.

Today she wore what he thought of as her librarian clothes, with her hair tucked up into a knit hat and boots covering her legs. He envied that leather being skin on skin with her shapely curves. He wondered what her calves would feel like under his hands as he skimmed up, heading for the promised land.

He shook his head, trying to clear the image. He had to stop this or he'd screw up and act on it before he explained. But he didn't get a chance to visit that idea for long. Instead of heading for the barn, Angel came toward the house, the big bag knocking against her side and her hands dug deep into her pockets. The wind blew stray leaf skeletons across her path and she waded through them as if she didn't notice. She focused on the path, and he swore he could match the uptick in her speed with the accelerated beat of his heart. He had the door open before she put a foot on the first porch step.

She looked up, her face troubled and cloudy like a winter storm. Her eyes met his, and she examined him with so much seriousness, she must have figured it out. Now she'd want an explanation about why he hid his truth.

"I have something to tell you." Her voice sounded small, like she dreaded what was to come.

He motioned her inside with a wave of his arm. "It's freezing out there. You should come inside. I have a fire going."

She still didn't move. "I don't think you're going to like it."

He came out to the top step, extending his hand. "Whatever it is, I'm sure it's not as bad as you think. Come inside. I've missed you today."

He nearly choked on the honesty in those words. He had missed her, and even if he wasn't working side by side with her, the fact that she was close helped. The words he needed to say were on the tip of his tongue.

She rose one step, and he came down another. She said, "I'm not the person you think I am."

That made his pause with his foot extended to meet her halfway. He couldn't imagine Angel being anything other than who and what she said she was. Former librarian. A painter with promise. A glowing spotlight hanging over his stage and lighting his world.

"None of us are, Angel. If I told you everything about me, you'd race for that car and reverse it all the way out the drive at top speed."

She frowned at that. "I can't imagine you having any secrets like that, Josiah."

It was her use of his given name that did it. He reached for her, pulling her up the final step between them, and lowered his head. When his lips met hers, one of them trembled, and he was pretty sure it was him.

Chapter 15

Angel promised herself she'd admit her objective, even as it filled her with embarrassment. All day long, she'd come up with reasons and excuses to delay making the trip here, but in the end, she had to come. She owed it to him. If he still wanted to carry things further once he knew, she'd be grateful.

But she never got a chance to say what was on her mind, because that slate wiped clean the second his hands gripped her arms and lifted her like she weighed nothing. She wasn't sure her feet touched wood as her arms tangled around him, feeling his searing heat through her coat despite the wind whirling around them. She forgot her best intentions of full honesty before she let herself act on the one thing she really wanted, because it seemed he wanted the same thing.

His lips, so firm and yet so giving, moved over hers, and even though her experience was severely limited, she knew he was good at this. Or at least, they together were good at this. If this was so amazing, what would the rest feel like? She was dying to know.

But not without telling him first.

His hands lessened their hold, but only so they could drift, one down her back to cup her rear and one up into her hair. She couldn't move away, and she had no desire to. When he let her catch her breath long enough to nuzzle her neck and send shivers down her spine, she stepped in closer. A vibration ran through him, and she realized with a start that he was out here in a t-shirt. The wind must be biting through him.

Pulling back, she forced a smile. "I'm dressed for this weather and you're not." Without any conscious plan, her gaze ran down his body and faltered at the obvious bulge in his jeans.

As if suddenly aware where her eyes stared, he glanced down too. "Look, ah, about that." His voice wandered off as he looked away.

"Oh, please, don't be embarrassed. I'm sorry, I don't know what I'm doing. You know, in that department." It was her turn to trail off in awkwardness.

His eyes snapped back to her and he straightened. "You are doing everything right, Angel. It's me that's wrong. I just – I can't – I'm not – " His voice broke on a note of anger and sadness that touched her heart. Was he as inexperienced as she was?

She closed the distance between them and took his cold hands in hers. "Don't worry, Josiah. We'll figure this out together. I have it on excellent advice that if we relax and take things as they come along, everything will work the way it is supposed to."

She knew her cheeks heated with those words, and she hoped he attributed that to the wind. She walked past him, adding a sway to her hips. When he jumped to be next to her and grabbed her hand, she knew they had to be on the right track.

>>>>>

"Everything is different with you." He hadn't intended to say the words out loud, but they hung in the air between them just the same. Her cheeks, still pink from the cold, and the cascade of hair down her back made her look like some fairytale princess in a kids' movie, and yet, she was real. Warm skin, gasping breaths, wide eyes shining and a tremble to her lips. He stumbled to get the words out.

'I have another life, Angel, one I'm trying to rebuild. You might know me as Kaane Scott. I am, or I was, a rock star.'

Except he couldn't squeeze the sentences past the lump in his throat. A lump hardened in other places too as she slowly unbuttoned the coat, keeping her gaze on him, and revealed the librarian underneath.

Except, except. He choked. No librarian in his recollection ever dressed like this, not even in secret sinful fantasies. The skirt was plaid, and that was the only thing conservative about it. A slit ran up the side, exposing the creamy skin of her thigh. The lacy top was more see-through than concealing, and its deep plunge left an open invitation to explore and learn more.

Angel dropped her coat on a chair. "I'm not very good at this. In fact, I have zero experience." As if to counter her words, she ran a finger down the line from throat to plunge and back up again.

Kaane gulped, trying to remember why she was on his hands-off list. "You're doing fine, amazing, actually. Any better, and I'd pass out." He attempted a chuckle, but it came out strangled.

A slow sway marked her advance, and if he had any doubts about whether she was as turned on as he was, her rapid breathing sending those beautiful breasts up and down in a crazy rhythm and the perky nipples lace couldn't hide provided the answer. Muse, she was his muse. He let the word chant in his head like the beat of a drum, but it was doing no good.

She stopped in front of him, her finger teasing that dip in the lace once more. "You're being kind, and I appreciate that. Kind and nice. That's who you are, a nice, kind man. I find that very appealing, Josiah. Can you please kiss me again?"

When her fingertips brushed his torso, the gasp blew out of him without control. Her fingers snaked up his arm, raising hairs in a shiver of response. His hands grabbed her waist, aching to travel up and up until they cupped those tempting globes dancing in front of him. He forced them to stay in place, even as he got lost in the deep blue pools of her eyes.

"You make me ache, Josiah. Kiss me."

The breathless words commanded and he was powerless to deny her. Hell, he couldn't deny himself, not when she licked her lips and left them too shiny to be legal. He lowered his head and inhaled her next breath.

She tasted like that first welcomed sip of water after a long performance, bracing, invigorating, life-changing. Warmth flooded through him, making the pressure in his jeans pound to a new tune, and his hands couldn't behave themselves. They crept up her sides until his thumbs grazed the underside of her breasts, and as they ran along the bottom of her bra, she inhaled sharply. Her lips opened and he dove in deeper with the invitation.

There was something he was supposed to remember, but his mind was a blank. Her tongue met his in a tentative touch, and that was all it took to sink him the rest of the way. His hands molded her breasts and he swallowed her moan. It was music to his ears.

Music. Muse. She was his muse, and if he had sex with her, it would ruin everything.

He dropped his hold, even as his hands ached to pull her in again. Stepping back had him tripping over his feet, off balance and unsure. When she raised her eyes in confusion, the dazed expression was something he was sure he mirrored. Every part of him ached with the need to wrap his arms around her, drag her off to bed, and make sweet music with her all night long.

But he couldn't. As long as he held her but didn't act on it, the words and notes would come. He was sure they would, but he hated like hell that this was the price he had to pay.

He didn't blink, couldn't look away, and stared into Angel's eyes with twin emotions of regret and longing. Her glazed look faded a bit, but she raised a shaking hand to her lips and pressed her fingers there as if she wanted to hold on to their kisses. A mistiness filled her eyes, and damn if he was going to let her cry. He didn't deserve one single tear from someone so sweet.

"You're killing me here." He wasn't sure if she heard his muttered words, because she didn't respond. When that single tear slipped out and rolled down her cheek, he wanted to kick his own ass. Instead, he reached out and closed his hands over hers, pulling them down and until their joined fingers hung between them.

"Angel, I'm not a nice man, and you deserve better than me. You don't know me." He forced himself to say the rest because he wasn't that strong. If he didn't tell her, he'd lose the battle and grab her again. "I'm using you, Angel, and you shouldn't have anything to do with me."

Her face shifted from sad to confused. "Using me? No, you're not using me. You barely touched me, and yet even that little bit was amazing. I want more, and you're stepping back."

>>>>>

She would not cry. She would act like an experienced, together woman and she wouldn't let on how devastated she felt by his rejection. But she couldn't help the single tear when it made its cold trail down her face. Attempting to free her hands to wipe it away and hide her expression, she gave a desperate pull at their entangled hands, but Josiah wouldn't let go.

"Angel, I have to make you understand," he said in a tone that sounded as anguished as she felt.

She tried for sage and knowing but was afraid she came off whiny. "Oh, I think I understand. You aren't interested, and I get it. I don't know what I can do about it, but I understand." She shook her head, though, because a part of her really didn't understand. How could she entice him into more when even kissing her seemed too much effort for him?

Glancing down at their hands, she wondered why he didn't let her go. There was no point in this contact if he didn't want her. Then she looked past their hands and noticed his body said differently. His mouth might deny it, but that attractive bulge in his jeans was interested in more than kissing her.

He lifted their hands and brought them to his mouth, that full bottom lip she wanted to run her thumb across and that talented upper one that made kissing him such a dream. One by one, he kissed each of her fingers, and each time he did, parts of her tingled and heated with pleasure. She wanted his mouth on every part of her, and once she had that, she might die a happy woman.

"You have to believe me. I think you're a beautiful, desirable and sexy woman, and I do want you. I just – can't." He shook his head, and a breeze from his sigh kissed the dampened skin his lips had, sending shivers down her spine.

"Why not? Are you married?"

He looked shocked. "God, no." He tried to pull away now, but this time she held firm.

"A priest?"

This time he chuckled and stopped fighting her. He shook his head again. "Despite reports to the contrary."

She shook her head too, not understanding. Her eyes tracked down his body once more, slower and with deliberate attention. When they landed on his crotch, she swore the denim jumped. Despite the seriousness of their conversation, she smiled.

"I was going to ask if you had, you know, a problem, but I can see that's not the case."

To her surprise, he pulled her in close and wrapped his arms around her in a tight hug, settling his chin on the top of her head. She felt his laughter trickle through her, heating their connection. If she got any hotter in the places they touched, she would explode.

Instead, she concentrated on how great it felt to have a man wrapped around her like he never planned to let her go. The weight of his body leaned into hers and she leaned in too, sharing the intimacy so foreign to her experience. And yet, it felt so right, like their bodies were made for each other, interlocking puzzle pieces snapping into place. Inhaling his scent, something electric and earthy clean she wished she could bottle and take home with her, made her giddy. The harder she giggled, the dizzier she became, until she was laughing right along with him. After long minutes that went by too fast, they both fell silent.

"You feel good like this." His words were quiet with a trace of sadness, as if he wasn't aware he spoke out loud.

"You feel good everywhere," she replied, trying to snuggle closer.

As if he knew what she tried to do, he pushed them apart. "I can't do this." He wiggled a finger between the two of them. "I care too much about you, Angel, to hurt you like that."

She had that vague, itchy feeling again, the sense that he knew her crazy secret and because of it, he pushed her away. His honorable nature was getting in the way of their shared pleasure. It fed her greatest fear, that nice men didn't deflower virgins, and she was going to remain one for the rest of her life.

Chapter 16

It was his own damned fault. Kaane got his wish, and it cursed him. Angel stepped away, and in the void, her music did too.

He heard whispers of it on the wind when she came to her studio to work, but she rarely approached the house. She offered him a tight smile when he came to the barn door and knocked before entering, turning her work away and standing in front of it with her arms crossed. The billowy painting shirts she wore never hid her curves, at least not now that he knew what they felt like in his arms, and he wished he could enjoy the vision of her without the barrier.

Most of all, though, he missed her friendship. The experience felt as new to him as his music felt old. Worn, washed up, tired. Even as he played the old songs for lack of anything else to do, he hated the dated, uninspiring sound.

And he dreamed about her. Lush, sensuous dreams, where her body rolled over and under his with deadly ease, and when he entered her, they both cried out at the perfection of it. He'd fallen into lust with her, and that kind of lust for a muse grew only as forbidden fruit.

Rodney thought he was nuts. "Dude, if she is your muse, you must keep her close, but not too close, if you understand what I'm saying. It makes the music even better." Kaane didn't explain that the music came out as love songs no band named Rebellion would be caught dead playing.

That wasn't the end of the unsolicited advice, as it seemed everyone wanted to weigh in on his life. Mac warned him to be honest. "You have to tell her who you are, man. I don't think you'll get the kind of shocked and stunned reception that you think. Angel isn't like that. In fact, you might have to explain to her who Kaane Scott is."

Even Powers shared a vocal opinion. "Honesty is a cornerstone of any relationship, Kaane. Without it, you have zilch. The sooner you tell her, the better off you'll be. Then you can see what the two of you can build together." As if he had a chance at that.

Vince, the old cynic, provided the most brutal assessment. "You're a dumb ass if you think you can get her out from under your skin, and a dickhead for getting into this situation in the first place. Tell her, beg her forgiveness on groveling knees, and hope she takes you back into her life. I speak from experience, my friend. It will not get easier, and there is no going back to the way you were before you met her."

Kaane had shot back his response without thinking. "I'm fine with how things are. My life was fine before I met Angel and it will be fine again."

Vince clapped a hard hand on his shoulder and eyed him with a pitying stare. "Denial, man, is the first step. You have a long path until you reach the fifth step, acceptance." He smiled as if he enjoyed watching Kaane stumble along the journey.

Not that he was going on any journey. No, he was fine as things were. He could admire her from afar, and his music would not suffer. As she left that evening, he stood in the window and watched her taillights long after they disappeared into the darkness. It wasn't until hours later when he slammed the piano shut hard enough to make the strings vibrate and the plate sing that he began to realize Vince, the old shithead, had been right.

Anger buzzed through him, and he didn't know what to do about it. He shouldn't need anyone or anything to write. It went against his nature to rely on anyone. He was the independent one, and if he wasn't so cursed with a run of bad luck, things would be fine. That's what this drought was, bad luck, and he would power through it like he did when he struggled as a kid in school or fought the disapproval of his parents on his career choice when he got older.

By the next morning, after a night filled with Angel taunting him in heavy dreams during an uneasy sleep, he was ready to beg.

The day had turned balmy, as if the cold winds had blown any trace of winter far north and warm spring pressed up into the void. He peeked into the barn's big door, convinced she didn't see him and sorry she didn't at the same time. Her hair was in a braid today. What would it feel like to unplait that braid, strand by strand, and run his fingers through the silky softness of those blonde locks? Or wrap the braid around his hand and pull her head back so he could press a stream of kisses to her neck? His lips burned at the thought.

As if she sensed him, she turned to watch him without speaking any acknowledgment. At this distance, he couldn't read her eyes and her expression seemed stuck in neutral. When he gave a wave, she didn't return it. Instead, she turned back to her work and lifted the brush, dotting it on the canvas in front of her as if he didn't even warrant a pause.

He slunk back to the house and crashed his hands down on the keyboard in a dissonant sound that would scare animals out of the woods. The emptiness inside him wasn't letting up, and when two hours passed without a sign of her or a decent phrase in his head, he thought about putting his fist in the wall again. This time, though, he was smart, and paced out to the construction area. Hefting a board in his hand and giving the workers a fast nod, he strode back to the house and smashed it next to the first hole. He didn't feel better when the vibration of impact raced up his arms and he had a second hole to explain.

Angel was gone by the time he recovered his sanity enough to look outside. The void yawned larger and darkness pressed into his brain. Drastic times, drastic measures. He pulled out his guitar, plugged in his amp, and gave up any appearance of working on new material. It only took one chord for him to take off on a soaring riff that ran away with him, and he blasted like that for an hour before his fingers quit.

When he stopped, the room echoed for a moment before falling into an empty silence. He didn't feel any better. He was soaked with sweat like he would be on stage, but he didn't feel the usual buzz of energy inside. If anything, he felt worse, and all he could see when he closed his eyes was the single tear trailing down Angel's face when he told her there was no way they could be involved.

It took every bit of resolve she possessed to act as if nothing had happened. She remained polite but kept her distance. Funny, but in her quest to get laid, the other wonderful things about Josiah had crept in under her skin. Appreciation for their discussions and his friendship, both of which she missed. The way his mind worked admittedly different from hers. His views on life and the world. The contemplative way he weighed things before answering her. His kind eyes and those hands she was certain would feel amazing on her.

She longed for him, but she stood firm. Pouring pent-up denial into her painting proved easier than she expected. Today was her turn to work in the gallery, and she planned to use it to hang her new exhibit. The trouble was, if Josiah saw it, he was bound to understand what it meant, and he'd already denied them any future.

Bettie hustled over as Angel climbed up the ladder. "I can't wait to see your new work. Can I take a peek?"

"I'd prefer not, at least, not until I have them hung up. There's an order to things, and I think it makes a greater impact when you see it as a whole." Or at least that's what she hoped. This was her first effort in this realm, and she hoped people enjoyed them.

Bettie shot her a curious look but nodded. "All right, dear, but be careful. I have to run out for a while, but Thomas will be here at some point. Do you want to wait until he's around, just to be safe?"

Angel shook her head and Bettie stood at the base of the ladder for a minute longer, looking up at her with concern. "You seem kind of blue, dear, and I don't mean your paints. Anything I can help with?"

While the older woman might be a huge busybody and a town gossip, she also had a caring nature that reminded Angel of her aunt. She'd grown up in Flynn's Crossing and had a nose for the news on the street. How many secrets did Bettie know?

Besides, what if she was on the same path? Was it a bad thing? Her aunt had loved someone, if the gossips were right, and yet she remained stubbornly single until the day she died. Had her aunt died a spinster virgin, like Angel was now thinking she might become? She feared Josiah was the one for her, perhaps the only one, and yet he pushed her away harder than anyone she knew.

"Oh my, look at the time. Got to run. Be careful on that ladder, dear." Her possible source of insider information scooted out the door before Angel had a chance to ask.

Over an hour later, she was satisfied with her exhibit. The pieces may not please many, but they were what had been inside her, crying to get out. Other things cried out too, but since she couldn't have them, she'd settle.

"Well that's different, huh? Not your usual style."

She spun to find Thomas standing behind her, examining the wall. He didn't look unhappy with the work, exactly, but the expression on his face wasn't excited either. She almost hated to ask, but she had to. "What do you think?"

His head drifted to one side and he stepped closer. "Good technique. Nice work on capturing emotions. The colors work."

A 'but' hung in there somewhere. She waited, forcing herself not to ring her hands. To her, these pieces felt raw and exposed, like when she dipped her brush in the paint and swirled, she gathered up her feelings. Spreading those emotions on the canvas for anyone to see was the hardest thing she'd ever done, but it felt right too.

Thomas shook his head. "I don't know, Ms. Reed. I just don't know."

"Don't know what, Thomas? You can tell me. If they aren't good enough, tell me and I'll take them down." She'd hang them at home instead, as a reminder of everything she hoped for and couldn't have.

"Oh no, don't get me wrong. They're full of good stuff. Your aunt was like that too, full of feelings and passion and life. I see a lot of her in you, you know. And it comes out in your paintings." He shook his head and turned away, pulling a handkerchief out of his pocket and taking off his glasses for a moment. She wasn't sure, but she thought he mopped at his eyes before giving a dismissive sniff.

"Thank you. I did put a lot of what I was feeling into them."

"So, Ms. Reed, tell me. You clearly have a thing for this guy. Does he feel the same about you?"

Angel turned back to the portraits on the wall, her eyes running over the faces of Josiah laughing, serious, contemplative, passionate. She couldn't bring herself to answer.

A burst of street noise gave her the break she needed, because if she analyzed them much longer, she might cry with the loss. It wasn't until Thomas gave his usual gruff greeting that she realized customers had come in. She grabbed the ladder and concealed her face, afraid her emotions colored as easily as her paints did a canvas. It wasn't until her gaze landed on her own reflection in the back hall's mirror that she realized how raw she looked. Nothing hid on her face, and the pain of being apart from Josiah seemed to etch every line and shadow. Thomas said she reminded him of her aunt. She had a new appreciation for the years her aunt had spent pining for someone she did not have.

But she would not pine. She would get over Josiah and move on, and maybe someday, she'd find someone willing to take a risk and be with her. Until then, she had a job to do.

"Hey, you have some new work hanging. Mind if I look?"

Thomas answered the man with his normal reply. "That's what the gallery's for, so look all you want, and spend some money too." She rushed out before he kept on. With his lack of customer service skills, Angel often thought they were lucky they sold anything at all.

She led with a smile and was immediately nervous when she caught sight of their guest. He was middle-aged, round at the belt line, and domed with a shiny bald head. He examined her portraits of Josiah with an intensity she found frightening. At any moment, she feared he was going to burst out laughing.

The man peered closely at the faces, then stepped back and continued to stare. He raised a camera on its strap and snapped a few shots of the portraits. He turned around as if searching for someone to help him and when he saw her, his face brightened. "Oh hi, do you work here? Because I have questions about these things." He waved a finger at her portraits.

"Yes, I work here."

"Oh, good. Listen, do you know the artist? Because I'd like to ask a few questions. I mean, the subject is so unique and secretive and I want to know more about him. You know, off the record of course."

She didn't understand the sly look that came over his face, or the finger he put next to his nose like it was a signal for something.

"I can tell you a little about these pieces."

The man nodded with vigorous bobs of his head and said, "Do you happen to know where these were painted?"

"Yes, Flynn's Crossing."

That excited the man enough to take a giant step forward. "And the subject?"

She hesitated, because the question was odd and his behavior even stranger. He bounced on his feet and kept fingering the camera with an almost lustful stroke. When she didn't respond, he added, "Please, I'm just doing my job. You know what it's like to work for a living, dog eat dog world and all that."

The words came slowly. "I believe the subject is a farmer who lives outside of town. I'm sorry, but that's all I can tell you."

The man dropped the camera back to its strap and clapped his hands. He reached forward and gave her an unexpected peck on the cheek, a move that had Angel backing away. She glanced over her shoulder, expecting Thomas to be coming toward them full of bluster, but the old man was nowhere to be seen. When she turned back, the man was snapping more photos of Josiah.

Deciding to be bold, she said, "Would you like me to provide you with the prices for these paintings?"

The man shook his head, giving her a grin that felt dirty as he patted the camera. "Naw, that's okay. I've got everything I need right here. Sure there isn't anything else you can tell me about the subject, like where he lives?"

She backed away, not liking the direction the conversation was taking in the least. She shook her head, and the man headed for the door on quick feet. "Thanks anyway. This is a start."

The sharp creak of the door closing underscored the sense something was not right, and she glanced back at her pictures with a silent apology to Josiah for putting him on display.

Chapter 17

Kaane stood in a corner of the elegant living room, his eyes flicking between the street outside the window and the people milling indoors. Powers pushed a drink into his hand, and he didn't even ask if it was loaded or not. He drank, only a little grateful his friend honored his wishes and kept it spirit-free.

"She'll come. Tess talked to her this afternoon. Tell me again what you did?"

What hadn't he done? After Angel never appeared yesterday, he couldn't answer her call fast enough this morning. But once her heard her words, he wished he'd let it ring to voicemail.

"I'm retracting my invitation for tonight, Josiah. I don't think it's right to give my friends the appearance of a date when we clearly don't have that kind of relationship." Her tone was so polite, she could have been a stranger.

He'd sputtered out a denial and yes, he'd begged to come with her. If she heard him, she didn't respond.

"You didn't come to your studio yesterday," he said next.

"Oh, I work at the gallery on Fridays. I'm sorry, do I need to tell you when I'll be on the property? I didn't think that was part of our agreement. We should write out our terms so expectations are clear on both sides."

She sounded so official and so distant. He wasn't sure what nonsense he said next because his head buzzed with worry. She was pushing him away, probably only fair since he'd done the same to her.

When she hung up, he'd quickly dialed Powers and begged there too. "Angel has uninvited me for tonight, but I need to come, man. I need to see her and apologize. What do I need to do to convince her to give me another chance?"

Powers stayed silent for a moment, and Kaane was on the verge of begging again when he said, "Tess knows who you are, Kaane. I mean, she knows who you really are. She's been troubled about this all along, and now that things have blown up in your face, I don't know how she's going to feel about allowing you to push the issue under our roof."

Push the issue? He would give it a full body shove. He needed to see Angel, and any price wasn't too high to pay for that privilege.

"Please, Powers. I won't get a chance to tell her the truth if I can't see her, and maybe it would be best if I did it in front of friends. She'll feel safe and might be more willing to believe me."

The man must have heard the desperation in his tone, because he relented. "I'll explain that, and as long as you plan to tell the truth, I think Tess will agree. Honesty, that's the key. She and I don't have secrets, not since we got serious. You might think about that." And he hung up.

Tess had been welcoming this evening, if not particularly warm, giving him a warning look as he came in the door and watching him with serious eyes. Angel hadn't arrived yet, and as if she knew it made him stew, she gave the watch on her wrist a casual examination.

"What if she's not coming? I don't think she's coming." He rubbed the glass in his hand and wished it was filled with something stronger that soda.

"Relax. She worked at the gallery today. She might want to go home and change clothes or something. She'll be here, or we'll hear from her, but either way, you'll know where she is."

"What if she won't talk to me?"

Powers regarded him gravely without responding. When Tess asked for help in the kitchen, Kaane was left to watch the street alone.

This had become so much bigger than his music. He'd been living a lie by not explaining his identity, but in return, he'd been accepted for his real self without the glaze of fame. Angel had seemed to like him, up to that time when he'd stepped back from her temptations. She had no way of knowing what that cost him, and she couldn't know he was doing it for her own good.

>>>>>

Angel trudged along Main Street with slow steps. She'd had high hopes for bringing Josiah along to meet her friends. It would be a date, like a real date, and things would move forward from there.

She'd pressed him for things he wasn't ready to give, and she didn't want to listen to his explanation. Not that he seemed to have one, but maybe she had been rushing him. She wore her virgin status like a mark of shame. Changing how she felt about that was something she needed to consider.

"Hello again."

She started out of her worries, noticing the man who'd visited the gallery yesterday. He sat at a table outside the bakery and lifted a coffee cup in her direction.

"May I buy you a cup of coffee? Or maybe something to eat?"

She shook her head with a forced smile and resumed walking. The last thing she wanted was another weirdo nipping at her heels. Glancing over her shoulder, she noted he stayed at his table but continued to track her progress. When their eyes met, he twiddled his fingers at her as if saying goodbye. She would bet he'd show up at the gallery again, and she dearly hoped she wouldn't be working when he did. The least he could do would be buy one of her paintings if they interested him so much.

That's what it came down to. She needed sales to be known, sales other than Josiah's. And she needed to broaden her perspective and offer other work. The portraits were done on a surge of emotion, feelings she now needed to quell. Josiah had been clear. He was not the man for her.

Turning into the walkway leading up to the old Victorian Tess and Powers now called home, she paused. The last thing she felt like was a party. She would again be the fifth wheel with the couples around her. They never made her feel left out or extra, but she was the only one without a special someone, and the feeling was lonely.

She'd thought she might have a chance for that with Josiah. Their conversations, swinging from serious to laughing and back again, never bored her. They found so many things to discuss. Even when they didn't agree, like on music, they could still find common ground. She missed him, and it had only been a day.

"Angel."

Her name in his voice made her look up and blink. Had she conjured him up from her imagination? He wasn't supposed to be here, and yet here he was, flesh and bone, standing at the top of the steps watching her with hungry eyes.

That gaze did her in, making her warm when she'd been shivering and trembling moments before. He came down the steps at a run and grabbed her arms, pulling her into an embrace that trapped her.

"I'm so glad you came. I was afraid you wouldn't, but they told me they were sure you'd come. I've missed you, Angel."

She pulled in a gulp of air, and with it, the heady scent she'd associated with him engulfed her. As her face pressed into his shirt, she could feel the rapid beat of his heart as if he was truly excited to see her. But it could be a sham. That thought had her pushing away, and he dropped his arms and stepped back as if she stung him.

"Hello Josiah. I didn't expect to see you here." She gave half a thought to turning around and heading home.

"There you are, Angel. We're so glad you could make it. Please, come in. Let's get you a glass of wine." Tess hurried down the stairs and linked arms with her, shooting a sharp look at Josiah as if admonishing him. He shoved his hands in his pockets and glanced up the street, then followed them slowly up the stairs.

Angel didn't want to be here now more than ever. It was difficult enough to think about Josiah and hide her feelings. But to have him here and face him all evening with her friends looking on? Just about impossible.

Inside the door, Powers enveloped her in a hug without words and turned her back over to Tess, who fussed with Angel's purse and coat. In a low voice, she said, "I'm sorry, I wanted to call you and tell you he was here, but Powers kept me too busy. He begged to come, Angel, and Powers agreed. The man says he needs to talk to you."

She had her doubts about how that would go, but she was determined to hide her disappointment. Giving her friend a forced smile, she accepted the glass of wine from Powers and sat down in a chair. When Josiah settled on a settee across from her, she gave him a polite nod, then turned to Tess with every intention of continuing their conversation.

But she never had a chance to utter a word as Josiah's voice cut across the room. "Angel, I have something I need to tell you. It's important. Can we go somewhere private to talk?"

She swiveled her attention slowly to buy herself time. What did they have to say to each other in private? He'd had his chance, and they no longer had that kind of friendship.

"You can use my office upstairs," Powers said.

As if he'd expected this, Josiah sprung up and extended a hand to her. She stared at that hand for a moment, then turned back to Tess and said in an undertone, "What do you think?"

Tess glanced between Josiah and Angel, uncertainty in her expression. "If you close things off between you, you'll never know what might be possible." Her gaze swung to Powers and softened.

Risks. Life was full of them, and Angel hadn't exactly lined up to roll the dice. Tess was right. If she didn't take a chance, she'd never know. She lifted her chin and rose, ignoring Josiah's hand. "Let's get this out of the way, Josiah, so we can all enjoy the evening."

Relief flooded his face as he began to smile at her. The chilliness in her expression must have gotten through to him, though, because the smile faded before it reached full wattage. That was just as well. When he smiled like she was the source of his sunshine, it did things to her resolve.

A fast knock sounded on the front door before it burst open, and DK and Vince tumbled into the room. Vince didn't even offer a greeting before saying, "Boy, that was weird. We parked the car and a guy rushed up to the window and knocked on it. And naturally, I asked what the hell he wanted, and he said he wanted to know who owned this house."

Tess and Powers exchanged an amused look. "That happens. People are intrigued by the architecture or they've heard the history of it and they want to know if they can tour inside."

Vince waved a hand, pulling DK forward. She said, "It was that guy who asked about famous people living around here. I recognize him from the gallery. Anyway, Vince told him this is a private home and he smiled like we were joking. He pranced off when Vince got out of the car and towered over him, though. My hero."

DK pulled her husband's head down for a quick kiss, and Angel felt that surge of envy. Tess had Powers. DK had Vince. She had a big question mark. She was ready to have this out with Josiah.

DK's face was flushed and she giggled as she and Vince broke off their clutch, and she spun to give Angel a hug. "I'm so happy you're here, Josiah or not."

Angel leaned in. "Well, you're getting your chance to meet him. He came by himself. Powers has done work for him and they know each other, so he begged to come too, according to Tess. Come on, I'll introduce you."

She turned her friend to Josiah, ready to go through the platitudes, when she noticed DK's face tightening in shock. "Oh. My. God. Angel, that's – "

Vince pushed his palm over his wife's mouth, and her wide eyes switched to him. He said, "That's Josiah Harmond, my love. I told you we knew him. You just don't remember meeting him. Josiah, good to see you, man. Do you remember my wife, DK?"

If his hand was a little slow to move off DK's mouth, Angel wasn't sure. Josiah's pointed stare landed on DK too, and her eyebrows lifted in questioning glares between the two men. Vince said, "Ok?"

She nodded slowly, and his hand dropped, equally slowly.

"DK, it's great to see you again. I hope you and Vince can come over someday and see where I've displayed that guitar you created. It's an amazing piece." Josiah grabbed DK's hand and shook it with exaggerated energy.

DK nodded slowly. "Josiah Harmond. Holy crap." She allowed him to pump her hand, and as he dropped it, she turned to Tess. "Can we talk?"

Angel watched the exchange with confusion. Meaningful, pointed glances flew between everyone in the room but her. No one said anything, darting looks at Josiah who examined his boots, clean today, with apparent rapt interest.

She linked through DK's arm and then through Tess's, and pulled both women toward the kitchen. "I'd like to talk to both of you." Neither one of them resisted. Behind them, she heard the buzz of male whispering, accented by a couple of Vince's colorful curses. She pushed closed the door and turned her friends to face her.

"Something strange is happening here, and I want to know what it is."

Tess and DK glanced at each other, then back at her. Tess said, "I think you need to talk to Josiah about this, Angel. He desperately wants to talk to you, and I think you should listen."

Beside her, DK nodded hard enough to set her pixie cut of red hair dancing. "I agree. Geez, he's, ah, he's, I don't know what to say." She shook her head and stared over Angel's shoulder at the door. "Yes, talk to him, but don't make it easy for him."

"What do you mean?" Tess turned with the question as if she was intrigued by the idea. Angel followed suit and added, "I'm not making anything easy for him."

DK leaned in and lowered her voice. "I think you should listen to what he has to say, and if you're still interested, pull out the full act. You know, temptress and siren and that little black number Roxy kept urging you to use."

Temptress. Siren. She hadn't even had the courage to put that little black number on again in the privacy of her own bedroom.

"He's going to try to tell you no, that he's not interested in sex, or that he's not ready or some such shit." DK covered her mouth as if she wasn't sure where the word came from.

Tess nodded. "Yes, even if he says no, if you're fine with things after you talk, go for it. He's obviously crazy about you. Maybe you just scare him."

That was so preposterous, Angel giggled. "No, I don't scare him. And I don't think he's interested in me in that way." She didn't need to explain which way she meant.

DK shook her head. "Nope, you do, and he is. I mean, look at the way he watched you, like he was a hungry lion and you were the gazelle. Once he tells you what's going on and why he's been acting like a stupid guy, if you're good with the explanation, dive in. Trust us, Angel, the water's terrific once you get the hang of the stroke, if you catch my drift."

All three women collapsed into laughter, Angel hardest of all even though she was sure her face colored at the suggestions. As they calmed down a bit, she grew more serious. Did she really want to do this? Josiah was a nice man, underneath the confusing mixed messages.

"I'm not sure this is right. I mean, taking advantage of him and all."

DK and Tess exchanged another look. They grabbed her hands and pulled her to face the door to the living room. Tess said, "Life is full of risks, and no man is who he appears to be on the surface. Take it from me."

Angel nodded, eyeing the door with a rising sense of confidence.

DK gave her a little push and said, "Do you want to become a thirty-four-year-old virgin?"

That was all the convincing she needed.

Chapter 18

Angel said she didn't want to wait for dinner. She wanted to have their discussion immediately, and she wanted to do it in her own home. "Are you coming?" Her no-nonsense question and march to the door had him diving for his coat and following. She wanted to walk, but Kaane didn't want to be exposed until he told her the truth. All it would take is one fan screaming out his name and it would all be over.

He pulled up in the driveway of a cute little bungalow a couple of blocks off Main Street. It had white shutters against the yellow siding and a white picket fence. He bet in the summer, wispy flowers tangled in the slats. This was the kind of place where Angel belonged.

Not at his place, with its cold walls and industrial feel. Only her art lit it up, like she lit up his life when she was around. Would she want to be anywhere near him, even using his barn, once she knew the truth? He didn't want to consider any option where she wouldn't.

He raced around the hood of the old pick-up to open her door, and she accepted his help with a nod most would call royal. A gentle serenity filled her face as she sailed along in front of him. If she was feeling any nerves about this, she gave no sign of them. He, on the other hand, was about to jump out of his skin. He glanced at a car traveling slowly up the street and looked away quickly.

He was naked as a baby today. No disguise, no pretense, and no way to hide how he felt. It was easy to tell that DK recognized him, and if Vince hadn't shushed her, Angel would already know.

How the hell was he going to explain this?

She unlocked the door and entered, not waiting for him or inviting him in. But the door didn't swing shut behind her and he took that as permission. He sought her out in the room's shadows, lit only by the streetlights' glow.

His thoughts scattered when she hooked her jacket on a rack by the door. He must have been missing her more than he realized, because that sway of her hips as she walked away from him to the window seemed even more enticing than before. The rattle of curtains on the rod marked the room's plunge into darkness. Blinded by it, he stretched out his arms to search out her form, and jumped when her hands closed on his shoulders.

"Let me take your coat." He didn't recognize her sultry voice. She worked the coat down his arms and threw it at a chair, missing with enough force to have it land on the floor. She stood in front of him with her face unreadable. The air charged with electric energy as her heated scent washed over him, and he couldn't move.

"We need to talk."

"We will talk, Josiah. Not here, though. Come, I have something to show you."

She pulled his hands, and he stumbled over his feet to follow her. When a stab of sneaky light from outside crossed her face, the smile that shown there had his heart stumbling too.

Now. He needed to say it now, before things got out of hand. Who was he kidding? They were already out of hand, and he was eating out of hers. She could pull him to the edge of a cliff and tell him to jump and he would.

She dragged him down a small corridor and into a room where a single light glowed. A bedroom, so feminine and soft, had him tripping once more, unable to find his balance. She dropped his hands and lifted hers to her hair, and the clasp that held it back magically disappeared. The curtain of curls fell over her shoulders and surrounded that perfect face. Her mouth pulled into a bow of a smile as she sat down, and she patted the bed next to her.

"Please, sit down. Tell me what's on your mind."

He'd never heard her voice take on that husky note, and yet it fit her like the dress she had on. The rich blue marked every curve and could drive him out of his mind if he wasn't careful. He was sitting on the bed without realizing he'd dropped exactly where she'd told him to be.

"I have something to tell you." His voice grated and he tried to clear his throat.

"I am sure you do. So, tell me."

She ran a hand down her side, as if smoothing material. He followed the movement with his eyes and wanted to trace it with his lips. He was dying here. He stuttered the words, because his throat was parched and he couldn't get his heart to settle into a reasonable beat. "I'm not the man you think I am."

Her movements paused as if she considered this. Her hands then rose like a pair of doves taking flight and fiddled with the buttons at her neck. One popped open, then another. "Most men aren't who they think they are," she said. Pop number three.

"Angel, you don't understand. I'm not a pig rancher or farmer or whatever the hell it is. I'm not building a big barn. I'm a musician and I'm trying to write music to record in what will someday be that studio. And you're my muse."

Her smile dimmed for a moment as if she was unsure how she felt about that. His words rushed on. "With you around, I've been able to find the words and the music again. It's different from what I used to do, different from the Kaane Scott people used to know, but it's still great. And I think you'll like it. I'll play it for you."

Angel tilted her head and regarded him with a thoughtful expression. "So, you've been using me?"

With a desperate groan, he admitted it. "Yes, I have, from the day I saw you and your paintings at the gallery to offering you the barn for a studio. I need to have you near me. My life is empty and bland without you in it, Angel. I can't write a damned thing without you."

She rose with the grace he'd come to expect of her, tapping a finger against her pursed lips. "So, you were using me without telling me. Why the change of heart? Why tell me now?"

Kaane raked his hands through his hair, unable to find the right words. He jumped up because sitting still wasn't an option and blurted out the truth, hoping to hell the guys were right. "This has become bigger than a muse and my music. Angel, you fill my life up with something I didn't even know I was missing. I won't say I'm sorry for making you my muse, but I am sorry it's come between us."

She ran her eyes up and down his body, that thoughtful gaze still in place. When her eyes landed on his crotch, he thought he'd jump out of his skin. A jungle beat pounded in the flesh behind the zipper, making it hard to think.

With that same seductive sway to her hips, Angel disappeared, and he drew in a deep breath. She hadn't kicked him out, hadn't laughed at him, and hadn't done the whole rabid fan thing. He might stand a chance at having her back in his life, because without her, it wasn't worth a penny of his vast fortune or the fame that created it.

Angel battled to breathe, wondering where the bravado came from. This was not her, and yet, it felt right. Josiah was clearly at the end of his rope, and that's just where she wanted him.

The story was sweet. She wasn't sure she was muse material, but if he thought so, that was good enough for her. She didn't have a clue who Kaane Scott was, so he might not be that famous after all, but if he thought he was, she wasn't going to deny him that either.

Her hands shook as she reached into the closet and her fingers closed on the black straps. She didn't have the nerve to put it on, but she remembered the advice Roxy gave her. Pushing air out on a deep exhale, she sauntered back into the bedroom on shaky legs.

Josiah stood where she'd left him, his hands fisted at his sides and his face a mask of doubts. If those doubts were for what was about to happen, she hoped she could make him forget them.

"Do you like this?" She held up the lacy black bit of next to nothing, a negligee the girls assured her would bring any man to his knees when he saw her in it.

Josiah gulped and nodded, his eyes darting between her and the nightie.

She dropped it on the floor.

"What are you doing?"

"That's where it's going to end up anyway. I'm simply skipping a step."

The shock on his face was a tangible thing, as if he couldn't breathe through it. Then his eyes narrowed to slits with a dangerous glint in them. If he'd had any other reaction, she might have laughed. But he leaped across the distance and his arms encircled her, driving her into him so hard that air left her with a gasp.

"I can't play games like this," he said with a low growl.

She tilted her head back to look at him, because pressed together like this, he couldn't deny he was attracted to her. He heated each of the places she hadn't known had been cold inside her, and she pushed further into him. "Who said this is a game?"

As if her words triggered something in him, he wound his hands in her hair, angled her face, and drove his mouth on to hers. The kiss wasn't anything like the mildly insane but comparatively tame ones they're shared before. She moved her lips, trying to taste more of him, and fisted her fingers in his shirt.

His tongue pressed against her mouth and she opened for him, unable to do more than feel. The way his hands tipped her head brought a deeper angle. His body pressed its impressive erection into her belly. The moan came from him, or might have been hers. She no longer knew where he ended and she began.

Josiah broke off the kiss with a muttered curse and screwed his eyes shut, shaking his head as if trying to dispute what was happening between them. She wasn't going to let him. He was the one she'd waited for and saved herself for before she even knew him, and he was going to teach her everything he could about passion. She would not deny either one of them that.

His eyes opened, the green fired with golden lights and aimed at her with fierce attention. How had she missed how hypnotic they were? She couldn't turn away, and every minute he held her and swayed with her in his arms only convinced her she'd been right to push things.

He shook his head again. "Angel, this isn't right. Didn't you hear me say who I am? You are so much better than me, and you deserve the right man, not me." His hands slid from her hair to her arms but the hard grip didn't lessen.

Angel lifted her chin in defiance and stared him the eye, not willing to back down. "Josiah, you are the right man. This, you and me, is right. It's better than right."

He shook her then, not hard enough to make it matter but as if he needed the movement to emphasize his point. "Call me Kaane. That's what all of the women call me."

That gave her heart a little pang, but she soldiered on. "I'm calling you Josiah, because that's who you are to me. And if you've had other women, all the better." At least one of them would know what they were doing.

He pushed her away then, stepping back and scrubbing both hands over his face. "You deserve to be protected from me, from all men like me. Besides, you're my muse, and you're taboo to me."

She wasn't his muse any more than a chair was. There was nothing in her to inspire someone to be creative. If anything, he inspired her. Choosing to misunderstand him, she turned to the bed, sat on its edge, and patted the blanket beside her. Josiah didn't move, his arms crossed in front of his chest in a gesture he might think of as refusal. To her, it looked like he was trying to protect himself. When he only watched her with darkened eyes, she leaned over in slow motion, allowing him a peek where the buttons gapped open. He hissed in response and was scrutinizing a bare wall when she glanced back.

Leaning over further, she pulled open the nightstand drawer. Removing the discreet box, she held it out to him. He glanced at it and away, then back again with wider eyes. "I hope I bought the right size," she said, using her best vamp voice. "By the look of things, I think I guessed correctly." When his eyes sprang up to meet hers, she slid her gaze down in slow motion, resting where the denim stretched away from his body, and she smiled in a way she hoped was sensuous.

The snap of his control might have been an audible thing, like teeth gnashing together or a sharp cry, but Angel didn't have a chance to analyze it. Josiah jumped across the space between them and tossed her back on the bed, pressing into her chest to chest, hips to hips, and limb to limb. If he wanted to imprint himself on her, he couldn't have done a more thorough job, and her delight warred with a flare of passion so intense, she moaned.

His face was inches from hers, their noses almost touching, and their eyes locked. "Tell me no, Angel." He shifted his body, and the weight of his erection pressed into her in a place that made stars appear in her vision.

Catching her breath was harder, but she managed a smile and said, "Yes, Josiah. Yes."

This time he groaned, and when his mouth came down on hers, the rugged ruthlessness of before was gone. His lips were gentle, caressing hers, then moving to her closed eyes, and around her jaw to her ear, then down her neck. The slow journey was so mesmerizing, she didn't register his hand cupping her breast at first, not until his thumb shifted across the tip. She moaned again because the feeling was so exquisite, she wasn't sure she could stand it.

"Make love to me, Josiah."

He didn't raise his head from the place where his tongue traced the lacy edge of her bra. "Call me Kaane."

"Josiah."

"You are going to be the death of me."

He knew he should stop. Forget the taboo. He should stop because he had too much respect for Angel to use her.

Except it was more than sex, and even in his aroused state, Kaane knew it. He had always been a sinner and his hook-ups were fast and public. But here he was, in the arms of a woman as beautiful and sweet as any he'd ever met, and she wanted him. The real him, not the rock star him. In his head, he'd already consummated their relationship, and once that happened in the flesh, her days as his muse were over.

The thought should have freed him to do what he wanted, take the woman as she offered herself and damn the consequences, but still, he hesitated. This was Evangeline Reed and he liked her, and not just the casual lust kind of like, but with the deep trust and respect of friendship and feelings he didn't know how to name.

He groaned into her hair, willing himself to move away, pull back, and keep her unsullied by his touch, but he couldn't. If this was the only time he touched her like this, every nerve would feel the heat for the rest of his life. How could he walk away?

"I don't know how to do this," he groaned into hair so soft, it could be made of spun dreams.

Her answering whimper came without hesitation. "That makes two of us. Just kiss me, Josiah. We'll figure it out as we go."

Could it be that she felt as lonely as he had? Did she feel something different in their physical connection, different from the other lovers she'd had? He pulled back to examine her face, but all he saw was excitement shining from her eyes, and he drowned in it. He might never write a song again, but it would be worth it to have this night in the arms of his Angel.

He caught her hitched sigh with a kiss. His fingers skimmed her creamy skin. He cupped her breast and thumbed her nipple through the lace. His lips explored hers, meeting the sweet tentative strokes of her tongue. She was his favorite candy and he could no sooner pass up the sugar than he could stop his heart. When he cupped a hand over her heat, he inhaled her desperate gasp. She was so responsive, so perfect, that his head spun. No woman had ever been like this with him, as if his touch was her first and their bodies discovered new music together. His fingers curled and stroked, and with each motion, she breathed faster.

"Oh my, I didn't realize it could be so amazing."

Had no man ever taken the time to satisfy her? She deserved to be worshipped, spread on an altar and feasted upon. He moved down her body, pressing his lips to exposed warmth and murmuring words of reassurance and adoration as her pants came closer together. When he could finally press his lips in a single kiss to her core, she cried out and bucked underneath him. He'd never seen anything more beautiful than her face in ecstasy.

His hands couldn't stay still. She was the perfect instrument he simply had to play. His erection throbbed hard against the zipper of his jeans, and he shifted to ease the pressure. He didn't want to rush things, even if it meant denying his needs.

But Angel seemed to have other ideas. She raised up on her elbows and rolled him off her. Her hair cascading in a madhouse curtain of curls as her lips landing on his with a ferocity that fired his blood faster. Control was going to be nearly impossible if she kept this up.

"Angel, please. You're driving me crazy." He grabbed for her hands, but she sat back and grinned down at him.

"That might be the nicest thing you've ever said to me." Her fingers pressed to her lips with a considering expression. "But you know, we're not done yet."

Her hands went to the button of his jeans and popped it open as if she'd done this a thousand times. He didn't want to think about Angel with other men, not when her fingers sliding the zipper down were slow torture. He'd picked a hell of a day to go commando. When she grazed the throbbing heat underneath, his hips levitated off the bed.

"Oh, this is interesting," she said, running a finger down and back up again, making his cock jump in response. Angel's wide eyes stayed on his crotch with a fascinated smile. She sounded so innocent when she asked, "Would now be a good time to get out those condoms?"

He nodded vigorously because he couldn't help himself. She popped open the box and pulled out a foil, flipping over the wrapper as it lay in her hands. Her eyes traveled over his body once more, and when her gaze landed on his instrument, she licked her lips.

Any more rapt attention and he'd come from that alone. He grabbed the silver packet and tore it open, and as he rolled it on, her eyes stayed focused on his actions. Her surprised squeak when he rolled her on her back and landed on top of her changed to delighted laughter. He grinned down at her, watching the chase of emotions on her face. The giggle died, replaced by a serious panting gasp.

"Are we going to do it now?" She wiggled her hips, leaving him in no doubt about what 'it' she was talking about. And god help him, it had been so long for him, he began to move into her on instinct.

"Josiah, that feels amazing," she said, lifting her hips as if trying to draw him in deeper.

"First you, Angel," he said, trying to reign himself in. She deserved more, so much more, but this he knew he could give her. His fingers found her core and rubbed, meeting her body's rhythm and the thrust of her hips. Soon she cried out again and grabbed him close.

"Please, now, please."

His breaths had long before changed to synchronize with hers. He teased her entrance and braced himself over her, kissing her with as much passion as he ever gave to his music. This astounding woman lay crazed and wanton under him, and his body only knew one response.

He sank into her slowly, the tight grip of her channel making him grit his teeth. Beneath him, he felt Angel stiffen. He dropped his forehead to hers and tried to slow things down.

"I'm sorry. Are you okay?"

She didn't say anything but nodded. Her teeth appeared and bit into her lower lip, and he had to do the same, licking the same spot and diving in for a deeper kiss. Another inch, another kiss, and another, until he was all the way home.

He pulled back far enough to see Angel's face. Her eyes were closed and a small frown line joined them. A light sheen of perspiration shown on her cheeks and her teeth grabbed that lower lip once more.

He never thought of himself as particularly well-endowed. Women came after him for his star status rather than his prowess, but he wanted to be the best possible everything for this woman in his arms. He pulled out slowly, and he watched her exhale as he almost withdrew.

The frown eased a bit, and he pressed in again. Her gasps matched his thrusts, until the sounds changed to moans. Her eyes opened and met his. The hazy lust he saw there did strange things to him, flipping his insides out and making him wish a thousand crazy notions. Her hips began to rock in time with his, and when he didn't think he could wait any longer, struggling to hang on, she cried out and gaped up at him with blind amazement.

He shook like the pounding feet of twenty thousand fans as he followed her over the crest, and never broke their shared gaze. He couldn't. Diving into the depths of her eyes was like diving into a bottomless pool of passion, something he'd never experienced with anyone else. When his body finally unclenched and he panted in time with her, he didn't want to look away either. Pressing a tender kiss and brushing the hair back from her face, he was surprised to see the tremor in his hand.

Tears pooled in Angel's eyes and as if they knew his weakness, they slipped out and ran into her hair. She inhaled sharply and her lips quivered. His confusion grew as she touched his cheek with fingers shaking as hard as his. She framed his face with her hands. Then she cried harder.

>>>>>

She had always been a woman who understood words, and yet there were none for this. Angel could only memorize the face she would remember forever.

"Angel, what's wrong?" Josiah shifted off her and pulled her across his body. He ran his hands up her back and into her hair, as if to comfort her. It would take her a long time to convince the tears to quit, she feared, and she shifted to examine the relaxed planes of his face.

"Will it always be like that?"

His face clouded in confusion. "Like what?"

She smiled despite the tears. "Perfection."

He grinned, but shook his head. "You'll have to tell me. Though I thought this time was pretty special."

He'd given her the perfect opening. It would be a good time to explain. But he looked so proud of himself, like he was the reason she felt the glow from her toes to her fingertips. He was, and somehow, she knew saying that would ruin the moment.

"It was amazing," she said in a whisper.

His grin faded. "For me too." He shifted them until they lay on their sides face to face, and he ran a hand down her body. His eyes stayed on his fingers, and she swore even if his skin didn't touch her, she'd feel that gaze as if he did. His hand traveled back up, cupping and caressing, until she heard herself panting with new energy. As if he could read that in her face, he leaned in and kissed her with urgency.

It was like that each time they stirred during the night. She'd had her chance at exploration too, and she found his skin must be as sensitive as hers. A run of her finger up his spine had him hissing. Her grasp of his cock made him moan. Each time they made love, it felt easier and got better, until she couldn't wait for that magic moment when he was inside of her, before they moved, when the world balanced on an edge of completion.

When she woke this time, she reached for him with a happy hum of anticipation. Her hand snaked across sheets, grasping at nothing but cold. Her eyes popped open in surprise, searching the faint light of the early morning.

He sat in the little chair next to the dresser, fully clothed. She couldn't read his gaze, and she held the sheet in front of her as she shot up.

"What are you doing?" The throaty huskiness of her voice didn't seem to carry far.

"Watching you." He leaned forward and clasped his hands in front of him, dropping his eyes from hers. "I should go. I have work I need to do."

Her muddled thoughts became even more confused. "Um, okay. I'll see you later?" She heard the eager hopefulness in her voice, but she was powerless to control it.

When his eyes slipped back up to meet hers, a tortured expression made the green that glowed so brightly last night seem dim. "Feel free to use the studio any time you want, Angel. I have some things to take care of, so I may not be around."

He rose then, and despite her nakedness, she jumped off the bed too. He stilled as if his boots were suddenly nailed to the floor, ogling her like he'd never seen her before. He seemed to need her comfort, so she pressed into him and lifted on her toes. Her lips grazed his, and a groan tore out of him. He kissed her without wrapping her in his arms, a hard kiss that held nothing back. With one last intense look, he spun on his heels and was gone before she could force her feet to move.

Chapter 19

"What have I been saying all these years? Men are scum."

Tess said, "Rox, my dear, it is time to put that phrase to rest. Give it a decent burial, as it were. You don't believe it any more than we do. Besides, he told her."

Despite the consternation on her friend's face as she waved the scooper of ice cream in response, Angel couldn't laugh. Yes, he'd told her, but it meant nothing to her. This wasn't her field of expertise, so she'd relied on research.

He'd said he was famous, but he didn't tell her how famous. After he left, after a long weepy bath and another hard cry, she fired up her computer and opened the search browser. She had few expectations about finding anything, but research was what she did best.

'Cain Scott.'

The cursor blinked for a moment before the engine responded.

'Showing results for Kaane Scott.'

Scrolling down the screen, her jaw had dropped open. One page later, then two, and then on and on. With so many sources and so many stories, she wasn't sure where to begin.

And there were pictures. His hair was often longer than it was now, and his face more haggard, but there was no doubt it was the same man. Her Josiah. He'd told her he was Kaane Scott, but the music legend meant nothing to her.

"How would I know who he was? I don't listen to rock music. I don't read gossip magazines. The name meant nothing to me." She knew she wailed the last words, and when a bowl filled like a mountain of Rocky Road appeared in front of her, all she could do was sniff. The selection was poetically appropriate.

"Come on, this cures all ills. At least he told you. I was ready to tell you, but I wanted him to man up and do it himself. He seemed like he was sincere." Roxy sounded like she had grudging respect for the fact he'd done it.

"Did you paint today? What did he say when he saw you?" Tess eyed her over her own bowl.

Angel dropped the spoon into a softening puddle. "He told me before to come to the studio any time I wanted. I have keys for the barn locks and the code for the gate. I haven't gone back." She was chicken, pure and simple. Afraid of what she might see in Josiah's expression. Pity, or embarrassment, or worse.

DK said, "You have to go back, Angel. Hiding doesn't solve anything."

The urgency in her friend's tone registered. "I'm not hiding." Exactly. She just wasn't ready to face him when her emotions were raw and she couldn't hide her feelings. She had a boatload of them for a man who clearly could have many women, and had. None of them would get clingy or attached. It was in her research. He never stayed with any woman for long and they didn't seem to mind.

DK removed the uneaten bowl and closed her hands around Angel's. "Was it okay? I mean, did he take things slow when you told him it was your first time?"

Angel shook her head. A clatter of ceramic landed on the table as Roxy muttered, "That bastard. Knives are too good for him. I'm getting the meat grinder."

Despite the pain cutting her heart in two, Angel had to laugh. "You can't do that, Roxy. It wasn't his fault. I didn't tell him."

Stunned silence made the room seem too quiet, until Roxy exploded once more. "You didn't tell him? That's almost as bad as him not telling you his name."

Tess sounded more consoling. "What Roxy is trying to say, Angel, is that sometimes, things can feel a little rough the first time, if the man doesn't know. It gets better, I promise."

Angel gazed up sharply, her mind wandering back to the sensation of being touched everywhere, inside and out, and the thrilling orgasms, and the unearthly feeling that overwhelmed her even now. Josiah – Kaane – had taken such amazing care of her that she swore he could read her inexperience.

"If it gets any better, I might not survive it," she said. It had been a night unlike anything she could even imagine, and her imagination was vivid. The possibility he could improve upon the extraordinary boggled her mind. He'd set a standard against which she would hold any other man.

Except she didn't want any other men.

"Wait. Hold it right there. Are you telling us it was great? Like fantastic, better than all of your favorite foods in one meal?"

Angel nodded shyly, taking in Roxy's astonished expression. "He said he had no experience of it, so I thought he was like me." But in her heart, she must have known that wasn't true. He had to know what he was doing. It was unbelievably perfect.

"Perfect? As in perfect, perfect?" It was DK's turn to sound incredulous, and Angel realized she must have shared that thought out loud. She nodded.

"That doesn't make any difference, not if the guy isn't one thousand percent committed too. You have to be willing to risk it all, and to walk away if it doesn't work out," DK said, toying with the spoon and pouring melting dessert back into her bowl in repetitive movements.

"Is that what you did? Walk away, I mean. Vince clearly came to his senses since he's as mushy as that ice cream around you."

DK nodded. "I drew a line in the sand and he stepped back from it. We had an agreement, and both of us were too stubborn to admit we wanted more."

"What changed that?"

DK examined Angel's face. "We have a mutual friend, our agent, and he realized what had happened after he talked to us both. He made sure Vince and I met again, and once I saw him, I knew. I never got a chance to say that to him until much later, because he begged me for another chance. Turns out, when a cynical guy begs, it's kind of sexy."

"I don't want Josiah or Kaane or whatever I'm supposed to call him to beg," she said. As soon as the words were out of her mouth, she realized it was true. He had to be willing to meet her on shared terms, though she had no idea what those might be.

"Yeah, well, beware the special efforts. I ended up conked out and in the hospital, and history nearly repeated itself before I came to my senses." Roxy began retrieving their bowls, giving Angel a wry smile as she passed.

"Why haven't you married Mac?" It was a question Angel had been dying to ask, because Roxy and Mac seemed destined to be together forever.

When Roxy stopped but didn't turn around, Angel rushed to retract the question. "Sorry, that's none of my business."

But her friend waved off her apology. "Let's face it. He's a major international star. I don't want to hold him back if he decides to go."

Tess and DK immediately voiced their denials, but Roxy only stirred the gelled messes in their bowls and shook her head. "It's better this way. I guess maybe I also enjoy it when Mac keeps trying to win me. Keeps him on his toes." She started forward again and dumped the bowls in the sink.

"I don't agree," Tess said with a marked frown. "Powers and I don't play games and he's never had to beg. He proved to me in a very public way how important I am to him, and he keeps showing me every day. That's sexy."

"But you two haven't married either," Angel said, so curious by now, any discomfort at being so nosey evaporated.

Tess raised a shoulder and looked away. "Let's just say that when your relationship is something that can't easily be explained, you aren't willing to complicate it. Powers and I are together forever, but we're not traditional people by any stretch of the imagination."

Angel tried to picture herself with a rock star. The canvas in her mind stayed stubbornly blank. Angel and Josiah, she could envision. Angel with Kaane, no.

Tess came around the couch and settled next to her, taking her hands. "So, what do you want to do about Kaane?"

She stared back at her friend, realizing with fresh tears that she had no idea.

>>>>>

Kaane paced the length of the room, pausing only when he came even with the piano. He jammed his hands down in dissonant chords, the resulting sounds a perfect match to the screwed-up feelings cutting him to pieces inside. When the doorbell's melody began, he slammed closed the keyboard, cutting off the notes with a reverberating screech.

"Kaane? You okay, man?"

The insistent pounding of a palm against wood joined Mac's voice. Kaane yanked the door open and reached out to grab his friend's jacket in a fisted clench. Mac's eyes widened as raised his hands in surrender.

"I come in peace, my friend, despite what Roxy says."

Kaane stared back for a beat, ready to snarl at the interruption to his jam of self-hate. Sympathy filled Mac's gaze, though he looked wary enough for the irony of the situation to register. Mac wasn't the enemy. Kaane was his own worst enemy and he had the scars on his soul to prove it.

He dropped his hands. "What does Roxy say?"

"That she'll let her knives do the talking the next time she sees you. Mind if I come in? You look like shit." Mac paced over to the dining chairs and dropped into one, regarding Kaane with interest.

"Is there a reason you're here?" Kaane wanted to wallow in his misery like those proverbial pigs he would never own. All he could see was Angel's crushed expression when he walked out her door. He decided it would be best to wait for her to come to her studio. He could apologize. He'd let a day pass, then another, unsure of what to do. He waited longer, but she hadn't shown up to paint.

"I wanted to check on you, see how you're doing."

Kicking a chair seemed like a good idea, so Kaane did it. That didn't release his frustration, and he eyed Mac, wondering if he'd be up to going a few rounds. As if he understood, Mac raised his hands again.

"Again, peace. Angel has the women. Who do you have to console you?" Mac tucked his hands under his chin and regarded Kaane gravely.

"What are you talking about?" But in his heart, he knew. He'd hurt Angel, and there was no way he could fix it. He righted the chair he just abused, dropped into it, and stared at Mac without bothering to hide the pain in his expression. "Is she okay?"

"No clue. To bring you up to speed, Angel called DK. DK called Tess. Tess called Roxy. The four of them are meeting up somewhere to discuss something. And after the knives comment, Roxy pulled two big cartons of ice cream out of the freezer and two bottles of wine out of the rack. Usually, a set of one means tears and comforting are involved, so this is much worse. Her last words were stronger than all men are scum when she stormed out the door."

Kaane cursed a litany of oaths. "When was this?"

Mac consulted his watch. "About two hours ago. When did you hook up?"

Two hours ago. But that meant Angel had been alone all this time. "Saturday night," he said, then realized what he'd admitted to. "Look, it's not what you think."

Mac shook his head and pinched the bridge of his nose. "No, it never is. That is, it is never what we think. It's what they think, and believe me, they have plenty of experience in this arena. All of us have screwed up royally at some point."

"I didn't screw up, we just sc- " He'd been about to say screwed, except he couldn't. It was so much more than that. This time he groaned out the curses and thought about slamming his head in the piano case to end his stupidity.

Nodding sagely, Mac eyed him with open sympathy. "Been there, done that, have the t-shirt, or at least I did, until Roxy ripped it to shreds."

A mumble of noise came from the front door. Mac rose faster than Kaane could. He opened the door and waved Vince and Powers inside. Looking up at them in disbelief, all Kaane could think of to say was, "Don't any of you work?"

Powers raised a skeptical eyebrow. "What were you doing?"

"Working," Kaane shouted.

Vince crossed the room and slapped his arm. "That's what we all say, man. That's the script for a moment like this. Tell me, you write anything?" He meandered over to the piano and tapped his finger on the blank pages arrayed across the top. "Nope, didn't think so."

Powers crossed his arms and broadened his stance. "Did you tell her?"

Kaane stood and mimicked his position. "Tell her what?" He could tell by his friend's annoyed expression that his belligerence wasn't going over well.

"Don't be a prick, Scott. Did you tell her who you really are or not?"

The air blew out of him, and he deflated back into the chair. No woman had ever called him Josiah in passion before, and he didn't know what the hell to do about the feelings that brought up in him. He covered his eyes, afraid his emotions were written on his face.

"I think we have our answer, gentlemen," Mac said, disappointment in his tone.

"I told her."

"What did you say?"

"I told her." He jumped out of the chair with his fists ready for a battle. "I told her, okay? And it didn't fucking matter."

The three men across the room darted uncertain glances at each other. Mac finally said, "What do you mean, it didn't matter?"

"She calls me Josiah. She's always called me Josiah and that's what she called me that night, even when I told her to call me Kaane. I begged her to." He shook his head and dropped back into the chair. Who was he kidding? Even if she had, he wouldn't have been able to stop, not when he had an angel from heaven here on earth in his arms.

"Begging time," Vince said.

"Fuck you."

Vince nodded with unusual seriousness. "Yup, I was where you are, man," he said, nodding to the array of Angel's paintings on the wall and fingering the poster. Kaane fought the urge to yank the cardboard from his hand. Only he had the right to run a finger over her smile and that paint smear. "I had a shrine to DK with everything of hers I could lay my hands on. If I'd been messed up enough to grab her undies on the way out, I might have framed those too." His wry laugh was anything but amused.

Mac added, "I am betting you want to make a grand gesture to show her how important she is, and I get that. Just be careful how you do it. Mine ended with Roxy injured, though since the incident triggered a big reveal that saved us, it probably worked out for the best." He swallowed, his gaze lost in the past. "When you see your woman on the ground, unconscious and bleeding, it takes years off your life, a life she had already saved. Mine."

Powers nodded his head. "And nothing like having her collapse in your arms because she's doing something brave in the face of tragedy and horror. Or having an inexplicable connection deeper than anything you can imagine, and having her say she's willing to walk away from you despite that." He rubbed a hand on his chest as if his heart still hurt with the thought.

But Kaane didn't believe any of them were right. His apology demanded a big gesture to express all he felt, and he only knew how to do it one way. It took him a couple of hours to convince them he would survive, for now. When they left, he pulled the wires out of the idiot doorbell and headed for the piano.

You wake beside me, tousled and dreamy from sleep,

Your hair wraps around me like it's me you want to keep.

And I pray that it's true, that you want me for your own.

There is no place on earth I would rather call my home.

Than you.

He tinkled the piano keys, trying to find the right note. Two days of this and it still evaded him. The hours he hadn't spent fighting the music block were taken up staring at Angel's face on the poster. He traced her cheek so many times, a spot was beginning to wear on the printing. If she sat beside him now, he'd be running his fingers over her face and down her neck and into her hair and anywhere else she'd allow it. If only she'd come to her studio.

When day turned to night, he picked up the phone to call her for the thousandth time, only to drop it again without dialing. Tomorrow, he vowed, he'd go to her house and convince her to give him another chance. Beg. He could do that. The plan gave him hope, and he nearly jumped in his van to initiate it now, but a glance at the clock, one in the morning, told him it was hardly the time to surprise her.

And then he must have dozed off, because he dreamed about Angel, pliant and willing beneath him. Her face as he stroked into her, pulled taunt with tension. Had he misread her? Was the pleasure he'd found in her arms one-sided? But she'd cried out as she came and her kisses afterwards were gentle and shy and decidedly innocent and pure.

Somehow, his conscious pulled him out of the dream with the thought. He lay sweaty and shaking and tight as the skin on a drum. He jumped off the couch because he couldn't lie still and crossed the room to the piano, banging his hands flat on the keys and producing a discordant noise that felt strangely gratifying. It reflected the wave of things inside him that he didn't know how else to express. His eyes focused on the clock. Three in the morning now. He wasn't going back to sleep, not when he knew he'd only relive their single night a thousand times and always come up with the same conclusion.

He'd fucked up.

He grabbed his pen and the notepad, scribbling as fast as his fingers could go.

I am not proud of all I've done, two hundred times or
*   more.*

Faceless women, countless times, and yes, I did keep
*   score.*

But then you came into my life and your face shown
*   warm and pure.*

Everything is new and different around you.

With you.

Three hours later, he had two more verses and a passable string of melody. It was far from perfect, and it still sounded like a bad love song. But he knew one thing for sure as he dropped off into an exhausted restless sleep. His muse might have left him, but she'd never leave his heart.

Chapter 20

Angel told herself she hadn't taken extra time with make-up she didn't usually wear, but she had. The clothes she selected today were ones she felt good in, to boost her morale, but hotter than anything a librarian would wear. She left her hair down and cascading in a way Josiah liked. When she looked in the mirror, she practiced a calm self-assurance she was far from feeling and lifted her chin with a hint of defiance that was new.

She'd had her first fling, an encounter so romantic, she still wondered if she'd dreamed parts of it. It was only a hook-up to him. The Josiah she knew might be caring and sweet, but Kaane Scott was not, according to the stories she'd read.

As her friends told her, you never forget your first. In her case, he might be her first and her last and her only, but she wasn't going to think about that. She'd be cool, together and nonchalant. He was never going to know how much his casualness hurt her.

She punched in the code at the gate, wondering if it would work. If he sought to avoid her, the easiest way was to change the numbers. It swung open like a yawning entrance to the great unknown. She drove through slower than her norm, gathering the thoughts she believed she had together but clearly didn't. When she parked at the barn, she sucked in a breath and forced herself to hold it until she got her racing heart under control. Only then did she step out of the car, keeping her eyes averted from the house. She was turning her key in the lock on the small barn door when she heard boots on the gravel.

"Angel, can we talk?"

Despite her resolve, her heart jumped in a painful beat at his voice. She had to be imagining the strain in it. If it bothered him that she was here, he might be preparing to evict her now.

"Angel, we need to talk." A hand wrapped around her arm with the brittle phrase, and she froze in place, only looking down at the fingers on the left hand, flatter than the right. Now she knew why. She'd read that online too. His fingers were broader where they pressed the strings on the neck of his guitar. Decades of music had changed him.

Her open scrutiny of his hand must have registered with him, because his fingers dropped away. She heard another crunch underfoot, and the heat of his body communicated itself to her without their touching. It would so easy to step back and let that unyielding form support her, but she was different now. One night had changed her, and she was determined it would be for the better.

"I've just come for some of my paintings and supplies. I'll be back for the rest in subsequent trips. If that's all right with you, that is." With a calm she wasn't feeling, she turned slowly, careful to keep her distance.

Josiah squinted bloodshot eyes at her. She would have liked to think he missed her, that her absence drove him as nuts as staying away had her, but his face held no expression. He could be on a partying bender. She'd read about those too. He could have other women dragging their fingers through his hair and setting it on end as it stood now. His fear of commitment was famous. Damn that skill of hers to research ten layers deeper than anyone else would readily go.

He shook his head then. "No, please continue to use the barn. I have no other need for it."

The clipped words dismissed it as unimportant. So that's how it was going to go. They had a business agreement and nothing more, like that one perfect night hadn't happened.

"Listen, Angel – " He stepped forward and put out a hand, and she moved back against the rough wood siding. The hand dropped almost immediately. His face remained empty of emotion, and she willed hers to be the same.

In the silence of their staring contest, a rock melody ring tone sounded from his pocket. He swore but didn't go for the phone. The song finally died off. His face didn't change, and Angel loathed the acceleration in her breathing that watching him like this brought on.

The tone sounded again, and as if its second pass added urgency, it seemed louder and more insistent. Cursing once in a harsh tone, he yanked the cell out of his pocket. "Not now."

He shoved it back, stretching the denim in a way that reminded her what aroused Josiah looked like. He didn't look that way now, and despite her better judgment, she slumped a little.

"Angel, we have to talk." His words were quieter. His face fell into sadder lines, and she nearly caved before remembering he had used her. That little voice prompting the memory that she'd used him too wasn't easy to stifle.

The sound of a revving engine cut across the stillness. The phone rang once more, and when he pulled it out this time, he looked down at it, his thumb poised over the face. Lifting it slowly to his ear as his empty gaze returned to her, he said, "I'm busy. Make it fast."

Angel had no problem hearing the booming voice on the other end. "I'm at the gate, and you are being an asshole. Either open up or give me the code. It wouldn't be the first time I've arrived when you've been indelicato with a bevy of women."

Josiah frowned and she did too. The revving sounded once more, and they both looked down the driveway at a dark form at the gate.

"What the fuck?" He looked at the gate, then back at Angel. "I haven't had a bevy of women around or any other woman at all since I met you." His face had changed, becoming something desperate.

She reminded herself of all the reasons why she needed to keep her cool. Her friends had been right. Be prepared to walk away with your head held high if it didn't turn out as you wanted. Don't compromise your values because in the end, that was all you had. And make him suffer. According to Roxy, that meant letting him believe whatever the outcome, you would handle it better than he did. Act as if you didn't care.

As if.

She raised a hand in a dismissive wave and turned back to the barn. As she did so, he grabbed her arm and spun her around. "Give me a chance. I'll get rid of him and then we can talk."

She tossed her hair over her shoulder in a way she'd seen movie stars use and shrugged with what she hoped was an adequate amount of boredom. "You have a visitor, and it's impolite to keep him waiting. As to the bevies, that does not matter to me."

He continued to watch her, and his face became unreadable once more as he dropped her arm. The revving sound magnified as he lifted the phone to his ear. He repeated a string of numbers, the same ones she'd used moments ago, as she turned for the studio. He said nothing as she slipped inside and shut the door behind her with a resounding click.

>>>>>

Of all the fucking stupid moments for Rodney to arrive. His sense of timing could not be worse. His wording upon his arrival, dangerous. And Kaane knew the moment the man laid eyes on Angel, he'd know. How could he not?

The sound of the motorcycle as it scattered gravel coming up the driveway drowned out his thoughts. The bike came to a stop without a skid where Kaane stood. The engine died, and the kickstand came down under a dusty boot.

Rodney didn't remove his sunglasses, the large frames dwarfed by his larger face. He lifted off his helmet and made a slow examination of the house and yard, his eyes resting last on Angel's car. At that precise moment, the woman came out of the barn with a large canvas in each hand and stopped when she caught sight of him.

A slow grin came to the big man's face as he said, "Well, now that I can understand."

Kaane didn't think he understood anything, and he was about to point this out when Angel propped her paintings against her car and came across the space between them with interest in her gaze. Was that bounce in her step new? She eyed Rodney with too much curiosity for Kaane's liking.

Rodney rose off the bike, his eyes directed at Angel. His glasses landed on his shiny dome of a head and he met her part way, his hand extended and wearing that shitty engaging grin. Angel's face lit up in a way Kaane hated as she took his hand. Hers looked too delicate to be in Rod-man's big paw, though Kaane knew that hand could be as gentle as a baby's when he played a riff.

"Rodney Moukou, at your service, ma'am."

He bowed, he fucking bowed over their joined fingers, and Kaane wanted to kick him in his leather-covered ass. Angel's smile widened and her eyes flicked over him in open examination. "Oh my, I love your ink. Tell me, did it hurt when you got it?"

The booming laugh was as hearty as it always was, and Angel's appreciative giggle made Kaane close his hands into fists. It wouldn't be the first time he'd come to blows with Rod-man, but it would be the first time over a woman.

"You are a breath of spring. What's your name, little one?" Rodney pulled her hand into the crook of his arm and turned them to the house, giving Kaane a knowing wink as he bent his head down to catch Angel's response. They proceeded up the stairs to the porch, already in deep conversation.

He had never been jealous of Rodney, not when the women who swarmed them like flies to their lightbulbs choose one man over the other. Not when Rod-man earned a Grammy for his songwriting skills in a major movie and Kaane was overlooked. Not when the critics weren't kind and said Rodney was the real voice behind the band's music, even as Kaane rightfully earned the credit.

But he sure as hell was jealous now. He took the steps two at a time to follow before Rodney had a chance to get Angel under his skin.

"But this is incredible art. How long did this one take?"

Angel's finger traced a dragon up Rodney's right arm. His bare right arm, because damned if he didn't have a cut-off t-shirt under his leather. The man drove a motorcycle in the damp cold without a jacket, and Kaane sincerely hoped it killed him. He was seeing red and hearing nothing but white noise, so he had no idea how Rodney answered.

Then the big man did the unthinkable. He lifted Angel's hand to his lips and he kissed the back of it. She blushed, a beautiful sight, except Kaane only wanted her blushing for him.

"Don't you have to be going, Angel? You were going to clean out your supplies."

Kaane hated the harsh tone in his voice, but he couldn't help it. Angel looked at Rodney with too much interest for his peace of mind and damn it, yes, he was overcome with jealousy.

Rodney's single word of warning rumbled out. "Dude," he said, with enough meaning in that tone to fuel a thousand miles of travel. But Kaane ignored him. His focus, his only focus, was on Angel.

She raised her eyes to his. He caught the stricken expression as it flashed across her face for a moment. Then it was gone, and in its place was a haughty maturity he hated to see. It was as if the light of joy went out in her eyes. She gave Rodney a polite goodbye, spun on her heels, and marched out the door without another word.

His visitor didn't say anything either, and Kaane didn't feel the need to break their silence. A few minutes later, Kaane heard her engine starting and the jangle of gravel as she accelerated down the driveway. As the sound faded away, Kaane searched his memory for a single time in his life when he'd fucked up so badly, and he couldn't think of one. When the other man in the room cleared his throat, Kaane looked up to find Rodney shaking his head as if sorely disappointed.

"Dude, that is no way to treat your muse, not if you want her to grace you with her wisdom."

As if he fucking well didn't know that.

>>>>>

She drove as fast as she could until she was sure no one had followed her. Proud of herself for not weeping outright, she sniffed and made it to the crossroads where Roxy's restaurant stood. Her friend's SUV was parked in the back lot and she pulled in next to it. That was as far as she got. She sat there, seeing nothing and wondering where things had gone so wrong.

Was it wrong to want what her friends had, a relationship loving and perfect even in its imperfection? Was she crazy for thinking the media misunderstood Kaane and that obviously, Josiah was sweet? Was it so unlikely that a rock star could care about someone like her, a lowly librarian with artistic aspirations?

Apparently, the answer to all those questions was yes.

"Do you want to come in? I have a sauce at a delicate point." Roxy held the screen door open with her hip, her hands busy whisking something in a pan. Beyond her, Angel could see forms moving around in the kitchen. She wasn't ready to face anyone she didn't know, not yet, so she shook her head.

Roxy turned back inside saying something, and a young woman appeared to take the pan and whisk out of her hands. The screen fell shut as she marched to the car, opened the passenger door, and slid in. One look at Angel's face must have told her everything she needed to know.

"That fuckwad. I am going to mince his dick. Then I'm going to filet Mac's ass for bringing him to the neighborhood."

Her face was thunderous and Angel had no doubt she meant every word. She appreciated the protectiveness, but she shook her head to stave off her friend's continuing rant.

"It's my fault as much as his, Rox. I wasn't clear on who I was or what I needed. I can't expect him to read my mind."

Her friend quieted and gave her an assessing look. "Should I get ice cream?"

Despite the tears that threatened to overflow unchecked, Angel chuckled. "I don't think this will be solved with ice cream or wine, but thank you for the offer." She sniffed and raised her chin, willing her tears to go away.

"What happened?"

Angel gave her the blow by blow, and other than a couple of muttered curses at key points, Roxy stayed silent. At the end of the story, she nodded. "Rodney is a force of nature, and two more different men would be hard to find. Kaane and Rod-man have been together in the band almost since the beginning. They co-write songs and do the arranging and from what I've heard, are the primary ones women throw their panties at during concerts."

Even if the thought made her blanch, Angel couldn't resist. "Women really do that? Like off their bodies?"

Roxy gave an apologetic grin and nodded. "Sometimes. Celebrity, the kind they have, makes it hard for them to be humble. Kaane has had a problem with that for a long time. His family expected something different from him. He pushed against the family expectations and took off for LA, where he and Mac met when they were both unknowns. They crashed at a little apartment a group of them shared to save money. From what I'd heard, they shared other things too."

Angel had no problem figuring out what Roxy meant by that. "But I thought you said Kaane and Rodney are different."

Her friend nodded. "They are. Rodney was a Rhodes scholar in something esoteric like Buddhist philosophy or Eastern religions. Kaane struggled to finish high school. Or perhaps that's not the right word. He wasn't interested in book learning so much as music. But you can't write the kinds of songs he does without a heavy dose of the smarts, so I bet if you dig deep enough, you'll find a closet philosopher there too."

Angel could see that. Josiah's angle on life fascinated her, from his statement that what goes around comes around to his steadfast belief that karma existed in every capacity of actions. It didn't mesh with what she'd read in her research. That Kaane lived life on the edge and didn't care about the consequences.

"Josiah's like that," she said, aware she was thinking out loud but unable to stop the flow of words. "It's how he goes from Josiah to Kaane that I don't understand."

Roxy nodded, turning to face the restaurant's back door with a contemplative look. "I wasn't completely open with you when you asked about why Mac and I haven't gotten married. He asks me. Boy, does he ask me. Some of the most imaginative proposals and the most romantic. He's supportive and a great cheerleader of my work and urges me to try new things all the time." She fell silent, staring at the dumpster as if seeking words there.

Angel put a hand on her arm, and Roxy turned back to her. "So why don't you say yes?"

Her friend gulped and shook her head. "It's crazy, really. I know he loves me like there's no tomorrow. On an intellectual level, I know this. But it's in here, where I read things and they hurt, that I can't resolve things." She touched her chef's coat above her heart, and Angel tightened her grip in support. "I guess part of me, that part hidden way down deep inside, is afraid that someday, he'll wake up and realize he's with this insecure girl who didn't question and didn't fight for him when she should have."

Roxy laid a hand over Angel's and squeezed. "Here's what I'm trying to say. You might want to look around, check out the world a bit, and explore things, now that you've spread your wings, so to speak. You could find other men that are more to your liking. More your type."

"But I'm not even sure what my type is."

Roxy gave a small smile. "Oh, you'll know. Like I knew. It's Mac or nothing for me, not that I haven't sampled some haute cuisine along the way. It was Mac at the beginning, and when we found each other again, I knew for sure. But there's still that little part of me that doubts he can possibly feel as much for me as I do for him."

Since Roxy LaFollette was one of the most self-assured women Angel knew, she had a problem believing this. And she herself was nowhere as courageous. She was the timid one, the librarian who would rather research and read about life than experience it, the artist who didn't believe in her own possibility of success. If Roxy couldn't handle this, how could she?

"Give it time. Wait for a sign that makes sense to you. Try things out and embrace the world, even other men. If Kaane-slash-Josiah is the one, fate will take care of things. Destiny is a bitch, but she's still our bitch."

It made sense. She looked at her friend, taking in the caring face with its twinkle of humor in her eyes. Shrugging, she sighed. "What do I do now?"

Angel squirmed under Roxy's examination for what felted like minutes, long enough for Angel to think she wasn't going to say anything. Finally, she nodded. Her voice was a whisper when she said, "Fight for what you want, Evangeline. Never give up if it's what you believe in. If you want Josiah, fight for him."

Chapter 21

"She is a beautiful woman. I can see why she's become your muse. Her inspiration is phenomenal."

Except Kaane had broken the code, wrenched the taboo to pieces, and now had to pay the price. And he couldn't tell Rodney about it.

His friend continued, "And of course, your relationship is strictly platonic since she is your muse."

Trust Rod-man to see through the haze to the core of his problems. Kaane said nothing, hoping the conversation would veer off in another direction.

"You are not having sex with her, are you?"

Rodney's troubled question hung in the air as Kaane sorted through the lyrics and scores on the piano's lid. Finding the sheets he needed, he whirled and waved the pages.

"I've got some good shit to show you. Really good, I think."

Rodney's barrel forearms looked particularly threatening, crossed at his chest in a way that drew attention to fierce tribal ink. "I will overlook your silence in response to my question, because I believe that is my answer. It is not the answer I had hoped to hear. And why do I think there is an 'except' after your last sentence?"

Kaane stopped waving, extending the pages instead. "Take a look. You tell me."

Advancing a pace, the big man took the paper and held the print to the light coming in the windows. He patted a pocket of his black leather vest and with gentle fingers, produced a pair of reading glasses. With them perched on his nose, he nodded, humming along softly with the notes on the page.

Kaane couldn't stand to watch, his nerves getting the better of him. He plopped down on the bench and ran his fingers over the piano keys in a random melody.

"Stop. You know I need to concentrate," Rodney said, his head nodding in a beat that approximated the song he studied.

Jumping up from the piano, Kaane marched over to the poster in its place of honor. He picked it up, fingering the spot that was becoming worn with his frequent fondling, the smear of paint on Angel's cheek. The cardboard was rough compared to the real skin on her cheek, the face he had spent hours caressing.

Except he'd ruined it. He sent her away with harsh words as if nothing mattered. Having her as his idealistic inspiration was one thing. Holding her flesh and heat in his arms, levitating to another atmosphere, was something else altogether.

Humming ceased behind him, as the cultured voice so out of place with the vision of the man said, "Ah, I understand."

He spun with the cardboard gripped in his fingers. "What do you think you understand?"

Rodney took off the glasses and examined Kaane with a frown. "You are sleeping with her. You know that this breaks the rules. The next time you attempt to write with her in mind, nothing will come."

"No, no, that won't happen. And I'm not sleeping with her. We took a shot at something and it didn't work out and now we're back to the way things were." Even he didn't believe the bullshit coming out of his mouth as he all but yelled the words.

"Prove it," the big man said, tilting the pages back in Kaane's direction. "Sit down and write something I haven't seen, right in front of me." He crossed to examine a set of watercolors on the music room's wall. "These are hers too? A talented woman."

Kaane bit off the curse he was about to scream. His eyes flicked to the painting that had become his favorite, the landscape with a single splash of color against an otherwise faded background, like an old photograph. He wasn't sure why it drew him in, other than the spark of light was like emerging hope in an otherwise dreary life. Kind of like him until Angel appeared.

Rodney must have followed his stare. He stepped forward and leaned into the picture, examining the signature before moving back and taking in the scene. He set his chin in a big hand and tilted his head, first one way and then the other. His gaze tracked back to Kaane, and he said, "I see."

"Will you stop saying shit like that? What the hell do you think you see? There is nothing to see. I like her work. I'm helping out a young artist, that's all." When Kaane stopped shouting, the room held an echoing remnant of his frustration.

Rodney simply chuckled with a knowing smile. "I'll be staying for a while to make sure you continue on track and keep producing. Of course, the band won't be recording this or what I suspect comes out of you next, but I think it bodes well for your new direction, my man."

"There is no new direction. We'll make this work, like we always do. Rebellion is due for a new sound anyway." Kaane stomped out of the room, but not fast enough to avoid the rumbling laugh of the man behind him. It almost made him turn again. He would welcome a few fists and a good wrestle even though he knew he'd lose, just to burn off the steam. But he also knew the truth.

Rodney was right.

Hours later, Kaane pounded his forehead on his braced arms, wishing he could turn back time. Take back the words he'd spewed at Angel. Restore her as his muse, back a week or more. But that would mean he'd have to skip the night of heaven in her arms.

What was it about her that was so special? It was like sex with her was transforming, like it was a brand-new experience. He wouldn't use the words Rodney had to describe it, a parting shot as he exited the music room.

"You're falling in love with her, my man."

But Kaane Scott didn't do love.

And yet he could not explain it. It was more than lust, though there was plenty of that. The thought of Angel's body under his hands hardened him even now, and he remembered every sigh, every moan, every throbbing moment of being with her, on her, in her. The look of surprised wonder on her face as she peaked was something he'd never forget. It was as if their shared experience brought something new to her too.

At least the words flowed again. Under Rodney's incessant needling, Kaane had ripped out stanzas and a refrain to a new song, so brutally honest and bone chilling in what it said that he couldn't second guess himself. When his friend read the verses, he gave that wise-ass smile again and had to comment. "This makes sense, given your circumstances."

Kaane was tempted to deck him. The only thing holding him back was the knowledge that Rodney would ward him off without any effort at the end of one well-muscled arm. He'd probably laugh his ass off too.

He lifted his head and glanced at the cell phone. He'd been tempted all afternoon to call Angel and beg her forgiveness. His stupidity seemed to grow exponentially with each passing hour. How long he'd spent gazing out the window to the place where she parked by her studio, he had no clue. When he returned to his sorry attempts at another song, the pages stayed stubbornly blank, as blank as his mind felt without the guidance only Angel could provide.

Snatching up the phone, he hit her speed dial number. He had no clue what he would say if she answered. It would be a small mercy if it went to voicemail. Then he could hear her voice but hang up without speaking. She'd never know what he was thinking.

"Hello?" The breathy tone held cautious expectation. She had to know it was him.

Pounding a fist on his head, he realized that of course she would know. Caller id. She knew his number. Light breathing punctuated the silence on the other end as she waited while he stumbled. It took him too long to collect himself, while she seemed to have no problem keeping things together.

"Josiah? Or should I call you Kaane? Is there something you need?"

She sounded so self-assured, as if she was already moving on from their brief affair. Her tone of boredom cut him deeper than anger or hurt would. He fumbled with the phone, nearly dropping it.

"Hey Angel. Sorry, I was having a problem with the phone." That sounded stupid, even to him. She didn't respond, so he rushed on.

"Listen, I would like you to come to dinner. That is, we would like you to come. Rodney and me. To dinner."

He'd always been smooth with the ladies, but whatever panache he might have deserted him now.

"Dinner?" She said the word as if the meal was a foreign concept to her.

"Yes, here."

It sounded like she placed her hand over her phone. A hint of a whisper sounded in the background before the hand moved and she was back on the line.

"What am I supposed to call you now?" Suspicion colored her words, and he couldn't blame her.

He was tempted to say she could call him whatever she wanted, as long as she came over. She could call him every rotten name in the book.

"You can call me Josiah. I like that you do. It feels more intimate."

Her continued silence told him that was the wrong thing to say. He rushed into the disaster, hoping to salvage something.

"So, about dinner. Rodney is fascinated by your art, and he'd like to get to know you better. He's not as scary as he looks. I think you'd enjoy talking with him."

The purr of words on the other end surprised him when they came.

"I don't think Rodney is scary. In fact, I find him fascinating. I would enjoy a longer conversation with him."

But she obviously didn't want to talk to Kaane.

She said, "What time would this dinner take place?"

Kaane did a quick mental search of the bare refrigerator and calculated the time it would take to pay Roxy's grocery store a visit. "Does six work for you?"

She agreed and hung up before he could say anything more.

Chapter 22

"I'm so glad you decided to join us, Angel. You have no idea how happy it makes me."

Kaane stood on the porch as she approached, making Angel glad she'd taken the time for hair and make-up. Just like a Hollywood performer, and in some ways, she kind of felt like this was an act. She didn't feel brave or anywhere nearly as together as her friends assured her she looked.

Fight for what she believed in, Roxy had counseled. Angel believed in Josiah, or rather, she believed she and Josiah deserved a chance to see how they worked out. Rodney or not, she was going to make sure she and Josiah had the beginnings of that chance tonight.

As if her thought of him conjured him up, the big man appeared at Josiah's shoulder and grinned at her. He walked down the steps nimbly for a man of his size and extended a hand to Angel. When she placed hers in his larger palm and expected him to shake it, he surprised her by lifting it and placing a soft kiss on the back. Behind him, she heard what sounded like a snarl from Josiah.

"You look quite lovely, my dear. I have to admit, if I had known Kaane was hiding such a gorgeous muse, I would have claimed feeling lost in a creative desert as well and thrown myself at your feet in parched thirst." He pressed another kiss to her hand.

She glanced up at Josiah from under her eyelashes, pleased to see tight lines of tension around eyes hidden by partially closed lids. He spun and went inside, not waiting for them.

Rodney leaned in and whispered, "Ignore him. He has no manners. That southern charm upbringing was lost on him. He never knew how to treat a lady."

Intrigued, Angel looked up at him. "Southern charm? He has no accent. Where is he from?"

"He hasn't told you? He came from a wealthy family in Charleston, South Carolina. He is the classic middle child, with a brother on each side of him in age. Ergo, the need to be noticed. This was before I met him, but I understand his accent was pronounced, until a producer turned him down because he sounded too regional. He worked hard to rid himself of it."

"I couldn't tell, and obviously, he didn't share anything with me. He doesn't like to talk about himself much." Her eyes traveled around the room they'd entered, seeking out the subject of their musings. His back retreated under the kitchen arch as if he knew he was the subject of scrutiny.

Rodney stopped and looked down at her with surprised humor on his face. "Really? That is most interesting. You see, Kaane loves to talk about himself, and it's rare he doesn't give someone the full rundown within days of meeting them. But of course, you're different. You're his muse."

Angel disentangled her arm and stepped back. Part of her wanted to follow Josiah, but she wasn't sure what to say. Could she win a battle for him, or was she fooling herself? And even if she did want to fight, did he? His absence with a dismissive greeting only pointed her back to Rodney.

She turned to find the big man watching her with keen interest. As he had before, his arms were bare and his clothes did nothing to disguise his muscular build and array of tats. But despite his good looks and his obvious interest in her, Angel didn't feel the same stirring of warmth that even thinking Josiah's name brought her. Rodney felt more like a friend, kind of like one of the girl tribe's men, an idea that strengthened her resolve.

Angel moved to the cushioned chair near the fireplace, making it clear she was happy sitting alone. She settled herself with as much grace as she could muster, and made sure the skirt rode up her thigh just enough to make a good impression. She glanced in the direction of the kitchen and let the fabric pull a little higher.

"Ah yes, our Kaane is in deep trouble, is he not, little one?"

Angel shot Rodney an innocent expression. "What do you mean?" Her eyes drifted back to the kitchen, where glass crashed and curses could be heard.

Rodney chuckled more deeply as he leaned on the fireplace mantle. "You are his muse, and as such, taboo. But that didn't make any difference, did it?"

"Tell me about this taboo. And I don't know how I can be his muse. We're friends, that's all." Though there was that whole night of amazing sex she couldn't wait to experience again.

"From what little he tells me, you two have shared many stories and he respects you. Yes, he's in over his head, and so, I am guessing, are you."

Another crash sounded from the kitchen, this one lasting longer and followed by silence. Angel half-rose from her seat, but Rodney waved her back. He hadn't moved away from the fireplace, but his eyes stayed on the arch. By the smile on his face, she thought he was enjoying himself.

Josiah appeared, mopping at a green stain smeared across his white shirt. Angel appreciated the fitted cut of the fabric, accenting his lean body and making his shoulders seem broader. The expression of marked disgust on his face was so comical, she grinned.

"Dinner will be delayed," he said.

"May we inquire as to what happened?" The cultured tone and formal words were out of keeping with his appearance, but she had to give Rodney credit. As if he knew exactly what would needle his friend the most, he chuckled on the end of the question.

Josiah's growl of frustration matched the twisted scowl on his face. "I dropped something."

"Something green. We can see that. Would you like assistance so that we can eat the remainder of the meal?"

"I dropped everything," Josiah muttered, loud enough for them to hear but in obvious disgust. He looked anywhere in the room but at her.

"Everything, as in the complete meal?" She had no problem reading disbelief in Rodney's tone, but it didn't matter. Josiah's inattention did, and despite her best efforts to look seductive and worldly, Angel feared she was failing in her role. Rodney stepped forward, but Josiah raised a warning hand, his eyes darting to Angel.

It was as if he just noticed her pose. His eyes widened and his nostrils flared, and Angel felt her heart hammer in response to the possessiveness in his expression. Then, as quickly as it flared, the light extinguished. It didn't stop him from flicking a blanket off the back of the couch and throwing it over her lap.

>>>>>

He thought a vein would burst in his skull. The pounding of his blood rang louder and beat harder than any percussionist's riff, and no amount of deep breathing would change it. As it was, Kaane could barely draw air.

That creamy thigh, with the blue bit of nothing above it only accenting skin he knew was even softer than it looked. His fingertips tingled with the memory of tracing that flow of warmth like the perfectly executed scale. Match that with the sultry smile and confident tilt to her head, and there was no doubt in his mind. Angel was daring him to lose his cool, and damned if he wasn't about to do it.

When the blanket landed in her lap, he couldn't keep the snarl out of his voice. "You must be cold."

She shook her head, eyes a little wider.

"Well, I guess I will need to ride to the rescue yet again. Pardon me, my dear. I have been enjoying our lovely conversation, and I look forward to continuing it very soon."

Kaane knew Rodney accentuated the class and education he had by the bucket load to aggravate him. Rodney leaned over Angel and took her hand in his. He said something in a voice too low for Kaane to understand, but he didn't need to hear the words to know their intention. Angel's cheeks colored in a warm blush and her lips opened in a perfect circle of surprise. Her eyes darted to Kaane's and back to Rodney in a nervous flicker. When the big man pressed a kiss to her temple, Kaane considered decking him despite their obvious size difference.

Rodney turned and walked toward him, his eyes traveling over Kaane's face as if reading his anger and enjoying the hell out of it. When he was shoulder to shoulder, he leaned in slightly and shared his thoughts in a low whisper.

"I am going to procure us a replacement repast, and it may take me considerable time."

"Cut the crap with the twenty-dollar words and the Harvard accent, you asshole," Kaane said, but like Rodney, he kept his voice low.

"It's Oxford, not Harvard," Rodney replied, dropping the accent and the attitude. "I think I'll be gone for quite a while. I'll bring us something in, say, about three hours. That should give the lovely Ms. Reed ample time to put you out of your misery."

Kaane swung a fist in the man's direction, but he was already four paces back and laughing. Rodney turned to Angel and executed a perfect courtly bow and was out the front door before three more seconds had passed. The motorcycle's big engine caught on the first acceleration and the rumble faded away a moment later.

The bike and the man might be gone, but the rumble remained, only this time, it rose in Kaane's blood as he continued to stare at the woman who was doing her level best to drive him insane. The trouble was, she was succeeding. As if she knew exactly what kind of effect she was having on him, she leaned deeper into the chair and crossed her legs the other way. It drew his fresh attention to the flesh above boots that people would consider modest, but Kaane decided should be banned for what they could do to a certain artist's shapely legs.

"This dinner was a bad idea," he ground out, even as he knew it wasn't the dinner that was wrong. It was him.

Angel gave him a pout, which only drew his gaze to her full mouth. His lips had enjoyed that mouth for hours, and yet it hadn't been long enough. He craved it again, like he craved her moans of pleasure and the sounds she made when she came. Damn it all, he wanted her again, and he had no idea what the hell to do about it.

"You're taboo to me."

Her expression changed to a puzzled frown as she tilted her head. The view that provided of her neck, the place he wanted to bury his face, made him inhale on a sharp note. As if she heard him, her chest rose and fell in a deep sigh.

"I do not understand that, Josiah."

"Call me Kaane," he demanded.

"Josiah," she replied, with so much defiance, he stepped toward her. She had to understand. If they came together again, it would be as he was, a washed-up rocker who had squandered his one chance at the future. Ideas jumbled in his mind. Had he ruined his career by violating his muse, or had he screwed up his chance at personal happiness by alienating the one woman he cared about more than anything?

>>>>>

"Call me Kaane," he said, taking another step toward her. Angel lifted her chin in a fresh show of defiance and hoped she looked more confident than she felt. Her insides tumbled and the jerk of her heart had to be loud enough for him to hear.

Inhaling a long breath once more and making an effort to hold Josiah's gaze, she stood and let her fingers run down her body as if her palms were damp. Not a problem, since they were, and her nerves pulsed out of control, but if she wanted the man, she had to play the part until he read between the lines of her act.

"Josiah, I do not understand this taboo nonsense. I also don't understand how I can be your muse. Muses are stunning, perfect creatures whose intention is to drive their creatives crazy. I am none of those things."

Would batting her eyelashes be too much? How did women flirt without making themselves into fools? She had no clue.

His eyes widened and a wild expression matched his clenching fists. It had to be anger, because lust couldn't be in the picture. Josiah worshipped her, and her heart hammered under that pressure.

"It's Kaane. Kaane. Kaane." With each insistent throb of his name, he took a pace closer, until his chest almost touched hers. The color in his eyes had all but disappeared in his intense stare, and his nostrils flared with rapid breaths. Angel felt her own rapid breathing match his, and she couldn't look away from the intensity in his glare, not if her life depended on it.

She huffed out a sigh of mock-resignation, difficult when blood thrummed in her ears. "Fine, Kaane, if you insist."

He nodded, but narrowed his eyes when she stepped into him instead of away. She prayed she wasn't misreading everything she thought she knew about him when she put a hand on his chest. His heart hammered under her palm in an echo of hers, and despite her intention to make this a seduction, she bit her bottom lip in indecision.

Did he have a right to know he'd been her first? Would that change things between them, if he knew? As Roxy would say, time to sharpen her knives and find out.

"I have to thank you, Kaane. You made everything special, so very special, and I'll never forget it." She gulped in air, hating the wispy breathlessness of her tone.

His hand came up to cover hers. "Why does that sound like you're saying goodbye?" Cool distance chilled his words, a sharp contrast to the tight hold he had on her fingers.

She shrugged again, wishing she could look away from his eyes. "It's only goodbye if you say so. It's completely within your power to maintain our friendship. There's only one condition."

"What?" The bite of the single word came in tempo with the stab of his heart under her hand.

"Don't put me on a pedestal," she said, tapping her index finger against his chest to accent each word in the statement.

He threw her grip away like it burned him and spun in two complete circles, moving back with each step. His hands flayed to the side until his arms extended, and his head leaned back, eyes closed, when he finally faced her again. The pose was one he used on stage, one she saw in a video she couldn't help watching now that she knew who he really was.

"Evangeline, no. You don't understand. I have already broken the rules with you, and it might have cost me my life. That taboo, it changes everything." He didn't open his eyes, his voice full of anguish.

"You're right, I don't understand, so why don't you explain it to me?"

Kaane didn't respond, staying in his pose for longer as she ran out of patience. He wasn't the only one with issues here. Angel's anger rose with each passing second. If he realized how far off that summit she'd fallen, maybe that would be the shove back into bed he needed.

Stepping in close again, she wrapped her arms around his neck and forced his head down. His eyes popped open and landed on her face in surprise. If he needed a shock to make him listen, she had one to give him.

"Thank you, Kaane, for being my first. You made it special, memorable, and something I will always treasure." When his mouth sagged at her words, she took advantage of it and pressed her lips to his.

The kiss turned hot the second flesh touched. Without warning, his arms locked around her and his head angled, deepening the kiss with a tortured groan. She smiled against his mouth. She did that to him. Little Angel Reed could take down the famous rock star who'd probably had hundreds of women before her, and she didn't even know what she was doing.

In the next moment, she forgot to think. Glee faded away to hunger, sharp and raw and more real than anything she could have imagined. He might want her to call him by his stage name, but there was nothing make-believe about the effect they had on each other. But even as he moaned again, his arms began to fall away from her.

Regret filling his face as he moved back, palms raised to ward her off. And that was all it took, because she'd had enough. Angel lifted her fingers to the top button of her blouse, proud of her hands for not shaking. She popped it open, dropped to the next one, and got exactly the response she wanted. The regret fled Kaane's face and a hungry expression replaced it.

"Stop." He ground the words out like they strangled him.

Her smile widened. Maybe, just maybe, she could be good at this seduction thing. "No," she said, and reached the next button.

His hands grabbed out. Was it bad of her to be happy they shook as they closed over hers? "Stop," he said again, but there was less conviction in the command this time.

Wiggling her fingers free proved to be remarkably easy. By the time she had the next button undone, his mouth dropped open and his breaths came in audible heaves.

"You are my muse," he whispered, though whether it was to remind her or himself, she wasn't sure. Her blood pounded south and pooled between her legs at the hunger in his gaze. She gulped, trying to stymy the nervous giggles that threatened to turn her seduction into an abbreviated joke.

His hands grabbed for hers again, but this time, he wrapped them around her back and held them at the base of her spine. She was ready for the heat, the whirl of feelings and the rapid acceleration of passion, the pulse of throbbing heat pressing into her belly. When his mouth settled over hers, the surprising gentleness in his kiss made her quiver with unending need.

"You make me want to do things, things that take a long time, hours or days." Reverence in his whispered words strengthened the shivers.

This was what she wanted, what she needed. Kaane, tracing his lips down her neck, interspersing little love bites with soft kisses and licks of her skin. When he ground his hips against hers, she felt every hard inch of him pressing into her, and her last sane thought was that she had succeeded. The glimmer of satisfaction left her on a low moan that matched his growl in desperation and hunger.

They were moving, though where they were going wasn't something she could track, not when Kaane kissed her like she was a precious treat and he was a starving man. She had done this to him. The knowledge made her bold, and when his mouth was again over hers, she reached up and nipped at his lower lip, loving the gasp of surprise he gave.

"What are you doing to me?" Wonder and confusion filled his tone. He lifted his head and stared down at her, a puzzled expression on his face. "What did you say before?"

Angel shook her head, not sure of why he was talking when she was a walking ball of lust ready to explode. Her nipples were sharp points pressing into his chest, and if that didn't communicate what she wanted, she made sure her lower half rubbed against him until he groaned again.

"I want to take this slow, to savor you, but I don't think I can do that," he said, strain making the words clipped.

"What if I don't want slow?"

His eyes blazed at that, and he let go of her hands. His fingers went to the next button on her shirt, closed over the edges, and ripped downward. He pushed her bra down and her breasts fell free into his hands, and he lowered his head to lick at one nipple before pulling it into his mouth. Every hair on her body stood up with the frisson of nerves, every pulse running to her core and heating up her apex until she cried out from the simple pleasure of it.

"Yes, like this. I want to feel you come like this, in my arms, raw and needy and powerful." He muttered the words as his mouth traveled to the other breast, giving it the same attention. One hand crept down and gathered her skirt, while the other wove into her hair and pressed her face against his shoulder. A finger surged against her undies in a way that made her chant, though she had no idea what she was saying. When he pushed the fabric to the side and his fingers entered her with his own groan, her words turned into a beg.

Whether she called him Josiah or Kaane, she wasn't sure. Whatever she said seemed to flame him hotter, and his palm ground against her in the spot that was sensitive beyond pleasure, harder, faster, until she cried out as a fire consumed her and made everything pitch into a bright, burning light. He didn't stop the onslaught until she sagged in his arms, unable to feel her legs and unable to hold on to him with arms as useless as noodles.

He buried his face in her hair, and she felt him shake. He whispered words she couldn't make out, and he shook his head as the trembling continued. Finally, something he said formed into real words.

"I am going to hell."

She pushed back and lifted his chin so that he couldn't help but meet her eyes. Every ounce of sincerity she possessed knew was in her response as she linked their fingers tightly. "No you aren't, not when you transport me to heaven."

He gave a sad half-smile and kissed her knuckles one by one, punctuating his words. "If I must dance with the devil for the rest of my life, this is worth it, Angel."

She reached behind her, unhooking her bra and letting the blue lace fall to the floor. Then she extended her hands to him, and as if he was in a trance, his came up slowly to grasp them. Tilting her head, she recognized the hunger in his eyes as much as the regret. She craved the first and wished to banish the second.

"Come, Josiah." She took a step back toward his bedroom, and he followed. "Let's visit heaven together."

>>>>>

The ringing in his ears didn't quit for so long, he wondered if the years of blasting percussion and screeching guitar chords had finally caught up with him. His hearing finally caved under the never-ending onslaught of noise. That idea should upset him, but he felt immeasurable peace.

Hair, soft and gentle as the spring breeze, tickled his nose. The pleasurable weight of female stretched over his body, legs wrapped around his thighs on the sides and wonderful orbs pressed against his chest. His brain was too scrambled to process thoughts. All he could do was feel, and the strength of those emotions scared the hell out of him.

Careful not to wake her, Kaane shifted Angel to the side, sliding out of her with more regret than he thought was possible. He didn't want to feel like moving away from her set him on a path to sure destruction. At a minimum, it would mean he could never rest in those arms, feeling that rapture, and know such deep wholeness again.

He threw the condom in the wastebasket with enough force to knock the can on its side. Avoiding his reflection in the mirror wouldn't make the pain recede. Combing his fingers through knots in his hair, ties that bound him to Angel in so many ways he was incapable of counting them, didn't bring order to his scattered ideas. When he stood still and stared at the tile floor long enough to send a shiver of cold over his bare skin, he looked up.

His face, haggard and creased past his years. His cheeks, sunken and cut as if he had lost a dozen pounds in the past few hours. His eyes, haunted, because he knew the truth, and he couldn't escape it.

Kaane Scott would never be able to write another song, and he was definitely going to hell for screwing his muse. But it had been so damned worth it.

The face in the mirror smiled, though Kaane wasn't sure what he felt on the inside. Wrapped around Angel, surging into her, swallowing her screams of pleasure and watching her face transform past its usual beauty to something otherworldly emptied his mind. No other woman had ever been like that for him. The only thing that came close was when he was one with the music, his music, the music he would never compose again.

The reflected face drooped into a deep frown. Something nagged him, something he knew he should remember. Angel, when she explained things before – well, before the last few hours. Their murmurs since then had been in turns playful, hot, and moaning. And frankly, once that first button popped open and she gave him that challenging smile with a pert lift of her chin, his big brain stopped processing anything that made sense. He was one walking bass line of heat and his little brain swelled to emphasize the point.

He looked down at himself. "Really? Even now? We have to figure things out."

His little brain twitched, probably hoping he'd forget what he needed to think about. What a dick.

It was there, the words hovering like a backstage pit viper hoping to have her way with him as soon as the last cheers of the crowd died off. There had been plenty of them over the years, the disciples, the rabid groupies, the nutcases. Plenty of others who wanted a piece of him too, from the paparazzi to the unethical managers to the up-and-comers who saw him as a meal ticket, not a person.

But Angel was different. She honestly had no idea who he was until he told her, and then she didn't even realize the importance of it. She looked at him with sunshine in her eyes, and that shining light inspired him to be better. A productive songwriter. A better man. A good person.

What had she said? Something that struck terror in his heart even as it made him swell with pride. Angel was an angel, and she'd chosen him.

"The bed is cold without you in it."

His gaze snapped up to take in the sight in the mirror. Angel lazed against the doorway, her hair tangled from his frantic hands and her lips swollen from his kisses. Her nipples shown like rubies from their long hours of lovemaking, and her lush curves called to his tingling fingertips. Her skin would be warm and soft, so very soft. He couldn't help but feel that same surge of unrestrained need, like the first set of notes when he debuted a new tune.

First.

His heart began to pound hard as stars appeared at the edges of his field of vision. He put out a flaying hand and gripped the lip of the counter until it hurt.

Her first.

"Josiah? What's wrong? You look like you're going to be sick." Angel's reflection drew closer in the mirror and he put out his free hand to stop her. She did, but not without touching his back, sending a convulsion of nerves down his spine.

"You said I was your first." The words came out without any strength to them, and he might be hyperventilating. The shooting stars grew in number and he closed his other hand on the counter.

Angel linked her fingers in front of her and retreated to the doorway. She looked uncertain for a moment, then her chin lifted with a single abrupt nod.

"Your first what?" He bit out each word like a snap of fingers. Bile made the taste in his mouth rancid, but not as sickened as he felt about what he'd done.

Angel lifted a pale shoulder in a shrug, but she dropped her eyes. Her gaze fell on every surface of the room, landing last on the knotted condoms spewed across the floor from the upended can. Four of them, to be exact.

"Help me out here, please. What did you say? What did you mean?"

Her head tilted to one side and she ran a finger up and down the door jamb's molded surface. Like she'd run her fingers up and down him before guiding him into her core, the wet heat of it making his throat parched even now. Despite his need to know, his body seemed to draw closer to her like she was a magnet and he was raw iron.

Her gaze finally couldn't avoid his when he put a finger under her chin and guided it upwards. Myriad emotions shifted the blues from the clear tones of a shallow lake to the rough waves of violent ocean and back again. She swallowed, a motion he felt under his fingers. Defiance finally won out, and she tilted her chin up further out of his grasp.

"It doesn't matter, you know. Not anymore." She lifted a bare foot as if she planned to step back, but his hands closed on her upper arms and anchored her in front of him. Her eyes shifted to the mess on the floor, and she bit her lower lip.

That did crazy things to his blood, heating it without conscious thought. He shook his head, trying to clear it. She did say what he thought she said. He couldn't be wrong about it.

Shaking her a little to get her attention, he said, "I did hear you right. You said – " He stumbled to a stop and gulped for air. "You said I was your first. Your first lover?"

That defiant tilt again, as if daring him to make something out of this. His fingers loosened with shock, and Angel shrugged free of his hands and stepped back twice before turning for the bedroom. He followed a pace behind, fascinated by the idea that a woman this sexy could still be a virgin. His eyes locked on the shape of her delectable ass as she bent to retrieve her clothes.

"Angel, stop." She didn't, so he stepped closer and whispered, "Please."

She halted the frantic yanking up of panties but didn't look at him. He pulled even with her and put a hand on the bundle of clothes she mashed to her chest. Despite the seriousness of what he had to say, his body responded to the heaving breasts just below the layers of fabric. One tug, and he could have his hands there. His body twitched with the urge to do just that.

He closed his eyes and focused, drawing on every time he walked in front of an audience and felt unprepared, or every time he sat down in the studio and didn't know what would wail out of him next. He could do this. He could make it right between them, because her courage was much greater than his desperation.

"You should have told me," he said, fighting to keep his voice even.

"I did. I did tell you." Anger tinged her words with a venom he did not expect, forcing his eyes open and on her. He shook his head in slow passes, thinking back. He was certain he would have remembered something like that.

Angel resumed dressing with sharp movements that told him more than words how much this upset her. That was the last thing he intended, but he had no idea how to fix this. Kaane Scott, hell-on-wheels rocker with a history of sex with more women than he cared to count, had never slept with a virgin. He thought he would have been able to tell. She was as much his first as he was hers.

Delivery of her next words was muffled by the position she tied herself in to hook her bra. "I did tell you, Josiah. But that's right, I told Josiah. Foolish me. I thought I was going to give my virginity to a nice farmer who was a little shy and almost as inexperienced as me. I thought it would be sweet for both of us. Instead, it rocked me from head to toe and after that, who cared about my pre-sex status?" She jammed buttons into holes, the blouse crooked.

Kaane fought the urge to stop her hands and line things up properly, but by the look in her eyes, he doubted she'd take it well. He paced closer. Her eyes traveled up his body in a slow sweep, lingering where he hoped she'd notice his profound interest in her even as they argued.

"Angel, please, don't misunderstand me. I just – I didn't – I can't – " His words dropped off, because he had no idea what to say.

She zipped the skirt shut with a brutal pull that made it sound like fabric ripped with the effort. A sneer he'd never guess she had in her curled her lip. "Go ahead, Kaane. Say it. If you'd understood my status, you would have fallen all over yourself laughing. You might even accuse me of something, something like wanting to lose it to a rock star so I could sell it to the tabloids. Or maybe I'd sue you for rape. Well maybe I'd have laughed at you. Have you ever thought of that? The formerly great Kaane Scott, reduced to bedding virgins because women in the know won't have anything to do with him."

Her chest heaved with her tirade and her eyes snapped with fury, and damn, she was sexy as all hell. Odes to her glory would never do it justice. Despite a rising sense of ill-ease, Kaane had to admit Angel in a piss was a glorious sight. Wonder at it made him grin.

"Oh, now I'm funny? Is that what you think of me? Go ahead, laugh. I'm sure everyone will agree with you and think it's very funny." A hiccup punctuated her sentence.

Funny? Hardly. Another audible gulp came from her lips and he realized she was losing a battle with sobs as she raced out the bedroom door. He started to follow, then looked down at himself. Semi-erect, his little brain pointed at Angel's retreating back as if armed to follow. He glanced around the tousled bedroom, trying to locate his jeans. A hint of denim peeked out from under a corner of knotted blanket. He pulled them on as he headed down the hall.

"Are you sure you are able to drive?" The deep voice came from the kitchen, followed by a much smaller tone and a distinct sniff.

"Angel, you can't leave." Kaane rounded the opening and drew to a fast halt as he took in the sight of Rodney with an arm around Angel's shoulders. The man looked up with a grim expression. Angel didn't.

"I'll arrange for the rest of my things to be moved and I'll return the keys to the barn. And I'll send you a check for rent for the past few weeks. If it isn't enough, too bad."

She spun away from Rodney and out the door without ever meeting Kaane's gaze. He began to follow, but a large hand that could make a guitar weep wrapped around his arm tight enough to stop circulation. "Let her go."

Kaane tried to shake himself free, but Rodney wasn't budging. "I need to go after her and explain. I can't let her leave like this. She has to understand."

An ominous silence followed, and the grip didn't lessen. Kaane swung around, thinking fleetingly of landing a punch in his friend's face to encourage a release. One look at Rodney's expression was enough to convince him he'd end up beaten just enough to communicate the guitarist's anger.

"What did you say to her? She's crying but insists she's fine. She's leaving when I'm not sure it's safe for her to be driving, but she declines help. She says, and I'm quoting, she hopes you're satisfied, you asshole."

Angel never swore, which sharpened Kaane's focus. He twisted, still held in place, and stared out the window. He couldn't see the driveway, but he heard the gunned engine as the car raced down gravel. A distant pause, and then she was gone. He sagged into Rodney's firm grasp, no longer fighting it, and the hand immediately released him.

Kaane shook his head. "I fucked up, Rod-man, fucked up royally." Worse than that, he wasn't sure there was any way to fix it.

Chapter 23

Even if it wasn't clear to Kaane, Angel had no doubts. She needed to remove her things from the barn, and she couldn't risk seeing him again.

"Angel, are you there?"

She started, remembering the phone in her hand. "Yes, Tess, Sorry. Do you think I could borrow your delivery van to pick up the rest of my things? If I go back and forth with everything in my car, it will take too many trips. I don't want to risk running into him."

"I'll do you one better," Tess said. "I'll ask Powers to do it. He has a good reason to be out there. Plus, he's got a crew of people who can empty your studio in a flash." The phone fell silent, then she added, "Are you sure you want to do this?"

Angel closed her eyes, fighting back the tears as she said yes and hung up. Working at the gallery was a special form of hell today. She wanted to rip her exhibit off the wall and dump it in the trash, but she couldn't do it when customers might come in.

Her eyes darted to the clock on the computer tablet and her fingers tapped impatiently on the counter. Willing time to move faster, she looked up with relief when the opening of the door brought street noise with it.

"Welcome to Sierra Shining. We are a cooperative gallery of local artists. If you have any questions as you browse around, I'll be happy to answer them."

The woman gave her a distracted smile and a nod, shifting the large purse on her shoulder. Her partner, a man who didn't bother to acknowledge Angel's words, circled the room, examining works on the walls in rapid succession. When the woman followed, she lingered longer and seemed to read the artists' signatures on each one with care.

"Ah, here it is. Wow, no doubt, is there?" The woman leaned close, and Angel was pleased to see her interest lay in her own watercolors. Even if she now hated the subject, the quality of her work pleased her. She wanted to destroy them, but she couldn't bring herself to do sever her final link to a man who'd come to mean too much to her. Resignation made her head ache.

"What can you tell us about this artist?" The woman pointed at a picture of Kaane done in a wild combination of neon greens and yellows. In the picture, Angel had captured him laughing outrageously. Her memory of that expression alive on the man did messy things to her gut.

The man's tone was sharp when he barked out a repeat of the woman's request. "Is that a difficult question?"

Angel startled and rushed forward. "No, not at all. I'm sorry, I was just thinking about when I painted that. I'm Evangeline Reed." She extended her hand, and the man looked at it for a moment before taking it with sudden attention that made her uncomfortable.

"You're the artist? Tell me, who posed for you?" The woman stepped close with a sly smile and leaned into Angel's personal space, blocking any view of the man. Behind the woman, Angel heard a click. She tried to look around the human shield, but the woman moved to the side with her.

"So, did you see him often? Did he pose formally? How long did this take? Did you get to know him well?"

Angel shook her head, trying to figure out what the man was doing.

"Oh, so you did these from, what, a photo?"

Embarrassed and uncomfortable with the rapid-fire questions, Angel retreated. "Memory. I did them from memory."

The woman's partner gave a growl of disbelief. "Come on, she obviously won't share anything useful, probably just a groupie. At least we have that other confirmation he's in the area. Now we just need to find him."

The man was already hurrying for the door, glancing in both directions when he hit the sidewalk before heading to the right. The woman paused, her face sympathetic. "Sorry, he's on the hunt and he gets rude when he's like that. We're just trying to find Kaane Scott, you see. You know, him." She pointed to Angel's pictures on the wall.

Because the statement surprised her, Angel's question popped out without control. "Why?"

The woman paused mid-step and looked over her shoulder. "Well surely you know, since it's been all over the entertainment media. He's washed up. No new songs in ages, the band spread everywhere doing their own thing, and the man himself in hiding. The outlets are paying top dollar for news about his slide into the gutter. We're betting on drugged out and shacked up with a harem. I don't suppose you'll tell me where he is?" The predatory gleam in her eyes changed her appearance into a feral thing.

Angel back-stepped and shook her head. "No, sorry, I painted that from a picture I saw. The same with the others. Sorry."

Her face now a mask of disinterest, the woman hurried out after her companion, yelling before she even hit the sidewalk. Angel watched her race in the direction of the man. Her heart thudded at a quicker pace than normal.

If she'd needed any confirmation about how different his life was from hers, she'd just had it. There worlds were galaxies apart. What did the great Kaane Scott see in quiet Angel Reed? Josiah was more her speed, but that wasn't who the man was. If she hadn't been told he was famous, she'd have had no idea until it was too late.

Except it was already too late.

Fight or flight? If this had been Josiah, there would be no question. She'd fight without hesitation. Kaane, though, was another story. He was out of her league.

By the time she met up with the girl tribe that evening, she was no closer to an answer, and their news didn't help matters.

"They all went?"

Angel looked from face to face, unable to believe what she was hearing. All three women nodded in reply. Roxy's expression was particularly grim.

"I told you, I want to use his dick to test my knives. I just sharpened all of them."

Angel wasn't sure if she should be worried about the potential for blood.

DK shook her head. "I have a hard time believing he was such a jerk to you. I mean, you laid it all on the line and he acted like, I am sorry to say, an asshole. Don't tell Vince I used the word. I'll never hear the end of it."

Angel shook her head and pulled an imaginary zipper over her lips. Tess rolled her eyes as Roxy swore in a colorful rainbow of expression. Tess gave the chef a hard look and said, "You're not helping here."

"I brought ice cream, house-made salted caramel mocha. And her favorite shortbread cookies. And wine." She lifted her hands as if this solved everything.

"This might require something stronger," DK said, waving a lecturing finger.

She couldn't let this go on any longer. "Stop, all of you," Angel said, her tone quiet but firm on the words. All three women froze and turned to her as one. "I don't need something to eat and I'm fine with tea, thank you. I need a solution. I can do all of the research in the world, but it's not going to help me figure out what to do."

Tess reached out to her, patting her arm before turning to the others. "You're right. She's right. We need to listen and be supportive and help her come up with an answer that works." She swiveled back and said, "What do you want us to say?"

Angel stared at her, and she was sure the puzzlement she felt showed on her face. "Want you to say? I need to draw conclusions based on the facts." She shook her head, trying to make sense of this.

"Not going to work," said Roxy, and DK nodded in agreement.

"Why?"

DK glanced at the others and pulled Angel through the small living room, pushing her on to the sofa. The other women arrayed themselves next to her on other furniture, and all leaned forward with serious expressions. DK cleared her throat and said, "You're thinking about this with your head, Angel, like a librarian. You need to channel your artist side and figure out how you feel."

How she felt? She felt hurt to her core and angry with Kaane and lonely without Josiah and confused about what to do next. There was that other nagging feeling, the one she didn't want to give voice to. Maybe she hadn't been as clear as she should have been that first time. Did he misunderstand the implications of this from her perspective because she hadn't told him what that was?

Not that she thought she understood his point of view on the muse thing either. She was no more a woman to be treated like a rare doll than the next. Nothing special made her off-limits, and if that bullheaded man would simply realize this and come to his senses, they could work on their future steps.

Like more of that amazing intimacy, and his kisses, and their shared moans and sighs, and that moment when the world blew up like a barge full of fireworks but it was impossible to close her eyes and turn away from the sheer brightness of it in Josiah's rapt expression. Her eyes closed tight to capture the memory and hold it closer.

"She's sighing. You're sighing. This isn't good, Evangeline." DK's face drew tight in a worried expression, one mirrored by her other friends.

In a quieter voice, Tess asked, "What are you thinking about? Your face, I have to admit, is getting a little too dreamy for you to be thinking about how mad you are at Kaane."

What could she say? She was angry with him. Maybe more to the point, she was mad at herself for having silly hopes and wishes about a situation she should have known from the beginning would not turn out like a romance story.

Standing and pacing to the kitchen, she filled a kettle with water and turned on the burner with a decided snap. This was silly. She was a grown woman and she had accomplished what she set out to do. She could no longer lay claim to the title of virgin. Why were the tea cups swimming in front of her vision as she reached for them?

"Aw shit, now she's going to cry. That means we're all going to cry, and damn it, I always feel like crap after we do that." Roxy's fingers closed over Angel's and took over the task of retrieving tea bags and spoons. Her sympathetic glance contrasted with her sharp words and tone, and she patted Angel on the shoulder before pushing her back toward the living room. "I've got this, girlfriend. Now you go have yourself a good cry, and then we'll figure out how to fry Kaane's balls and serve them up on a platter."

Despite the trail of tears now coursing down her cheeks, Angel couldn't stop the giggle of laughter. Her friends smiled with encouragement, making her lift her shoulders in a bravado she was far from feeling. She didn't want Kaane. She didn't need Josiah. It was impossible to imagine having any relationship with a man she wasn't even sure how to address.

"Well, that didn't last long. She's crying again. My friend, you have it bad. Tell us what we can do to help." DK put an arm around her shoulders, Tess patted her back, and Roxy held a box of tissues in front of her face.

Friends. She had friends, and these wise women would help her figure out what went wrong and how she could avoid any entanglements again in the future.

Reaching for a tissue, Angel said, "I need to do some research on how to keep my distance."

The others glanced at each other and burst out laughing.

"No, come on, I'm serious." But even she had to grin at their mirth. "I don't want Kaane to think of me as any sort of obligation. After all, he really didn't know."

That stopped the laughter abruptly. Tess asked, "What do you mean, he really didn't know?"

Angel squirmed as understanding bloomed on their faces. In a flat voice, DK said, "You didn't tell him beforehand."

Angel shook her head slowly, feeling the heat of a blush rise on her cheeks. "I kind of said something, but I might not have been clear. No, I definitely wasn't clear."

Roxy dropped the tea cup to the table with a crack of ceramic on wood. "Well hell, this changes everything."

Kaane crossed his arms and widened his stance, unwilling to move unless they forced him. And oh yeah, they just might do that.

"You're not removing anything," he said for the third time.

Powers glanced to Kaane's right, where Rodney leaned against the barn. The two men exchanged a grim nod, and Rodney pulled away from 11 and sauntered to stand next to the other men.

It wasn't enough that Powers was here, ready to retrieve Angel's art and supplies at her request. He'd enlisted Mac and Vince too, and the three of them arrived tight-lipped and angry. Now with the desertion of Rodney, Kaane stood alone against them.

"Come on, Kaane, let us move her things and we can all get a beer and discuss it. Angel's got to have her stuff back. She doesn't want to see you man." Vince extended a hand as if trying to defuse the situation, but Kaane made a point of ignoring it.

"When she wants to get it, if she really wants to, she'll come around," Kaane said, with more confidence than he was feeling.

His repeated voice mails to Angel had gone unanswered. He drove by her house, but the windows were dark and her car was not in view. He even went so far as creeping around the garage and trying to see in the windows, risking being caught as a prowler. Everyone would then know what a sorry case he was. Stalking the gallery had the same results. The old man gave him a weird look of satisfaction, like he knew Kaane had gotten what he deserved.

No, what he deserved was Angel. Angel sure as hell deserved something better, but she was stuck with him. The certainty of it grew with each passing minute, and Kaane wasn't willing to give up, not when a lyric was difficult, not when his future was, and not where Angel was concerned either.

Mac stepped forward next. "Man, I have never known you to be like this. Stubborn about your music, yes.

Determined to take down a story about you that isn't true, yes. Even fighting to keep your career afloat when things are sinking isn't something you shy away from. But this? I don't understand." He shook his head, the bafflement on his face so true that there was no way it was an act.

Kaane shifted, because it all hit a little too close to home. But instead, he barricaded the barn like his life depended on it, and maybe it did. He couldn't string three thoughts together without Angel in them, and his heart was a barren winter landscape without her in view. It was more than his music. She was his life.

All he needed was for her to see how great they could be together. She could paint in his barn, and he could write music in his studio, footsteps away from her. When their creative energies dwindled, they'd come together like two lightning bolts and refill with a new surge of power.

Who the hell was he kidding? He was a stubborn ass. He was also deathly afraid Angel would tell him she didn't need him anymore, and he'd be without her, not just as his muse, but more importantly, as her man.

Her first. Why hadn't he treated those words with the respect they deserved? That answer was easy. He was a dickhead.

Powers swung the key to the locks, Angel's keys, on the end of his finger like a metronome. His mouth pulled into a grim line and his eyes weren't looking friendly. He said, "Kaane, you are outnumbered. Besides the point that none of our women will let us in the door unless we accomplish our mission, we can't understand how you could hurt a smart, sweet woman like Angel. Her name is no misnomer, as I'm sure you know. How the hell could you make her cry?"

The picture of Angel running to her friends in a weepy mess brought him a pang of regret greater than anything he'd ever been sorry for. At the same time, he hoped the news would spur someone to action. He deserved to have the crap beaten out of him. Maybe that would allow sense to take its place, and maybe then his heart would quit leaping every time he heard a car on the distant road.

Powers glanced to his right and left, pushing the keys into his pocket. "Gentlemen, shall we?" Mac and Vine shouldered in tight next to him and the three of them advanced.

"Oh, allow me." Rodney stepped around them on nimble feet, reminding Kaane of the big man's favorite contact sport. He'd wrestled in his native country and continued to train when he was in England. If Rod-man wanted to move him, he was screwed.

Kaane gave up the aggressive stance and dropped his hands to his pockets. He glanced down the driveway, willing a certain sedan to lumber up the road and park behind the advancing man. He thought he heard a crunch of gravel, but he was sure his sleep-deprived mind might be making that up.

Rodney stopped a pace away and looked him square in the eye. "You are being an asshole. Do you agree?"

Kaane nodded, and Rodney took a step closer. "So, you'll move then?"

He shook his head, lifting his chin. Just so there would be no doubt, he said, "No, you'll have to make me move."

Rodney looked like he might be trying to hide a grin. Without warning, a big fist landed with a thud right above Kaane's belt buckle, pushing out any air with a shocked gasp. He began to crumple as pain set in, fiery and low and making his dick throb in agony.

A shocked pause might have happened, or time might have stood still while Kaane stared at the guitarist he'd rarely ever seen in a temper regard him with flashing anger in his eyes. It took a moment to remember he deserved this, and probably much more.

"Hey, come on, hold on, man," Vince said as he grabbed Kaane's left arm. Powers had his right in the next second, but that didn't keep Kaane from falling, his hands covering an injury so all-consuming, he couldn't breathe. Damned if the pain wasn't growing into an all-out body throb of intensity. Kaane's vision blurred. His head might be lolling on Vince's shoulder, and he might be drooling on the tight grip of Powers' hand, but he wasn't sure.

"That was impressive. What kind of punch was that?" Mac stood with a hand on his chin, having a casual conversation with Rodney as if nothing unusual had happened. Kaane tried to focus, but even squinting didn't help. Shit, it hurt everywhere.

His former friend's voice followed in its usual confident cultured tone. "It's an acupressure point related to the vagas nerve that controls bodily functions. Hurts like hell, but it wears off in a while with no lasting damage. Kaane needed a wake-up call. There was no reason to do anything to make that nice woman cry. I can't figure out what is wrong with him."

Through the thin slits of his eyes, Kaane could tell both men were shaking their heads as if they didn't understand it. He didn't understand it either. What made him think he deserved his beautiful Angel? He was a sick bastard, and now he felt like one too.

"Hey, there he is. Look at him, can't even hold himself up. Hey Kaane, over here."

"What the fuck?" Mac's furious words tore Kaane's attention away from the ache making his body weak to the shaded darkness of two figures a distance away up the driveway. He couldn't see them clearly and couldn't tell what they were doing, but the actions of his friends communicated a problem. Rodney was already jogging toward them, with Mac not far behind him covering the ground with surprising speed.

"What should we do?" Powers hissed the words.

"Let's get him inside. Hurry." Panic roughened Vince's tone.

Kaane felt himself being half-carried and he tried to dig in his heels. They would move her things. Angel would no longer have any reason to come here if they took her art with them.

"No," he tried to say, but it came out in a moan. His feet dragged on the ground and each bump jammed like a fresh punch to his gut. His nerves were on fire and despite the need to block their progress, all he could do was groan.

"Are you getting that?" A woman's voice yelled the words in excitement.

"Hell yeah." Triumph made the man's reply a screech.

"Now wait a minute," Rodney said from a distance, and Kaane tried to turn his head to see what was happening.

"Nope, don't look. And stop fighting this. Trust us, dude, you want to be behind closed doors with the blinds pulled shut. Let them take care of it."

His big toe on his right foot jammed into concrete and wood as Powers and Vince pulled him up his front steps. His left hand knocked into a post on the porch and Vince swore. It took two tries for Powers to work the door latch and handle with his free hand, and the three of them fell face-first into the entry while more shouting erupted behind them.

"Are they gone?"

Half an hour later, Kaane massaged his bumped hand, not because it hurt, but because it gave him something to do other than what he wanted. And that was to pound it into the wall and create a string of holes from one corner to the other. Vince stared at the motion with a mournful expression on his face, and repeated the words he'd said three times already.

"Man, I'm sorry I banged up your hand. Is it okay? You keep rubbing it."

Kaane waved the hand in the air and flexed fingers in response. His body had recovered from Rodney's blow with remarkable speed. His emotions were another story, and none of that was about the wake-up call he knew he deserved.

Pacing bled off some of his nervous energy, but it did nothing to calm the rage. "It's nothing, so stop asking." He swung back to the men by the front door. "How did they find me? I'm so careful. I don't bring anyone back here and I don't advertise where I live. Fuck, I even disguise myself when I go into town. How did those jerks find me? Unless someone who knows I live here told them, of course."

Rodney and Mac exchanged a level stare, with neither face giving anything away. Without breaking that link, Mac said, "Maybe they followed you from town. Dumb luck, seeing you on the street and trailing after you. For all you know, they might have put a tracking device on your truck or something." He hesitated, saying with more force, "I don't think anyone gave you away."

Rodney shook his head, though if in agreement or denial wasn't clear. Kaane resumed his pacing, only to come face to face with a towel in a bundle. Vince hung it in front of his hand. "Here, put this ice on it. Maybe a doctor should look at it. We have a buddy, we could call him, and he'd make a house call. Fuck, I don't want to be responsible for you not being able to play again."

Kaane tried to push the towel away, but Vince was just as adamant, until it was easier to accept it than throw it on the floor. The cold did feel good on his fingers.

"If he can't play, it will have nothing to do with a little tap on his hand." Rodney's delivery sounded in calm, deep tones, making Kaane swing around to stare at him. "He won't be able to play because he thinks his music is gone."

A silence so complete that the ticking of the wall clock sounded like a gong followed his words. Kaane could only stare in disbelief. He thought Rodney was on his side.

"Gone? Like writer's block, except for music? You know that's a myth, right? You need to find the right inspiration, man. The notes will come." Vince nodded in time to his words, as if accenting the point.

"Have you isolated yourself too much? I mean, you rarely go out and you live alone. What do you do for inspiration? Where do you find your ideas? Even as an architect, I need to explore other people's work, and not just buildings, to find new designs." Powers leaned forward and put his chin on his linked hands, his gaze narrowing.

Mac waved a hand to quiet them. "I don't think that's what Kaane's talking about, is it? You mean your muse. You lost your muse and now you don't think you can write any more. Is that it?"

That wasn't what was important. He needed to find out how the paparazzi found him, because like ants, when you saw one, there was a nest behind it. That's all he needed crawling all over him as he struggled to bring Angel back to him once more. Josiah's life wouldn't be invaded by vermin like Kaane's was.

Rodney responded before Kaane could think of a way to detour the topic. "Oh, he knows his muse. He is on very good terms with his muse. Or at least he was, until he screwed up. And he broke the taboo, so that about clinches it."

"That's not it," Kaane shouted, but no one was looking at him. Instead, the other men stared at his guitarist with varying degrees of curiosity.

"What?" Powers changed the hand clasp and leaned further.

"Who?" Vince's eyes were wide with that look of discovery journalists got when they thought they were on a hot trail.

"Why?" Mac swung back to meet Kaane's gaze, his expression sober with understanding.

Throwing the towel down on the hardwood with enough force to scatter ice cubes to all corners of the room, Kaane swore a string of profanity that even had Rodney's face breaking into an appreciative smile. Vince said, "Wow, I think I just learned some new words."

"Seriously? You guys are the worst excuses for friends I could ever imagine. My songwriting is not the issue here." Kaane kicked a frozen nugget for emphasis, sending it racing past Rodney's scuffed boot.

As he followed the progress of the cube across the floor with his eyes, Rod-man said, "So if you think there's a song in it, write it. If you think you're in pain, write about it. If you're angry at the papas for their moral bankruptcy, put it into a tune. But stop blaming that nice woman you don't deserve for not filling your head with music. That's on you and you alone."

Mac broke in, "But you heard them. They said – " He broke off as Rodney glared at him, then jerked his shoulder.

"Oh man, you can't write songs? Wow, that must be hard. Kind of like having no construction contracts, I suppose. I remember what that felt like, back in the day." Powers nodded in apparent understanding.

"I can write. I can write just fine. Look, you're missing the point." Kaane shot a frantic glance at Rodney, but his friend wasn't looking at him. His gaze was instead focused on the front door, contemplative in that way he had when he was about to issue a zinger of a reprimand.

Vince said, "What do you mean, he broke the taboo? And who's the muse? I need details, guys. There's a story here."

In unison, Kaane and Mac said, "There's no story."

Kaane swung around to find Mac still staring at him in sympathy. When their eyes met, Mac nodded. A moment later, he disappeared in the direction of the music room, Kaane on his heels. He had to stop him. Once he saw the room, he'd know for sure that Kaane had lost it. He registered the shuffle of feet behind them with only half an ear of attention.

"Mac, look, there's nothing to see. Let's just drop it and focus on what's important. How did they find me?"

But Mac didn't slow down and Kaane found his own feet dragging enough to allow Vince and Powers to pass him. Only Rodney lingered behind with him, matching his slower pace.

"Maybe it's for the best, Kaane. Maybe they can help. After all, they've known Ms. Reed for a lot longer than you have. Perhaps they can tell you how to make things right." But he looked uncomfortable, like he didn't believe his own words.

"Holy shit. Look at this place. It's a shrine. DK told me Angel sold all of her work to one customer, but I didn't realize it was you." Vince's loud tone carried over the scrape of their feet on the floor.

"All I can say is, wow. You have it bad, my friend." Powers swung from the poster's place of honor, and from his expression, Kaane figured he now understood too.

"It's not important. I thought Angel was my muse. Obviously, I was wrong, since I haven't really been able to write a damned thing since I met her."

"I disagree." Rodney's voice was a steadying quiet in the overcharged atmosphere. "I read the lyrics you left on the piano, and they are good. Not what you've been doing the past few years. Different, a new direction. But good, and I might even say some of them are great. Of course, we'll have to see how they sound with the notes behind them and I doubt the band will be on board with this, but there is hope for you. I would say you found your muse, Kaane, but you still broke the taboo."

"What the hell is the taboo? And I still want to know more about you and Angel, because damn, she's a very nice woman, and you're, you're – " Vince waved his hand as if he didn't know how to finish the phrase, but Kaane did.

"I'm a dick, and I know it."

The men nodded as if they each understood the depth of his failure. "How involved are you?" Mac asked the question with what sounded like desperation.

"Very." The one word conveyed more emotion than he wanted to give away, but Kaane couldn't hold it back.

"And how committed?"

He didn't hesitate. "Completely." More than losing his privacy, losing Angel was causing the pain and fury in his heart. Pain, because he knew better now, and Angel deserved much better than him. The fury was all for himself.

"If the papas have found me, they might chase after Angel too, and I'll do anything to protect her. I can hire security, but I think that would only make things worse." Kaane's eyes fell on the poster, on the dab of paint on her cheek, the one he caressed on the photo before he could touch it in real life. His fingers tingled as if her skin was under his hands now. Yes, she deserved better than him, but he could change.

"Unless they found her already," Rodney said, his voice even lower.

Kaane glanced up at him to find Mac and Rodney exchanging another meaningful stare. Without looking away, Mac asked, "How angry was Angel with you, Kaane?"

Only one word summed that up nicely. "Very."

Both men turned to him, and he heard Powers and Vince step closer too. Rodney cleared his throat in apparent discomfort and said, "I think you have a bigger problem than you believe, my friend."

"What do you mean? Have they found Angel already? Are they harassing her? Is she in hiding? I have to find her and protect her. It's my fault they're after her. Shit." He ran a hand through his hair and yanked to focus himself, his feet already moving toward the door. There weren't many places she'd run to, he assumed, and with their help, they could cover them all.

"Kaane, stop." Mac's voice held authority as well as sadness. Since his old friend would understand better than any of them what was at stake, the command was surprising. Mac had his share of troubles with the media trailing his every step in the past. He had to understand how important it was to protect Angel. She wasn't part of that public world and her innocence alone would make her an easy target for the kind of vitriol the press liked to dish out about people like him. They could destroy any chance he had of making things right with her. He needed a chance to apologize, and to show her things could be different. He wanted her in his life for whatever she was willing to give him.

"What did those goons say?" His voice caught as he stared at Mac. The sorry expression on his friend's face made his words trip over themselves as he continued. "What did they say? Have they dropped their stories on her? She'll never understand. I have to protect her."

Mac's face dipped into discomfort as he put a restraining hand on Kaane's arm. His grip was tight, as tight as his grim expression when he said, "Kaane, the paparazzi said Angel told them where to find you."

Chapter 24

Her friends were right. She couldn't do enough research if she lived to be a hundred to figure out what went wrong with Josiah-slash-Kaane. Kaane. It was easier to think of him by that name since his famous persona was the one that was real. The sweet, shy farmer was a figment of her romantic imagination. Kaane had just been using her, probably because he needed a temporary outlet, and face it, she made herself convenient.

No, she refused to think of herself in those terms. Angel had to be honest and admit she had an agenda too. He'd ticked that off her list. He'd made it magical, even when he didn't know. His face as he realized what she'd been telling him all along communicated that.

She couldn't stop thinking about his face, not in any of its forms, in joy or in passion, contemplation or rest. At least she didn't have to think about what to do with her paintings of him. According to Thomas and Bettie, every single one of them had sold as soon as people realized their subject, and the gallery's growing waiting list wanted to know when they could expect more.

At least there, she had no problem making her decision. Her art life was over. She hadn't been sure what to tell the guys when they brought her supplies from Kaane's barn. Their taciturn delivery of those items was one more puzzle in a long line of them. While their faces were kind, they said little. Only Mac talked at any length, and that was to encourage her to continue to develop her craft, even going so far as asking if she'd consider taking a commission. She had stuttered a vague response that had him smiling with what looked like relief, something she didn't understand. She thought she'd said no.

Her paintings. Her art. It was silly to assume she could make a living at it. After all, if Kaane hadn't been crazy enough to think of her as his muse, she'd have sold nothing.

"Ms. Reed? Angel? Your ESL class?" The head librarian leaned into Angel's field of vision and waved.

"I'm sorry, I was deep in thought. I'll come out right now."

The other woman nodded and hurried off, leaving Angel alone with the notepad she'd been using to catalog new books to label and shelve. This was work she knew, work that she could probably do in her sleep, and much more appropriate for her than thinking she could create art.

Her friends had disagreed. DK tried to persuade her the hardest of them all. "You are an artist, no matter what the subject of your pieces, Angel. It isn't about the subject but about how you bring that content to life. Am I less of an artist because I create pieces for corporations to put in their office entrances? Those works are no less art than the things I do because I have a wild idea to make something no one may ever buy."

She had a point, but that didn't inspire Angel to pick up her brushes. No, she was better off here in the library where she had her feet firmly underneath her, living in the background and learning about life from the pages of books. Someday, a librarian would retire. She could work here full time. Or she could sell her aunt's house and move away, preferably someplace where magazines with rock stars' faces on the covers were never sold.

The class nodded and chanted their greeting to her in English, and Angel forced a smile to her face. The first half an hour passed in a blur. The faces in front of her held no confusion, so whatever she was doing, she must have been doing right, but she had no idea. She prayed for the time to fly by so she could go home and hide.

A knock sounded and the librarian appeared in the doorway. The hassled toss of her head wasn't unusual, but the confused starry expression was. She patted her hair with hands that shook and her words came out in a torrent. "Ms. Reed, excuse me class, but Ms. Reed, you have a visitor. I think you need to see this person." She emphasized the last two words with an intent gleam to convey her insistence. "I mean, I am sure you want to see this person, if you know what I mean."

Again, she gave the meaningful look that Angel couldn't assign any significance to. She glanced at the men and women around the table, all of whom were watching the older woman with a mixture of fascination and anxiety. No matter who waited outside, the class came first.

"Thank you. Can you please ask whomever it is to come back later? As you can see, we're busy at the moment. We have work to do." She circled her finger to indicate the room, and turned away from the door to return to their discussion.

A hand closed on her arm, and a chorus of gasps sounded from the people around the table. Their eyes widened, some in confusion and some in recognition, and Angel could understand their surprise. She hadn't expected the older woman to be quite so insistent. Fingers dug into her skin with enough force to make her freeze, marshalling her retaliation while tempering it for public consumption.

"Ms. Reed, we have to talk."

The voice whispering in her ear wasn't that of the older woman. No, it was the one person she'd just been thinking about, and the only person she could guarantee she didn't want to see again, ever. Except, she was glad he was here.

"You're Kaane Scott," said a man, his voice cracking into a deeper accent in his excitement. The nervous giggle of a couple of women followed, and a younger one fanned herself in rapid movements.

Kaane stood so close, she could feel the rapid puffs of his breath on her cheek. His expression remained neutral, though the lines at the corners of his mouth deepened as if he compressed his lips to keep from saying more.

"I understand that congratulations are in order. You sold all your paintings at the gallery, yet again. And this time, I didn't have to slap down a credit card, even if I did have something to do with their success."

How could he be so brutal? Did he think the whole world revolved around him? This was a side of him she had never seen, and given a choice, she'd prefer never to see it or him again.

"Let me go. You are making a scene. This is a public place, and I work here."

His fingers loosened but stayed on her arm, changing from firm grip to light caress, a feather touch she felt through her sweater. His face softened too, and a turbulent light came to his eyes, almost obscuring the green as his pupils dilated. She felt her own heart rate kick even higher in response. She couldn't look away, and neither, apparently, could he.

"We need to talk," Kaane said, and even the timbre of his voice made her shaky. What was it with this reaction? She should be able to control it and turn off any attraction. It was only chemistry, and if she found the right formula for an antidote, she could fight it. Based on the expression in his eyes, she doubted Kaane would give her a chance to do that research now.

An older student pressed in close, a pen and paper extended. "Please, Senor Scott, an autograph for my daughter? She will never believe I met you." Others joined the tight circle, forcing Kaane to drop her arm as the crowd grew more excited. He nodded and made noises, but he wasn't looking at them. His eyes stayed on Angel as she shrank away. When her fingers closed on the doorknob, she didn't look back.

She fled the room, shutting the door behind her, as voices lifted even further in a litany of questions. She doubted the fans would let him leave without pumping him for every bit they could get, and that might be a good two hours if she was lucky. It would give her enough time to get home, throw a few things in a bag, and hit the road to who knows where. The destination didn't matter. Getting out of town without talking to Kaane did.

Less than half an hour later, Angel was ready to flee. Her friends' warnings rang in her ears, but they could not change her mind. She was going, and hopefully, Kaane would forget all about her. She was sure the only reason he showed up was to chastise her about the paintings. He'd see the benefits of her leaving first soon enough.

Tess hadn't been so sure. "I'd be happy to pick up your mail and your paper, but are you sure this is what you want to do? Kaane has had three days to think about what happened. Maybe he's come to his senses and wants to set things straight with you."

The setting straight part, undoubtedly, but she doubted it was about things she wanted to hear.

"Oh, I am sure he wants to talk, but I think it's so he can rid himself of guilt. Or out of obligation, to make sure I don't hold it against him. Hold something against the famed and fortunate Kaane Scott, isn't that rich? Or maybe he's afraid I'll sue him."

She bit off the words, forcing her voice to stay even and the tears on her cheeks not to show in her voice. Tess had said more, but she didn't register the words. Her friend's insistence that she think this over and hear him out was a waste of time. Angel wanted nothing to do with him.

That little voice inside, though, wouldn't stay quiet. She was as much to blame as he was. She should have told him and made it clear before they'd ever made it to bed. Refusing to think about the lovemaking didn't make things easier, because then it was all she thought about.

Assuring Tess she'd check in from wherever she ended up, she disconnected. The phone stayed silent, which she found a little surprising. She half-expected Tess to rally the girl tribe into a series of calls intended to convince her to stay. They'd all faced issues with their guys, and none of their relationships came easily or without pain, but this was different. Those men cared about their women. She was just a notch in Kaane Scott's bedpost, and a temporary one at that.

Her footsteps carried her to the tiny kitchen. She'd told Tess where she would hide her key and asked her to help herself to everything in the fridge. She didn't know when she would return, if ever. This place now held too many memories, and she couldn't stand to look around the space, not when she saw Kaane's ghost in every corner. A fresh start in another part of the country was a reasonable prospect. Trying to ignore the pang she felt at that thought made her sick to her stomach.

Slipping out the front door, she was happy to see that no tall, rangy rock star stood in her path. She could imagine him there too easily, his arms crossed and his face looking mysterious. But he wasn't there. She should be happy about that. Walking more slowly around the front to the driveway, the wheels on her suitcase made a squeak that sounded as forlorn as she felt.

"Going someplace?"

Angel froze at the words, her surprised gaze landing on someone she would never have expected to see. Mac leaned on the hood of her sedan, his arms crossed and an expression of casual interest on his face.

Her hand fluttered, recognizing she'd done the damsel in distress thing to cover the jump in her heart. Forcing a smile to her face, she put her feet in gear and continued forward.

"Mac, you are perhaps the last person I would expect to see here."

He nodded. "That's why everyone decided it was best that I come."

Her feet stopped clicking on the sidewalk again. "Everyone?"

He lifted himself off the car and came toward her. "Well, let's see. Powers didn't vote because he hasn't answered his voicemail yet."

Confusion made it hard for her to follow his words. "Vote?"

He nodded, putting a hand under her elbow and turning her back toward the house. "Why don't we sit on the porch and chat for a while? If you still want to leave after you hear what I have to say, okay. But I'd like you to listen first."

Angel allowed herself to be steered back up the steps, and she dropped into one wicker chair as Mac creaked into the other. He extended his legs and folded his hands on his stomach, gazing not at her but at the front yard. "Spring's going to be amazing this year, don't you think? Look, your flowers are starting to come out. This yard is a sight when everything blooms. Did you know your aunt let me use it as a set in one of my movies?"

Taking a deep breath to steady her jumping nerves, Angel said, "Why are you here, Mac?"

His face turned to her in a movement she was sure he had used in many a film, but the frank honesty in his expression was real. "I told you why. There are some things I think you should know."

"Not that why. I understand why you think it's important for me to listen. But why you?"

He grinned that big movie star grin, and she had a pang of emotion wishing Kaane was more like Mac. Mac was hugely important, and yet, when he hung around with the gang, he seemed like just one of the guys. Kaane seemed like, well, a rock star.

Except when she knew him as Josiah. She missed that man more than she could say. Tears threatened again, and she flipped her wrist over to look at her watch, as if time mattered.

"That isn't hard to explain. Tess felt your spirit wasn't settled by your decision to leave. She checks on things like that, you know. She called DK because they thought if anyone could make you understand how relationships can suck before they work out, it was her. DK and Vince had a strange history that I'm sure you know about. But DK thought Roxy would be better able to explain things, because despite everything she says, she's come around and realized that people are capable of change. When we're in the spotlight, our public sides are often based on the expectations of our audience. Our private selves, though, are another matter. With Roxy's help, I melded together both parts of myself, public and private, into something that feels authentic, and someone she loves. I consider myself a damned lucky man because she gave me a second chance."

His frank expression was kind and thoughtful as he tapped his lips and continued to watch her. Angel couldn't help but reflect on what each of those women had told her about how their relationships had evolved. She shook her head, dropping her eyes to her fingers twisted around her car keys in her lap. "That doesn't explain why you're here."

Mac chuckled. "Well, DK got her blowtorch out with Vince's blessing and Roxy sharpened her knives again, and the last thing I heard, Tess was driving the three of them over to Kaane's place to, as they put it, teach him a lesson. I think Tess said something about a curse too. Vince and I are just waiting for Powers to get home to go over and mop up the blood and guts. Which left me with time on my hands."

She didn't know when she jumped to her feet, but her phone was in her hand and she tried to pass Mac's feet when his words registered. "Hey, I'm joking. Damn, I'm sorry. Roxy was right. You both have it bad, don't you?"

"Both of us?" She hated the small sound of her voice. Pushing more volume into it, she continued, "What do you mean?"

Mac stood too, putting a gentle hand on her arm. The touch forced her to look at his face, and the sincerity there made her pause. "Angel, I've known Kaane Scott since both of us were trying to make names for ourselves in LA. We shared an apartment with a rotating array of guys and everyone was trying to make it. Back then, even as Kaane was trying to get a band going and trying to book gigs other than the corner bar on drunken weekday nights, he always had time to help everyone else. Some of those people took advantage of him, and over the years, his big heart got him in trouble more and more."

Mac guided her back to the chair and leaned against the railing, facing her. "When I got my first big roles, Kaane was delighted for me. When Rebellion took off, I was so happy for him. We've stayed connected all these years, not because it's easy or expedient to do so. No, it was because the same thing drives both of us, a passion for our craft. I loved acting, but after a certain point, it didn't feel as necessary anymore. I knew I could be good at something else, maybe better than I am at acting, and that's directing. I made a change."

Angel didn't want to hear this, didn't need to know how Mac had changed his life, because that wasn't the point. Kaane, the Kaane she knew, was only in it for what helped him. She jumped up again and retraced her path to the top step.

"Angel, hear me out, please. Just like I did, Kaane reached that certain point, but for him, it meant he couldn't write music anymore. His inspiration dried up, which he took to mean his talent was gone too. If you love him, and I think you might, fight for what you want. If in the end when the credits roll he isn't that one and only for you, you gave it a chance. Talk to him. That's all we're suggesting."

She narrowed her eyes at him. "All of you?"

He tilted his head to one side. "Well, Roxy still isn't convinced, but I can probably get her to put the knife set back in the kitchen for a while."

She wanted to believe in the possibilities Mac suggested. A life full of love, of art, would be a dream. That life with Josiah in it felt real. With Kaane? She wasn't sure.

"And Angel, don't give up on your art, either."

"How did you know?"

Mac's eyes lit with understanding. "Because we're artists, all of us. It feels easier at times to walk away than to struggle, and I'm not talking about the monetary cost. It's hard to be creative without refilling your well. Love does that, nurtures us and provides the fuel we need to keep creating. I think you and Kaane give that gift to each other."

Angel shook her head but offered a reluctant smile. "How did you become so wise?"

An easy laugh burst out of her friend as he rose from the seat. "Roxy would disagree with you on that score, and I prefer to think of it as the benefit of years of hard knocks. Learn from my mistakes, Evangeline. Go to the gallery. Think about Kaane. He's a good man, and you make each other better. Think about that before you leave."

Still uncertain, she put her suitcase in the trunk of her car and made the short drive up Main Street. The back door squeaked its welcome as she entered the gallery. No one called out as she drifted inside, and she didn't call out either. If she decided to leave, it would be better to avoid questions.

She was afraid she could too easily be swayed into believing in fairy tales. Josiah-slash-Kaane. Her art. A passion-filled life.

She stood in front of the wall where her work had hung. Empty of art with a 'more coming soon' sign once again taped to the wall, it waited for her to find her inspiration for what came next. It felt like a fork in the road, and she had no idea which direction to take.

"Well about damned time you got back in here."

Angel smiled at the old potter's cranky tone. "I am sorry I've been missing, Thomas. I had some things to work out in my head."

The man harrumphed and eyed her skeptically. "Work out in your head, huh? Little girl, let me tell you that when it comes to romance, working it out in your head just leads to grief and missed opportunities."

For Thomas, this amounted to a long-winded speech and much more personal than he'd ever let on. Turning away from her blank display area, she eyed him with marked interest. "Why Thomas, is romance in the air for you?"

He looked taken aback at her statement, then shook his head hard enough to make the cap he kept on his white hair go flying. When he grabbed it off the floor, his cheeks were flushed a bright red.

"Had my chance. Blew it, because I was too stubborn and too proud. Thought I had all the time in the world." He squinted at her with sudden intentness. "You know, sometimes I squint my eyes and I think you're her from back then."

Angel blinked, confused by his words. She thought his interests would focus on Bettie. Though they fought like crazy and talked trash behind each other's backs, she'd always believed they had an honest affection for each other.

"You don't know, do you?" Thomas said, in a much quieter voice than he ever used. The red was fading from his cheeks, leaving him pale and for the first time she'd noticed, looking his age. She fought the urge to wrap an arm around him to allay the forlorn expression.

"What are you talking about, Thomas?"

His eyes drifted away from their shared gaze and turned to the street, though it didn't appear he noticed the activities outside. A heavy sigh came next, followed by a rapid scratching of his thick thatch of white hair before the cap descended again with a vehement shove.

"Your aunt. I had a crush on Miss Reed from the first day she arrived in town. She came to teach school, you see, and she was the most respectable and serious young lady I'd ever known. All that college education and big city experience put my nose out of joint. I didn't want to like her, you see, not at all. I thought she was probably uppity and I'd never understand what she was talking about." His eyes snapped back to her and narrowed. "You must take after your pa."

Angel barked out a laugh, because that had been her greatest burden growing up. With each passing childhood year, her parents would comment on how much she looked like the photos of her father at the same age. Never her mother, and she spent hours staring at her reflection in the mirror, wishing for the willowy grace and gentle smile. Instead, she got big eyes and big curves. Then her mother died, and hoping she measured up to her mother's big heart became more important than looks.

"I thought so," the old man said, nodding. "Jenny and your pa must have looked a lot alike because I see the family resemblance. You're the image of Jenny when she was your age, and she was one handsome-looking woman. Plus, that brain under her bun of blonde hair was a lot like yours. I tell you, when you first came into the gallery a year ago, I nearly croaked at the sight of you. Thought the maker had come to get me and I was in heaven. Not a bad idea for a guy like me."

He chuckled and pulled a handkerchief from his pocket, mopping at his eyes.

Sympathy for his pain and empathy for what he must still be feeling coursed through her. This kind of love she understood. Unrequited, heavy with regrets and potent with feelings while you and your love circled the sun on two different planets was too similar to her situation with Kaane to ignore. "Thomas, why didn't you and Aunt Jenny make it work?"

He huffed and sighed, looking anywhere but at her. She noticed the sheen of unshed tears as he wiped his eyes again. When he finally looked up, grim determination made his expression fierce.

"I didn't do my part to make things work. We got along fine, but I had this crazy notion that Jenny, with her smarts and such, would never be serious about a man like me. I didn't go to college, worked whatever jobs came my way, and never had the security of a house I owned in those days. It wasn't until many years later that I found my calling in clay. But by then, too much time had passed. Now Jenny and me, we were polite and friendly to each other, but I couldn't help but be embarrassed because she was this spirit on the mountain top and I was in the dirt at her feet. It was foolishness on my part and I know it, but a man's pride is an awful thing."

He pulled in a huge breath as if the long soliloquy exhausted him. His finger came up in admonishment. "Don't make my mistakes. Pride won't keep you warm at night, give you a family of your own, or bring you peace in your aging years."

If he only knew how different she and Kaane were, he wouldn't be saying this. Perhaps he thought Kaane was more like the person he first played at being, Josiah. Did that make her the prideful one? She didn't like to think so, but so much had happened in the past weeks to challenge her view of herself, she wasn't sure.

"But Thomas, he's not what you think. Not Josiah, I mean. He's someone else, and lives in a world so foreign, I'm surprised I even understand the language." She gave a self-conscious laugh, aware it wouldn't fool anyone for long when tears brimmed in her eyes.

Thomas waved a disclaiming hand and smacked it on the counter hard enough to make her jump. "Now listen to me, young lady. I know exactly who and what that young man is. Sure, he's a big music star and he's hiding out here in Flynn's Crossing, but he is trying to find himself. You have to respect a man who knows things aren't working like they should and is trying to find a new way of doing business. And those reporters who were chasing after him, well, back in my day, we'd call them yellow journalists, if you understand my meaning."

She felt a single tear run down her cheek and swiped at it. "How do you know all this?"

Thomas laughed again, but his voice was gruff when he replied. "Ms. Reed, I keep my thumb on the pulse of this town. It's given me acceptance and a home for odds-on half a century or more now. You think that old biddy is the only gossip in this shop? I've passed Bettie a long time ago on feeding that machine. Plus, I've turned into a modern man, and I'm not as behind in my ways as I let people think. When he slapped that black credit card on this counter, I did some digging on the computer, and I've known who he was for quite a while. Question is, did you? And if you only found out recently, does that really make any difference to what you feel?" He poked a gnarled finger at her. "Think on that while you're working for the rest of today. I'm tired, and I'm going home. These dang emotions wear me out."

With that, he turned and rambled to the back door, only pausing when his hand was on the knob to give her a wink.

"Don't tell Bettie my secrets, okay? I like her to think I'm a bumbling old idiot. Don't get to have that much fun anymore otherwise."

He chuckled at her nod of agreement, and seconds later, he was gone. Angel felt the silence of the gallery press in on her with a heavy weight. Her eyes strayed to the clock on the wall. Three hours left to the work day. Thankfully, the town seemed quiet this afternoon, but that didn't seem like such a blessing when it left her with too many heavy thoughts.

Her friends were right. If she wanted something bigger in life, she had to be willing to step out from behind the research desk. Her eyes fell on the blank wall allotted to her. If she wanted to create art, she had to paint. Thinking about it, even making excuses for it, would not be the answer.

And if she wanted the man she loved, she'd have to fight for him, even if it meant crossing the line to someplace outside her comfort zone. Honesty and truth came first, and perhaps the rest would follow.

Chapter 25

It had taken him nearly an hour to settle the fans and autograph their papers and answer their excited questions. They gave him some hope that no matter what music he created next, there would still be a small following. But none of that would matter without Angel at his side. He wasted no time in calling her friends the minute he could break free.

"She's left town, Kaane." Tess seemed genuinely sorry she couldn't help him when he asked where Angel was going. No one knew. Her house was locked up tight and no one answered the door. Her car didn't sit in its usual place. Gone.

She couldn't be. They had things to work out. He hadn't understood before how important it was to clear the air between them. In his heart, he'd never wanted to believe Angel would give away his secret. Seeing her hopeful gaze settle on him at the library confirmed it. That wasn't who Angel was.

Pushing her away by blaming her was the easy way out. Then he wouldn't have to admit to the feelings that swamped him when the hope faded and tears filled her eyes. The sharp pain in his soul when he admitted to himself how much he'd hurt her didn't abate. It was wrong to blame her when he should only blame himself for not being honest from the beginning. He wanted Angel back, not only because she was his muse, but because he loved her more than anything. He had to find out if he still had a chance.

She could be anywhere by now. The idea had him frantic, racing with no destination, other than the woman he loved. Kaane cursed long and hard, with enough volume to bring attention to himself from some young guys loitering outside a bar at the end of Main Street. One of them must have recognized him and hit his buddy, pointing at Kaane and stepping toward him. He growled a fresh round of curses at them and gave them an aggravated stare, and that was enough to stop them in their tracks, whispering. He didn't have time for any more delays.

He scanned the street, hoping to catch sight of the waterfall of blonde curls, when his gaze settled on the gallery's bright sign. He wasn't sure why he hadn't thought of that, other than he wasn't thinking straight. He reversed directions, breaking into a jog as he passed the loitering gang. Their shuffling had him turning to find they were only twenty feet away and gaining. He stopped, putting on his best rock star smirk. He didn't need to bring any more trouble Angel's way.

The boys halted two paces back, obviously delighted to have his attention. One mimicked his posture with a smirk of his own. The kid couldn't be much past the legal drinking age. He said, "Hey, Scott, your music sucks, you know that?" He nodded at his chuckling buddies as if he'd just scored major points.

Kaane tilted his head and stared at him. Maybe his music did, in fact, suck. Maybe it had sucked for a long time. It wouldn't suck in the future, of that he was certain. Even if he never found Angel again, he had enough pain and feelings built up to last him a lifetime of songs.

He stepped closer to the men, and they stopped tittering. "You know what? You're right. The music I've been making has sucked for the last few years. I got complacent, and I thought I knew it all. I thought it didn't matter as long I just showed up. But guess what, guys? Life is about more than that. It's about growing and reaching and stepping in shit and learning to clean it up yourself. It stinks. I know this all may be hard for you to understand, given that you have the world figured out and all. But hear me when I say this. Things suck. Things change. The music I produce in the future won't sound like the old Kaane Scott. Now fuck off."

The leader blinked like he wasn't sure he understood English, and around him, his band of buddies took a couple of steps back as Kaane took another pace forward. The kid looked him up and down and gave a single nod with quiet words. "All right then."

They turned as a group and walked away, and when they got even with the bar, they kept walking. Kaane had to smile. He was sure they'd try to sell their encounter to a tabloid or at a minimum, put it on social media. Hell, one of them might even have been filming it. But he was satisfied with himself. Fuck them and fuck the world if it didn't understand he had changed.

Only one thing was important, and that was finding Angel and explaining. Shit, not explaining, listening. He had to hear her words and listen and make her understand that he was listening. And then he needed to wrap his arms around her and apologize and make her understand they had a future together. He quickened his pace to a jog once more that carried him to the gallery. Maybe the owner would know where else he could look for the woman he loved.

She heard the gallery door open and close, followed by the measured walk of boots across the old concrete floor. "Welcome to Sierra Shining. Please feel free to browse around. We feature the work of local artists. I'll be happy to answer any questions you have."

The footsteps stopped. Glancing in the mirror, she felt satisfied that her face showed none of the pain and worry from the last hour. After Thomas left, she stared at her blank wall until customers came in. They distracted her for a time, and on their way out, one told the other, "I'm so disappointed they didn't have any of those Kaane Scott pictures. I mean, I was kind of hoping he'd be hanging around too."

The words cut through her resolve to keep things calm, and the tears began without warning. Her thoughts were jumbled, straying to Kaane at every opportunity, until she craved a long drive to try to think things through. As soon as she closed the gallery for the day, she'd get behind the wheel and see where her muse took her. Luckily, that time would come soon enough. Another hour, and she could be on her way, though what waited for her at the other end was an abyss of the unknown.

But until then, she had a job to do. She tried to think of positive things, like what kinds of paintings she would work on next. Kaane's face kept swimming into her mind's perspective, solemn or laughing, intent on his work or distracted, dark with passion or bright with glee. She'd found her passion, all right. Now, she had to let him go.

Turning out of the back office, she brushed at her skirt and checked the bun of her hair, hoping she didn't look too disheveled. Even if her insides churned with the unresolved, she didn't need to appear that way to the world. She rounded the counter, blinking hard at her shoes and clearing her throat. "I'm sorry to keep you waiting. What can I help you find today? We have many different mediums and styles to enjoy."

The customer didn't reply, and she looked up from her firm examination of the floor. He stood to the side, next to her blank display space. His stance was wide and his hands clenched and unclenched at his sides. He took a single step forward, and a glow from overhead fell on his face.

"Kaane." She realized his name came out strangled and her voice was weak but it was the best she could do. He took another single step toward her. His expression was neutral, like someone she didn't know, and yet she thought his eyes shown in a brighter green, the kind of light they had when he held her in his arms and kissed her.

As if her lips remembered, they tingled, and her hand came up to cover her mouth. She dropped back against the counter, wishing she felt more prepared. Kaane's fists clenched tight, hard enough for her to notice the blood draining and their color turning white.

"Angel." She could read nothing in his tone.

"You found me." She hated the whisper of her voice. She pushed herself upright and fought to sound strong and determined. "Why are you here?"

Something flickered across his features, though she couldn't tell what feelings they might be. He glanced at the blank wall and said, "You sold everything."

She nodded, though she wasn't sure he saw her movement. "Yes."

"You should paint more."

Not sure where this was going, she gave a distracted wave. "I haven't decided if I'm going to paint anything. Maybe I'll go back to being a librarian." In her mind, she finished the thought. The library was safe. People were another thing altogether.

His voice was a trace quieter when he said, "No, you should paint. I'm not trying to be a shit about this. You sold everything because they were good representations of a subject people wanted to see. How much longer they're going to want them is a big fucking question mark, but for now, I'm still popular. You have a good eye for portraits. Do more of them."

"Kaane, you don't like people profiting from your fame. You love your privacy above almost everything else. The only other thing you hold in higher esteem is your music." She fell silent, because if she kept talking, she might give away how much that list of priorities hurt.

His face swung around in slow motion, and this time, there was no denying the emotions flooding his expression. Anger, pain, remorse, reflection, and slowly, regret.

"You don't get it, do you?"

She shook her head. He took two steps back, and she felt the sting of his retreat. "But I think I now understand why you are the way you are."

As if her words were funny, he smirked and put a kink into his posture. She recognized the pose immediately. It was his favorite rock star persona come to life, and it hurt even more to see him distance himself from her with his status.

Spinning away, she fought for control over a mix of sadness and rage. She didn't know what to say to apologize for her little omission. And after everything they shared, why did he treat someone he once called his muse in this way?

"I'm sorry you find that amusing, because I certainly do not. I am also sorry I inadvertently exposed your location to the press. I didn't think anyone would search for you in Flynn's Crossing, and I didn't think they'd recognize you from my paintings. I didn't know who I was painting when I did them. And I'm sorry I didn't make myself clearer that first time." Her first time. The sting of it, the beauty and joy muffled by his later anger, made the tears pinch once more.

"Oh, but Angel, you had no idea. It's my fault. I didn't explain how things are for someone like me. You had no way of knowing. And I mean it. Your work is great, and you should paint whatever you want, including me, if your muse speaks to you that way. Like I said, the market may be short-lived."

She wanted to ask him what he meant. She longed to look at his face and see if he meant any of those pretty words, but she didn't want him to see her cry. His footsteps headed for the front door. This was it. She didn't have long to hang on because he wasn't far from his escape. Just once, she wanted to say the words out loud and see how he'd react. If he laughed at her, so be it. At least then she'd know for sure, and she could feed every ion of pain into her paintings for years to come.

At first, she wasn't sure she heard it over the hard beats of her heart as it shattered. It was a slight tune, a single note, then another. A hum of notes, a murmur of words she couldn't make out. The metallic rumble of lock cylinders followed by the rip of cell blinds being pulled down over a front window. The other side came next, and boots scraped as he turned. The humming grew louder and his words became clear.

If I could paint, I'd paint this perfect moment.

If I could write, I'd capture your smile in flowery words.

If I could dance, I'd never be still for showing you,

Just how much I care.

For you.

Her gaze snapped up and crashed into his. Was he mocking her? He had no reason to say he cared for her. But that's not what his eyes said. They were soft and gentle and a little shy, like the Josiah she first met. The green glow drew her in, and it wasn't until he stood in front of her that she realized she'd drawn closer too.

"Kaane, why are you singing that song?"

He gave a flip of his head that she'd seen him do on videos, an arrogant habit usually followed by a wink. He didn't wink at her, instead staring intently without blinking.

"Call me Josiah."

She shook her head, unable to process it. "I don't understand."

He gave that half-grin, stepping into her personal space and grabbing her hands. Rubbing fingers across her palms in an almost frantic motion, he leaned in. "Call me Josiah. I love it when you call me by my given name. Please."

She sucked in oxygen, feeling like she couldn't breathe. "Josiah. But I still don't understand."

He lifted their joined fingers to his mouth and he kissed her knuckles one by one. The feel of his lips reminded her of the first time he made love to her. But was it love?

His voice crooned again.

I know I'm a long shot, not the man you think I am.

I'm not who and what I've led you to believe.

But darlin', this washed up shell could be so much more,

If you would only believe

In me.

She didn't want to hope, because there was no way to research that. No way to count on something she couldn't verify. No way to believe something she couldn't test against facts.

Except she did believe it. Now, while his emotions bled one after another across his expression and his fingers clenched her harder. He moved their hands and pushed her palms flat on his chest. The fast thump of his heart made her pulse leap, and as if he recognized that, she felt the pace accelerate.

"I know you think it's just a song, Angel, but please believe me when I say it's so much more than that. It's my pledge to you. You see, I've researched this and I have it on the highest authority that I am rock star crazy mad in love with you, and I'll love you long after my last note fades away."

She couldn't look away from the sincerity of his feelings. Under her hand, his heart did crazy loops and bumps and she found hers matching the rhythm. He smiled, and her lips pulled into an answering grin.

"Josiah Kaane Scott Harmond, I love you too."

He gave a chuckle and a sheen of tears magnified the green of his eyes. "That's a lyric I'd like to hear on long-play again and again."

When his lips met hers, she forgot the words to the chorus and everything else. She forgot everything, except that they loved each other.

Epilogue

"They are good."

Kaane nodded, smiling and tapping his foot as the young band jammed under the cover of the tented stage. "Yup. Who would have thought we'd come to this, eh, Rodman?"

The big man shrugged, smiling too. A crash of cymbals offstage made them glance in the direction of the main building. The Rebellion drummer and his enclave of students huddled together. Two girls had given all the boys, their drum man included, a run for their money. Women could do anything, as Kaane had come to learn. When the right one came along, a man could do anything too.

Maybe this had been the greatest surprise of the last few months, that he'd learned of options he'd never even knew existed. Here on an August weekend, Kaane was entertaining a multitude of locals and fans from far away in a field on his ranch. This summer had featured a camp for local youngsters who wanted to be rock or country musicians, and in addition to Rebellion, other professional artists came through to teach clinics or give lectures or sit around and jam with the kids. Weekly performances, big names and newbies, drew regular crowds, and the gate would be used to fund local school music programs. It had been Angel's idea, and of course, she was right.

As if thinking about her made her appear, she slid under his arm and stood on her toes to kiss him. She looked nothing like a librarian today. Her shorts were cut-off jeans. Flip-flops showed off pink nail polish, something she said she'd never done before him. Her shirt had a billowy effect that made him want to slide his hands underneath and check out what its demure outline hid.

But most of all, it was the warm blue eyes shining up at him that made him want to yell at the top of his lungs that he'd found it. The muse wasn't a person or an image. The muse was love.

"Hey handsome. They're pretty amazing, aren't they?" She waved a hand toward the stage, and as if the band of youngsters knew she was looking, they turned as one and hit the final note of their creation grinning like fools. Angel was like that. Everyone wanted to make her smile, and Kaane couldn't blame them.

He leaned down and gave her a quick hard kiss. It would have to hold him, because it would be hours until this gig ended and hours more before they had their home to themselves once again. The barn, Angel's studio, was the only space off-limits. She worked there tirelessly while he wrote scores in the studio, and they fell into each other's arms at night for often x-rated dinners. Or they went out, and he didn't bother to disguise his identity any longer. The paparazzi were having a field day.

As if to punctuate that point, a shutter clicked in rapid succession. Kaane broke the kiss, intending to make sure the photographer was legit, and came face to face with Mac wearing a big grin and carrying a little camera.

"You too look good together. I think I need you for my next film. I'm calling it 'Painting Panting Music'."

Kaane laughed and Angel giggled, though she hid her face in his shirt. She was still shy of his celebrity sometimes, though that all disappeared when she thought anyone was taking advantage of Josiah. He loved that fierce protectiveness about her too.

"Listen, watch over Angel for me, okay? I have work to do. You ready, Rod-man?"

"Josiah, I do not need watching over. Honestly, you'd think I'd never been in a crowd before. Men." Angel's last huff was accompanied by laughter, this time with the ring of her friends accompanied by his friends circling around.

Rodney swung the guitar strap over his broad shoulder. "You sure about this?"

Glancing over, Kaane grinned. "Hell yeah. What's the worst that could happen? Angel will be the only one who claps."

If that was the case, so be it. He was okay with whatever the future brought. He'd made good music in the past, and he'd make good music again, and it didn't matter what size of audience he had, when Angel stood by his side.

As the Rebellion members settled into position, Kaane took the mic. "Thank you again for coming today. Wasn't that talent amazing? Terrific group of young people, and I'm sure we're going to hear more great things from them in the years to come."

The crowd drew closer. The press, some he'd invited and some who'd bought tickets, had cameras raised and cell phones at the ready. Everyone wanted the scoop.

Kaane Scott and Rebellion were going to play on this final night of the music camp, and rumor had it that they were playing something new.

"I want to dedicate this song to love. Young love. Old love. Unrequited love. Realized love. Love in any way, shape or form. We hope you enjoy it. Ladies and gentlemen, 'Angel's Song'."

The crowd's rumble of commentary at his words drained into the background as Kaane closed his eyes. He pictured Angel's face in its many expressions. Her love in the many ways she showed him every day. His unending happiness that he had her in his life. He would never again give her any reasons to leave. He hit the first chord, and one by one, the band's instruments joined in.

If I could paint, I'd paint this perfect moment.

If I could write, I'd capture your smile in flowery words.

If I could dance, I'd never be still for showing you,

Just how much I care.

For you.

Success can seem so far away, it's only a shimmer in the distance.

Every cell in me beats in time with every breath of you.

Everything is different with you.

I know I'm a long shot, not the man you think I am.

I'm not who and what I've led you to believe.

But darlin', this washed up shell could be so much more,

If you would only believe

In me.

Success can seem so far away, it's only a shimmer in the distance.

Every cell in me beats in time with every breath of you.

Everything is different with you.

You wake beside me, tousled and dreamy from sleep,

Your hair wraps around me like it's me you want to keep.

And I pray that it's true, that you want me for your own.

There is no place on earth I would rather call my home.

My home is you.

Success can seem so far away, it's only a shimmer in the distance.

Every cell in me beats in time with every breath of you.

Everything is different with you.

Everything is different with you.

Love, everything is different with you.

In that breath after the last note sounded, in the nanomoment before the crowd's roar of approval swelled, Kaane met Angel's eyes. Her expression said it all. He mouthed the words, as if she didn't know.

'I love you.'

She nodded with a wide smile and blew him a kiss, and he reached out to catch it and place it over his heart with a grin he knew would never end.

THE END

About the Author

I love to hear from readers, so feel free to contact me through my website, www.yvonnekohano.com, or directly on Facebook as Yvonne Kohano, on Twitter @yvonnekohano, and at yvonne@yvonnekohano.com. Please leave an honest review of this novel at Amazon, Goodreads, or your favorite book discovery site of choice.

A HOLT Medallion Award of Merit recipient in Romantic Suspense, Yvonne enjoys channeling her characters' voices and passions as they overcome real world problems and discover love. Her Flynn's Crossing contemporary romantic suspense series is set in a fictional northern California foothills town not unlike the one where she used to live. Of course, the beauty and wonders of the Sierra Nevada Mountains and the surrounding counties play costarring roles in her work.

The first six books in the Flynn's Crossing series follow the developing love interests of the girl tribe, a group of successful women who work through real world conflicts and challenges to find acceptance and love - with some suspenseful happenings thrown in! In the next six books, single guys in the wolf pack find their true loves, but not without their own issues to conquer. Periodically, Yvonne will be adding seasonal novellas to the series, featuring the first-person voice of a character from one of her previous books experiencing an event that we can all relate to.

www.ingramcontent.com/pod-product-compliance
Lightning Source LLC
Chambersburg PA
CBHW031059270626
47155CB00027B/2681